I0580195

THE COURTROOM CORONER

THE COURTROOM CORONER

BOOK FIVE OF THE
FENWAY STEVENSON MYSTERIES

PAUL AUSTIN ARDOIN

THE COURTROOM CORONER
Copyright © 2020 by Paul Austin Ardoin
Published by Pax Ardsen Books

All rights reserved. No part of this book may be used or reproduced in any manner whatsoever without written permission from the publisher, except in the case of brief quotations embodied in critical articles or reviews.

This book is a work of fiction. Names, characters, businesses, organizations, places, events and incidents either are the product of the author's imagination or are used fictitiously. Any resemblance to actual persons, living or dead, events, or locales is entirely coincidental.

ISBN 978-1-949082-16-6
First Edition: May 2020

For information please visit:
www.paulaustinardoin.com

Edited by Max Christian Hansen and Jess Reynolds

Cover design by Ziad Ezzat of Feral Creative Colony
ziad.ezzat.com

Author photo by Monica Toohey-Krause of Studio KYK
www.studiokyk.com

10 9 8 7 6 5 4 3 2 1

TABLE OF CONTENTS

Alack, what heinous sin is it in me
To be asham'd to be my father's child!
But though I am a daughter to his blood,
I am not to his manners.

—WILLIAM SHAKESPEARE, *THE MERCHANT
OF VENICE*, ACT II, SCENE 3

1

8:30 AM

CHAPTER ONE

FENWAY STEVENSON SET DOWN THE BLACK PLASTIC FINGERPRINT KIT at her feet and pulled the equipment room door shut behind her. She locked the deadbolt, then returned her ring of work keys to her purse. She fumbled with the molded polymer handle of the kit before picking it up, then hurried down the hall. Streaking past the coffee cart, Fenway began to push open the glass door to exit the City Hall building.

"Fenway!"

She closed her eyes and grimaced.

As she turned toward the coffee cart, she saw her stepmother nodding at her, standing next to Piper Patten. Charlotte and Piper had only been working together for the long weekend, and the difference between the two women was striking.

Charlotte, a trim blonde of medium height in a professional yet flattering tan wrap dress, stood holding a large paper coffee cup in front of the sign reading PICK UP HERE. The dress looked chic and expensive—it probably cost more than Fenway made in a month. She could have passed for her late twenties, but when she smiled broadly, her eyes did little to mask the fatigue and anguish of the last week, showing the pain of her thirty-six years. She waved in greeting and Fenway raised her hand in response.

"Hi, Charlotte."

Piper, on the other hand, was a young, willowy redhead. In contrast to Charlotte's fashionable elegance, Piper dressed in ill-fitting navy slacks and a beige-and-turquoise striped top, her light makeup not hiding her freckles. She carried a ratty black canvas backpack. Her eyes were tired, too, but from the challenge of working long days over the Veterans Day weekend, not from distress.

"I was hoping we'd catch you before the arraignment," said Charlotte, "but you weren't in your office."

"I had to refill my fingerprint kit," Fenway said, gesturing to the office door she'd locked. "Why didn't you go to Java Jim's?"

Charlotte clicked her tongue. "It looks like it's going to rain. Besides, I figured you'd be around these buildings somewhere." She took a sip from her cup and made a face.

Fenway looked out the front windows at the threatening skies outside, then glanced at Piper. "Busy weekend?"

Piper nodded. "But productive. I'll tell you what I found later."

"Come over to the courthouse and meet the lawyers when they arrive," Charlotte said to Fenway as the barista handed a drink to Piper.

Fenway shook her head. "I can walk over with you, but I need to be in the courtroom for Professor Cygnus's arraignment right at nine."

Charlotte tapped her foot. "I can't believe they'd put his arraignment right before Nate's," she murmured. "It'll be a circus."

Fenway shook her head. "Judge Miller has already banned cameras from the courtroom. I know this is the closest thing Estancia's had to a celebrity scandal in years, but it won't be that bad."

"If you have until nine, maybe we can go over some of the items I found this weekend," Piper said.

"I can wait until after the arraignments," said Fenway.

"Let's not wait," Charlotte replied. "I haven't gotten an update either."

Fenway couldn't think of how to exit gracefully, so the three women stepped over to a small round metal table with three wrought metal chairs a few yards behind the coffee cart.

Fenway sat down and looked at her cover-girl stepmother and the thin redhead, suddenly feeling self-conscious. She shifted in the chair and couldn't decide what to do with her hands. Fenway's hair frizzed in the mid-November damp air, and her grey blazer and black slacks were practical but not exactly flattering. She set down the fingerprint kit on the table as Piper began.

"I think I've found a way to prove your dad didn't make the murder-for-hire payment he's accused of."

"And just in time for the arraignment." Fenway sat up straight. "Have you identified another suspect?"

"Not yet, but let's not get ahead of ourselves." Piper leaned forward. "So, we know that most of the prosecution's case relies on the fact that fifty thousand dollars was paid to Peter Grayheath from an account supposedly belonging to your dad."

"Right."

"Now, I'm not sure how they'll prove that money was expressly a payment for killing your Russian lit professor in Bellingham, but I have to think they've figured out how to do that."

"So what proof did you find?" Charlotte said, tapping her manicured fingernails on the side of her paper coffee cup.

"I've got the screenshots and the server logs showing that the computer that opened the account under your dad's name is the same computer that moved the money between several of the local businesses and the master account in the Caymans. It couldn't have been your dad!"

Fenway groaned. "Piper, that just shows that the same person was one of the central people in the money laundering scheme. If the prosecution found that, I bet they'd bring him up on a bunch of additional charges." Fenway looked at her stepmother.

Charlotte nodded. "That makes sense. Unless you can prove that the computer used wasn't Nathaniel's, I'm afraid it won't help."

Piper tapped her foot excitedly, but kept her voice calm. "It's true, simply proving it's the same computer won't help. Fortunately, there are timestamps on the server during the online transactions."

"So?" Charlotte said.

"So—your father can prove he wasn't at a computer when those transactions were made."

"He can?" Fenway asked.

Piper said, "Well, he might not be able to, but I can. I've got security camera footage from the mansion. I've got a couple of traffic cameras showing him driving. A credit card receipt from a restaurant. For most of the transactions from that account—and for the big one that really counts, the fifty-thousand-dollar transfer—I can prove he wasn't at a computer."

"Won't the prosecution just say he could have done it from a mobile phone?"

"That doesn't add up either," Piper said, "because the IP address specifies the operating—"

"Well, well, well," a voice cut in.

They all looked up into the face of Assistant District Attorney Jennifer Kim. She was smartly dressed in a light gray suit. Though barely over five feet tall, she cast a long, angry shadow over the table. Fenway suppressed an urge to shiver.

"As a law enforcement officer, Coroner Stevenson, you shouldn't be consorting with either a fired county employee *or* the wife of a defendant whose arraignment starts within the hour."

"Perhaps you should mind your own business," Fenway said, "and stop finding excuses to listen to the defense's strategy conversations."

"Perhaps I should investigate you for—"

"For what?" Fenway said, rising to her feet. She drew herself up to her full height, her five-foot-ten frame towering over the ADA. "For being related to someone who's been falsely accused? For continuing to talk to an employee whom you wrongfully forced out? Do you *really* want to see this to its conclusion?"

Jennifer Kim bristled. "If you meet with *anyone* before the arraignments today, Fenway, it should be me. Since you're the arresting officer of Professor Cygnus, the judge could ask you questions. It's my job to make sure there aren't any surprises."

"Had you asked me," Fenway said, "I would have agreed to meet with you. But I'd have said the same thing I'll say to you now. I will tell the truth, the whole truth, and nothing but the truth."

Kim shook her head and set her jaw defiantly, but took a step backward. "At some point, Fenway, you'll have to decide if you want to be on the side of law and order, or in the morally gray morass where Miss Patten and your father's..."

Fenway tilted her head.

Jennifer Kim chewed on her tongue for a brief moment, then said, "...*second wife* seem to live."

"Second wife," Fenway said, nodding curtly. "Interesting choice of words. I'm not sure what his previous divorce has to do with it, but rest assured I'll take your advice under consideration, Jennifer."

They watched her walk away, through City Hall's front doors and toward the courthouse.

"Huh," Charlotte said. "For a minute there, Fenway, I thought for sure you were going to defend my honor."

Fenway glanced sideways at Charlotte. She'd been after Fenway's father's money for a long time, and Fenway figured she'd have fleeced him in a divorce long before now—but they'd been married for an entire decade. Fenway turned her head toward the clock on the lobby wall. Only ten minutes before the start of Professor Cygnus's arraignment. She wouldn't have time to drop off the kit in her office. "I should get to the courthouse."

"Okay," Charlotte said. "We're meeting with the lawyers soon, so I guess we'll see you at Nathaniel's arraignment."

Fenway picked up her purse and the fingerprint kit, then walked out the front doors before cutting diagonally through the amphitheater toward the courthouse. Rain fell lightly as she got halfway across.

A small group of college students gathered near the courthouse entrance, some wearing *Nidever Forever* sweatshirts, a few wearing

Shakespeare-themed T-shirts, most carrying picket signs. FREE CYGNUS NOW—the same thing they chanted—was lettered on several of the signs, although COPS GONE CRAZY was painted on one. Fenway recognized a few of the student-actors from *Othello* and the North American Shakespeare Guild, including Xavier Go and Amanda Kohl, the two students playing Othello and Desdemona. They stood near the front of the group, chanting but not holding signs.

Fenway gave the picketing students a wide berth, but the student holding the COPS GONE CRAZY sign started barking at her.

"Hey—you!"

Fenway kept walking.

"I know who you are," he called, taking a few steps toward her. Fenway could see him out of the corner of her eye, taller than her, white, and dressed in a blue Nidever polo shirt with heavily styled light brown hair. "Don't you ignore me!"

She was almost within arm's length of the door when he stepped in front of her.

"Let me pass," she said, softly but firmly.

"Not until you tell us what you did to frame Professor Cygnus," the kid said loudly, jostling her fingerprint kit.

"Get out of the way, asshole," Xavier Go growled, appearing at Fenway's elbow.

"Not until she—"

"I was there," Xavier said. "She treated him fairly. Just because I think Professor Cygnus is innocent doesn't mean *she* should be harassed."

"Oh, sure, your kind have to stick together, don't you?" the kid sneered, planting his feet.

Amanda bumped his shoulder, and although she was a good foot shorter, she threw the kid's center of gravity off, and he stumbled.

"I don't know what decade you think this is," Amanda said, "but you're literally fifteen seconds away from the cops showing up and arresting you for interfering with an officer of the court."

Fenway slipped behind Amanda and opened the door. The kid said something Fenway couldn't hear, but Xavier stiffened and snarled.

"Every night and twice on Sunday," Amanda responded, as Xavier followed Fenway in. Amanda walked in right behind him and closed the door.

"Everyone in The Guild is protesting Cygnus's arrest," Amanda grumbled, "but he's not even part of The Guild. I'm sorry you had to hear that."

Fenway and Xavier both got in line for the metal detector.

———

The three of them stepped into the new courtroom, and Fenway's eyes widened. She had hoped it would be an improvement over the old cafeteria in City Hall, which had been remade as a cramped, ugly courtroom in the sixties.

In contrast, the new courtroom was stately and gorgeous, all dark wood and art deco brushed nickel lighting. It looked more like an architecture firm's conference room than a courtroom—excepting, of course, the traditional layout. The gallery was large, with about a dozen rows of seats and perhaps ten chairs per row on each side—over two hundred seats in all. The imposing judge's bench, a wall of solid mahogany from the floor of the dais to the top of the desk, threatened to overwhelm the room. Both the jury box against the wall on the right and the witness stand on the opposite side were made from the same dark mahogany as the trim, the bench, and the wainscoting. Two large, square columns extended from floor to ceiling, interrupting the back two rows of chairs—one from the middle of the left side, the other in the middle of the right.

The lack of windows in the courtroom was almost disconcerting. Nowhere could a glint of sunlight make it inside. The design clearly placed the large judge's bench as the unquestioned focal point of the room.

Fenway sniffed. The smell of new varnish and paint wasn't exactly overwhelming, but it did serve as a reminder that the room had just opened and the two arraignments would be the first proceedings.

The gallery was packed and buzzing. While arraignments were hardly ever well attended, Professor Virgil Cygnus, who'd put Nidever University on the map, and Nathaniel Ferris, the oil magnate and Fenway's father, were being arraigned back-to-back. Fenway scanned some of the faces, wondering who was a looky-loo and who was a reporter.

Xavier and Amanda went down a row near the back on the left side, and for a moment, Fenway considered sitting with them. Since the judge might call upon her, however, Fenway thought she'd sit close to the front, so she kept walking up the center aisle.

A trim white man in his early forties, with sandy blond hair and a black sheriff's department uniform tight on his muscular torso, sat in the middle of the front row on the right side of the gallery. He turned to face her, caught her eye, then pointed at the empty seat next to him.

Fenway lifted her fingerprint case to shoulder height and stepped in front of the people in the front row. "Excuse me—sorry." The woman at the end of the first row was Professor Cygnus's wife, Judith, who looked pale and weak, and scrunched her face up in annoyance as Fenway squeezed between her and the railing separating the gallery from the defense table.

She almost called him *Craig*, then remembered the rumor mill. "Thanks, Sheriff," she whispered. She sat in the open seat next to him.

"My badge was the only thing that saved your seat," he whispered back. "You brought your fingerprint kit?"

"I refilled it, then got waylaid by Charlotte when I tried to go back to my office."

McVie gave Fenway a crooked smile. "I like that you're prepared for anything."

Fenway rolled her eyes. "I sure wasn't prepared for this courtroom to be so nice."

McVie tried to suppress a grin. "I know. The electricians and audio teams worked a long time to make sure the new courtroom would be ready for the big arraignments this morning."

Fenway turned her body, looked around the rest of the gallery, and gave a start. "Hey, Cynthia Schimmelhorn is here."

McVie turned. "Oh. Yeah. Didn't Judith Cygnus say that she was one of his students way back when?"

"Yes. I guess she still supports him." She thought for a moment. "I guess I had a couple of professors in college who I'd show up to support, too." She paused. "How is the Nidever community taking the news? Is it just the group of students out there, or is the whole campus up in arms?"

"Too soon to tell," said McVie in a low voice.

"It's definitely a black eye for the university."

"But it's a win for us."

"For us?"

"For law enforcement. The professor's scholarship fund was turning over *millions* every month—it was the biggest laundering operation in the county's history. Of course it's a win."

"You might think so," Fenway said, remembering the protestors, "but it didn't help community relations."

Jennifer Kim was already sitting at the prosecutor's table on the judge's right side, going through her notes, her briefcase open in front of her.

A tall, heavyset Latino man with a mop of salt and pepper hair, an unkempt mustache and an unruly goatee, entered through the doors. Looking disorganized in a rumpled navy blue suit, his gray-and-burgundy paisley tie slightly askew, he sauntered down the center aisle, a slight hitch in his step. Round, thin-framed glasses perched on his bulbous nose, and his bright, alert gray eyes watched everything closely as he went through the gate and set his briefcase on the defendant's table in front of Fenway and McVie.

The side door opened heavily, and the bailiff brought in Professor Virgil Cygnus. The orange jumpsuit made the respected Shakespeare scholar look old, hiding his powerful arms in the loose-fitting outfit, but his eyes were bright. The bailiff motioned to Cygnus to sit, and as soon as he was satisfied that Cygnus wouldn't go anywhere, he walked to his spot in front of the judge's podium.

"All rise," he said.

Fenway and McVie stood up with everyone else.

"Dominguez County Superior Court now in session, the Honorable Didi Miller presiding." The judge, a short but wiry woman with tight black curly hair and Buddy Holly glasses, stomped up to her seat and asked everyone to sit down.

"I like Judge Miller," McVie whispered to Fenway. "Low tolerance for bullshit."

Judge Miller talked briefly about her views of the high-profile case, her expectations of nothing but the lawyers' best behavior, and her warnings to the audience, stating she'd order anyone who interrupted the proceedings to leave. She looked pointedly at the Nidever students near the back. Xavier and Amanda slunk down in their chairs.

"Thank you, Your Honor," the defense attorney said.

The clerk got up from her chair. "Criminal cause for arraignment. Counsel, please state your appearances."

Jennifer Kim stood quickly. "Jennifer Kim for Dominguez County. Good morning, Your Honor."

The judge swiveled her head to the defense table.

The defense lawyer stood, Professor Cygnus following a half-second afterward. "Evans Dahl for Mr. Cygnus."

"Good morning," Judge Miller said, nodding to the professor. "Sir, can you state your full name for the record?"

Cygnus nodded. "Virgil Devonte Cygnus, Your Honor."

The judge smiled, tight-lipped. "Thank you, Mr. Cygnus. This is an arraignment hearing. I'll read the indictment. It's fairly straightforward." The judge held a few sheets of paper, adjusted her glasses, and read. "'Count one, murder in the second degree. Between Tuesday, November sixth of this year, at approximately eleven P.M., and Wednesday, November seventh of this year, at approximately two A.M., within the jurisdiction of Dominguez County, the defendant Virgil

Devonte Cygnus did knowingly and intentionally commit the murder of Jessica Marquez with malice aforethought, as defined in California Penal Code one-eight-seven.'" She set the papers down. "See? I told you it was straightforward." She pushed her glasses up on her nose. "Counselor Dahl, have you discussed the charge set forth in this indictment with your client?"

"I have, Your Honor."

"And will your client be entering a plea at this time?"

"Yes, Your Honor. He pleads not guilty."

The judge nodded. "So entered." She turned to ADA Kim. "Is there discovery?"

"Yes, Your Honor," said Kim. "It will go to the defense by Friday at the latest." She looked at Dahl. "The parties expect to engage in plea discussions."

"When do you expect to have those discussions?"

"Perhaps they can begin on Monday, Your Honor. I expect they'll take at least a few weeks."

"Will both parties be ready for trial after that?"

"Pending discovery, Your Honor," said Dahl.

"Yes, Your Honor," said Kim.

"We'll be running into the Christmas recess," the judge said. "So we'll schedule the trial January second—that's a Thursday. Sorry if that ruins your New Year's Eve plans, but justice is a cruel mistress. And maybe that will incentivize you to negotiate the plea before you pop the champagne and kiss your sweetie at midnight."

"Thank you, Your Honor," said Kim.

"Regarding bail—" the judge began.

"Yes, Your Honor," Kim interrupted. "This is a serious crime, and given the defendant's—"

Judge Miller held up her hand. "Half a million dollars," said the judge. "Is there anything else?"

Kim blinked hard. "No, Your Honor."

Evans Dahl opened his mouth, then closed it. His jaw tightened. "No, Your Honor."

The judge banged her gavel. "Next case."

The bailiff left out the side door.

Judge Miller tilted her head. "I can see many of you were here only for the first arraignment. And it looks like many are here for the second arraignment. So let's take a fifteen-minute recess so everyone who wants to leave can leave, and everyone who wants a seat can find one." She banged her gavel again, then stood up and stalked off through the side door.

Almost everyone in the gallery stood, then headed to the center aisle and began filing out. Fenway turned around to watch. Xavier and Amanda kept sitting near the back on the prosecution's side, talking to each other in hushed tones, serious looks on both their faces.

"That was quick," Fenway said, a knot in her stomach. She shouldn't be this tense for her father's arraignment.

"Just the way Judge Miller likes it," McVie replied. "Short, sweet, and drama-free. Everyone here hoping to see a circus just realized they wasted their time."

"She ran out in a hurry," Fenway said.

McVie smirked. "Rumor is she's on a cleanse."

Fenway lightly elbowed McVie in the ribs. "Maybe *that's* why she was so quick."

ADA Kim walked over to the defendant's table and started a conversation with Evans Dahl, not five feet in front of Fenway. She could hear snippets of what Kim said in a low voice—"plea bargain," "give up names," and "money laundering" were all plainly audible.

The side door opened and Nathaniel Ferris walked in. The bailiff behind him had a confused look on his face as he saw the court in recess.

A dash over six feet tall, Ferris's good looks had barely faded in his sixties. He wore a black tailored suit and walked confidently, head up and shoulders back, as if his name were on the courthouse. Ferris raised his hand in solemn greeting, and Fenway followed his eyes, turning around and craning her neck. Charlotte and Piper had entered the courtroom as well. Charlotte took a seat about four chairs in from the center aisle, three rows behind Fenway, and Piper sat in the row behind her.

"You okay?" McVie said in a whisper.

"Sure." She turned. "I don't know why I'm nervous. I know this is mostly a formality."

McVie leaned forward, putting his hands on the railing above the ironwork. "You haven't seen your father in court before. It's understandable."

Fenway narrowed her eyes. "Hey—you're supposed to be sitting on the prosecutor's side, not behind the defendant. You *are* the sheriff, aren't you?"

He gave her a sheepish grin. "Well, yeah, but since I'll be out of this position in six weeks, I figured no one would care. Besides, I knew you'd be a little nervous. I thought I'd give you some moral support. And it's hard to do that from the prosecution's side."

"Tell that to Jennifer Kim. She gave me a talking-to about sitting with Charlotte and Piper this morning." Fenway cleared her throat. "Where's his lawyer?"

"She's probably out in the hall. The recess is another ten minutes, right?"

"Right." Imani Ingram was one of the best criminal lawyers in the business. Fenway scolded herself for her creeping doubt.

"I can give you a dozen names."

Fenway's head whipped around at the bold statement from Cygnus.

He stood up, nodding enthusiastically. "Maybe *more* than a dozen," he said.

"If he gives up these names," Dahl said pointedly, "this will make your career, Jennifer. Maybe we should start talking deal."

Jennifer Kim frowned. "Unless the good professor can provide enough evidence to secure a conviction, a dozen names are useless to me. Now the professor, on the other hand—there's more than enough to make my case against him. A murder conviction for a big name like Virgil Cygnus? I don't think I'll have any problem with my career."

"I wouldn't be so confident." Dahl scoffed. "By the time the case is over, everyone will know that Professor Cygnus was just doing Jessica Marquez's bidding. It was a disaster from the start."

"The victim isn't on trial, and you better not think you can bring up her past." Kim folded her arms.

"You mix the ingredients properly, and any jury can be swayed," Dahl said with a smile.

The ADA shook her head. "I know you're not above doing that kind of thing."

"You catching this, McVie?" Fenway whispered, opening her purse and searching through it for her phone, but watching the scene in front of her closely, hanging on every word.

"Yep," McVie said in a low voice. "Jennifer's playing hardball. If Cygnus actually gives up both names *and* evidence, we'll finally get somewhere with the money laundering investigation."

"I have proof to go with those names," Cygnus said. "Think of how many arrests you'll get out of this. The Cayman accounts are accessible if you know where to look. That alone should give you enough to go on, especially after I give up the mastermind behind this."

"You're acting like prosecuting a massive conspiracy is a walk in the park," Kim said, turning to Cygnus. "You'll have to testify, you know."

"As long as I can spend the next few months with my wife," Cygnus said. "I think the district attorney will be very interested to know who's behind the murders and behind all the laundered money."

Kim cocked her head toward Evans Dahl. "Counselor, won't you advise your client to keep those names to himself until he can work out a deal?"

Dahl smiled. "I've advised him of his rights, Ms. Kim. In the courtroom, in an interview room, wherever. The professor wants to cooperate."

"I can give you the name of the person who coordinated the use of the scholarship fund right now," Cygnus said. "Do your research. If it checks out, then I'll negotiate for my freedom in exchange for the names of the big players behind the scenes."

Fenway pulled her phone out of her purse and tapped on the voice memo app—then the phone slipped out of her hand and onto the tile floor with a clatter.

"Negotiating in the courtroom is highly irregular, Professor," Kim said.

Fenway leaned to her left to grab her phone off the floor—

Bang. Bang. A high-pitched *snap* next to her right ear.

The shots had come from the rear of the courtroom. People screamed. McVie grabbed her shoulders and pulled her down. She smacked her head on the ironwork in front of the row and saw stars. McVie shielded her body with his.

Feet scrambled as people ran for the doors, sprinted for the exits, hid behind their seats. Screaming and yelling, pushing chairs, shouting at each other, all trying to get out of the courtroom.

The weight of McVie's body on her back, his breath hot in her ear.

"Count to thirty before you get up," he whispered. "I love you, Fenway."

And then McVie was up, walking across the rows of chairs, barking orders for people to stay down. Fenway caught him out of the corner of her eye as he raced out of the courtroom, pulling up his radio, crackling and buzzing, requesting all units to respond. And then he disappeared as the heavy double doors began to close.

This is exactly why I shouldn't be categorized as a peace officer. McVie's instinct was always to run *toward* the fire, while Fenway lay motionless in fear on the floor.

Wait.

Did Craig just tell me he loved me?

She turned her head and looked through the ironwork barrier that separated her from the defense table.

Virgil Cygnus's sightless eyes stared back at her.

II

9:15 AM

CHAPTER TWO

The screaming stopped after what seemed like only a second or two. The large double doors slammed shut, echoing through the room. There was a loud, low clicking sound, like a large piece of metal sliding into place.

Fenway couldn't tear her gaze from the professor's dead body, his eyes boring into her soul. With effort, she blinked. Tears leaked out of the corners of her eyes, running down the side of her face.

Two shots.

Okay.

She'd forgotten to count to thirty, but things seemed to have calmed down.

She took a deep breath and pulled herself up into a crouch. Her forehead hurt, a sharp pain where she'd hit it on the ironwork. Walking low and awkwardly, she pushed through the swinging gate then got on all fours and crawled toward the defense table. Jennifer Kim and Evans Dahl were both sitting on the floor, the petite well-dressed woman and the large rumpled man with the same dazed looks in their eyes.

"Were either of you hit?" she whispered.

Dahl shook his head. Kim blinked three times.

"Were you hit, Jennifer?"

Kim pursed her lips and gave a slight shake of her head.

Fenway scooted over to the dead body of Virgil Cygnus. Near his temple was a bullet wound, a dark red hole that the shadow of the table partially concealed. She put two fingers on his neck at the jugular. Fenway wasn't surprised at the absence of a pulse.

He was about to name names.

Fenway raised her head and sniffed. Maybe a faint smell of nitroglycerin, but with the new paint and varnish competing in her nose, it was hard to say for sure. She looked up, but the defense table blocked her view, making it hard to determine if gun smoke still hung in the air.

With her back to the judge's bench, she looked to her left. On Fenway's side of the defense table, Jennifer Kim and Evans Dahl sat on the floor, only a foot or two away from Cygnus's body. Turning her head, she saw her father, sitting with his legs sprawled in front of him. He put a hand on his chest and took a deep breath, then turned his head and caught Fenway's eye. A look of relief spread over his face.

Fenway pulled herself up to her knees so she could survey the whole courtroom. No one holding a gun. No one threatening anyone. Fenway set her jaw—there wasn't an immediate threat.

"Has anyone been hit?" Fenway called out.

In the gallery, several people began to get to their feet.

Judith Cygnus, the professor's wife, had fallen in the center aisle, and now was struggling to stand. Xavier disentangled himself from Amanda, and the young man hurried over to help the recent widow up.

Cynthia Schimmelhorn stood in the rear of the gallery near the center aisle, leaning on the backs of the row of chairs in front of her. Even after the gunshots, nary a hair was out of place in her elegantly styled updo, her silvery hair pulled back out of her face. Likewise, her makeup, a light application of subtle reds and pinks that accentuated her northern European features, was perfect.

A white man stood with his hands on his hips in the middle of the aisle a few feet away from Schimmelhorn. Wearing a fitted charcoal gray suit, white dress shirt, and a garish multicolored tie, he was slender and of medium height, but had the wiry, strong build of an acrobat. Fenway tried to remember where she had seen his face before.

She touched her forehead where she'd hit it, and pulled her hand away just as quickly. It still hurt.

"Charlotte?" Ferris called.

"I'm here," said a voice from between two rows on the defense side of the gallery. Charlotte stood, a little tentatively, but when no one seemed to fire another shot, she rushed through the swinging gate and Ferris swept her into a desperate embrace.

Piper popped her head above the row of chairs behind where Charlotte had been sitting. Fenway nodded at her.

"Look around, everyone," Fenway said. "Is anyone still on the floor? Is anyone injured?"

Two rows in front of Cynthia Schimmelhorn and the man in the dark suit, a brunette woman who looked to be in her late forties pulled herself up so that her eyes were visible over the back of the chair in front of her. "Is it—is it over?" she said.

Judith Cygnus stiffened at the sound of the woman's voice. Xavier, who was helping Judith into a seat, flinched, then looked up. He shot a glance over at Amanda, who narrowed her eyes.

"Xavier, is that you?"

"Yes, it's me, Professor Nedermeyer."

Ah—Leda Nedermeyer. The head of the English department at Nidever—and, supposedly, Professor Cygnus's lover for over a decade. About five foot five and rail-thin, she wore her wavy light brown hair in a chin-length asymmetrical cut that looked a decade too young for her. With a frazzled look in her eye as she looked around the courtroom, she pulled herself up to a standing position and wrapped her off-white cardigan closer around her front. It made sense that Nedermeyer would not only be at his arraignment but sit near the back, away from her lover's wife.

Near where the shots came from.

Another movement at the rear of the courtroom, but this one from the far end of the prosecution's side. Shadows shrouded that corner, and the figure, dressed in black slacks and a dark gray sweater, stood near the wall. Her dark, straight tresses hung in front of her face. She moved into the side aisle, almost catlike, and then walked to the side door. She pulled the handle, but the door didn't move.

"Rose," Fenway called, more like a statement than anything.

The woman froze and looked up at Fenway. Yes, that was Rose Morgan, all right. Fenway hadn't expected to see her ever again, not after Cygnus had almost killed her, and certainly not after she'd picked up the USB stick and fled into the night. But here she was in the flesh. With the man who threatened her life dead on the floor.

Rose nodded. "Hi, Coroner."

Fenway opened her mouth to say how surprised she was to see her, then thought better of it. "Are you okay? Were you hit?"

"I'm fine. Not a scratch."

"Anybody back there with you?"

"With *me?*"

"On the floor, maybe? Anyone between the rows there?"

Rose craned her neck, looking between several of the rows. "Not that I can see."

Fenway nodded. "Good."

"Ferris!" the man in the charcoal suit shouted. "Is this your idea of a joke? Do you think this is how you cut and run?"

Nathaniel Ferris, standing in front of the prosecutor's table, pulled away from Charlotte and narrowed his eyes at the man. "I don't think you know what you're talking about, Bryce." He took three steps toward him.

Ah, yes. Fenway remembered him now. Bryce R. Heissner, chief operations officer of Ferris Energy—Fenway had seen his picture on the website. Obviously here to see what would happen to the founder and chief executive.

"Shooting a gun in a courtroom!" Heissner snarled. "You've embarrassed the company, Nathaniel, you've embarrassed yourself—"

Fenway grimaced. Her father hadn't even been on the side of the courtroom from where the shot had been fired. "Mr. Heissner,"

Fenway said sharply, "this is not a time for baseless accusations. Now, do you see anyone who's been—"

"This is all Nathaniel's doing," Heissner said.

"I had nothing—" Ferris began.

"Gentlemen!" Fenway belted, and both her father and Heissner were quiet. "I'll ask again—do you see anyone else injured or hurt?"

"We're all fine," Xavier said.

"Wait," Ferris said. "Anyone *else?*"

"Professor Cygnus," Fenway said. "He was shot."

Judith Cygnus and Leda Nedermeyer both gasped. Where they were sitting, neither of them could see the professor's lifeless body, partially blocked by the defense table.

Judith Cygnus stood and took four cautious steps forward. Her husband lay in front of her, his legs splayed at an unusual angle. Judith's hand clasped over her mouth. Fenway rushed toward her and caught her as she sank onto the floor, tears spilling down her cheeks. "Virg—oh, dammit, Virg," she keened, bringing up her other hand too, burying her face in her palms.

Fenway looked up. Leda Nedermeyer was standing now, her hands halfway in front of her like they were floating unattached to her body, as if she didn't know what to do with them. "Vir—Professor Cygnus is dead?"

"I'm afraid so," Fenway said.

"I swear," Heissner growled, looking at Nathaniel Ferris, "if you *are* behind this, you're sure as hell going down with the ship. I promise you that."

"A man is dead, Bryce," Cynthia Schimmelhorn said softly. "Stop making this about your righteous indignation."

"Did anyone see the shooter?" Fenway asked.

Cynthia Schimmelhorn looked around the room, craning her neck, and the others followed suit. No one spoke.

"No one?" Fenway asked again.

Schimmelhorn turned in the aisle and faced the double doors. She pushed the crossbar on the left door, but nothing happened.

"We're locked in," said Leda Nedermeyer.

"It appears so." Cynthia Schimmelhorn tried the right door, but it, too, held fast.

"Lockdown protocol," Piper said. "Gunshots fired in a public building. We're in active shooter mode."

"Which means what, exactly?" Charlotte asked.

ADA Kim cleared her throat. "It means that the doors automatically lock until there's no more indication of a threat."

"The side door too?" Charlotte said, walking to the metal door near the prosecution table and trying the handle. It didn't budge.

"The side door too," Piper replied. "And that one's a steel door."

Fenway looked up and took in the full layout of the courtroom. She'd noticed the full use of mahogany and brushed nickel before, but she noticed the details this time.

The front of the judge's bench was dark wood, decorated simply with outlines of rectangles in mahogany trim, each about a foot high and two feet wide. Fenway couldn't tell if the rectangles were separate panels or not.

The side door, the one Nathaniel Ferris had entered, was in the wall on the prosecution's side. Fenway assumed it led to the holding area and to the judge's chambers. Next to the side door, on the far side of the witness stand, two steps, about five feet wide, on the far side of the witness stand, led up to the dais.

On the right side, beyond the defense's table, matching steps between the low wall of the jury box and the outside edge of the judge's bench led up to the dais. Behind the jury box stood two flagpoles, one with the United States flag, trimmed with gold on the outside edge, and the other with the California state flag. The desks for the prosecution on the left and the defense on the right matched, solid Craftsman-style dark mahogany tables with three brown leather-padded straight-backed chairs behind each.

Fenway turned and surveyed the gallery. The gate in the middle of the gallery divider, about four feet wide, swung both ways, and served as the front of the long, wide center aisle. The large double doors stood at the rear of the center aisle, with a large clock on the wall with art déco numerals underscoring the aesthetic. But the green exit sign above it and an industrial-looking push bar mechanism didn't match the design of the rest of the room.

Neither did the two large white metal grilles stationed in the back wall, three feet above the floor and at a distance of about five feet on either side of the double doors. The grilles were roughly two feet square. Fenway blinked. They resembled the in-wall speaker enclosures in the "concert hall" room at her father's mansion, but larger. Maybe they were vents or doors for electrical panels. The back aisle was clear of chairs all the way across. At the end of the back aisle, on the defense's side, an archway in the side wall led to—what? A closet? An exit? Another room? Maybe somewhere the killer could hide? She'd have to check it out.

Much of the courtroom looked luxurious and expensive, but Fenway wondered if the rest of the furniture and decorations were simple veneers and faux nickel as well.

She raised her head and scanned the room again. Two shots from the back of the courtroom, almost directly behind where she'd been sitting. But she'd leaned over, and there was that odd *snap* at the same time. She shook her head. It had all happened so fast. Was she sure about what she heard and saw? She wasn't that familiar with the acoustics of the room.

Judge Didi Miller had called a recess, with many of the gallery-goers in the aisle, either going out or coming in, meaning only a handful of people had been sitting.

Had there been anyone sitting behind her in any of the dozen rows? Charlotte and Piper, and possibly Leda. Other than that, she didn't know. She was paying attention to what Cygnus was saying, not what was happening behind her.

"All right—where did the shots come from?" asked Ferris, stepping into the aisle.

Fenway shook her head. Only her father could be a murder suspect and think he could command a room where another murder had just taken place.

"Dad," she said sharply, "I think I can take it from here."

He turned to look at her, eyes wide with surprise, then his gaze softened as he nodded.

"This is ridiculous," Cynthia Schimmelhorn said. "We all went through a metal detector before entering the courtroom, yet someone got a gun in here. Are the police officers really so incompetent?"

Fenway bristled. She knew the guards, and she knew they were capable. If there had been a flaw, it was in the design of the system or the implementation of the protocols—not in the way the guards had executed the implementation.

The shooter had been accurate. Professor Cygnus had been killed by a head shot. The information he promised—naming who was behind the money trail, the phantom oil tankers, and the multibillion-dollar conspiracy—would never be delivered.

As angry as she was at Schimmelhorn's statement criticizing the officers' competence, one thing was certain: someone *had* gotten a gun into the courtroom.

For all she knew, the killer could still be in the room. "Are you sure no one saw the shooter?" she said.

A dozen heads swiveled, looking all around the room. Then Schimmelhorn said cautiously, "I might have. I was sitting in the last row."

"On which side of the courtroom?"

"Oh—the right side, where I am now. Behind the defense. And the gun sounded right next to me. It was chaos right afterward, of course, but I did see a man in a black sweatshirt run out." She shrugged. "But I don't know if he was the shooter."

"Show me where you were sitting."

Schimmelhorn took several steps to her right, hesitated, then paused at a chair on the aisle side, right next to the large square column. "Here."

"And was the shot on the left side of you or the right side?"

Schimmelhorn closed her eyes. "It was behind me—but I'm not sure which side."

"In the back aisle," Fenway said.

Leda Nedermeyer narrowed her eyes at Cynthia Schimmelhorn. "I'm not sure about that," she said quietly. "I didn't see the shooter either, but I don't remember anyone like that behind the last row."

Schimmelhorn glared coldly. "Professor Nedermeyer, I hate to disagree with you, but I know what I saw."

"Yes, yes," Nedermeyer said, nodding. "Of course. I could be wrong. There was quite a crowd." Her eyes glazed over for a moment.

Fenway studied the last two rows of chairs, interrupted by the columns. Witnesses often didn't recall accurately, especially during chaos. But *no one* seeing the shooter? That would have only happened if the killer had hidden behind the four-foot-square column, which blocked the view to the center aisle.

Fenway looked at ADA Kim, sitting motionless, and Evans Dahl, still on the floor near the body. Maybe it was just the shock of someone standing between them being shot in the head, but she had to make sure they were okay before she started her investigation.

"Mr. Dahl? Ms. Kim?"

Evans Dahl grunted. Kim was silent.

"Jennifer?" Fenway repeated. Kim continued to stare, dumbfounded and horrified, at the body of Virgil Cygnus.

"Jennifer!" Fenway said sharply.

Kim jumped as if shocked. "Sorry—sorry. No—I'm not injured. I didn't get hit."

Fenway tried to give Kim a reassuring smile, but she had gone back to staring at Cygnus's twisted, unmoving body.

Fenway turned to Evans Dahl, whose legs were in an awkward position on the floor behind him. He took off his round-rimmed glasses and wiped his face on his suit jacket sleeve.

"You weren't shot either, right, Mr. Dahl?"

"No—but I did something to my leg."

Fenway crouched next to him. "The left one or the right one?"

"Left," Dahl said, wincing. "My ankle, actually."

"Does it hurt right now?" Fenway held her hands out in front of her, about eight inches above his ankle.

"A little. Kind of a throbbing pain."

"What about numbness or tingling?"

"None."

"Can you move it at all?" Fenway asked.

Dahl moved his foot and grimaced.

"Did you hear a noise when you fell?"

Dahl gave Fenway a game smile. "Well, there was the gunshot."

Fenway nodded. "But nothing from your ankle? A pop or a crack or anything like that?"

"I don't think so, but, you know, I had a lot of other things to pay attention to."

Fenway asked him a few more questions, then gingerly pulled his sock down to the top of his shoe. He grimaced every time Fenway touched the area. His ankle had yellowed a half shade.

"I think it's a sprain, Mr. Dahl, but from what I see, and from what you've told me, I don't think it's broken. It'll bruise pretty badly —you can already see it starting to discolor. If you can't put weight on it in the next half hour or so, we may need to take you to the hospital."

He swore under his breath and blinked hard behind his glasses. "I hate hospitals."

"If you have someone to help you get into a car, this might be something they can take care of at one of those medical clinics," Fenway said. "Although they might send you to the emergency room anyway."

"You used to be a nurse, right?"

"Nurse practitioner, yes."

Dahl nodded. "Can I move to a seat? Maybe something where, uh —" He motioned with his head to the professor's body lying next to him.

Fenway bit her lip. It wasn't ideal to move him. If he *had* broken a bone, any weight at all on the ankle could worsen the damage—and the pain. But sitting that close to a corpse wasn't ideal either.

"Yes," she said. "Let's get some help."

She got to her feet, then looked around the room and caught Xavier's eye. "Xavier—can you help me lift Mr. Dahl?"

Xavier nodded, stood, and walked up the aisle through the gate. Fenway crouched on Dahl's left side, placing his arm around her shoulders. Xavier did the same on the other side, and together they hefted the defense attorney upright. Dahl held his left foot off the ground and winced. Amanda hurried over and held open the gate while Evans Dahl was led, half-hopping, half-hobbling, to the aisle seat in the second row on the prosecution's side. He sat down heavily and Xavier disentangled himself quickly and took several steps back.

"Are you all right, Mr. Dahl?" Fenway asked.

Dahl turned to his left and carefully lifted the leg with the injured ankle onto the seats next to him. "I think so. I'll keep it up on the chair, shall I?"

"Yes," Fenway said. "And take your shoe off." Ice would be best, and maybe ibuprofen, but at least he could rest and elevate his ankle. She straightened up and turned halfway toward the rest of the room. "Anyone have ibuprofen? Advil?"

Amanda raised her left hand, as if she were in class, and with her right hand dug in her purse until she produced a small travel-sized pill pack that she gave to Fenway.

"Thanks, Amanda." She tapped two pills out into Evans Dahl's hand and was about to ask for some water, but Dahl tipped his head back and dry-swallowed the ibuprofen.

Nathaniel Ferris turned around in the center aisle, trying to get eye contact with everyone he could. "Anyone else injured? No?"

Fenway stepped in front of him. "I got this, Dad."

"Right, sorry."

"What do we do now?" Rose said from the corner. "We're on lockdown? Until when?"

"I don't know," Fenway said. "It's possible the shooter ran out with the rest of the gallery in the confusion." She raised her head and watched Rose in the shadows behind the large column on the prosecution's side. Could Cynthia have mistaken Rose's dark hair for a hood? Cynthia Schimmelhorn seemed like the kind of "nice white lady" who wouldn't care about the difference.

Fenway shut her eyes tight. *No.* That was jumping to a conclusion about Cynthia Schimmelhorn that might lead Fenway down the wrong path. She was getting a headache from the knock to her head. She hoped it wasn't affecting her judgment.

"Well, I *did* see the shooter run out," said Cynthia Schimmelhorn under her breath. Defensiveness glinted on Schimmelhorn's face. Maybe it was unfair to jump to conclusions, but Fenway planned to examine Rose more closely anyway.

"So the shooter could be anywhere," piped up Amanda.

"I suppose," Fenway said, "but since no one else has been shot, and no one's holding a gun on us, I think the danger has passed." Fenway felt a chill up her spine. There was no evidence the danger had passed. McVie had run out after the gunshots, and Fenway assumed he was pursuing the shooter. But if he had falsely assumed the shooter had run out the double doors, the danger was still in the room.

As if reading Fenway's thoughts, Leda Nedermeyer said carefully, "But if the shooter didn't leave, it means he's still in here with us."

"Or she," Xavier said. "There's twelve—no, thirteen of us in here. And only four men. If the shooter's in here, it's more likely to be a woman than a man."

Amanda elbowed him and gave him a disapproving look out of the corner of her eye.

"What?" Xavier said. "It's a numbers game."

"It's not *any* kind of game," Fenway said. "We're in lockdown. We have no choice but to wait until the all-clear."

"That's not very reassuring," said Professor Nedermeyer.

"I'm sorry," Fenway said, "but it's the best I've got."

From her spot in the center aisle, she looked around at the motley group and wondered if any of them would make decent witnesses.

A little voice in her head said maybe a few of them would make decent suspects, too.

Her father, waiting for arraignment on his own murder charge, might be a good suspect. But Fenway knew him well enough to know that this wouldn't be a tactic he would employ to get out of a murder charge. He'd use the legal system to his advantage and a high-priced lawyer like Imani Ingram. Exactly what he *was* doing, in fact.

Was Charlotte a good suspect? In spite of her annoying Barbie-doll exterior, Charlotte was not only savvy, but quite a good shot. She'd been sitting behind Fenway, too. Fenway had seen the targets that Charlotte brought home after an hour at the gun range. Charlotte was also a realist and might gauge her husband's chances at being convicted better than he would.

Fenway sighed. She'd have to include her father and Charlotte in the suspect pool, although she couldn't think of why either of them would target Cygnus. Unless he was about to point the finger at one of them.

Fenway turned and looked at the two lawyers, Evans Dahl with his leg elevated, and Jennifer Kim, struggling to her feet. She knew that neither ADA Kim nor Evans Dahl had pulled the trigger, but it didn't mean they didn't have someone do it for them. What were the chances that either of them had been behind the shooting? It didn't make sense. The courtroom was their bread and butter. Of course, Piper didn't trust Jennifer Kim at all. But was that just because Kim insisted that Piper resign?

The Ferris Energy contingent—Schimmelhorn and Heissner—was an unknown quantity. From what Fenway knew, Schimmelhorn had taken Cygnus's Shakespeare class years ago, and she loved him like a surrogate father. And as for Heissner, he was here for Nathaniel Ferris, not for Cygnus. Unless there was something in their past Fenway didn't know about, neither of them had a motive. But both of them had been behind Fenway at the time of the shooting, so it could have been one of them.

Xavier Go and Amanda Kohl still, despite what happened when

their director had been arrested for murder, seemed to be romantically involved. But Fenway had heard that *Othello* had not gone well after the arrest. Two women ahead of her in line at the grocery store had been discussing how poor the performance Saturday night had been. The student-actors would certainly be disappointed, if not downright angry. Would either Xavier or Amanda be upset enough at Cygnus that they'd want revenge?

And of course Professor Cygnus had both a wife *and* a mistress. Both seemed genuinely shocked that Cygnus had been shot and killed. But as Fenway knew, hell hath no fury like a woman scorned, and Judith Cygnus fit that category. She was battling cancer and losing, and she looked frail. But perhaps she wasn't as weak as she let on.

Leda Nedermeyer didn't seem the type either, but love and hate were closely related—and if she'd been waiting for ten or fifteen years to be with the man she loved, there was no telling what she might do.

Rose Morgan was a major wild card. She was a liar, a cheat, and a fraud, as Fenway had uncovered. Rose had worked directly with the money launderers to monitor their enterprise at Central Auto Body as the owner laundered several million dollars. If Cygnus *had* named names instead of getting shot in the head, there would likely be questions for Rose Morgan. There might be an end to her employment, or even a threat to her life. So perhaps keeping Cygnus from blabbing was in Rose's best interest. There was a difference, though, between keeping two sets of books and committing murder. Especially a brazen shooting in a crowded courtroom.

No way was Piper involved in the shooting. She was the one who uncovered the whole conspiracy to begin with. And Fenway trusted her completely.

Twelve people in the courtroom. Fenway made thirteen. And she knew for sure that *she* hadn't fired the shots.

If the shooter—or the person who had hired the shooter—was in the room, at least three of them would make excellent suspects. Cygnus's wife, his lover, and Rose Morgan.

But this was all conjecture. The guards or McVie or one of the sheriff's deputies might have captured the shooter. Maybe one of Fenway's sergeants, Dez or Mark, would have rushed over from the Coroner's Office and assisted with the arrest.

Fenway itched to know more. She pulled out her cell phone to see if McVie could tell her what was going on.

If she had heard him correctly when they were both on the floor right after the shooting.

And if he had caught the shooter. Perhaps it *was* the man in the hoodie Cynthia Schimmelhorn had seen.

No service.

She swore softly under her breath.

"So," Cynthia Schimmelhorn said, "we're stuck here until we get some sort of all-clear signal?"

"I'm afraid so," said Fenway. She was torn—she itched to know more, to start collecting information. Yet without contacting McVie or Dez—or *someone* from the outside world—she hesitated to take the first step. She walked back to her previous seat in the front row.

Conversation in the courtroom was bubbling at a low volume. She examined the chair she'd sat in. The seat and back were a dark wood veneer, which saved money compared to real wood chairs but would look awful in six months. She clicked her fingernail against the chair's legs. Aluminum treated for a brushed nickel look. She tried to pick up the chair, but the chair leg was snapped to the leg of the chair next to it. She'd have to pop out the chair on the side before she could pick up one in the middle.

She glanced over at Judith Cygnus, who had moved from the front row and was now sitting a few rows behind Fenway on the end. Tear tracks stained Judith's cheeks, but she blankly stared forward now. Fenway turned her gaze toward the rear of the gallery, with Xavier and Amanda one seat apart from each other, each of them reading a textbook. Rose Morgan stood behind them, her dark eyes watching Cynthia Schimmelhorn, who, along with Bryce Heissner, skulked near the double doors, their conversation low.

Fenway looked across at Evans Dahl, red-faced with his leg up. She could do nothing else for him, not at the moment. She hoped the ibuprofen would at least take the edge off the pain.

At any second, they could announce an all-clear.

The moment of the shooting flooded into Fenway's head.

Cygnus's voice. *I think the district attorney will be very interested to know who's behind the murders and behind all of the laundered money.*

It was a grandiose statement from a stage director attempting every last drop of attention from the moment. And it had been his last.

Then the two shots.

And the odd *snap*. Had that been a ricochet?

But it had been so loud.

She played the moment and cleaved the milliseconds in her mind, but nothing came clearer.

She had a sinking feeling in the pit of her stomach.

Should she be keeping her eye on everyone in the room? She was only one person, and there were twelve others. She could ask Jennifer and Piper too, but she didn't want anyone to be more on edge than they already were. Fenway had no idea how long they would be locked in.

At least she could gather some evidence and ask some questions. It would keep her mind off the professor's dead body on the floor in front of the defense table.

CHAPTER THREE

Fenway opened her eyes and turned her head. Everyone was still in the same spot except for Rose Morgan, who sat on the floor, her back against the rear wall, shrouded in shadow.

Fenway focused on the ratty backpack sitting on the chair next to Piper. There was a mountain of evidence against Professor Cygnus on the laptop in there. She took a few steps and caught Piper's eye. "Hey."

"Hey, Fenway."

Fenway's shoulders were tight, but she forced herself to smile. "Kind of weird, you not being on my team anymore."

Piper nodded. "Not as weird as Professor Cygnus getting shot and killed right in front of us." She cocked her head. "Are you okay?"

"Yeah." Fenway shuffled her feet and pointed at Piper's ratty backpack. "You have your new laptop in there?"

"Yes."

"Can you use it to help figure out what's going on?"

Piper hesitated.

"You want me to talk to your boss first?" Fenway asked.

"Uh—yeah, I guess I do." Piper chewed on her bottom lip. "You know that the paint in the courtroom blocks cellphone signals, right?"

"Oh—no, I guess not. So that's why my cellphone wouldn't work in here. There's actually *paint* that can kill a signal?"

"Yeah—the team consulted me on some of the security measures when they were figuring out the construction." Piper's eyes lit up. "The paint reduces signals significantly. Wi-Fi and radio and TV, too. EMF-shielding paint, they call it. Fifty liters for three hundred bucks."

"I didn't even know anti-cellphone paint existed."

"The manufacturers put a special type of nickel-cobalt alloy in it. Some security experts think it's a waste of money and that you can just mix iron oxide in regular paint, but I disagree. See, the molecules of the nickel and cobalt vibrate at the same frequency—"

"I don't need a chemistry lesson right now, Piper."

"Right, sorry."

"How do we get connected to the sheriff?"

Piper nodded. "Yeah—okay, near the clerk's station here, there should be an Ethernet port."

"Like an old-school wired connection?"

"Right."

"Your brand-new laptop doesn't have an old-school Ethernet port though, right?"

Piper rolled her eyes. "Like I'd ever buy a laptop without the proper dongles." She turned and picked up her backpack from between the rows, then hurried through the gate to the front of the courtroom. Fenway followed.

Her father and Charlotte, standing together in front of the prosecutor's table, followed her with their eyes. Fenway tried not to notice. She still was angry with her father, and even though Charlotte had taken her advice to hire Piper, she had no idea what to say to either of them.

Piper recoiled when she saw Cygnus's dead body in front of the defense table. "Oh, holy shit."

Fenway put a hand on Piper's shoulder. "Sorry. But we've got to do this. It's an active shooter scenario."

Piper took a deep breath. "I—I knew he was there. I just—crap,

Fenway, I don't think I've ever been that close to a dead body before. I certainly have never had to *work* so close to a dead body, anyway."

"Yeah, well, I've never been in an active shooter situation in a public building."

Piper's eyes, like ADA Kim's, were still fixed on Cygnus's dead body.

Fenway scanned the side of the dais below the judge's bench. There were two panels, about six inches wide by four inches high. One panel was on each side of the bench, each the same matching mahogany as the dais. She chose the one on the prosecutor's side, farthest from the body, and knelt down. Digging a thumbnail underneath the edge of the panel, she pried it up.

Bingo. Two power outlets, two microphone jacks, two USB ports, a couple of video ports—and, all by itself, an Ethernet jack.

"Here it is."

Piper hurried over with her bag, getting out a plastic adapter box shaped like a shark fin. She pulled two power cables out of her bag, then a coiled gray cable and a USB cable. Within thirty seconds, she had the adapter box and the laptop plugged in, and cords running from the laptop to the box to the Ethernet jack.

"Impressive," Fenway murmured. She'd had her back turned to everyone else for over a minute, so she straightened up and turned around. No one seemed to pay any attention to her except her father.

"How are you doing?" he said.

"Okay," Fenway replied. "Considering."

Nathaniel Ferris nodded, then, taking Charlotte by the hand, led them around the back of the prosecutor's table to sit.

Piper sat on the floor, legs tucked behind herself, and opened her laptop. She clicked around for a moment.

"You doing okay, Evans?" Fenway asked the lawyer, who was still sitting in the second row with his left leg up.

He took off his round-rimmed spectacles and wiped his face with his sleeve again. "Do we have any water in here?"

Fenway looked around but didn't see a water fountain.

"Judge Miller might have a bottle up there," Evans said. "Maybe a couple, since she was planning on being in the courtroom all morning."

Fenway walked around the side of the judge's bench to the back, and sure enough, there were two unopened bottles of water on the desk. There was another panel set into the wood above the desk. When Fenway pried the cover off, she found jacks and plugs set up identically to the one below on the step.

"I found another plug set up here," Fenway said to Piper. "You might be more comfortable sitting." *And being farther away from the dead body.*

"Oh—uh—is it okay if I sit up there?"

"Not during court, but now? Sure."

"All right. Let me get my settings taken care of."

"Can you communicate with McVie?" Fenway asked, stepping down from the dais, going around the witness stand, and then leaning across the rail to hand the water bottle to Dahl. "Maybe from an instant-message program?"

"Yes, and I've already texted him from my laptop. But I want to see some stuff." She clicked around some more, typed, paused, and typed again. "Okay," she said in a low voice. "Here are the feeds from the courthouse cameras."

"What?"

"They didn't turn off my username and password yet. They turned off my remote access on Friday, but I figured if I was using a trusted computer inside the building, I might still have access. And I do."

"That new laptop is a trusted computer?"

Piper's lips twitched as she tried to hide a grin. "As far as the system is concerned, anyway."

"I'll have to forget everything I see here, won't I?"

"Shush. Do you want to see the feed from the courthouse cameras or not?"

"Yes."

Piper clicked one final time, and two screens showing wide-angle camera shots came on. "All right, this is last week, when they tested the system. You can see the workers installing the plugs and ports. One camera on each side of the court, both facing the judge."

"When did the courts start recording their proceedings?"

"Uh—I think the California Supreme Court made that decision a long time ago. It was intended for appeal review, but also to reduce the number of violent incidents in the courts."

"Like this one."

Piper shrugged. "Reduce, not eliminate."

Fenway nodded. "Do you have footage from today?"

"Sure do." Piper clicked again.

A black screen. A second later, the other screen also went black.

She frowned. "That's weird. Maybe if I...." Piper typed a couple of commands and hit *Enter* with a flourish.

The screens flashed, then went black again.

"I don't understand," Piper mumbled. She opened another video file. "This one's from yesterday."

"The courts were closed for Veterans Day yesterday."

"I know, but I need to figure out what went wrong."

More black screens.

After another ten minutes of searching, Piper found the end of the feed. On the video recording of Sunday afternoon around three o'clock, the first camera flickered and went dead, followed about thirty seconds later by the failure of the other.

"Interesting," Piper murmured.

"What?"

"Well—if it had been an equipment failure, most likely both cameras would have failed at the same time. The fact that it went about half a minute between failures possibly means that someone disconnected the camera feeds, one right after the other.

"Where would they have done that?" Fenway asked. "Certainly not at the cameras themselves."

"I don't think it would be possible. The cameras are mounted in the ceiling."

"Was anyone here over the weekend?"

"Not that I know of. Everything was finished last week. Not unless something was overlooked."

Fenway folded her arms. "Let's interview each person in here. Someone must have seen something. Even if they didn't know it at the time." She glanced up at the ceiling, at all the nickel-plated lights. "Is the audio working?"

"What do you mean?"

"The cameras were disconnected, sure, but that doesn't mean that the audio was disconnected."

"Huh." Piper dug through her backpack and pulled out a set of corded earbuds. "Let me see if I can hear anything."

She plugged the headphones into the laptop, clicked several times, and listened intently for about fifteen seconds.

"There's nothing here," she said. "That makes sense if whoever unplugged the video was in the control room—the audio probably was disconnected at the same time."

"I would assume," Fenway started, "that whoever turned the video off wanted to *do* something they didn't want recorded."

"That makes sense." Piper sighed. "I wish I had my old computer setup back. I mean, this laptop is super-fast and top-of-the-line, but I miss the two big monitors."

"Hopefully, we won't have to deal with this for too much longer. I bet McVie is arresting the shooter right now. I predict Dez or Mark or one of the bailiffs will open up those double doors any second now and tell us it's all over."

Piper smiled and shook her head. "It's like you've never worked for a public service organization before."

"Can't be any more bureaucratic than working for the hospital was."

"Don't hold your breath. Things move glacially at City Hall. Even if you *are* dating the sheriff." Piper elbowed Fenway jokingly. "McVie will focus so much on catching the bad guy that he won't even remember you're in here until after he submits the paperwork."

"Hardy har har." Fenway looked back at Piper's laptop screen.

Piper's fingers paused over the keys on her laptop.

"What is it, Piper?"

"Well," Piper said, "I'm not sure my new boss would want me to tell you this, but over the long weekend, I found out more information about the payments to and from Global Advantage Executive Consulting."

"What? Why didn't you say anything?"

"I was planning to tell you after your father's arraignment, when you and McVie were together."

Me and McVie together. Fenway closed her eyes and for a moment, they were on the floor again, his confession of love in her ear. Fenway took a deep breath and opened her eyes. "That makes sense. Let's take another stab at talking with McVie, and if we can't reach him, you might as well tell me now—I don't know how long we'll be in here."

Piper nodded and clicked on her messaging app. "McVie hasn't responded to my message yet. I'll ping him again." She typed a brief message and clicked.

A swoosh from the computer told Fenway the text had been sent. "I wish there were some other way to communicate with him. I mean, in crisis situations like this, I'm sure there are communication plans in place, right?"

Piper bit her lip, her brows knit. "There must be. Shall we look?" She disconnected her laptop and brought it to the desk of the judge's bench. She and Fenway searched through the drawers. The first dozen were empty, and Piper stood up after finding nothing in one of the bottom drawers. "What about walkie-talkies? Bailiffs have those, right? That must be something we can find in here."

The back wall behind the judge's bench had several low cabinets. A cord led from a wall plug through a small hole in the back of a counter next to the witness stand. "Isn't that the spot for the bailiff?" Fenway asked Piper.

"I don't know. I guess so."

Fenway pointed. "Is that a cabinet too?"

"Maybe?" Piper cocked her head to the side.

Fenway walked to the side of the counter and ran her hand around the side. She pushed slightly, and the whole side of the cabinet swung open. "Abracadabra."

The door opened smoothly, revealing three walkie-talkies docked in a charging station. A small green light shone brightly next to each of them. There were five empty spaces in the dock as well.

"That'll be better," Fenway said, grabbing one of the walkie-talkies. "Hopefully McVie has one of the others."

"There's one problem—" Piper began as Fenway turned the dial to the on position and turned up the volume.

A crash of static greeted their ears.

"Dammit," Fenway growled, turning down the volume. "Walkie-talkie frequencies too?"

"All electromagnetic and radio frequencies," Piper said.

"Pretty much anything that's not plugged in, then. Why even *have* the walkie-talkies in here?"

"They get charged in here, I guess. But walkie-talkies have stronger signals, especially if another walkie-talkie is close. You might be able to find a spot in the room that works."

"I *might?*"

Piper shrugged. "It's worth a shot."

"Okay." Fenway pinched the bridge of her nose and shut her eyes tight. "So how else can we get communication out of here? Is there a land line somewhere?"

"Not that I see. I think the clerk's area was supposed to have one set up, but maybe the order hasn't come in yet. I can try a software phone—I've got a couple of apps that might work."

"Okay. While you try that, maybe there's a spot in the room where all the planets align just right, and we can get a trace of a signal, either for our phones or for the walkie-talkies."

Piper nodded. "I'll see if anyone else is responding to texts besides McVie. Maybe Dez. I bet Rachel's in her office, too—reporters must be all over this."

"Yeah, good idea." Fenway turned the volume up about halfway, so the static was a low hum, and began to walk carefully around the courtroom.

"What I want to know," Evans Dahl said from the second row, his eyes glinting, as Fenway and her crackling walkie-talkie passed in front of the gallery divider, "is how someone cooked up a plan to get a gun in here in the first place."

"It's quite obvious that they got past the guard and the metal detector, isn't it?" Cynthia Schimmelhorn said from the back.

Fenway set her mouth in a line. She hadn't checked the perimeter for open doors or other ways into the courtroom that didn't go through the metal detector, but hoped that McVie or one of the other law enforcement people would find something. She couldn't imagine what the guard was going through after hearing a gun was in the courtroom.

"I wonder if the shooter got out," Leda Nedermeyer piped up.

"The protocol is to shut the building down immediately," Piper said. "So it's not very likely they escaped."

"Yes, well," Bryce Heissner said huffily, "it wasn't exactly plain sailing, was it?"

Piper shrugged and turned back to the laptop.

"And anyway," Heissner said, walking up the center aisle of the gallery, "how would *you* know what the building protocol is, anyway? You can't be more than—what? Seventeen?"

"I'm twenty-four. I was on the security planning committee during the design phase."

Heissner let out a snort. "Well, you all really run a tight ship here."

Fenway bristled. Not only had Piper *not* been on the implementation team, ADA Kim had insisted on Piper's resignation before the weekend, when the final walkthroughs were happening. She wrenched a smile onto her face as she passed Heissner. "Sorry—would you mind being silent for another few moments? I'm trying to find a spot where I can get a decent signal."

"A decent signal?" Heissner looked confused.

"Oh, for heaven's sake," Cynthia Schimmelhorn said. "Have you paid no attention? There's no reception in here. No phones, no Wi-Fi, no radio signals."

"My cell doesn't work?" Heissner pulled his phone from his pocket and stared at it without comprehension.

"No," Fenway said.

"Is that legal?" Heissner asked.

"I assume it is," Fenway said, "but even if it isn't, it doesn't change the fact that we're all stuck in this room together without reception. So, please, Mr. Heissner, don't say anything for another minute or two so I can hear the walkie-talkie."

Heissner harrumphed and glared at Fenway but said nothing. She kept walking up the aisle toward the double doors. The static changed for a half-second and lowered in pitch. She stopped in her tracks, raising the walkie-talkie over her head, then lowering it all the way to the floor. A short *pop* interrupted the buzzing halfway down to the floor, but there was no additional change in the static.

Fenway continued moving methodically. Cynthia Schimmelhorn watched her take careful steps until she stood in front of the double doors. When she turned left to go behind the last row of the gallery, Fenway could feel the woman's eyes on her.

The wall curved gently, and Fenway slowly walked past a white in-wall speaker enclosure, and the static was loud all the way to the side wall, where the back aisle ended.

She looked to her left. Next to the narrow side aisle was a small nook. She peered through the archway. The tiny, oddly-shaped room was only about six feet wide near the entrance, with an angled wall that narrowed to about three feet. Two chairs, the same dark wood seat and brushed-nickel legs, were in the small space. Was this a closet that hadn't been finished? An architectural mistake?

Fenway sighed, staring at the angled wall. Would her search for a spot where she could communicate with the outside world be fruitless?

She rotated her head. McVie may have saved her life by tackling her to the ground, but the pain from the bump on her head was down-shifting into a dull throb. Starting to raise her arms above her head to stretch, the static swooped from a low thrum to a high pitch, not unlike the sound of a theremin. Even in the awkward position, her arms bent at the elbow and her hands level with the top of her head, Fenway spun the walkie-talkie slowly in her hand and the squeal's volume decreased.

This was it!

She pushed the call button.

"Coroner Fenway Stevenson in the new courtroom," she said. "Can any officers hear me?"

She released the button and the loud squeal was back, but after raising the walkie-talkie an inch, a fuzzy voice came through.

"Hey, Fenway, you sure know how to get out of a weapons search."

"Dez!"

"Hi, Fenway. I'm glad you're okay. McVie thought Professor Cygnus was hit."

"Yeah. Professor Cygnus. Shot in the head—it looks like he died instantly."

"Oh." Dez paused, and after a moment of static, continued. "Is anyone else hurt?"

"Looks like the defense lawyer sprained his ankle. I banged my head a little. Everyone else seems to be okay. Any injuries out there?"

"Nope. I'm out here with two hundred of my closest friends. I'm sure glad I got the industrial vat of hand sanitizer at Costco last week."

Fenway chuckled, a sense of relief flooding her. "Oh, man, am I glad to hear your voice. Do you know what's happening?"

"The courthouse is on lockdown—as soon as the shots were fired, the guards initiated the security protocol. Kept everyone inside before the doors locked automatically."

"Oh—good. Did anyone get a look at the shooter?"

Dez scoffed. "You would think with a hundred people walking in and out of there, someone would have seen something. But no one saw anything—or if they did, they're not saying. Lots of confusion. Everyone seems to think the shots came from the back of the room, though."

Fenway closed her eyes and remembered the two pillars interrupting the last two rows. "There are two big pillars near the back of the room—maybe the shooter stood behind one of them."

"Pillars? Are those really big enough to hide a whole person?"

"They're about four feet wide, Dez. So probably."

"Okay—I'll check in with you throughout the day. Cell coverage is really spotty in the building, so we're relying on walkie-talkies."

"Our cell phones don't work at all in the courtroom, and I'm contorting myself just to get this crappy walkie-talkie signal."

"Oh. Maybe we'll figure out another way to communicate with you."

"Piper's got a text app on her laptop—so far, that's the only way she's been able to get messages out."

Dez sighed. "We didn't have much of a police presence in the building before the doors all locked—so no one's getting in or out for a while. Me, McVie, the bailiff, the guard at the security entrance. That's about it."

Fenway clicked her tongue. "So I don't suppose anyone has a time frame on when we can get out of here?"

"McVie is leading the questioning right now. Once we know more, we can let you know."

"Well, hurry up. There are a dozen people stuck in the courtroom besides me."

"Who's in there?"

"My father and Charlotte, Jennifer Kim and the defense attorney, Cygnus's wife and his"—Fenway almost said *mistress* but caught herself —"uh, colleague, two of his students, two Ferris Energy board members, Piper and me."

"And a partridge in a pear tree."

Fenway lowered her voice. "And Rose Morgan is here, too."

"What? Isn't she in Mexico by now!"

"I know—I don't understand why she showed up either. Do you think I should arrest her?"

There was silence on the other end, and a slight hum. Then Dez came back on. "—talk to McVie. See how he wants to do this. I don't think we have enough to charge her on."

"She attacked me in Cygnus's office last week, remember?"

"She threw a book at your head. I'm not sure that will be enough to give her more than a slap on the wrist."

"But it will let us hold her until we can figure out what else can stick."

Silence again, only for a moment. "I'd rather get McVie's take on this."

"Fine." Fenway cleared her throat. "So, even if we can't leave the building, can we at least leave the courtroom so he can question everyone?" Fenway released the button and got a loud buzz of static. She turned the walkie-talkie about forty-five degrees in her hand again.

Dez's voice melted in once more. "—separated into groups. So no, not for a while."

"You broke up there for a minute."

"We've separated them in different rooms, and once we've searched them all, we'll question them separately. You won't be able to leave for a while. Maybe an hour if you're lucky. McVie wants to keep your group separated too."

"Why?"

Then it hit Fenway—hard enough to make her knees wobble.

They hadn't found the gun.

No one who had left the courtroom in the shooting's aftermath had been permitted to leave the building—but not one of them had a gun in their possession. She knew Dez and McVie, and maybe the guards and bailiff, would thoroughly search the building—vents, ducts, trash cans, drawers—anywhere big enough to fit a gun. They'd probably already started.

But if they still couldn't find it?

That meant the gun was still in the courtroom.

And the killer was in with them too.

CHAPTER FOUR

FENWAY TRIED TO THINK OF ALL THE PLACES TO HIDE A GUN IN THE courtroom. She steadied herself against the angled wall with her hand. "Dez, do you want to get updates from us?"

The audio crackled. "Yes. We should set a time to talk again. If we're lucky we can—"

And the walkie-talkie buzzed angrily with static again.

Fenway raised and lowered it, but the whine didn't return, and neither did Dez's voice. She tried in vain to find another position where the sound would come in.

Okay.

She clicked off the walkie-talkie.

She panicked, breathing fast, so she closed her eyes and concentrated on breathing more slowly, getting herself under control little by little. She couldn't go out into the open courtroom area showing her fear. She had to think. She had to have a plan.

She needed to tell someone.

She knew for a fact that the shooter wasn't either Jennifer Kim or Evans Dahl—Fenway was watching them talk to Cygnus moments before he was shot. Fenway could tell one of them, maybe. Fenway trusted Piper too, and although she hadn't seen Piper when the shots were fired, she was positive that Piper hadn't done it.

Ugh—but she was *assuming facts not in evidence*, as the two lawyers might have said. So maybe Piper wouldn't be the sounding board for now. And besides, Piper was a gearhead, not a police officer. She might panic if her life was in danger, as she had once or twice in the past. Her judgment might be compromised.

Surely ADA Kim had dealt with similar situations before. She must have had to at least *prosecute* something when the police couldn't find the weapon in question.

She walked out of the nook and into the open courtroom, behind the last row of seats in the gallery, toward the double doors.

"Well?" Cynthia Schimmelhorn said, exasperation touching the corners of her mouth. "You were talking to *someone* in there. When are we free to go?"

Fenway shook her head. "The doors will still be locked for a while. No one was able to leave the courthouse. They've searched—" Then Fenway stopped. She didn't want to give away anything she didn't have to. "They're searching everyone now."

"Searching everyone?"

"For the gun."

Cynthia crinkled her nose and nodded. Fenway walked up the center aisle toward the judge's bench. Jennifer Kim was still sitting on the floor, staring straight ahead.

Hmm. ADA Kim had been in shock after the shooting. Fenway had chalked it up to being so close to the victim. Maybe the bullet being only a couple of feet away had bothered her. But Kim was tough. She should have snapped out of it by now.

"Jennifer?"

Kim didn't move.

"Hey!" Fenway snapped her fingers. "Come in, Jennifer!"

"Oh—sorry." Kim cleared her throat and smoothed down the skirt of her suit.

Fenway watched her for a moment, then sat down next to her. "So," she said in murmur, "the sheriff's office is searching for the gun right now. But they haven't found it yet, and I think the gun is still in the courtroom."

Jennifer Kim cocked her head. "Jumping to conclusions, Fenway?"

Fenway shrugged. "As a law enforcement representative, I *have* to assume that the gun is in here. The safety of these twelve people has to come first."

Kim nodded. "That makes sense. What did they say to do?"

"I lost contact with Dez before I could ask for advice on how to proceed. I got a feeling we'll be in here a while."

Another nod from the assistant district attorney.

"You and I are the only representatives of the county in here. We'll need to take control, make sure everyone else sees that we know what we're doing. That we're competent enough to get everyone through this. Otherwise, I can see someone like Rose Morgan going off the rails."

Kim looked up. "Off the rails?"

"She won't want to be cooped up in here at all, and she certainly won't stand for it being another four hours."

"Four hours? It'll be another four hours?" Jennifer's eyes glazed.

"No!" Fenway hissed, then brought her voice back down. "I don't *know* how long it will take. Dez said it would be an hour—I hope it's only another fifteen minutes—but they've got two hundred people to search and interview. And I don't want the killer getting antsy with a gun. If the killer's trying to figure out how to answer our questions and stay one step ahead so we don't suspect anything, no one gets antsy. It'll be a better situation for us. Safer."

"What makes you think the killer won't go shooting up the room when you start asking questions?"

"Because," Fenway said, "the murderer obviously thinks they're clever. They snuck the gun in here. They shot the gun with two hundred people in the same room—and *nobody saw them do it.*"

"The shots did come from the back of the room."

"Right, and those corners aren't well-lit. And visibility is limited on the side of the columns in the back row." Fenway thought for a moment. "Most people were facing away from the shot. But you weren't, were you, Jennifer? You were looking that way."

Jennifer shifted uncomfortably. "Uh, I don't really remember. I was looking at the professor, not the back wall."

"You didn't see anything out of the corner of your eye or anything like that?"

Jennifer set her mouth in a line. "I don't think so. Not that I remember, anyway."

Fenway leaned back against the wooden panel of the judge's bench. "I don't remember much either." *Except for hitting my head.*

ADA Kim frowned and closed her eyes.

"All right then, what's our plan?" asked Fenway. "Maybe we need to search everyone's purses, pockets, everything like that. Then interview people."

"How would we do that? It's an open courtroom. Everyone can hear what's going on. If the killer *is* in here, they'd answer all your questions. They could set you off on a wild goose chase, shifting blame off themselves."

"Fair point." Fenway scrunched up her face, then pointed to the back corner by the archway to the nook. "The acoustics back there deaden pretty much everything. Cynthia Schimmelhorn was sitting ten feet away, but she couldn't hear details of the conversation. So that's a perfect area to use. We can keep everyone on the far side of the gallery while we question people in that nook."

Jennifer looked unconvinced.

"What?"

"I don't know. I mean, if you actually come up with some evidence to use, can't the whole interview be tossed out on privacy grounds?"

Fenway shook her head. "You're the lawyer, not me, but I think we have a situation where there's a compelling right to know the answers that supersedes the individual's right to privacy."

"I disagree."

"Come on, Jennifer, it's like you're not even *trying* to catch this murderer. The killer's in the courthouse, maybe even this courtroom. If the gun search comes up empty, the killer *will* get away. They'll be in their car on the way to Mexico or on the next flight to Khartoum."

"I'm fine with catching a murderer. You apparently don't care if they walk on a technicality."

Fenway bristled. "This isn't—" Then she held up her hands. "Okay, you know what? Let's argue about this later. Let's do the search now. If someone in here has the gun, this discussion will be moot anyway." She stood up.

"All right, everyone, if I can have your attention," Fenway said, her strident, clear voice carrying over the whole gallery.

Jennifer scrambled to her feet.

"The assistant district attorney and I will conduct a thorough search of all your belongings. Backpacks, purses, pockets. Anything that can hold anything, open 'em up, turn 'em inside out, let us see 'em."

"We're searching everyone?" ADA Kim whispered to Fenway.

"Everyone," Fenway said. She shifted her eyes to Rose Morgan, who had moved to the other side of the gallery, near Cynthia Schimmelhorn and Bryce Heissner. "We'll start with this side of the room." Fenway pointed at Rose. "Your right, my left. Jennifer, will you—"

Then Kim's eyes rolled back in her head, and she began to collapse.

Gasps and shouts from the gallery pinged all around.

Fenway jumped behind Kim and caught her left shoulder and right hip before she hit the floor. Her medical training kicked in. Vaguely aware of the people rushing from the gallery, she slid Kim out of her arms to lay her on the floor, flat on her back.

Kneeling at Kim's side, Fenway studied her face. Kim's lips weren't blue. Her breathing didn't seem labored. The others crowded around her.

"Is she okay?"

"What happened?"

"Did she hit her head?"

Fenway stood up and made her five-ten frame as large as possible.

"Give her room!" she barked. "She needs some air." She put her fingers on Kim's neck. The heartbeat was strong—a little fast. Unusual, perhaps, in someone who'd fainted, but she was stressed. "Xavier!"

"What do you need?" Xavier pushed between Leda Nedermeyer and Bryce Heissner.

"Pull Jennifer's feet up—about twelve inches off the floor—and hold them there."

Xavier crouched down and picked Kim's feet up. "Twelve inches?"

"Yep, right there, that's perfect."

"Will she be all right?" asked Charlotte.

"She doesn't have any signs of trauma," Fenway muttered. "Breathing is normal. She should come back to us in a few seconds."

Ten seconds passed, but it felt like an hour, and it seemed like everyone held their breath. Finally, Jennifer Kim's eyes fluttered, and she gasped and shuddered.

Fenway sighed with relief.

Jennifer blinked. "What—what happened?"

"You fainted," Fenway said gently.

Jennifer frowned. "Is—is someone holding my feet?"

"You can let go now, Xavier."

"Right. Sorry." Xavier set Kim's feet down.

"Blood flow," Fenway said. "Elevating a fainted person's feet—"

"I—I get it," Kim said. "Feet. Blood flowing to my core and brain and stuff." She pushed herself up onto her elbows. "How long was I out?"

Fenway looked around from her kneeling position at the other faces. "What do you think? It was only a minute or two, right?"

Most of the heads nodded.

"I think I can stand back up now," Kim said.

"Don't rush it," Fenway said. "Most of the time, it takes a good ten minutes to fully recover."

"I'll be fine."

"We don't have access to medical aid," Fenway said. "I'm a licensed nurse practitioner, but I can only do so much. So stay on your back for ten minutes. Hey, Piper?"

Piper's head appeared above Fenway and Jennifer, over the judge's bench. "What do you need?"

"Can you set a timer for ten minutes?"

Piper's head disappeared, and Fenway heard a few keyboard clicks. "Done," Piper called.

"Okay, since everyone is up here, stay up here. We'll search your bags now."

"The hell you will," Bryce Heissner said. "My briefcase contains documents with proprietary information." He pointed at Nathaniel Ferris. "I can't have you sharing that information with your father."

"Mr. Heissner," Fenway said, "don't you and my father work for the same company?"

Heissner affixed a steely gaze on Ferris. "Not for much longer."

"What the hell does that mean?" Ferris said, turning toward Heissner.

"It means that unless the arraignment results in the dismissal of all felony charges, you're out, Ferris. The board convened yesterday and voted you out."

Ferris set his jaw. "You're kicking me out of my own company? The company *I* founded thirty-five years ago? What happened to 'innocent until proven guilty'?"

"Listen, you asshole, you've been skating on—"

"*Gentlemen.*"

Fenway looked for the firm, calm female voice. It belonged to Cynthia Schimmelhorn, who was still standing in the gallery area. She stepped forward confidently.

"Mr. Ferris, you've carried the company capably for many years. But we can no longer ignore the events of the last six months."

Ferris seethed. "You've wanted me out so you—"

Schimmelhorn held up her hand, and like magic, Ferris shut his mouth. "You've made bets on criminals, Ferris. Murderers and cheats and liars. Not only have they been unscrupulous, but they've been caught. I'm afraid the board members aren't the only ones who have lost confidence in your leadership. We've lost customers. I'm sure you've seen the op-eds calling for your resignation."

Fenway swiveled her head toward her father. His face was beet red. Charlotte was behind him, her body stock-still and her eyes wide.

"We've done a century's worth of damage control in the last few months for you, Nathaniel," Schimmelhorn continued. "I looked it up —this county averaged two murders per year over the last ten years. Except for last year. We've had six murders the last year. Now Professor Cygnus makes seven. You've been involved in *all* of them in some fashion."

"What do you mean?"

"The killer worked for you. Or your wife was arrested for the murder—"

"She was innocent!"

"—or the victim was your doctor, or *you've* been arrested for hiring a hit man." She stepped up to the closed gate between the gallery and the front of the courtroom, and gripped the top rail with her right hand. "Most of the board didn't see it before, but it's become clear to *everyone* that Ferris Energy can no longer be a viable company if you continue to serve in a leadership role. You're toxic, Nathaniel." She folded her arms and stared right at Fenway. "Some of us have known it for a long time."

Fenway felt the heat rise to her face and clenched her jaw. No, she wasn't getting along with her father, and yes, he'd had his lawyers work their magic so her mother got nothing. Yet this rich, entitled white lady was speaking *for* her, purposely widening the rift between Fenway and her father. She struggled to contain her anger but couldn't help herself.

"Don't pretend you know what's in my head, Ms. Schimmelhorn," Fenway said sternly. "Yes, my father and I have a complicated relationship, but I'd ask you to kindly stop putting words in my mouth."

Cynthia Schimmelhorn cocked her head, the tranquil calm radiating from her body in waves. "My dear," she said. "I don't have any idea what you're talking about. I'm referring to myself. I have known for years that your father would sell out his own mother—or his own daughter—if it meant he could get an edge over the competition."

"Come off it, Cynthia," Nathaniel Ferris snarled. "Yes, you won a seat on the board a few years ago, but you don't even bother to stick around after meetings."

Schimmelhorn shook her head. "Have you forgotten that I was the CEO of Petrogrande Western when Ferris Energy conducted its hostile takeover eight years ago?"

Ferris's eyes turned down.

"You see, Mr. Ferris," Schimmelhorn said, "you don't think of me as an experienced executive in the oil industry. You think of me as the token woman on the board."

Ferris stepped back. "Petrogrande Western was a long time ago. You've been away from day-to-day management for a long time."

"Doesn't seem to make a difference to you when it comes to the other board members. Just me." Schimmelhorn's eyes sparkled. She was clearly enjoying this.

Ferris's face hardened as he lifted his hand up and pointed a finger at Schimmelhorn. "You—you've been trying to undermine me ever since you joined the board."

Schimmelhorn smiled. "Now why would I do that, Nathaniel? I'm a stockholder, just like everyone else. I wanted to change Ferris Energy into a good corporate citizen. Not one that was just concerned with short-term get-rich-quick schemes that would blow up in our faces in five years. Being a responsible steward is about the long term, not the quick buck." She laughed, a biting, derisive sound, and Ferris winced. "It's a lesson that you haven't learned yet, and I fear you won't learn it until you've lost everything."

"What do *you* know about Nathaniel Ferris?" Charlotte said haughtily. "You lost your company in the buyout, and you want revenge. You're trying to find anything you can to justify your anger—to justify what you've done to wreck the company."

Schimmelhorn chuckled. "Even if that *were* true, honey," she said, "it's still a business decision. One the board has already voted on. Let's see how your precious husband feels on the *other* end of a hostile takeover."

"You're out, Ferris," Heissner said. "And the murder charge triggers a clause in your contract that eliminates your golden parachute. I hope you've saved up for that expensive lawyer because you're not getting any more from Ferris Energy."

Ferris staggered as if he'd been punched in the gut, grabbing onto the prosecutor's table for support.

"And now," Cynthia Schimmelhorn said, "I think I'd like to be the first to volunteer for a search."

————

Fenway pulled a high-quality cloth handkerchief from Cynthia Schimmelhorn's Paola Sacci handbag. Then she removed a Salvatore Ferragamo baby-blue bifold wallet, a set of keys with a BMW fob, a mobile phone (a just-released model), a silver compact mirror, a small tube of hand cream, two expensive lipsticks, a credit-card-size packet of blotting linens, a pair of Oxford Vaughan sunglasses, and a tin of breath mints. She laid them all out on the prosecutor's table.

"Is everything satisfactory, Coroner?" Schimmelhorn asked.

Fenway ran her hand along the sides of the designer handbag, as much for the delicious feel of the leather against her skin as to check for any hidden items in the lining. "Everything appears to be in order," Fenway said, giving the handbag back. "You travel fairly light."

"I don't like redundancies."

"Fair enough," Fenway said. "Who's next?"

"Bryce," Schimmelhorn said, placing all the items back in her purse, "empty your pockets and open your briefcase. Let's get this over with."

Heissner hesitated. "But I don't think—"

"I have every confidence that Miss Stevenson is a professional and that anything proprietary will stay confidential. Isn't that right, Miss Stevenson?"

"My duty is to the safety of the citizens of this county, then to the law, as I'm sure you know, Ms. Schimmelhorn. Anything in the briefcase that affects anyone's safety or the law will be dealt with appropriately, proprietary or not. I suspect you know as well as I do where the line is drawn between the rules of evidence and the right to privacy. I'll respect that line."

Schimmelhorn laughed. "My goodness, such drama."

Fenway narrowed her eyes. "A man is dead, Ms. Schimmelhorn. No one's found the gun yet."

"Of course, I'm sorry." She turned to Heissner. "All right, Bryce, you heard her."

Frowning, Heissner removed the contents of his pockets: a thin leather wallet; a key ring with six keys, a U.S. Navy decorative coin, and a Lexus key fob; a travel-size package of facial tissues; a mobile phone; and a handful of change. Fenway inspected the group of items on the table. Heissner turned both pockets inside out. Fenway nodded.

He lifted his briefcase up to the table, placed it on its side and unlocked it. Fenway snapped the clasp open, lifted the lid, and sifted through envelopes, papers, and file pockets.

"Satisfied?" Heissner said softly.

"Thank you," Fenway said. "Your suit jacket, please."

Heissner's scowl deepened, but he pulled a checkbook out of his suit jacket pocket.

"Sorry, Mr. Heissner, I meant for you to please remove your suit jacket. I need to feel the pockets and the lining as well."

Heissner took off his jacket and handed it to Fenway, who patted down the pockets.

"I don't see the point of all this," Heissner grumbled. "I could have one of those ankle holsters."

"Excellent point." Fenway handed the jacket to Heissner, then bent down and patted his right ankle, moving up to his calf.

"Hey!"

"Now your left one," Fenway said.

"Don't touch me!"

"Bryce," Schimmelhorn said, gently but firmly.

"Right, right. Sorry, Miss Stevenson."

"You're clear." Fenway patted his ankle and stood.

Heissner breathed impatiently as he gathered his things.

Fenway looked at the group. "Who's next? Rose?"

Rose set her jaw. "I notice you're not including yourself in this search."

Fenway cocked her head. It was true. Fenway had been too close to the action for her to be a viable suspect, but few people in the room had seen Fenway when the shooting happened. "I guess I wasn't," she said. "Sure, fine." She walked over to the gallery seat in the first row, reached over and grabbed her black faux-leather messenger bag, then emptied it on the table. Her messy life was there for all the world to see. Three near-empty lipsticks. A folding wallet with receipts sticking out of the sides. A key ring with about a dozen keys on it, including one for both her mother's foreclosed house in Seattle and the old Nissan Sentra Fenway no longer owned. Two granola bars. A broken earring. Two USB charging cables for her phone—and the phone itself. And finally, a small pink plastic case.

"What's in the case?" Heissner said. "Bullets? Maybe *you* have the gun and it's small enough to fit in there?"

Fenway looked up into Heissner's face. "You really don't know what this is?"

"You need to open it up. You made me open up everything in my briefcase."

Still staring in Heissner's eyes, Fenway opened the case and showed him the contents. Three tampons.

"Oh, for God's sake, that's disgusting." Heissner's mouth turned down like he'd sucked on a lemon. "Well, that certainly explains why you're being so nasty to me."

Fenway narrowed her eyes. "Anyone else need to see my tampons?" Fenway said, holding the case above her head. "They've got organic cotton cardboard applicators!" Her voice turned singsong. "They're in a cute pink case and everything!"

"Now you're just trying to embarrass me. Put those away."

Fenway made an exaggerated ninety-degree turn toward Piper. "Tell me, Piper, was your period especially heavy last month?"

Piper's hand was over her mouth, eyes squeezed shut in laughter.

"Boy, mine sure was." Fenway put her hands on her hips and affected a voice like she was in a television commercial. "It was like I opened a vein. I bled so much I filed paperwork to open an official investigation."

"You made your point." Heissner's voice was icy.

"I even called in the blood spatter analyst from San Miguelito. He was like, 'the only crime here is wearing white after Labor Day!'"

"That's enough," Heissner said, his face red.

"Those probably aren't the last feminine hygiene products you'll see during this search," Fenway said. "And if you think my period is to blame for your unhelpful attitude, I'm sure all the women here would be more than happy to share detailed accounts of a time in their lives when they wished their tampons had been more absorbent."

"I went camping once and left my tampons in the tent before starting out on a ten-mile hike," Amanda ventured. "I ended up burying those shorts because they were attracting vampires."

Standing next to Amanda, Xavier, like Piper, covered his face in laughter.

"Who's next?" Fenway said.

"I'll go next," Amanda said. "My tampons of choice are 'super-plus,' and I've got a really cute tote for them." She pulled a wildly decorated purple-and-silver nylon bag out of her purse. "Look! Butterflies!"

CHAPTER FIVE

One by one, everyone in the courtroom emptied their handbags, backpacks, and pockets onto the prosecutor's table. Fenway had intended to search Rose Morgan first, but she kept far enough away that there was always someone closer to the table who agreed to be searched first. Fenway's father had very little in his pockets: a fancy money clip with a few credit cards and a driver's license, and a ring with only two keys, one for his Mercedes S500 and one for his home.

His phone was in Charlotte's purse, a well-organized handbag with similar luxe items as Cynthia Schimmelhorn, although it was clear their aesthetic tastes were wildly different.

Amanda and Xavier had nothing out of the ordinary. Piper's backpack was full of cords and connectors and small devices, but none of the dozen pockets held any weapons.

Judith Cygnus had five different medications in her purse, as well as a white handkerchief with blood on it. Fenway gestured to it on the table. "What's this?"

Judith shrugged. "I got a nosebleed just before I came into the courtroom. It happens all the time now that things have progressed."

She laughed. "I honestly don't know how Virg thinks we'll make it to that clinic in Mexico—"

And then her face fell, pain evident in her eyes. Fenway grimaced, but while Judith was getting control of her emotions, Fenway patted down the insides of her purse.

"Listen," Judith said, "but—could you maybe move Virg's body somewhere else? I mean, that's my husband, dead on the floor."

"Oh," Fenway said, handing the purse back to Judith, "I'm really sorry, Mrs. Cygnus, but as soon as the doors open, we'll need to collect evidence and the body needs to stay where it is."

"You're serious?"

"I'm really sorry," Fenway said again.

Judith frowned and shook her head. She turned and stepped to the side, rearranging the contents of her handbag.

Leda Nedermeyer's purse was even messier than Fenway's. In addition to her wallet and keys, the handbag contained three empty eyeglass cases, two packs of tissues, a tube of sunblock, five bottle caps, a travel-size toothpaste, three paperback books (a scholarly-sounding title discussing the natural world in the works of John Milton, *Pride and Prejudice,* and a romance novel with a shirtless, deeply tanned, heavily muscled man holding an alabaster-skinned heavy-lidded blonde on the cover), two prescription pill bottles, two packs of gum, and a minibar-sized bottle of cinnamon-flavored whiskey. She muttered to herself as she put everything away.

Judith Cygnus passed by, between Fenway and the prosecutor's table.

"Hey!" Leda said sharply, then there was a muffled thump. Fenway turned her head. Leda Nedermeyer's purse lay on the floor, the contents scattered and the tiny bottle of cinnamon whiskey rolling down the aisle.

"Oh!" Judith said, feigning surprise. "I'm so sorry. I get so dizzy from these cancer treatments, you know."

Leda glared at her but said nothing as she bent down to pick up the contents of her purse, although she didn't attempt to go after the bottle of cinnamon whiskey.

The only ones who hadn't been searched were Evans Dahl, Jennifer Kim, and Rose Morgan. Fenway walked through the gallery gate and halfway down the center aisle. Rose was sitting by herself in the back corner.

"All right," Fenway said to Rose, beckoning her. "It's your turn."

"Sorry," Rose said, "I don't consent to a search."

Fenway narrowed her eyes, then walked down the back aisle.

"I don't have a gun," Rose said. "I don't have any weapons—but I don't consent to a search."

"Everyone in this room now thinks you have a gun in your purse. Or your jacket."

"Be that as it may, you can't compel me to give up my personal property for search without a warrant."

"Or a reasonable expectation that you have a weapon," Fenway said.

"Nice try, but this doesn't meet the Supreme Court standard," Rose replied. "The reasonable expectation only applies to public schools."

"It's a public building."

"It's still not a school. You want to forcibly search me, go ahead. When we're out of here, my first call will be to my lawyer. I seem to remember he did pretty well when you tried to hold me without evidence last week."

Fenway crossed her arms. "You're right, of course. Okay."

She turned and headed up the center aisle.

"She refused?" Jennifer Kim said.

Fenway nodded. "All right, Jennifer, what do you want to do?"

"I don't know. If she *does* have a gun, we obviously want to take it from her. But if she *doesn't* have it, and she has anything else, or if there's something in here she says is embarrassing, we could get sued—or accused of violating her civil rights."

"But the law is on her side, right?"

"I know that's not a risk my boss would want me to take right now." She looked at Fenway. "You don't *think* she's got a gun, do you?"

"Come on, Jennifer. Look at all of the people in here. You see anyone else who's a better suspect than Rose?"

Kim stared hard at Rose for a moment. "Honestly," she murmured, "I thought it might be your father."

"My father? He was in front of the prosecution's table. Totally wrong angle. I would have heard it from that direction—you would have, too."

"Yes, I guess you're right. He might have had someone do it for him."

Fenway scoffed. "Like who?"

"Like your stepmother."

"Charlotte? Don't be ridiculous."

"Ridiculous?" Kim put her hands on her hips. "She's got a gun registered in her name. And I don't know if you've ever seen the targets from the gun range after she goes there, but there's a nice cluster around the bull's-eye in almost all of them. She's a good shot."

Fenway was taken aback. "When in the world did you get her targets from the gun range?"

Kim shook her head. "I know you're a busy woman, Fenway, but have you honestly forgotten—"

"Oh, right. When she was arrested for murder. Still, I didn't realize you were on the case."

"I wasn't. But I saw pictures of the targets. We were joking that she should teach some of our officers how to shoot."

"So." Fenway leaned on the prosecutor's table with both hands. "You think Charlotte did it, and I think Rose Morgan did it."

"Honestly? I think the shooter slipped out of the courthouse without us catching them. I bet they're a hundred miles away by now."

Dez had made it sound like no one escaped before the whole courthouse was locked down, but Fenway had no way to clarify that. Someone could have gotten out. *That'll wreck my perfect record of catching murderers. Oh, well. The streak has to end sometime.* "So what'll we do about Rose refusing to be searched?"

Jennifer shrugged. "I'm not sure quite how much we *can* do. She's within her rights to refuse."

"Doesn't the state's interest in preventing a murder outweigh her right to privacy?"

Jennifer shook her head. "We can't reasonably assume that a murder will happen. I don't want to argue that in front of my boss. I won't be responsible for opening us up to litigation like that."

Fenway scoffed. "You'd rather put all of our lives at risk?"

"Look, Fenway," Jennifer said, "I appreciate that you're trying to do something constructive instead of letting everyone stew in their own juices while we're in here, but the odds are good that the shooter escaped. The double doors didn't shut for about fifteen seconds. I think even your favorite B&E suspect over there—" she acknowledged Piper with a nod of her head "—understands that this building was designed to keep people *out*, not prevent their escape once they're inside."

"I don't like it."

"You don't have to like it. You have to follow it, though."

Spoken like someone who's lived on the wrong side of a previous decision. Fenway nodded. "So that leaves you and Evans."

"I will also claim Fourth Amendment privilege," Evans Dahl said. He didn't look comfortable in the chair, even with his foot up. "Especially as I have paperwork for other defendants in my briefcase. I don't want the prosecution—or anyone in county law enforcement—to get their hands on that."

"Surely your pockets and your suit jacket—"

"Bring Judge Miller back in here, and I'll have no choice but to do what she says," Evans Dahl said, pushing his round-rimmed glasses up on his nose. "Until then, you're not getting anything from me."

Jennifer Kim screwed up her face. "I think I have to side with my legal colleague and decline based on the Fourth Amendment, too."

Fenway was aghast. "What? You actually *performed* some of the searches with me! Are you telling me you're a complete hypocrite?"

Kim walked around the prosecutor's table and grabbed her briefcase. "Not a *complete* hypocrite. I didn't force Miss Morgan to comply and then refuse myself. In fact, I didn't force *anyone* to comply."

Fenway opened her mouth and closed it again. She couldn't believe this was happening. "And what about interviewing people in here? You refuse to do that too?"

ADA Kim squinted, then shook her head. "No, you're free to ask me questions. I don't have a problem with that. I suppose I might plead the fifth if you ask me the wrong kind of question."

Fenway was glad she'd trained to be a nurse practitioner instead of a lawyer. Both Evans and Jennifer—and Rose, too, for that matter—seemed insufferable and smug. She wondered if that's what she was like when anyone had a medical question.

Folding her arms, Fenway closed her eyes and went over everything in her mind. Part of her wanted to search for the second slug as Cygnus had only been hit once. But it was a needle in a haystack—the second slug could be anywhere. If it wasn't buried deep in a wall or table, it might have ricocheted. Her time would be much better spent talking to everyone.

"We're going into the interview portion of our morning next," Fenway announced to the group. "I'll ask you questions like what you saw this morning, both in the courtroom and on your way here. If we can get a full picture by piecing together your reports, we might be able to get some actionable information to the sheriff." *Or find out if the killer is still in the room.*

She looked out over the people in the gallery. They mostly looked bored, except Rose. Her eyes darted back and forth between Fenway and the back row, and she sat forward in her chair, as if she were expecting to spring to her feet.

Again, it was Cynthia Schimmelhorn who stepped forward to go first. "Good. Something to occupy my time rather than staring at the wall. Where shall we conduct this interview?"

Fenway pointed to the nook in the corner. "It's not the best, but it's likely the most private spot in here. At least people won't be able to tell what we're saying. You couldn't make anything out when I was on the walkie-talkie, right?"

"Correct."

Fenway turned her head toward Piper, who was still working on the PC at the judge's bench. "Any luck communicating with McVie?"

Piper looked up. "What?"

"I asked if you had any luck getting ahold of McVie."

"Oh." Piper shook her head. "Not yet."

Something told Fenway that Piper wasn't working as hard as she could to communicate with McVie. Shifting her weight from foot to foot, Fenway didn't press it any more. "Okay. Keep working."

Then she found Xavier, who was sitting back in the gallery with Amanda's head on his shoulder. "Hey, would you give me a hand with these chairs?"

"Oh. Uh, sure."

Fenway grabbed her purse, walked into the nook, and arranged the two chairs to face each other. It looked more like a quiz show set up than an interrogation room, which Fenway supposed was okay.

Cynthia stuck her head in. "Are you ready for me, Miss Stevenson?"

"I think so." Fenway motioned to the chair in the center of the room, as she took the chair next to the wall, facing out. "Let's get to it." She reached down and pulled her phone out of her purse.

"I didn't think you had any signal in here," Cynthia said.

"I don't, but I don't need a cell connection to record." Fenway opened the voice memo application and clicked on the record button. "The date is November twelfth, 9:32 A.M. Coroner Fenway Stevenson interviewing Ms. Cynthia Schimmelhorn."

She raised her eyes to the stately woman in the chair across from her. "Do you consent to having this conversation recorded, Ms. Schimmelhorn?"

"I—uh, yes."

"Great." Fenway leaned back in her chair. "Can I get you to state your full name for the record?"

"Cynthia DiFazio Schimmelhorn."

Fenway snapped her fingers. "DiFazio! Like the DiFazio Theater at Nidever. Was the theater named for you before you were married?"

Schimmelhorn blinked. "Uh—no, actually. Well, in a sense. I did make the donation, but I requested that the theater be named after my late father."

"Oh—I'm sorry for your loss."

The older woman smiled. "It was over a decade ago, dear."

"Right. Anyway, can you tell me about your relationship with Professor Cygnus?"

"My *relationship?*" Schimmelhorn's mouth dropped open.

Fenway furrowed her brow. "Sure. He was your professor when you were at Nidever, right?"

"Oh." Cynthia Schimmelhorn visibly relaxed. "Well, yes, he was."

"Changed your life, from the stories I hear." Fenway attempted a half-smile, trying to get the posh woman to open up a bit, although she wasn't quite sure what she could use.

"He—he did. I was, perhaps, not the best student. I had issues with, well, authority." She cleared her throat. "I'm not sure why I'm telling you this."

"You were close with him."

"No." Cynthia shook her head. "When I was a student, perhaps. Not lately."

"I've been to the theater. It can't be more than five years old. You mean to tell me that you donated enough money to construct a five-hundred-seat theater and a four-story classroom building attached to it, and you're not close with Professor Cygnus?" Fenway squinted. "You named your daughter after the character you played, too, right? Nerissa?"

Schimmelhorn popped back in her seat as if she'd gotten an electric shock. "How did you know that?"

"Because I was investigating a murder last week, and your name kept coming up." Fenway rested her chin in her hand. "So how much had the two of you talked recently?"

Cynthia shifted uncomfortably in her chair. "Recently?"

"Sure. Like, say, the last six months."

"I don't—I don't really remember."

"You don't remember?"

"A couple of times, I think. We must have run into each other at a restaurant."

"Really? With his wife sick at home, he's going out to a restaurant?" *Oh, right, he's got a mistress too.* Fenway wondered if Cynthia knew about Leda Nedermeyer and wanted to ask about her. However, the nook wasn't private enough to ask her without risking either Judith or Leda hearing it.

"Perhaps it was in line at one of the local coffee roasters. Whatever it was, it was in passing."

"Had you heard anything about the money that the scholarship fund was laundering?"

"Certainly not. We simply exchanged pleasantries."

"You didn't ask how *Othello* was going?"

"No, I don't suppose I did. I don't really remember."

Fenway looked at Cynthia, who had an exasperated look on her face but betrayed no other emotion. Fenway folded her arms. There was something here that Cynthia Schimmelhorn wasn't telling her. Unfortunately, without a door that closed, it might be hard to get *anyone* to reveal secrets. So Fenway changed tactics. "When did you get to the courthouse?"

Schimmelhorn dropped her shoulders, probably relieved that the questioning was moving on to something else. "I pulled into the lot at seven forty-five or so."

"Over an hour early for a nine-o'clock arraignment?"

"I was meeting Bryce. We needed to go over a few things."

"Like what?"

Schimmelhorn smiled. "I apologize, Coroner, but I'm not at liberty to discuss business conversations in a forum where everyone can hear."

Fenway nodded. She took deep, even breaths, keeping herself calm, but perhaps interviewing people in the nook wasn't that good an idea after all.

"You met Mr. Heissner inside the courthouse?"

Schimmelhorn shook her head. "No. We met at Java Jim's."

Fenway cocked her head. "The one next to the courthouse?"

"No, the one on Third Street."

Nodding, Fenway continued, "Ah yes, I know that Java Jim's well. How long did you stay?"

"About twenty minutes. We walked to the courthouse together."

"And did you go through the metal detector together?"

"Yes. Well—not exactly *together.* I went first, then Mr. Heissner."

"Of course. And the two of you were with each other the whole time?"

"Yes. The whole time."

"You walked into the courtroom together?"

"Ah." Schimmelhorn nodded. "Yes. The two of us definitely walked in together."

"And where did you sit?"

Schimmelhorn pointed at the wall that separated the nook from the full room. "Right on the other side of this wall. Last row, next to the column."

Fenway cocked her head, trying to remember where in the room Schimmelhorn had been sitting before the arraignment. "Did you say you were on this side of the column or the side closest to the center aisle?"

"The center aisle."

"You showed up forty-five minutes early and took a seat in the last row?"

Schimmelhorn folded her arms. "Sometimes I have to take phone calls. I didn't want to disturb the proceedings if I had to exit."

"But there's no cell service in here."

"I didn't know that, did I?" Schimmelhorn snapped. "I wouldn't have sat so far away if I *had* known." She shook her head. "I was trying to be polite."

Fenway nodded and leaned forward. "Did you see anything suspicious, either before the arraignment started or afterward?"

"Hmm." Schimmelhorn looked up and to her left, as if trying to remember. "Well—as I said, there was a man in a black sweatshirt with a hood standing next to me."

Fenway nodded. "Right. A hoodie."

"Yes. I'm not sure if the sweatshirt said anything on it, but he stood in the row behind me."

"I thought you said you were in the last row."

"I mean, he was standing in the aisle behind me."

"He didn't take a seat?"

"I don't know. As soon as the courtroom started to fill up, he went away. I assume he sat down, but I didn't see where."

"Did you see him again?"

"No."

"What about him seemed suspicious to you?"

"I—I don't really know. He didn't seem like he was dressed appropriately for court, for one thing. And he seemed nervous."

"What did he look like? Tall? Short?"

"He was medium height, I suppose. Maybe five-foot-eight. I hate to say this, but perhaps his skin was a bit on the darker side."

Fenway's annoyance crept up. "You mean he was black."

"No! No." Schimmelhorn shook her head. "I'm sorry. I'm not very good at this. He seemed to me to be either Hispanic or perhaps Palestinian."

"Latino or Middle Eastern, you say?"

"Maybe not. I don't know all the nationalities. He had dark hair, and I thought he might be in the wrong place." Cynthia considered this a moment. "Maybe he was the relative of someone else who was getting arraigned in another courtroom."

"Or maybe the relative of one of the victims."

Cynthia brightened. "Yes! Maybe a relative."

"Did you see a gun?"

"No."

"Where were you when the shooting happened?"

"Sitting in the back row, as I've said, Miss Stevenson."

Fenway blinked. She was off her game. "That's right, I remember now. You said the shots came from behind you, didn't you?"

Cynthia nodded.

"So you're saying the shooter was in the aisle between the back row and the wall."

"I'm just telling you what my impression was, Miss Stevenson."

Fenway had the same impression; the shots came from behind her. People had been walking in and out using the center aisle, which likely would have blocked any shot from the prosecution side of the courtroom—or made it significantly harder, anyway. "Tell you what—why don't you show me where you were standing when the shooting started?"

"Yes." Cynthia Schimmelhorn stood and smoothed the skirt of her suit. Fenway picked up her phone from the chair and followed her out of the nook and into the open courtroom. The others sat on the far side of the gallery. Xavier and Amanda huddled together, talking, as did Nathaniel and Charlotte. Everyone else stared, eyes slightly unfocused.

The last row of seats was on their right, and the curved wall was on the left. The large white in-wall speaker enclosure was about ten feet further down when Schimmelhorn passed the four-foot-square column and stopped, placing her hand on the back of the first seat. "Right here."

Fenway nodded. "And you say the shooting sounded like it was behind you?"

"Yes. Although I can't be sure it wasn't across the aisle. It didn't sound like it was on this side."

"Loud sudden noises can play tricks on your ears," Fenway said, but she was scouring the floor with her eyes. She stopped the phone's recorder, knelt down to search, but the overhead lights cast dark shadows under the rows of seats.

Why hadn't anyone seen the shooter? People were coming and going through the center aisle—two loud shots? Someone must have seen something.

She stood again and looked straight ahead to where Cygnus had been standing in front of the defense table. It was a clear shot—although she wondered if Jennifer Kim would have been in the way.

Hm. Was there another angle?

Fenway looked at the large, square column. She took several steps backward to the center aisle. She couldn't see the other side. As she walked down the aisle, the far side of the aisle remained hidden until she was almost even with the gallery gate.

She stopped and cocked her head.

There hadn't been anyone that close to the front—not that she remembered, anyway. And when the shots were fired, she and McVie had hit the floor. They didn't look to see where the shots had come from.

Had the shooter really been that lucky?

Walking back to the column, Fenway stepped to the side closest to the side wall. She looked toward the front of the room to the defense table and noted that the seat she was sitting in was also aligned. If she had heard the shots directly behind her, the shooter could have been standing close to this spot.

Turning on her phone's flashlight, she knelt and started shining the light on the floor.

A glint of light from behind one of the chair legs.

She squinted. A shell casing.

CHAPTER SIX

Fenway reached out her hand. Then, when her fingertips were only about an inch from the casing, she pulled her hand back quickly. She stood and walked to the front of the gallery, putting her phone in the half-pocket of her slacks. Opening her fingerprint kit, she got out a pair of blue nitrile gloves and an evidence baggie.

The hushed voices of conversation stopped, and Fenway felt eyes on her. She turned, and everyone—except Piper, who was still working on the computer at the judge's seat—stared in her direction.

She cleared her throat, snapped the gloves on, and walked to the rear of the courtroom again. Squatting, Fenway took a picture of the shell casing with her phone camera. Picking up the brass, she turned it over in her hand—9MM LUGER FC was stamped on the bottom of the casing.

She dropped it in the clear evidence bag and, still kneeling, wondered how she'd make sure the bag followed an acceptable chain of custody. She only had her purse and her fingerprint kit, neither of which had a lock, and neither of which would be a proper place to store evidence. With everyone's eyes on her, she knew she couldn't depend on subterfuge either—it was clear to all those in the courtroom that Fenway had discovered something worthy of being in an evidence bag.

Cynthia Schimmelhorn peered around the column. "What did you find?"

Fenway looked up at Cynthia. The older woman's face was impassive, not even casually curious.

Hold on a minute—even though everyone knew there was evidence, they didn't know what the evidence *was*. They didn't know it was a shell casing—it could be a button or a piece of dirt or a paper clip. She balled up the baggie around the brass and gripped it in her fist. "It's probably nothing," Fenway said, "but better safe than sorry, right?"

Schimmelhorn nodded and tilted her head as if she were about to ask a question, but kept silent.

Fenway turned toward the front again and watched as her father, his suit jacket draped over his arm, walked delicately toward the defense table. He stepped in front of it, crouched down and draped his jacket over Cygnus's body.

He stood up, put his hands on his hips, and whispered. Fenway jumped, startled.

"There you go, Professor. I hope that gives you at least a little peace."

His voice was loud, as if he were standing right next to Fenway.

She looked at the ceiling. Fenway had seen acoustic tricks before, usually in cathedrals or museums, where you could whisper in one spot and hear it in another spot on the other side of the room. It usually had to do with parabolic ceilings focusing the sound waves. Fenway looked up. The ceiling was designed in squares and rectangles, but a section over Fenway's head was shaped like an ellipse and rose more toward the center of the room. Above the defense table was a similar elliptical shape.

"Dad," she whispered.

Now it was Ferris's turn to jump. He spun around, a look of bemusement on his face.

"Say something, Dad."

"What's going on?" Ferris whispered back.

"Some weird acoustic thing is happening. It's the way the ceiling is shaped. Parabolas or something."

Ferris's eyes widened. "Does this have to do with the murder?"

Fenway shrugged and leaned her left shoulder on the square column. "I'm really not sure." But she was sure. The killer had heard everything discussed at the defense table. While Fenway could barely make out the conversation even though she was in the first row, the killer, who had no doubt stood right where she was standing, could hear Cygnus talk about naming names as if they were right next to him.

"Do you need anything else?" Ferris asked.

She shook her head, then walked up the aisle, everyone's eyes still following her, to the judge's bench area. Without making it obvious, she tried to look for places where she could secure the evidence bag. Maybe one of the cabinets behind the judge's bench. She wasn't sure if any of the cabinets locked, or if they did, if she had access to a key. She was so lost in thought she jumped again at the sight of Professor Cygnus's dead body, now with Ferris's coat draped over it.

Piper would probably have an excellent idea of where to keep evidence, especially since she had been on the security design committee of the courthouse, but since she'd been forced to resign the Friday before, she was no longer a county employee and wasn't allowed to have knowledge of the chain of custody.

But Jennifer Kim could. As much as Fenway was angry at Kim for being the one to force Piper out, she *was* a county employee and technically a law enforcement representative. She could legally enforce the chain of custody. Not only that, but she had a locking briefcase, too.

Fenway hesitated. A little voice inside her head whispered that she shouldn't trust Jennifer. But how loud was that little voice just because Fenway didn't like what Jennifer had done to Piper? She looked around the courtroom again, but there were no other options.

"Jennifer? Could I see you a moment?"

Jennifer Kim got up and walked through the gate to where Fenway stood. Motioning with her head toward the corner, Fenway turned and walked behind the judge's bench and next to the wall, where the American and California flags both stood in their floor-mounted poles.

Kim gave the corpse a wide berth and shuddered as she went past, then crossed her arms. "Are you sure we can't move the body?"

"Come on, Jennifer, you of all people? We move the body and anyone we arrest for the murder has a built-in appeal on the physical evidence."

Jennifer nodded. "So you wanted to see me?"

Fenway looked out at the courtroom; no one seemed to be paying attention to their conversation. "I found a shell casing under the last row of seats," she whispered. "I think the shooter was on the nook side of that column. That's one reason no one saw the shots." Fenway stopped before telling the ADA about the acoustic anomaly. Even though Jennifer Kim was a sworn officer of the court, Fenway didn't trust her. At times, she seemed almost maniacally focused on following the law closely, and at other times she forced Piper to quit or threatened Fenway for talking with Charlotte.

"Oh!" Jennifer Kim jumped slightly. "What—what will you do with it?"

Fenway shook her head. "I have no idea. I don't have a place to secure it. Neither my purse nor my fingerprint case lock. You have a briefcase, right?"

Jennifer hesitated for a moment, then nodded.

"What? Isn't that the best place for it? You're an officer of the court. We can't follow chain-of-custody rules to the letter in here, but in your locked briefcase, can't we get pretty close?"

Kim hesitated before answering. "Since I'm a prosecutor, it might look suspicious. Whoever we arrest for the murder of Professor Cygnus could argue that because I had access to the shell casing, I somehow tampered with the evidence to fit the theory of the crime."

"We don't have a theory of the crime."

"Well, I know that, Fenway, but the defense could argue that we were trying to capture a specific person all along." Kim tilted her head. "Aren't you the one saying that Rose Morgan is the most likely suspect? What do you think her lawyer would do if her fingerprints turn out to be on that casing?"

That was a problem—the casing. Rose Morgan had been on the other side of the aisle, hadn't she? It would have been difficult for anyone to shoot Cygnus from that side of the courtroom—and while shell casings can eject forcefully, would it have gone all the way across the aisle through a potential maze of people? Maybe Rose hadn't been on that side of the room at all—in the mêlée afterward, she could have crossed over the aisle easily.

It might have been easier just to leave the courtroom.

Exasperated, Fenway grunted. "Fine. I get your point. I still need to figure out where to put this. Somewhere safe."

"Maybe you should put it in your fingerprint case, then put the case in one of those cabinets."

"Or—doesn't the courtroom have something they use to store evidence?" Fenway snapped her fingers. "I bet they do. Piper would probably know—she was on the security committee to design the courtroom."

Jennifer screwed up her mouth. "That won't work. We can't let a civilian know where we're storing evidence."

An idea popped into Fenway's head. "It depends on how we ask her. If we say, 'Hey, Piper, we found some evidence. Where can we store it?' Then no, that's against the chain of custody guidelines. But if we say, 'Hey, Piper, where do they store the evidence used at trial?' then we're asking a reasonable question."

"Do you honestly think Rose Morgan's lawyer wouldn't sniff that out in about five seconds?"

"It's not against the chain-of-custody guidelines, is it?"

"No," Kim admitted.

"So if it follows guidelines, we're good."

Kim shook her head. "I can't believe you're willing to suggest *this*."

"I wouldn't ordinarily suggest it, Jennifer, but we don't have a lot of options. Given the choice between securing the evidence in a place that follows the rules and twenty other places that don't, I'll take chain of custody every time."

"Fair enough." Jennifer thrust her chin at Piper, still glued to the laptop, typing away. "You go talk to her. She can't stand me."

"For good reason."

Jennifer Kim pursed her lips.

Fenway walked to Piper, who sat at the judge's seat, typing furiously, the screen filling with text—obviously a command line interface. She bent over slightly and whispered near Piper's ear.

"You have a second?"

"Almost." She finished typing the line and hit *Enter*. "Okay."

"So do you know if there's some sort of evidence locker in the courtroom for when they need to store evidence for trial?"

"Is that what you were doing? Getting evidence and now you have to find somewhere to secure it?"

"I can't answer that question. Do you know or not?"

Piper smirked and nodded. "Down by the clerk's station. Under the table, there's a small safe for evidence. It was meant for guns, jewelry boxes, smaller items like that. At least, I'm pretty sure that's where they installed it. I didn't see the implementation blueprints, but it was part of the final design we submitted." She paused. "Before you go look for it, do you want me to see if I can get to the blueprints?"

"Not if you aren't supposed to have access to them."

"Isn't this a life or death situation?"

Fenway rolled her eyes. "You want an excuse to go digging around somewhere you shouldn't. And I know you're on my father's payroll. So no."

"You don't trust me?" Piper batted her eyelashes.

Fenway chuckled. "Not enough to risk my job and my reputation when it comes to you digging up the truth. Besides, it's probably faster to go check myself."

She walked around the side of the judge's bench, down the three steps, and to the clerk's station. She looked around for a moment but didn't see anything that looked like a safe. However, in the smooth mahogany of the judge's bench, a thin line in the shape of a rectangle—about three feet wide by a foot tall—was in the wood about at head height for a person sitting at the clerk's station. Fenway ran her fingers around the rectangle; it felt like a panel. She tried to pull the edges of the box and attempted to get her fingernails underneath. After a moment she remembered that pushing the flush door of the cabinet had activated a spring to open it. Sure enough, when she pushed the right side of the rectangle, it popped out slightly, and she caught the ridge with her fingertips and slid it to the side. Opening the panel revealed the beige metal door to a small safe, slightly smaller than the panel. Its rough, mottled paint didn't fit with the smooth, rich finish of the mahogany which gave a stateliness to the judge's bench. Fenway didn't disapprove of the aesthetics, although she wondered how much that single hidden panel had cost the taxpayers of the county.

The door had a single-line display that said READY in light green digital letters, and a numeric keypad underneath. Two small circular LED lights to right of the keypad were labeled ARMED and OPEN, but were both dark.

"Great," Fenway mumbled as Jennifer Kim walked up behind her. "I'm sure I won't be able to get into the safe without a code."

"I can see if I have the code on my laptop," the ADA said. "I know that evidence locker is for us to use during trial. Someone must have sent it to me. Maybe in an email."

"Really?" Fenway said. "If I can't use your briefcase, how in the world can I use an evidence locker that you have the code for?"

Jennifer Kim shifted uncomfortably. "Well—the county guidelines specify evidence lockers as a satisfactory location to store physical evidence and keep the chain of custody. My briefcase isn't."

Fenway shook her head. "I bet the people who made these rules never worked in law enforcement." She sighed. "Fine. Go see if you have the code in an email."

Jennifer walked through the gate to the seat she'd chosen in the gallery.

Fenway looked up and saw Piper's head sticking over the top of the judge's bench.

"You found it," Piper said.

"Jennifer's seeing if she has the code." Fenway laughed. "It would be funny if it was just one-two-three-four."

"Don't worry, I changed the safe from the default. Nine-nine-three-one, zero-two-eight-five."

"What?"

Piper rolled her eyes. "Nine-nine-three-one, zero-two-eight-five."

"Eight digits, huh?" Fenway turned her attention to the keypad and punched in the numbers: 9-9-3-1 hit three of the four corners on the pad. All the numbers in 0-2-8-5 lined up vertically—quite pleasing. The green light next to OPEN lit up, and the door released with a soft click.

She looked back up at Piper. "They didn't change the code after they installed it?"

A slight smile touched the corners of Piper's mouth. "It's probably best that you don't mention that to anyone."

Fenway placed the evidence baggie with the shell casing in the safe, then closed it. The red light next to ARMED lit up, and the display changed to IN USE.

"How much did this safe set us back in the budget, Piper?"

"I didn't spec it out, but these are surprisingly affordable. It's not the gadgetry in front that's expensive—it's the quality of the materials and how difficult they are to break into. I hope they didn't skimp on the quality there. Okay—I'm still trying to get McVie to respond."

Fenway nodded, and Piper's face disappeared.

She's doing more than trying to connect with McVie. Fenway hoped that Piper wasn't getting any information using access that she shouldn't have. Although, as Fenway pulled the mahogany wood panel back over the door of the safe, hiding the watchful eye of the red LED, that was probably too much to ask.

CHAPTER SEVEN

Fenway walked up the aisle toward the double doors. No one watched her this time; everyone was back to doing their own thing. The clock above ticked past nine forty-five.

Leda Nedermeyer was reading *Pride and Prejudice.*

Judith Cygnus sat with her head resting on her palm, her elbow on the arm of the chair, dozing.

Jennifer Kim had removed her laptop from her briefcase and was tapping away, probably to get Fenway the code. Fenway stepped up to the assistant district attorney and whispered, "Don't worry about it. I got the code."

"You did? From where?"

Fenway smiled. "A lady never reveals her secrets."

"Does that mean you got through to McVie? He definitely has it. Piper didn't see the code, did she?"

"The point is, Jennifer, we have the evidence safely locked up until the lab can get ahold of it, and you don't have to worry about digging through your email to get the code."

Fenway kept walking.

Evans Dahl had removed his rumpled suit jacket, pulled his brief-case onto his lap, and was reviewing papers.

Nathaniel and Charlotte Ferris were sitting next to each other, Charlotte's head on his shoulder, talking in low voices, their fingers intertwined. Fenway almost did a double take. She'd always assumed her stepmother was a gold digger who cared much more for her father's vast fortune than his feelings. But as her father's fortunes had taken a turn for the worse over the last several months, and even with him on the verge of losing his company and possibly his freedom, not only did Charlotte remain steadfastly by his side, but the two of them also seemed to grow closer. The love they showed seemed to be back to the bloom of a new relationship. Fenway's stomach tightened.

Amanda was looking at an e-reader with a notebook on her lap, and Xavier was reading a dog-eared paperback of Jean-Paul Sartre's *No Exit*. Fenway almost laughed out loud.

"Homework?" she asked.

"Figured we might as well," Xavier said. "It looks like we'll both miss our first class today."

Rose Morgan sat at the edge of the gallery by herself, staring off into space. Fenway would ask Rose next, although she wondered how to convince Rose to talk to her, especially since she wouldn't even give up her purse to be searched.

Bryce Heissner had his arms folded, an angry expression on his face, as if Cygnus had been inconsiderate enough to get murdered and incon-venience him like this. Fenway decided to interrogate him after Rose.

As Fenway reached the end of the aisle, she turned toward Cynthia Schimmelhorn, who still stood where Fenway had left her. They hadn't finished their interview.

"Apologies for how long that took, Ms. Schimmelhorn. I wasn't expecting that to be so complicated."

"You found some evidence, then?"

"I believe so." Fenway cleared her throat. "After the shots were fired, what did you see?"

"Well, not too much, to be honest."

"No?"

"It was—it was sort of a blur. People screaming."

"Did you see the man you described to me earlier?"

Cynthia shifted her weight. "No."

A stab of annoyance pricked at Fenway. "So why did you think he was the one who shot the professor?"

A crease appeared between Cynthia Schimmelhorn's eyes and her mouth turned down at the corners. She blinked several times and shifted her weight.

"Never mind, Ms. Schimmelhorn." Fenway started to turn away, then said, "I'm sorry—one more thing. I was sitting directly behind the defense table, and the professor said something about naming names in a money laundering scheme. Do you happen to know anything about that?"

"What?" Schimmelhorn's mouth dropped open.

"I said—"

"I heard what you said. I don't know if I can believe it!"

Fenway cocked her head. "You can't? But surely you're aware that Ferris Energy has been taking 'ghost ships' in one of their ports for over a year now. I was under the impression that part of the reason you want my father to be fired from the company is the lack of oversight he's provided."

Schimmelhorn stayed silent.

"Of course, it could be the mere appearance of impropriety, but a member of the board with your intelligence and foresight should at least have some actionable data at your disposal before you kick out the founder of the company." Fenway leaned against the wall and folded her arms. "But then perhaps you're in a power struggle for control of Ferris Energy, and you're looking for any excuse to try to kick him out."

Schimmelhorn stared at Fenway for a moment, mouth agape, then chortled. "It's quite surprising how much you've uncovered in your investigations." She nodded. "Yes, of course we know that there are insiders who are performing illegal activities inside Ferris Energy. We didn't believe that local police had the resources to ferret out the criminals without putting themselves—or us—in harm's way. That's why the board put in a discreet call to the federal government. We've been cooperating with the U.S. Attorney's Office down in Santa Barbara."

"Really?" Fenway straightened up. "Normally they try to coordinate that kind of thing with local authorities. Make sure no one steps on anyone's toes."

"You mean the U.S. Attorney never contacted you about this matter?" Schimmelhorn asked. "I never thought to inform the sheriff's office. I assumed it would all be coordinated from the top down." She gave Fenway a level gaze. "I don't want to speculate, Miss Stevenson, but perhaps the U.S. Attorney was unwilling to provide details to the daughter of the CEO of the company at the center of the investigation."

Fenway paused. That made sense. After all, a paper trail led right to her father's bank accounts for the murder of her Russian lit professor. It wasn't connected to the money laundering—at least, Fenway hadn't made any connections yet—and he maintained his innocence. Fenway, for once, believed him. But it looked bad from the outside, so of course she would be excluded from a federal investigation.

In fact, from the U.S. Attorney's perspective, she would be in the perfect position to cover up any murders. She shuddered with horror. If Nathaniel Ferris *had* been behind all this—the embargoed oil, the camouflaged supertankers, the sale of the fuel to the East Timor rebels, the complex network of money laundering over a *billion* dollars, and the murders of the people who had threatened the scheme—she knew he would have contacted her to convince her to either cover up his wrongdoing or at least look the other way. But he never called her to cover anything up—which cemented his innocence in Fenway's mind.

If her father was being set up to take the fall for a murder he hadn't committed, she could be set up too. Manufacturing false evidence wasn't outside the realm of possibility with the people who were *actually* running the show.

She blinked. Cynthia Schimmelhorn was standing in front of her, looking at her expectantly.

"Did you see anything after the shooting, Ms. Schimmelhorn?"

Cynthia shook her head. "I'm sorry, but I don't remember much. The gunshots seemed loud to me, but I figured it was because we were in an enclosed space, not because the shots were fired in the area around me."

"Where were you looking when you heard the shot?"

"I was—uh, let me see. I suppose I turned my head to see if I could locate the shooter."

"Toward the aisle?"

Schimmelhorn paused. "That sounds right."

Fenway cocked her head and studied Cynthia Schimmelhorn's face. It was impassive. She wasn't certain about what she'd seen, yet she wasn't worried about providing incorrect information to the police. Or whatever authority Fenway was. But perhaps the steely countenance was her default. After all, Schimmelhorn had lost her daughter to suicide a few years before, and she was a female executive in a man's world. She must have needed to force down her emotions to thrive in her career.

"You don't remember, do you?" Fenway said quietly.

Schimmelhorn blinked.

"The human brain can process an amazing amount of information, but when some of that information is traumatizing, it will wall it off so your conscious mind can't access it." Fenway's voice was gentle. Her psychology professors would object to the horrific overgeneralization, but Fenway was concerned about solving the murder, not about being completely accurate in describing brain function. "So it's understandable if you don't remember what happened." She leaned forward slightly. "You stood less than five feet away from where the shots were fired, Ms. Schimmelhorn. I understand if you can't remember what happened, but it's important that you're honest with me. I can't solve the crime if you give me wrong information."

Schimmelhorn pursed her lips. "You're right," she murmured. "I can hear the shot in my head, but I don't remember anything else until the click of the doors locking."

Fenway nodded and put a comforting hand on Schimmelhorn's arm. "All right. Thank you. That's all for now."

Schimmelhorn nodded. "If I remember anything—anything at all—I'll let you know. I'm sorry." She turned and walked slowly back to the left side of the gallery, where she took a seat behind Bryce Heissner, who was still leafing through his briefcase.

Fenway scanned the eleven people sitting there—Piper was still perched at the judge's station. She leaned against the back of the chair in front of her and took a deep breath. *Might as well get this out of the way.*

"Rose?"

Rose Morgan looked up. "Sorry, Miss Stevenson," she said. "I won't be talking to you without a lawyer present."

Fenway set her jaw. It was a long shot, but she might as well take it. "Mr. Dahl is a criminal attorney. He could step in for you if he doesn't mind."

Evans Dahl looked up at Fenway over the top of his glasses. "What?"

"I'd like to question Miss Morgan about what she witnessed this morning and what her relationship with the deceased was."

Dahl shook his head. "I decline."

Rose Morgan called out. "I decline too. I already have a lawyer. One I like. One who I'm positive has my best interests in mind."

She shot a look over to Evans Dahl, who looked uncomfortable but tilted his head. "Too many cooks spoil the broth, Miss Stevenson. I won't step on another lawyer's toes."

Perhaps Morgan and Dahl knew something Fenway didn't—it wouldn't be impossible. But then Dahl grimaced and shifted his weight in the chair, moving his lower leg into a different position. Ah—he must still have quite a bit of pain in his ankle.

Fenway turned her head to Bryce Heissner. "All right. Looks like you're next, Mr. Heissner."

He glared at Fenway. "Maybe if *she'll* wait for her lawyer, I should, too."

Fenway shook her head. "Miss Morgan and I have a bit of a history. A few days ago, I told her she was under arrest, and she ran away. So I can understand why she's a little reluctant to talk to me."

"She wouldn't let you search her bag, either."

"Right, but like I said, we have a history." Fenway put her hands on the back of the seat a row behind Heissner and leaned forward. "Don't tell me that *you've* resisted arrest, too?"

Heissner scoffed. "Of course not. But I don't have to talk with you."

Fenway nodded. "You're well within your rights. See, right now, I have my eye on the woman who I caught doing a lot of sketchy things last week."

"Hey," Rose said, "you can't—"

"It's a matter of public record," Fenway said coolly, although she wasn't quite sure if the sheriff's office had made the reports public or not. She still stared Heissner in the eyes even though she was talking to Rose Morgan. "You can assert your innocence to anyone you like, just like you don't have to talk to me without a lawyer." She softened her voice and cocked her head slightly. Heissner drew back slightly. "You'll never guess who's at the top of my list of suspects for the professor's murder." She straightened up and stretched her arms over her head, and her spine lengthened and made a couple of quiet but satisfying cracks. "It's not a problem. I'll just tell the sheriff's office that you wouldn't agree to talk. Since you're a material witness, you can simply wait at the sheriff's office until your attorney arrives."

Heissner paled. "You can't do that."

"I'm not doing *anything*, Mr. Heissner," Fenway said. "The law is the law. Talk to me now, while we're not going anywhere, or talk to the sheriff down at the station after you've spent a few hours waiting for your lawyer to show up. It's pretty straightforward."

Heissner harrumphed.

"Oh, for the love of God, Bryce, just talk to the coroner," snapped Cynthia Schimmelhorn. "You don't constantly have to keep measuring your dick with everyone who asks you to do something."

"Dammit, Cynthia—"

"*Bryce.*" Schimmelhorn's voice was sharp as she leaned forward in her chair and her gray eyes burned. "*Talk to the coroner.*"

Fenway, whose head had swiveled toward the sound of Schimmelhorn's voice, beckoned Heissner to join her in the nook.

He looked from Rose to Cynthia to Fenway, then back to Cynthia. Cynthia pursed her lips and motioned toward Fenway with her head. Bryce Heissner sighed and closed his briefcase slowly and deliberately, staring at Fenway as he did so. He placed his briefcase delicately on the seat beside him, then stood up slowly, brushing imagined crumbs off his suit, straightening his tie, and rearranging his suit jacket.

"Stop *preening* and go interview," Schimmelhorn hissed.

"Oh, let it go, Cynthia," Heissner said. "You may be the most vocal member of the board of directors, but you're not my boss." He picked up his briefcase and slowly walked toward Fenway, like a toddler who was intentionally trying to drag things out.

Fenway walked ahead of him, and by the time Heissner turned the corner into the nook, she was already seated, holding the phone in front of her, the recording app loaded.

She clicked the record button. "The date is November twelfth, 9:52 A.M. Coroner Fenway Stevenson interviewing Mr. Bryce Heissner."

She looked at Heissner, who grunted and took a seat across from her. "Do you consent to having this conversation recorded, Mr. Heissner?"

"What the hell, right?"

"So that's a yes?"

"Oh, we're being formal? *Affirmative,* Coroner Stevenson, I consent to having this conversation recorded. That better?"

Fenway raised her eyebrows. She could already tell this would be a slog. "Can you state your full name for the record?"

"Bryce Robert Heissner."

"Mr. Heissner, would you state your occupation?"

He cleared his throat. "I'm the chief operations officer for Ferris Energy."

"Where were you when you heard the gunshots?"

"I was standing in the back row."

"Standing?"

"I was stretching my legs."

"On which side of the courtroom?" Fenway asked.

"This near side. The defense's side, I guess."

"And on which side of the column were you standing?"

"Um..." Heissner furrowed his brow. "The side closest to the center aisle, I suppose."

"So you were standing almost immediately behind Ms. Schimmelhorn?"

"Yes, I suppose so."

Fenway nodded. *That's almost exactly where Cynthia Schimmelhorn said she heard the shot fired.* She tried to keep her face impassive. "Did you see who fired the gun?"

Heissner shook his head. "No."

"Where did it sound like the shot came from?"

He shook his head. "I lost most of the hearing in my right ear when I was in the Navy. I can't place sounds very well."

"Oh—when were you in the Navy?"

"About thirty years ago." He puffed out his chest. "Made it to Lieutenant Commander before I left to go into private industry."

Fenway studied Heissner's face. "Did you see anything out of the ordinary?"

"No."

"Ms. Schimmelhorn said she saw someone in the back aisle who looked suspicious. Did you see anyone?"

"Before the shots? There were a few people walking, trying to come into the room, trying to get out. I don't remember anyone looking nervous or suspicious."

Fenway nodded and paused briefly. "Did you know the decedent?"

"Jeez. Fancy words. I didn't really know him at all."

"So why were you at his arraignment?"

"I needed to meet Cynthia this morning. She and I had some paperwork to go over."

"What about?"

"How to fire your daddy." A slow smile spread across Bryce Heissner's face. "You know, before the arraignment today, I figured we should play this really close to the vest. But now, you know the board of directors has recommended firing Nathaniel Ferris with cause," Heissner said, raising his voice. Fenway cringed. Everyone in the courtroom would be able to hear Heissner's pronouncement, which she was sure was the point. "It's not like he's kept things level—he hasn't been able to keep his involvement with murderers and thieves under wraps. And it's bad enough that his own *wife* was arrested for murder—"

"She was innocent!" protested Fenway.

"—but now he himself has been arrested for murder. He would have been arraigned for it, too, but he made *damn* sure that he turned this into a debacle."

Fenway's jaw dropped. "You're saying that my father killed Professor Cygnus so he couldn't get arraigned for the murder of Solomon Delacroix?"

"Had him killed, yes."

"That's a ridiculous motive."

"According to you." Heissner chortled. "Sure, you make it seem like you and your father don't get along, like he's at odds with you over all the high-profile arrests you've made of his political appointees and employees. But when the chips are down, he knows he can count on his little girl to make evidence disappear or to convince a crowded courtroom that the angle of the trajectory couldn't *possibly* have come from that direction. And the entire county trusts you because you're the coroner. You won re-election in a landslide. Plus, you've got some fancy master's degree in forensics. But blood is thicker than water, Miss Stevenson. Oh, and it's a nice touch, using your mother's maiden name instead of your father's last name to really cement the popular misconception that you can't stand him."

Fenway blinked. She wasn't sure how to respond to Heissner's accusations.

"You don't have to say anything," Heissner said, a snarl on his lips. "The board has been cooperating with the assistant district attorney, and she would have introduced many more charges than a single murder indictment. Your father's in deep water. If his arraignment had been held, I guarantee your father wouldn't have gone home today. He wouldn't go home *ever.* Three more counts of murder. Conspiracy to commit murder. Fraud. Racketeering. And selling fuel to the rebels in East Timor? To a group on the terrorism watch list? I don't know if the U.S. Attorney wants to add treason to the charges, but 'aiding and abetting a terrorist cell' has a certain charm to it, right?"

Fenway's stomach dropped, and the room began to spin. This was so much bigger. She'd suggested that Charlotte hire Piper to dig into the trail of evidence that Fenway was sure had been planted. But this? This was another level completely. This might be beyond what even Piper could fight against.

Heissner's face was full of crazed glee as he stood up and stuck his head around the corner of the nook. "Did you hear that, you bastard? You're being brought up on a dozen different charges. You'll rot in jail while the Feds and the county fight over who gets to fry your ass."

Charlotte's voice shimmered with concern. "Nate—don't—"

Fenway was on her feet and scooted around the corner in time to see her father storm past the four-foot-square column and head toward the nook.

"You know those are damn lies," Ferris said.

"And I bet your wife pulled the trigger, too!" Heissner yelled. "I've seen those targets from the gun range. Some man you are, using your wife to do the dirty work."

Ferris got right in Heissner's face. "You've got a funny way of clawing your way to the top."

"Don't make me laugh," Heissner said. "We might have stopped this long before now if you weren't so busy pimping out your daughter to the sheriff so he'd look the other way."

Ferris's jaw clenched.

"Dad—" Fenway shrieked. A flurry of movement of her father's fist. Heissner had his eyes focused on Fenway, a sneering grin on his face, and never saw the blow coming. Ferris's uppercut connected with Heissner's chin.

The scene was in slow motion. Heissner's whole face rippled with the punch, the skin from his mouth to the receding hairline of his forehead condensing and expanding, up and down like a spring that had been stepped on.

Heissner's head snapped back, and he fell over the chair he'd been sitting in. There was a crack as the back of Heissner's skull smashed into the wall of the nook. He let out a sharp yelp of pain that almost drowned out the sound of tearing cloth as his suit jacket sleeve caught on the arm of the chair.

Voices from the gallery and footsteps. Charlotte, Jennifer, Xavier, and Amanda all came running.

"What the hell happened?" Xavier exclaimed, rushing to Heissner's side.

Charlotte had a look on her face like she didn't know whether to yell at her husband or kiss him.

Fenway looked at Jennifer, whose face slid from concern for Bryce Heissner into guilt. Fenway set her jaw. "You're adding a bunch of charges to my father's arraignment?"

"I couldn't tell you, Fenway. You're too close. You've got a conflict of interest."

Fenway shook her head. "The coroner's office has been investigating the murders that have happened over the last week, as well as the accident at the Ferris Energy plant, and you're telling me that instead of reassigning my office due to a conflict of interest, you let us flounder away? Did you obstruct my sergeants from doing their jobs? Withhold information?"

Jennifer Kim looked at her shoes.

"It's one thing if you thought I should recuse myself, Jennifer, but you wasted our time. And you wasted the taxpayers' money."

"We couldn't risk you telling your dad we were onto him," Kim said softly.

"Couldn't risk—" Fenway's mouth dropped open in disbelief. "Listen here, Ms. Kim. My father abandoned me when I was eight years old." She clenched and unclenched her fists. "He never paid my mother a cent because he had expensive lawyers and my mom had *nothing*. He missed my school plays. My high school graduation. Even my college graduation."

"It doesn't—" Kim started weakly.

"You don't think I *want* to see him to pay for what he's done? You think I'll have some sudden change of heart and *not* push for the maximum penalty if he's done something like this?"

"I think he's the only family you have left," Kim murmured.

Fenway blinked. It was true, but that didn't mean she'd look the other way. Far from it.

"And you think I want him to be the only family I have left? You don't think I wish every day that it was *him* who'd died of cancer in that hospital and not my mom?" Fenway shook her head. "You may care about the appearance of impropriety, but you sure don't care about getting at the truth." She pointed at her father, who stood with his mouth hanging open. "You think I'll let him get away with assault when we get out of here because he's my father?"

"No," Cynthia Schimmelhorn interrupted. "You're going to let your father get away with it because Bryce was insulting and uncouth and deserved to get punched in the face."

Fenway looked at Cynthia and burst out laughing. "Yeah, you're right." She waved her hand at Jennifer Kim. "Do what you've got to do, Jennifer. I couldn't stop you even if I wanted to."

She pushed past her shocked father, who was holding his left fist as if it were sore, and walked toward the aisle. She had to get away from ADA Kim, her father, Charlotte, and Bryce Heissner. Maybe she'd hide out with Piper behind the judge's bench. The interviews hadn't gone well, and not having a closed-off, soundproof area made the subjects tighten their grips around what they were willing to say in public.

Fenway reached out her left hand and touched the back wall as she walked. She didn't know where she would go to get the alone time she needed to reset herself. The wall had the slightly gritty feel associated with new paint, but it felt cool to the touch as well, probably because of the anti-radio signal paint underneath the top coats. She lifted her hand before her fingers touched the minor scratches in the paint around the bottom corner of the audio speaker enclosure.

Fenway took a right turn up the aisle toward the front of the courtroom, then stopped in her tracks.

Minor scratches in the paint.

Were there minor scratches in the paint when she'd first seen the back wall?

Maybe. If the installers put in the speaker enclosure after the painters were done. If the audio technicians hadn't done the job correctly, or if they hadn't gone back to touch up what they damaged.

It was probably nothing. Fenway had probably overlooked it the last time.

And besides, even though the scratches looked relatively recent, that didn't mean anything. She wouldn't be able to tell the difference between a scratch made last week and a scratch made half an hour ago. And even if those scratches *were* made half an hour ago, what significance could it possibly have?

Fenway took another two steps and stopped again.

When Jennifer Kim had fainted, everyone had turned their attention to Fenway, trying to revive Kim. No one had been paying attention to the back wall.

It would eat at her until she knew for sure.

She looked up at the judge's bench. Piper was watching Fenway curiously.

Fenway sighed. What the hell—it's not like she was going anywhere.

She turned around and walked back to the speaker enclosure along the back wall.

She peered at the scratches on the bottom left. Two scratches: one in a stretched z shape, the other a swoosh that turned slightly up at the right-hand side. It's possible that when the audio installers slid the speaker into the wall, the enclosing frame was slightly out of position, so one of the mounting screws could have made those scratches.

But the scratches were heavier on the left side than the right. As if whatever had damaged the paint had been pushed hard then dragged to the right as it got lifted up. If the scratches had been made from trying to shove the speaker enclosure in the wall opening, wouldn't they be deeper the closer they got to the wall opening as the frame was being pushed in?

It certainly didn't prove anything, but it *was* unusual.

Fenway studied the edge of the enclosure frame. Where there should be screws, there were only holes.

That was enough to pique Fenway's curiosity. There were many scenarios in which the scratched paint and the missing screws could be innocently explained away, but it's not like she needed a warrant.

She put her hand up to the edge of the frame and caught the edge of it with all four of her fingertips. The frame easily gave way and pulled out about eight inches.

At the bottom of the wall opening was a ledge.

On the ledge was a black handgun.

III

____

10:00 AM

CHAPTER EIGHT

Fenway stood for a moment, holding her breath, staring at the handgun that had been hidden behind the speaker enclosure. She hadn't been prepared for this. No evidence bag, no gloves, nothing.

Soft footsteps on the carpet stopped next to her.

"Oh." It was Charlotte's voice.

Fenway tensed at her stepmother being so close. "I'm as surprised as you."

"That's a Sig Sauer P226," Charlotte whispered.

"How can you tell?"

"Double stack magazine instead of the single stack of the P220, and it's got about an inch more barrel than the P229."

"I didn't know you knew your guns so well."

Charlotte shrugged.

Fenway pointed to the recessed lettering. "It also says 'Sig Sauer P226' on the barrel."

Charlotte smirked. "Well, yes. That was a dead giveaway."

Fenway turned to her. "Can you do me a favor?"

"Sure."

"Go and grab my fingerprint kit. It should be next to my purse."

Charlotte nodded and strode purposefully up the aisle.

Fenway shook her head as if clearing the cobwebs out of it, and turned her attention back to the handgun. She eased up on the pressure she had on the speaker enclosure, but it started to slide back—and silently, too.

Unusual, for sure. It's not like this speaker enclosure would be pulled in and out frequently. So why the need to have it slide—and so smoothly, too?

Fenway closed her eyes. When had these been installed? Piper had said they'd finished over the weekend.

Friday morning was when Professor Cygnus's arraignment had been announced. Her father's, too.

She remembered waking up in McVie's bed, tangled in his sheets, finally together with him the way she'd dreamed about almost since the moment she met him. And he'd felt the same way.

The phone call waking them up, McVie rolling over to answer it even though Fenway was trying to distract him. The arraignment would be the day after the Veterans Day three-day weekend.

Did she love him too?

Maybe she hadn't heard him correctly. It had been loud; a man had been shot and killed—McVie likely thought he was pursuing a gunman but didn't know what danger he might run into.

She squeezed her eyes shut and tried to block out everything but the speaker enclosure and the gun.

Who had ordered the installation of the speaker enclosures? And when? Perhaps Piper could find out.

Whose fingerprints would she find on the gun? Since no one in the courtroom had gloves on, she couldn't rule anyone out.

Charlotte walked toward Fenway, holding the fingerprint kit lightly by her beautifully manicured fingernails.

"Thanks," Fenway said. "Set it next to my feet for now." She motioned to Jennifer Kim with her head. "Can you come over here?"

Kim hurried behind Fenway. "What do you need?"

"Hold this open for me."

"Okay." Jennifer Kim reached out and gripped the side of the speaker enclosure with both hands.

"It'll try to slide back in if you don't grip it firmly," Fenway said.

"Don't worry, I've got it."

Fenway took her hands off, and Jennifer was right: she had it. The spring-loaded mechanism didn't faze Jennifer at all as she held it open.

"Do you know if this was part of the original audio design?" Fenway asked Kim, putting on another pair of gloves and getting an evidence bag for the gun.

Jennifer shook her head. "I don't know anything about the audio design of the courthouse. I wasn't on any of the design committees. I'm just as lost in this new courtroom as you are."

"Kind of an unlucky start, isn't it?"

"What, a murder in the new courtroom on the first day?" Kim nodded. "Yeah, I guess it really couldn't get much worse from here, huh?"

"No, I guess it couldn't. Maybe an earthquake or terrorist attack."

"Or a tornado full of sharks. Something like that."

"Right." Fenway reached out her gloved hand and took the Sig Sauer, placing it in an evidence baggie.

"Holy shit," Jennifer Kim said under her breath. "That was in the speaker enclosure?"

"It sure was," Fenway muttered. "And you feel how easily and silently this slides in and out?"

"Yeah."

"Someone spent a lot of money to get this sliding mechanism in here, and they made sure that it was as quiet as possible." Fenway looked at the gun in the baggie and looked at the hole in the wall with the ledge behind it. "Seems like a lot of trouble to go through."

"I don't know," Kim said. "Maybe it was opportunistic."

"Opportunistic? Like whoever shot Professor Cygnus just *happened* to pull on the speaker enclosure and find the perfect hiding place for a gun?"

"Well, no, that doesn't make much sense." She paused. "Can I let this go now?"

"In a second—I have to test for residue on the ledge." Fenway put the bagged gun into the fingerprint kit and looked at Jennifer as Piper walked up to them. "Do you know when the metal detectors were set up?"

"They were installed yesterday," Piper said. She held her open laptop in one hand and typed with the other. A long Ethernet cable trekked down the center aisle behind her. "I figured you'd need access to some of the information I was able to pull up."

"I hope you were authorized to access this data," Jennifer said icily.

Fenway rolled her eyes. "Jennifer, we're talking about trying to solve a murder with limited resources here. I think we're allowed to provide a little wiggle room."

Piper shook her head. "No need for wiggle room. I didn't need any authorized access to get into this. All public records. You have to know where to look." She smiled at Jennifer Kim, half amused and half mocking. "Sorry to disappoint you. I know it's your lifelong dream to see me behind bars."

"It's where your boss would have gone after the arraignment," Kim said to Piper.

Fenway grunted, reaching down and grabbing the cylindrical plastic container of gunshot residue pads. She unscrewed the lid and carefully pulled one out, wiping the ledge with the pad.

"The metal detectors were installed yesterday," said Piper, tapping on the laptop keyboard. "Two officers performed a sweep of the courthouse building yesterday morning, and after about forty-five minutes, they didn't find anything."

"What about the audio service?" Fenway looked at the pad. Several small spots on the pad were turning a bright blue. The gun had been recently fired—which indicated that it was likely the murder weapon.

"Everything was installed about two weeks ago by a company called Yesterday Audio," Piper said, reading from the screen.

"Yesterday Audio?"

"I guess they specialize in antique radios, tube amplifiers, turntables, that kind of thing. They were out of here the day before Halloween." Then Piper squinted at the screen. "Wait—hold on. That's not quite right. They reported a recall on the speakers they'd installed and asked for access to the building to replace them."

Fenway's ears perked up. "When did they report that?"

Piper clicked a few times. "Saturday morning. About ten o'clock."

"You can let it go now, Jennifer." As Jennifer Kim eased the speaker enclosure back in place, Fenway turned back to Piper. "That's odd that it was over the weekend. And were they able to get access to the courtroom?"

"Yes. It was authorized on Saturday morning—"

"By who?"

Piper clicked another four or five times. "Hang on. Huh. That's weird."

"What's weird?"

"Signed off by Jennifer Kim."

Fenway's head swiveled to the ADA.

"*You* authorized Yesterday Audio to come in and reinstall these speaker enclosures?"

"Uh..." Kim blinked several times. "What did I supposedly do?"

"You signed off on the audio company coming in and replacing the speakers."

"Oh—well, what, that was Saturday? Oh, right. I had to prepare for not one, but *two* arraignments for the most famous people in town. I had my hands full, and so did my staff. Someone said there was an issue with some equipment safety recall, so I signed it. I didn't know it was the speaker enclosure." Kim set her jaw. "But look, even if they told me it *was* the speaker enclosures, and even if they'd told me they were installing a sliding drawer mechanism, I wouldn't have batted an eyelash. Wiring, electrical work, appliances —if the people who installed say there's a safety issue, I let 'em fix it."

"But why did *you* sign off on it?"

"Because no one above me was working on Saturday. It was just me."

"Just you? High-profile cases like these and your boss doesn't come in?"

"You'll notice that he's not at the prosecution table either. It's the boring arraignment part of it. The trial? Yeah, you can be sure that he'll be first chair. But this is the arraignment. He's back in his office taking questions from the press, probably."

"So who came to do the replacement?"

"What do you mean?"

"Who was it? Or was it more than one person? Did they have names?"

"Oh, honestly, Fenway, I didn't even see. Someone came in and handed the clipboard to me. I think I was on the phone." Kim tapped her foot. "Okay, yes, maybe that's not the best way to do business, but I was swamped. I couldn't do one more thing."

"Well, I think I know how the gun got into the courtroom. It didn't get past the metal detector this morning."

"It didn't?"

"No. The audio company brought the gun in. Inside the speaker enclosure."

"But there were still metal detectors here on Saturday." Kim frowned and crossed her arms.

"That's true, but the speakers have big magnets in them. They wouldn't have put them through the detectors. They might have searched the boxes they were in, and I'm sure they had the audio installer walk through the metal detector, but no one checked for weapons *inside* the speaker enclosure.

Jennifer Kim shook her head. "You mean that I signed off on the people who brought the gun into the courtroom?"

Fenway tilted her head. "It's possible. It's only a theory, and it's a lot of conjecture, but it seems like a reasonable scenario." She started to snap off her gloves, then reconsidered. While she had the gloves on, she wanted to see if she could find the second bullet.

The first bullet might be recoverable too, if it had been a through-and-through, but from the back of the gallery to the front of the defense table had to be thirty or thirty-five feet, easily, and she didn't think the 9mm bullet could go all the way through a person's head from that distance. She tried to remember the rows and columns of the calculations from the class where she studied the mass and force of different projectiles, but it wasn't coming to her.

Still, it was worth examining the body again for an exit wound.

Fenway picked up the fingerprint kit and her eyes scanned both the mahogany façade of the judge's bench and the back wall. She pushed her way through the gate, Piper following her trying to pull the ridiculously long Ethernet cable out of the way.

"What are you doing?" Piper asked.

"Looking for bullet holes."

"You thinking it was a through-and-through?"

Fenway shook her head. "No, but I should check."

"Well then—"

"Piper," Fenway said, as quietly as she could, as she crouched over the head of the dead professor, "how many shots did you hear?"

"Two," Piper replied, keeping her distance from the dead body and trying to look calm but failing.

"Right. And were the shots 'bang-bang'—quick and right next to each other—or was there a short pause?"

"Uh, I'm not sure. Maybe there was a little pause."

Fenway nodded. "The professor was only hit by one bullet."

"Oh. So you're looking for where the second bullet hit?"

Fenway grunted in assent. "I think it hit the front panel of the judge's desk somewhere. And if we can find the bullet—unless it ricocheted off somewhere—we might be able pinpoint where the killer was standing." Fenway looked over her shoulder. Most of them had moved from the gallery and were crowded in the back, talking to each other. Only Evans Dahl, Leda Nedermeyer, and Judith Cygnus remained sitting in the chairs in the gallery. No one was paying attention to them. "I'm going to examine his body again. Just to make sure I didn't overlook a second bullet hole."

Piper spoke in a whisper. "Sounds like you think it was one of the people in the courtroom."

Fenway grimaced. "Ordinarily, I'd say no. A shooter would want to leave the scene as soon as possible—McVie certainly thought the shooter left the courtroom. But there's something that bugs me."

"What?"

"The gun—and I'm positive that's the murder weapon—was placed in its hiding place *after* the shooting. I can't imagine that anyone would have had time to put the gun behind the speaker enclosure *and* leave the courtroom."

"I don't know, Fenway," Piper said carefully. "There was a lot of confusion after those gunshots. Sure, the shooter would have to be quick, but I bet it could be done. Especially with enough practice." Fenway carefully lifted Cygnus's head. The bullet wound was a clear red splotch that had made a mess of his temple and the surrounding area. She carefully scoured his head with her eyes. She searched through his thinning hair, then his neck and throat—although she was sure the angle of the projectile wouldn't result in an exit wound so low, but it paid to be thorough. It was as she suspected: there was no exit wound. When the body got to San Miguelito, Dr. Yasuda could dig it out of his skull.

Fenway then studied the rest of Professor Cygnus's body. If that second bullet had hit him, it would have been lower. Given where Fenway had been sitting, it could have been his lower torso. Maybe as low as his thigh, although he was behind the table.

Piper kept silent as Fenway searched for a bullet rip in his clothing and the sight of any blood, but again found nothing.

"It's got to be in that wooden panel," Fenway said. She put Cygnus back into the position she found him and stood. She got her phone out of her pocket and turned the flashlight on. She briefly worried about the battery, but Piper had enough cords to recharge it if she needed to. Besides, they'd probably get out of here in the next hour. She hoped.

Wait, no. No they wouldn't. McVie and the other officers were looking for the gun—the gun Fenway had found in the back wall.

"Piper, did you message McVie that I found the gun?"

"Not yet."

"Do it now. He needs to know that they can stop looking for the gun out there because it's in here. And if he doesn't respond, try Dez or Rachel or someone else." She paused. "And see when they'll open up the courtroom now that they know we found the gun."

"Right."

Piper disappeared with her laptop back up to the judge's bench, pulling the Ethernet cable with her. It snaked around Fenway's ankle. Looking down, Fenway stepped over it as she kept shining the phone's light on the front mahogany panel of the judge's bench.

There it was. A shadowy pockmark with the faintest hint of brass, about three feet off the ground.

She shined her light closer. Surprisingly, it didn't go through the judge's bench—the mahogany must be solid and not a veneer. She wondered how much *that* cost the taxpayers.

Fenway turned her head around to look at the back of the room. She closed one eye. It was a straight line from the bullet hole in the wood, right past the gallery seat in the front row that had been Fenway's, all the way to the seat in the back row where she had found the shell casing.

Hmm. That line of sight *was* right where Fenway had sat. Maybe that's why Heissner thought she was a good suspect—though he was so far away, he couldn't have seen or heard anything to make him think Fenway was the shooter.

She examined the bullet hole again. There was no way she was getting the bullet out of the mahogany. It was too far in. Maybe the San Miguelito CSI team could do it. Or maybe they'd have to cut around the bullet. She knew from her class that forensic teams often had to cut out the portion of the wall with the embedded bullet in order to preserve the bullet's shape.

She sat down, took her gloves off, and exhaled.

"You okay, Fenway?" asked Piper.

"Yeah. Found the bullet hole. Judge Miller was lucky that it didn't go all the way through the wood. She might have gotten one in the leg."

"Even luckier that she wasn't in the room."

"Oh, right." Fenway touched the bump on her forehead again. She usually connected those dots. She'd need to pay closer attention.

"…bulletproof fiberglass." Piper finished.

"What?"

"Behind the wood panel, there's a layer of bulletproof fiberglass. It's in the jury box and the witness stand too."

"You're kidding."

Piper shrugged. "Can't be too safe, right?"

"I mean, I've heard of bulletproof glass in armored cars, but in courtrooms? I didn't know it was in the budget."

"It was surprisingly affordable. I spec'd it out myself. It wasn't the U752 level eight, of course, but it'll work."

"The *what* level eight?"

"Level eight protects against armor-piercing bullets from sniper rifles. I figured there wouldn't be a whole lot of people bringing sniper rifles in here."

"You know, for not knowing anything about guns, you sure know a lot about guns."

"I don't know how to shoot them effectively, but you need anything else, I'm your girl." Piper's laptop dinged. "Oh, all right, here's McVie's response now." She ducked her head back, then audibly sighed. "Well, that's no good."

"What is it?"

"He says they've reviewed camera footage, and they're sure the shooter is still in the building."

"The cameras all worked except the ones in the courtroom?"

"I guess so. He says that even though the gun turned up in here, they're not letting anyone go until the shooter is caught." Another ding. "And he says the system's locks are all tied together. They can't unlock the courtroom doors without opening the outside doors too."

"We're stuck in here until they let *everyone* out? Are you kidding?"

"I wish I were."

"That doesn't seem right."

"You should have seen the price of the multi-zone locking system. We never thought we'd justify the expense."

"You spec'd a multi-zone locking system too?"

Piper shrugged. "I'm good at research."

Fenway stood and lowered her voice. "Let's hope you're good at figuring out how to get to the outside world before we all go crazy in here."

Piper bobbed her head from side to side. "At least you found where the shooter stashed the gun. Now if the killer's in here with us, they won't have their weapon."

Fenway nodded. "True." She looked across the courtroom at Rose Morgan. "But I wish they'd open the doors so we can either interview Rose or take her into custody. I think we'd all feel a little safer with her out of the courtroom."

Piper stared over at Rose. "You don't think she's a little too obvious of a suspect?"

Fenway rolled her eyes. "And Dez says *I* watch too many cop shows. I think Rose is just obvious enough."

Piper shook her head. "I don't think so."

"Well, she's obviously hiding something."

"I don't have a lot of faith in our justice system if you think when anyone exercises their Fourth Amendment rights they automatically have something to hide."

"This isn't just anyone," Fenway said. "Rose stole the USB drive from our last murder victim's office. She ran away after I tried to arrest her. She assaulted me."

"She threw a hardbound edition of *The Complete Works of William Shakespeare* at you. I'm not sure I'd call that assault."

"It's enough to get her a night in jail."

Piper was silent for a moment. "Hey, Fenway, speaking of USB drives, did you take a look at the anonymous gift I heard *someone* left on your desk on Saturday morning?"

"It's amazing you didn't get caught." Fenway nodded, but frowned. "I started going through the files you copied, but there's so much information on there. I didn't get very far, but I know it's important. I was planning to work on the files more today, after the arraignments." She glanced at the clock on her phone. "Half past ten. I should have been working on them by now."

"You have the USB stick with you, don't you? I think I saw it when you emptied out your purse."

Fenway nodded. "I copied it to my home PC over the weekend. I didn't want anything to mysteriously happen to it at the office."

Piper tilted her head, a quizzical look on her face.

Fenway leaned over the tall judge's bench and whispered, "We think there's a mole in the sheriff's department."

Piper recoiled. "What?"

"I know. I didn't want to tell you before because we're trying to keep it hush-hush."

"A mole for what, exactly?"

Fenway shook her head. "We're not sure. We believe whoever it is let Robert Stotsky into Dylan Richards' jail cell to kill him."

"Wait—you're telling me that this has been going on for *six months?* You knew there was a mole in the department for six months and you didn't think to tell me?"

"We don't know for sure, Piper. And we didn't know who we could trust."

Piper looked at Fenway incredulously. "You can trust me, surely."

"No one knows about this but me and McVie. Dez and Mark don't even know about it. Well—Dez has figured it out, but I didn't tell her. And you know how much I trust both of them. Rachel doesn't even know."

The corners of Piper's mouth turned down. She went back to typing.

They were silent for a moment. Fenway turned and surveyed the gallery again.

Rose Morgan was still sitting morosely in the back, staring with unfocused eyes at the wall to the right of the flagpoles.

Evans Dahl still sat with his left leg on the chair next to him, looking more uncomfortable. Sweat formed on his brow, and he was blinking quite a bit behind his glasses. Fenway wondered if he needed another couple of ibuprofen.

Leda Nedermeyer stood up, a stricken look on her face, and made her way slowly over to Judith Cygnus. Hmm. The mistress and the wife —Fenway wondered if Nedermeyer would apologize or argue. She caught Jennifer Kim's eye and motioned with her head toward Nedermeyer. Kim turned to watch, then nodded at Fenway.

"Well," Piper said, concentrating on the screen, "while you've been interviewing Ms. Schimmelhorn and Mr. Heissner, I've been doing some more digging into the payments made between all the parties involved in the embargoed oil transport. Including Global Advantage Executive Consulting."

"Is that—is that legal?"

Piper grinned. "I've still got a valid username and password into the network. And per the wording in my separation agreement, I'm officially a county employee until the end of my unused vacation period."

Fenway gaped at her.

"I know. California is an accrual state. I guess the county used a template that didn't take that into account. Kind of a loophole."

"But you weren't planning to point it out to them."

Piper's grin widened—then faltered as her eyes focused behind Fenway.

Fenway spun around in time to see Judith Cygnus slap Leda Nedermeyer across the face. The English department head seethed with anger, drew herself up to her full height, and pointed at the professor's widow.

"You can't get away with that, you bitch! *You're* the one who killed him!"

CHAPTER NINE

Fenway rushed over and pulled Leda Nedermeyer away from Judith Cygnus.

"Get your dirty hands off me," Nedermeyer shouted, shaking out of Fenway's grip. "She's the one responsible—she forced him into it."

"I didn't force my husband into anything," Judith Cygnus spat, holding the side of her face where Nedermeyer had slapped her. "And it's not like I *could*, anyway."

"If you hadn't *insisted* on those treatments—"

"If *you* hadn't started an affair with a married man, you *bitch*, you wouldn't even be in this courtroom today."

Leda's jaw opened and shut.

"Yes, it's true, I did want those expensive cancer treatments," Judith Cygnus said, "but don't blame me. Blame the greedy insurance company. Or the money launderers. Or, you know, the actual killer."

Leda was silent.

"But no, you blame me instead. The cancer patient. The woman who's been married to Virg for forty-one years. Just because someone murdered him and now you can't ride off into the sunset with him when I die. Boo hoo. Cry me a river, Leda."

"He worked his ass off for you. You knew he was getting money for your treatment and he wasn't telling you where it was coming from." Leda pointed an accusatory finger at Judith. "You're not stupid, Judith. You didn't want to know."

Judith gave Leda a tight-lipped smile. "I have to admit, you're right. I didn't want to know." She crossed her arms. "But he's a grown man. *Was* a grown man." Her voice hitched, but she continued on. "It's not like I was in any position to stop him. I couldn't get even him to stop screwing you, after all. Even though I was supposedly the love of his life. Even when I'm dying of cancer. He still had his late-night 'staff meetings.'" She set her jaw. "So if I couldn't even get him to stay faithful to me, what makes you think I could have stopped him from laundering money through his precious scholarship fund?"

Leda's pale face flushed beet red all the way to her ears, and she started to gasp and shake. Fenway reached out to grip her by the upper arms. At the first touch, Leda spun around and started crying, the tears coming loud and sudden, as the shorter woman sobbed on Fenway's shoulder. Fenway hesitated, then put an arm around Leda's back and began to gently guide her toward the side, away from Judith.

"It's just," Leda whispered between gasps, "it's just that I loved him *so much.*"

"I know," Fenway said, nodding, feeling her shoulder dampen with the older woman's tears. "I know."

"It's not fair," Leda murmured. "I spent over a decade of my life on him. Years when I should have been falling in love and getting married and having a family." She sighed. "Don't ever fall in love with an older man. It hurts too much."

Fenway patted Leda's back, trying not to think of the fourteen-year gap between her and McVie.

"You okay?" Fenway said as gently as she could.

Leda sniffled and nodded.

"You'll say nothing else to Mrs. Cygnus today, Leda."

"But I—"

"No, Leda, you can't. I mean, I won't be able to arrest you or anything, but it's not a good idea. Virgil Cygnus is gone. I know it hurts. I've lost people who have meant the world to me, and I've been there."

"I can't even go to the funeral," Leda said, a fresh set of sobs welling up inside of her, making her breath hitch. "No one wants me there."

Fenway nodded, thinking again of how she started her romance with McVie before he had started divorce proceedings—before he and his wife had even officially separated. She didn't want to acknowledge that she'd been in Leda's shoes. And if McVie hadn't left Amy, if instead they'd stayed together for the children, or for financial reasons, or for convenience, would Fenway be unable to stay away from him, the way that Leda had been unable to stay away from Professor Cygnus?

And had Cygnus told Leda he loved her? Had Leda felt betrayed?

Leda staggered down into her seat and put her head between her knees. Fenway looked up, desperate to see if anyone could soothe the brokenhearted English Department head. Fenway had gotten the gun and bagged it—but it needed to go into the evidence locker as soon as possible, and Fenway needed to be there, watching over it.

"I'm so sorry," Fenway said, "but I have a murder investigation to conduct. Will you be okay?"

"The love of my life died in front of me," Leda choked out between sobs. "I don't think I'll be okay ever again."

Fenway nodded.

"Go," Leda said. "You can't help me. No one can help me."

Fenway gave Leda what she hoped was a reassuring pat on the shoulder, then stood up and made a beeline for the gun. She wondered why she hadn't thought of it before.

"Can I have your attention, please?" she called out to the room. People lowered their voices. Bryce Heissner and a few others loitered near the back of the room. Cynthia Schimmelhorn had moved to a seat in the prosecutor's side of the gallery. Nathaniel Ferris and Charlotte were sitting in the back row. She caught her father's eye, and he looked up, and soon everyone else, even Rose Morgan, was looking at her.

"Thanks," she said. "Since we found the gun in the courtroom, there's a possibility that the killer is still in here."

People murmured.

"It's a possibility, not a foregone conclusion. But we can determine that no one in *here* is the perpetrator. Then we can contact the sheriff and get them to open the doors. Maybe go back to our jobs in time for that important meeting, or back to Nidever University in time to make your afternoon classes." She caught the eyes of Xavier and Amanda, who both nodded.

"How do you propose to do that?" asked Bryce Heissner. The sneer was still in his voice. Her father apparently hadn't punched it out of him.

"I've got some GSR pads in my case," Fenway said.

"GSR?" Amanda asked.

"Oh, sorry—gunshot residue. Firing the weapon put a significant amount of it on the shooter's hands. It might not be visible to the naked eye, but it'll be there." Fenway held up the evidence bag. "I used one of the pads to determine that the gun we found had recently been fired. And now, since none of you are wearing gloves, and none of you have washed your hands with a weak bleach solution since the shooting, I'll test each of your hands. If you were the one to fire the gun, the pad will turn blue."

"What if the killer got hand sanitizer or something?"

Fenway shook her head. "Doesn't get rid of all the residue." She stepped next to her fingerprint kit case on the table and began to leaf through it. "I'll first use the pad on myself. Yes, I picked up the gun, but I was wearing gloves when I did it. I may have a miniscule amount on my hands, but nothing that would rival what actually would be on my hand had I been the one to fire the weapon."

"And I'll go next," said Jennifer Kim, stepping forward.

"Great, thank you, Ms. Kim," Fenway said, continuing to search through the kit. "And if we get through everyone and no one has gunshot residue on their hands, we'll contact McVie." There wasn't room to hide the GSR vial in the kit—where was it? "I can't promise that he'll open the doors, but it will indicate strongly that the killer isn't in here. And we can get the gun to the lab for further... um, further analysis." Fenway furrowed her brow. The GSR pads were in a cylindrical vial. It shouldn't be that hard to find. But it wasn't in the kit.

"Are you looking for the jar you had those white pads in?" Kim asked.

"Yeah—I know for sure I packed a brand-new vial in here this morning."

"You left it on the floor next to the speaker cabinet," Kim said, gesturing behind her.

"Oh—right," Fenway said, although she thought she *had* put it back in the kit. As she went through the gate and toward the speaker enclosure, she wondered if she'd forgotten that she'd taken it out of her kit again. She shook her head. She wasn't even thirty yet—she shouldn't be having memory lapses. Or maybe it was because she'd hit her head.

She turned the corner past the last aisle.

The floor was empty under the speaker enclosure.

Fenway stopped in her tracks and tried to remember, the bruise on her forehead gently throbbing. Maybe she hadn't left it on the floor. Maybe she'd put the GSR pads on the shelf in the speaker enclosure instead.

She walked up to the front of the speaker enclosure and opened the side with her fingertips again. But the shelf was empty. No vial.

Where could it have gone?

She stared at the empty shelf, holding the speaker grate open with her right hand. She tried to retrace her steps. Okay—she'd wiped the shelf clean. Then she'd—

She blinked. She hadn't held the pad with the rapidly spreading blue spots in her hand for more than a minute or two, had she? She didn't think so. And she'd obviously taken off her gloves at some point. Could she have been paying attention to something else?

She tried to remember if she'd taken the vial out of the kit and brought it over to the speaker.

No.

She remembered—she'd unscrewed the lid while holding the vial over the bag. She took out a pad, and....

Hmm.

She'd been focused entirely on finding out if that ledge contained gunshot residue. She must have done *something* with the vial. Back in the bag, or on the floor? Jennifer Kim said she'd put it on the floor. And maybe she was in a good position to notice, since she was holding the enclosure open and out of the hole in the wall. She might have been staring into space, looking right at the vial on the floor for the five or ten minutes Fenway had her standing there.

Well, it didn't much matter now. The vial was gone.

And with it, any chance of swabbing everyone's hands and maybe getting out of here in time for lunch. Lunch at Dos Milagros—the warm, spicy carne asada tacos would hit the spot on an overcast, dreary November day like today.

Fenway shook her head as her stomach growled. "Focus," she muttered to herself.

She slid the speaker enclosure back into the wall, then knelt to look under the seats. Maybe it had slipped out of her bag—but no such luck. As calmly as she could, she walked to the front of the courtroom again, up to the judge's bench. She could see the concern on Piper's face, peeking out above the laptop screen on the judge's desk.

"What's wrong, Fenway?"

"I can't find the GSR pads. They were in a vial, and I could have sworn they were still in my fingerprint kit. Now they're not there. Jennifer says I put it on the floor back under the speaker enclosure, and it's not there either."

"Okay—slow down. You're breathing really fast."

"Sorry, sorry." Fenway forced herself to inhale slowly, trying to get to the count of ten, but only reaching four. But her second inhalation got up to seven, and her third hit ten. Her heart eased its pounding in her ears.

"I've never seen you that close to a panic attack," Piper whispered. "What are you worried about?"

"Nothing," Fenway said, giving Piper a weak smile. "I'm mad at myself for misplacing that vial."

But that was a lie.

If someone had taken that vial—whether from her unattended fingerprint kit or from the floor—it meant that someone in the room didn't want anyone to know there was gunshot residue on their hands.

Finding the gun had made it more likely, but the stolen GSR vial confirmed it: the killer was *definitely* still in the courtroom.

———

Fenway emptied her purse and her fingerprint kit on the prosecutor's table, but the vial of GSR pads was still nowhere to be found. She stared at the array of items. Was she really reduced to the everyday stuff in her purse and a kit full of work tools?

She raised her eyes from the table and looked at her father, several rows back in the gallery, sitting with Charlotte. Stress lines stood out on his brow as Charlotte put her head on his shoulder, the corners of her eyes drooping.

After the revelation of all the additional charges—besides the murder charges that Fenway didn't think would stick—her father must realize that he wasn't going home that night. That he might not go home ever again.

Even if he were to somehow get bail, or even if he were to beat the false charges—assuming they *were* false—he had no more job, no company to call his that he built from the ground up. The board had taken that control away from him.

Nathaniel Ferris closed his eyes and leaned against Charlotte slightly, too. He looked like he was at peace, even with the small telltale stress creases in the skin of his forehead. But the two of them supported each other.

For richer or for poorer, in sickness and in health.

The bottom dropped out of Fenway's stomach, and she gripped the table for support. It didn't make sense. She'd thought for years that her father and Charlotte weren't *really* in love. That she was using him. That Charlotte hated that Fenway was in her husband's life—that is, when she thought about Fenway at all. That Nathaniel Ferris only gave a shit about having a hot piece of arm candy. Vapid. Airhead. Slut.

Ugh. The evidence against all of that was sitting right in front of her, and Fenway could barely process it. If her father *had* fallen in love, and if Charlotte had loved him too, really and honestly and truly, she couldn't hate their marriage. She couldn't hate their relationship. She couldn't really even hate Charlotte.

Fenway focused her attention back on the items scattered all over the table and began to hastily put them back in her purse and in the fingerprint kit. First the purse items: the wallet, the keys, the tampon case.

Then the fingerprint kit. The stab of pain and fear about the missing GSR pads. Then the container of fingerprint dust and the brush that went with it. Then the inkpad and a large stack of cards for left hands and right hands.

Hold on a second.

She might not have had the GSR pads, but she *did* have something else. The fingerprint dust.

Since no one had worn gloves—not that Fenway had seen, anyway —the gun might have the killer's fingerprints on it.

And she had a dozen suspects—thirteen, counting herself—who she could easily fingerprint.

Yes, it was true that the gun had a lot of rough surfaces from which it would be impossible to lift fingerprints. Yes, it was also true that fingerprint analysis from the naked eye wasn't nearly as accurate as lab analysis. So there was no way to make an identification with the tools that Fenway had that would stand up in court. But she didn't need to.

She knew the killer was in the courtroom. Though she might not be able to tell if the fingerprints matched, her analysis might be good enough for reasonable suspicion. It might even be good enough for McVie to take someone into custody.

Assuming, of course, that the killer didn't cause any trouble. That they didn't have another hidden weapon on their person, or that they didn't try to think of a way to get away from them. Thirteen people remained in the courtroom. Only one of them had pulled the trigger. She didn't want to endanger anyone else's life.

The killer could refuse to give their prints, of course, but that might look bad in front of everyone. Peer pressure was sometimes stronger than self-preservation.

She sighed. *Well, first things first.* She'd have to fingerprint the gun. She examined the prosecution's table. The large, well-lit surface would be an excellent work area, but it was out in the open, in front of everyone.

She looked around the courtroom: no locations were hidden from view, and no flat surfaces existed in the gallery. The nook was hidden well enough and had two chairs, but contained no flat surfaces adequate for working.

The jury box? Nothing.

Ah—of course, the judge's desk. Flat and well-hidden. The killer might not see what she was doing right away. She didn't know how she'd take everyone's fingerprints without tipping off the killer, but she'd cross that bridge when she came to it.

Piper had her laptop on the far right side of the desk. Was there enough room to fingerprint the gun without getting the dust all over Piper's laptop? Maybe. Fenway would have to risk it—otherwise the killer might realize what she was doing.

She placed the evidence bag with the gun carefully on the far left side of the desk, then took a pair of blue nitrile gloves out of her kit and slipped them on as silently as she could. Piper looked up from her keyboard, a questioning look on her face, but Fenway silenced her with a finger to her lips. Piper nodded, reached in the kit, and handed Fenway the brush and the jar of fingerprint dust.

Taking the Sig Sauer P226 cautiously out of the evidence bag, she set it on the table. The mottled sides of the grip created an impossible surface for obtaining fingerprints, but the sides of the front of the barrel and a few areas on the front of the grip were smooth. The chances she'd get something usable were low, but since she couldn't find the GSR pads, this would have to do. If the killer had grabbed the barrel to put the gun on the ledge behind the speaker enclosure, she might find something to check against other fingerprints.

She brushed the dust lightly over the side of the barrel and the area around the front of the grip. The trigger was too thin to grab any prints.

She got out her phone and turned the flashlight on.

Two smudged prints were unusable.

She turned the gun over and applied the dust to the other side as well. Shining a light on the barrel, Fenway blinked. There, above the Sig Sauer markings, was about half a print—clear and unsmudged.

She took a piece of fingerprint tape and carefully put it over the print, then affixed the tape with the transferred print to a card from her kit.

She exhaled loudly—she'd been holding her breath as she put the tape on—and stared at the card. The ridges of the fingerprint ran continuously from one side to the other without any backward turn, but with a noticeable bump in the middle.

She closed her eyes tight and tried to remember her fingerprinting class, grasping for the words that described what she was looking at.

Tented arch.

It was, as fingerprints went, a fairly unusual pattern. Fewer than one out of every twenty fingerprints had them, and for the bump in the center to be so dramatic—if someone in the courtroom had this type of tented arch, it would almost assuredly be a match.

Fenway swept as much of the dust off the tabletop and into her gloved hand as she could, and dumped it into the trash can underneath the desk.

"Fenway?" Piper asked in a quiet voice.

"Yeah?" Fenway whispered back.

"I know you're busy, but I need you to take a look at this."

"Can it wait, Piper? I'm trying to figure out how I can get everyone's fingerprints without making a big announcement."

"I don't know if it can wait. I found a way to prove your dad didn't make that financial transaction to the hit man."

"Do you have another suspect?"

"Well—not really. But you know how the evidence that your dad killed your old professor hinges on the fact that he paid Peter Grayheath to kill him?"

"Yeah?"

"So before the arraignment, when we were getting coffee, I told you that the computer used to open the account under your dad's name is the same computer that moved the money between the local businesses and the master account."

Fenway nodded. "And I said that's what the prosecution *wanted* to prove."

"And then Jennifer interrupted us. I found timestamps on the master server for the transfer to Grayheath."

"So?"

"So—at that exact moment, your father was being caught on camera out around town. He walked past an ATM on Fourth Street when the transaction was initiated, and a security camera caught him entering a French restaurant when the authorization went through."

"You think that will prove his innocence?"

Piper nodded. "I do."

Fenway paused. "Okay, you got my attention, Piper. First, though, let me see if ADA Kim has any ideas on how we can get the fingerprints from everyone without tipping off the killer."

Piper nodded, then furrowed her brow. "Is someone eating Indian food?"

Fenway tilted her head, then laughed. "Fingerprint dust. Cumin aldehyde. You can smell that over the new paint?"

Piper shrugged and went back to her laptop.

Fenway scanned the courtroom. Cynthia Schimmelhorn and Bryce Heissner were in the back row on the defense side, roughly where they were seated during the arraignment. Rose Morgan was in the back row on the prosecution's side.

Leda Nedermeyer was in the sixth row of the prosecution's side, all the way next to the wall. Judith Cygnus sat in the third row, next to the center aisle. The two women had turned their heads away from each other.

Nathaniel and Charlotte Ferris were still lost in their embrace, eyes closed in the second row. Huh. Maybe her father had finally gotten it through his head that his hours of freedom were numbered.

Amanda and Xavier were about two-thirds of the way back. Xavier had his notebook out and was writing in it. Amanda leaned back in her chair, her eyes closed, a paperback open face down on her lap, holding her place.

Evans Dahl was in the third row, leg still up on the seat next to him, looking paler and more sore. Fenway wondered if his discomfort was due to his painful ankle or if he had a different medical condition. She'd check on him after talking with Kim, who stood in the center aisle, leaning against the side of a seat, staring at the speaker enclosure in the back wall.

Fenway steeled herself and strode toward the assistant district attorney. She stood next to Jennifer Kim for a moment. The assistant district attorney had a faraway look in her eyes.

"You okay?" Fenway asked.

Kim smiled sadly. "You ever wonder how different your life would be if you hadn't gone into law enforcement?"

"I'd probably be finishing up my second twenty-four-hour shift in a row. Exhausted and hoping I wouldn't catch some weird avian flu from one of the snot-filled toddlers who came in with their worried parents."

Kim laughed softly. "I wanted to go into propulsion engineering," she said. "I loved physics in high school."

"Wait—you wanted to be an actual rocket scientist?"

Kim shrugged. "Things turned out differently."

"You got into law by accident?"

"Oh, it was no accident," Kim said, looking up at the ceiling. "I could tolerate being the only woman in the propulsion engineering major for just so long. It's not like my fellow students or my professors wanted to make it any easier for me."

Fenway nodded, and the silence stretched between them for a moment. "You haven't seen the GSR pads, have you?"

Jennifer shook her head. "You still can't find them?"

"I thought I put the vial back in the fingerprint kit, but when I went back five minutes later to look for it, the pads had disappeared."

"The whole vial?"

Fenway nodded.

"Maybe you misplaced them. Maybe you thought you put them back, but you didn't."

"I don't think so," Fenway murmured, shaking her head. "And even if I had, where would I have put them? I've looked everywhere."

"They'll turn up."

Fenway shook her head again, more emphatically this time, then took a step toward the ADA and lowered her voice. "Jennifer, I think the killer took them."

"You think the murderer stole your GSR pads?"

"Yes."

"Wouldn't it just be easier to take the entire case?"

Fenway cocked her head. "The vial would be easy to conceal in a purse or a pocket—especially now that I've searched everyone. You couldn't hide that big fingerprint kit."

Kim turned her head slowly, looking at Fenway's face for the first time since she'd walked up. "No, I don't believe that. The killer might have left the gun in the wall behind the speaker enclosure, but then they took off. They're out in the courthouse, trying not to look guilty."

"Even if that's the case," Fenway said, "I've got a partial print on the gun. A *good* partial—about two-thirds of a full print. If we fingerprint everyone in the room, we can see if we have a match."

"Partials are always iffy in court," Kim said.

"If we make an identification, though, McVie will know who to take to the station. We can make sure they don't get away, and they'll get screened for gunshot residue. Whoever it is will get questioned in a proper interrogation room. Where the recordings are almost *guaranteed* to be admissible."

Kim scrunched up her mouth but didn't say anything.

"Are you okay with me taking everyone's fingerprints?"

"I don't know."

"I'll round that up to a yes. Now, ideally, we could do it without letting the killer know we're taking fingerprints, but I can't think of how best to do it."

"Why don't you want the killer to know?"

Fenway widened her eyes. "Because the killer might still be dangerous. Yes, there's twelve of us and one of him—or her—but I'd rather minimize our risk."

Jennifer Kim considered it for a moment. "Maybe, but you've got the gun now. That makes the murderer far less threatening, don't you think?"

Fenway was silent for a moment. *People do crazy things when they're backed into a corner.*

Jennifer cleared her throat and changed the topic. "Usually, when we try to trick people into giving us their fingerprints, we'll give them a soda can or a water glass or something. That might work for one person, or maybe two if you do it at the same time, but there's no way that will work on thirteen people."

Fenway looked around the room. "Everyone is touching things, though. We could take fingerprints from the books that Xavier and Amanda are reading. The same thing with Leda Nedermeyer."

"You can't be sure that those aren't contaminated with other fingerprints," Kim pointed out. "If the killer picked up Amanda's book when she dropped it earlier, for example." She folded her arms. "No, it's got to be something where you're positive you're getting the right print. You'll have to use your fingerprint cards and deal with the killer potentially trying to get away."

Fenway frowned.

"Look, the killer no longer has their gun. I don't think they snuck one past the guards, either—not if they went through the trouble of bribing the audio installation company to put the gun in the speaker enclosure during installation." Kim leaned back against the chair again. "So I don't think they'll use lethal force. And you said it best: there's a dozen of us. Those are favorable odds."

Fenway put her hand through her thick, curly hair and scratched her scalp. "I don't like it," she said, "but I can't think of any way around it."

ADA Kim set her jaw. "We should divide and conquer. I'll start on the defense's side. You start on the prosecution's side." She gazed over Fenway's shoulder at Nathaniel Ferris and Charlotte. "Think you can get them to agree to the fingerprinting?"

Fenway nodded. "Yes. My father has been telling everyone he's innocent. I can't imagine he won't relish the opportunity to clear his name."

"Even if he's guilty?"

Fenway sighed. "I don't know how many times I have to tell you— he wasn't anywhere near where the shot was fired."

"And I don't know how many times I have to tell *you* that I'm not taking your word for it."

Both women went to the judge's desk to get fingerprint cards from Fenway's kit. "Should we announce what we're doing?" Kim asked.

"No way," said Fenway. "If we make an announcement, someone is sure to point out that they don't have to give us their prints—then no one will do it."

"Maybe we shouldn't ask. We're on shaky legal ground."

"Come on, Jennifer, you know as well as I do that we can *ask*. They can say no. So let's do the ones least likely to say no first. I'll start with my father and Charlotte. Maybe you can start with the brain trust from the Ferris Energy board of directors. They seem to trust you. We'll save Rose Morgan for last—I think she'll be the most likely to raise a stink."

"That sounds like it could work," Kim said, nodding. She brought herself to her full height—at five-foot-three, she was more than half a foot shorter than Fenway—and smoothed down her suit jacket. She grimaced and looked for a moment like she might throw up.

"You okay?"

"It's fine. Haven't eaten today. I was running late this morning." She pointed to Fenway's forehead. "Did you hit your head?"

"What?" Fenway touched the spot. It was still tender. "Oh—yes. When the bullets were fired."

"You okay?"

"I'm fine." Truth be told, she wasn't feeling great, but she chalked it up to being so close to a dead body. She hoped they would get out soon.

"All right, we might as well do this. You have more than one ink pad?"

Fenway held up three. "I used to get made fun of for being over-prepared."

They split up the fingerprint cards, eight each of the left hand and eight each of the right. Fenway took a deep breath and took the circuitous walk behind the judge's bench behind Piper, down the steps next to the witness stand, to the gallery gate, two rows in front of her father. He still had his arm wrapped around Charlotte.

"Hi," she said.

Nathaniel Ferris opened his eyes. He gave his daughter a tight, tired smile. "Hey, Fenway." He glanced at the ink pad and the finger-print cards in her hand. "I see you're still hard at work. I take it you want to take my fingerprints?"

Fenway nodded. "Found a print on the gun."

Ferris patted Charlotte on the shoulder, and she stirred. They both began to stand.

"No," Fenway said, stepping through the gate. "Do it sitting down. I don't want to call too much attention to us doing this."

Charlotte gave Fenway a quizzical look.

"Because first of all, if the killer is still in here—and I hope they're not," she quickly added, "I don't want to broadcast this or give them time to prepare."

"And second?" asked Charlotte.

"Well—look, there are probably a couple of people who will refuse, and if we make a big production out of it, then they might convince *everyone* not to give out their fingerprints."

Charlotte shrugged, taking two of the cards and balancing them on the wide wooden armrest of the chair. "Mine are already on file, and I know *we* didn't shoot Professor Cygnus." Fenway opened up the ink pad, and Charlotte gamely placed each of her fingers on the pad, then the cards, taking care to center her prints in each of the boxes.

It struck Fenway that Charlotte was being respectful of the process, and more than that, respectful of Fenway's job. She wasn't fighting the request, or telling Fenway that fingerprinting was a waste of time, or asking Fenway when they'd be able to go home. A knot formed in Fenway's throat, and she forced it down with a hard swallow.

"Here you go." Charlotte handed the cards back to Fenway, reaching for the handkerchief Nathaniel Ferris proffered.

"Your turn, Dad," Fenway said, not looking in his eyes as she handed him the cards, then held the ink pad for him.

He followed the same order Charlotte had.

"Oh—Charlotte, I wanted to ask you something."

"What?"

"I heard something strange during the shooting. You know guns and ammunition and stuff like that, right?"

"Sure."

"There were two shots, but also a loud snapping noise."

"A snap? Low or high in pitch?"

"High-pitched. Maybe a ricochet or something."

Charlotte crossed her arms. "Where did it sound like it was coming from?"

"Right next to my ear, but I think the acoustics of the room were playing tricks on me."

Charlotte slowly shook her head. "Right next to your ear, huh?"

"Uh—yeah, I think so."

"I didn't hear it, so I can't tell you for certain, but it sure seems like the noise a bullet makes."

Fenway's face fell. "A bullet? Right next to my ear?"

Charlotte nodded, and Ferris's head snapped up.

His eyes were wide. "A bullet? Right next—"

Fenway put a hand on Ferris's shoulder. "Shh, Dad—quiet."

He looked around, then lowered his voice. "Do you think someone took a shot at you?"

"I don't know, Dad. I just found out the sound might be a bullet. I don't know anything yet."

"Who'd want to shoot at you?"

Fenway shook her head, her curls moving side to side. "I can't even process this now. Stop making me worried. It could have been any number of things. And you heard Charlotte—it might not even have been a bullet."

Ferris gave the completed cards to Fenway. "Listen," he said quietly, "I want you to be careful. Maybe it wasn't intended for you, and maybe it wasn't even a bullet. But *be careful.*"

Fenway scoffed.

"What?"

She shook her head. "Sorry. It's just—you weren't around to tell me to be safe when I was growing up. It—" Fenway stopped and chose her words carefully. "It's weird that you're telling me to be safe. I don't need you to protect me now."

"I'm sorry, Fenway." Ferris lowered his eyes. "I wish there were something I could do to get back to a good starting point with you. With us."

"I know, Dad," Fenway said miserably. "I have no idea what that is, though. I've been so mad at you for so long, and everything you've done—I know you're trying to make it better, but for some reason it makes me angrier. I know you're trying."

"I am, Fenway. I *am* trying."

"Just because your intentions are good doesn't mean your actions are," Fenway said. "We have a lot of work ahead of us to get to a decent relationship."

Ferris was silent.

Fenway cleared her throat. "Anyway, I have a killer to catch. Maybe we can go back to see a family therapist once this is all behind us."

Ferris smiled. "Assuming I'm not rotting in jail for the rest of my life."

"You've got a great lawyer, and you've got Piper on your team now. My money's on you." Fenway turned before another knot could form in her throat.

She walked down the side aisle, then through the next row, finally planting herself two seats away from Judith Cygnus.

"Hi, Mrs. Cygnus."

Judith Cygnus's keen eyes focused on Fenway, and she put down her purse on the seat between them. "Hello, Miss Stevenson. Quite a situation we've found ourselves in, isn't it?"

"Indeed." Fenway looked closely at the older woman's face. No grief touched her eyes.

Judith Cygnus spoke as if Fenway weren't there. "I don't know whether to laugh or cry, myself. I was so worried about what Virg would do without me. Now I suppose I can die in peace."

Fenway, taken aback by the candor, pretended she hadn't heard it. "I need your fingerprints, Mrs. Cygnus."

"My fingerprints?"

Fenway nodded. "We're trying to eliminate suspects."

"Surely you don't think I—"

"We're looking at all possibilities," Fenway said, "and we can eliminate you as a suspect with your fingerprints."

"Oh," Judith said, eying the fingerprint cards and the inkpad. "All right, then, if it will eliminate me as a suspect." She held her left hand out to Fenway.

Fenway took each of her fingers in turn, carefully getting the prints inside the box on the proper cards.

When she was done, Judith Cygnus tutted. "Do you have a cloth for my hands?"

"I'm sorry, Mrs. Cygnus, I don't. I had to make do with what I have with me."

Judith clicked her tongue and tilted her head to the side but carefully removed a tissue from her purse. "This is nasty stuff. It really gets everywhere." She made a face. "Smells like curry, too."

"Yeah, it does, sorry. But I appreciate your cooperation." Fenway stood.

"I knew, Miss Stevenson."

Fenway paused. "I'm sorry?"

"I knew about Virg and Leda from the beginning. Virg was not a man who could keep his passions bottled up, and I'm afraid Miss Nedermeyer was caught in his web." Judith thoughtfully cleaned each finger with the tissue, the white material turning gray with the black ink. "I suppose I was angry at him about the situation—but not at her. How could I be? I'd known it wasn't in his nature to be faithful, and I married him anyway."

Fenway was quiet.

"I don't have the head for theater that Virg did. Nor the interest. He and I were a match in many ways, but not that one. And he and Leda were horrible together, except when it came to Shakespeare." She chuckled to herself. "Before he started his affair with Leda, I would attend every performance, then we'd go home and I'd have to listen to him spout off about all the actors who hadn't hit their marks or said their lines perfectly, and he'd talk about a new realization he'd made about the play. I found it perfectly boring. And for him to have so much emotion wrapped up in it—well, it was exhausting. It would have put me to sleep if Virg hadn't kept me up all night talking about it.

And then—well, my dear, the passions would enflame him, and I'd get even *less* sleep after that."

Fenway blanched but kept her face neutral.

"Then Leda came on the scene, and she was just as enflamed about the performances as he was. I came opening night, and the three of us went to a late-night diner afterward, and after an hour of Virg and Leda hanging on each other's every word, I excused myself and took a cab home. I knew the two of them would sleep together that night, and as much as I hated the thought of my husband with another woman, part of me—*most* of me—was flooded with an intense relief. The six weeks of hell that I'd endured every year was now another woman's problem."

Judith stared off into the corner of the courtroom, above the flagpoles. "I knew he still loved me. I knew he'd never leave me. But I also knew that there was this part of him that *had* to have an outlet for this. And I couldn't fulfill it for him—and I had no interest in filling it for him."

Fenway wished she had turned on the recorder on her phone.

"Part of me wanted to be the kind of woman who'd be jealous enough to kill him." Judith's eyes unfocused. "But it seemed like such a waste of energy. I was free to have my own affairs, or simply have six weeks to myself. If I weren't so ashamed about it, it would have been perfect."

"You felt ashamed?"

Judith sighed. "It was all over the campus. I'd meet people at university functions, and they'd look at me with pity in their eyes. *That* was the shame. That I was some poor, ignorant woman who couldn't control my husband."

"But you didn't do anything about it."

Judith smiled. "It sounds so banal, but one year, I had an affair with my tennis instructor. He was much younger than me. Younger than Leda, even. I remember thinking he'd be so, I don't know, *vital*. But he didn't care about anything. There was no passion there. He didn't even try, just because he was young and handsome, I suppose."

Fenway was silent.

Judith's eyes came back into focus, and she startled at Fenway, who sat a seat away from her. "Oh. Anyway, listen to me, rambling on." She paused. "I knew you were interviewing people, and I knew that his affair with Leda would come up."

"I—I appreciate your honesty."

"You know I don't have long to live, Miss Stevenson. If I had killed Virg, I'd tell you. I wouldn't want to drag this out, waste all that money on an investigation, and for what? The cancer will take me in another six or eight weeks if I'm lucky. And without Virg, even that much time doesn't feel lucky at all."

CHAPTER TEN

Fenway took fingerprints from Amanda and Xavier without incident. When she was finishing up with Xavier, she looked across at ADA Kim, who was closing the ink pad. Bryce Heissner wiped his fingers off, turned his back on ADA Kim, and walked to his seat.

Fenway stepped into the aisle. "So no problems so far?"

Jennifer shook her head. "Not so far."

"Who's left?"

"Who's *left?*" ADA Kim asked incredulously. "I just got started. I haven't done fingerprinting in a while. I messed up Cynthia's the first time I did it."

"Oh. So you've done her and Bryce?"

"Yes. How many have you done?"

"Five. My father and Charlotte, the two students, and Judith Cygnus. I was planning to print Leda Nedermeyer next. That leaves Rose Morgan, who I figured would go last."

"Why are you saving her for last?"

"If she's innocent, since everyone else has gone before her, she'll give up her fingerprints. If she's guilty, she won't."

ADA Kim shook her head. "It won't be that easy. She's been associated with a lot of crimes recently. She won't give up her prints, even if she *is* innocent."

"Still, it's worth a shot."

Kim bobbed her head from side to side. "And aren't you forgetting some people?"

"What, like Piper Patten?"

Jennifer Kim shrugged. "She was in the right place to take the GSR pads that you lost."

"The angle wasn't right for the shot, given where she was sitting in the gallery."

"Even so, Fenway, it would pay to be thorough."

"Fine, yes, you're right. But let me be the one to do her fingerprints. She thinks you have it out for her, and she'll be much more cooperative with me."

"As long as we get *all* the fingerprints."

Fenway turned and walked up the side steps next to the witness stand, then behind the judge's bench to where Piper was sitting.

"Leda Nedermeyer and Solomon Delacroix were both at UCLA at the same time," Piper said.

At the name of Fenway's former professor—the man her father was accused of murdering—Fenway felt the floor drop out from under her. "What?"

"He was a graduate student there, and he taught the discussion sections for a couple of big literature lecture classes. I'm looking to see if Leda was enrolled in any of his sections."

Fenway's chest tightened, and her pulse raced. "And you think—"

Piper set her jaw. "Men who do... who do *that* kind of stuff don't often have a one-off, Fenway. He recorded it with you, for God's sake. Chances are really good that it wasn't his first time—you know, forcing himself on someone. Probably wasn't anywhere close to his first time."

Fenway swallowed hard. "And you think he might have forced himself on Leda Nedermeyer?"

Piper clicked and typed, then clicked again. "It's possible. Look—I have to establish reasonable doubt that your dad didn't kill Professor

Delacroix. When I lift up some rocks, you might not like what crawls out. Will you be okay with that?"

"Do what you have to do, Piper," Fenway said faintly. It was almost an out-of-body experience.

What crawls out.

McVie still didn't know that Fenway had been raped. He still didn't know that her father was accused of killing her rapist.

He'd said he loved her—but could Fenway really love him back if she hadn't told him about this?

Fenway's life was messy and complicated enough. How would he react if he knew? How would he see her?

"I need—" Fenway started, but her voice broke as the fear washed over her.

The name-calling she'd experienced as a kid.

The men who looked at her hungrily when they eyed her on the dance floor.

The hot water scalding her as she sat on the floor of the shower crying after it had happened.

"Are you okay?" Piper whispered, and Fenway sank to her knees behind the judge's desk so no one else could see her break down, the hot tears springing to her eyes. The room spun.

Then Piper's hands were on her shoulders, then they were both kneeling on the floor, Piper holding Fenway as she tried not to sob. "I'm so sorry, Fenway. I'm so sorry. I shouldn't have brought it up. I'm such an asshole."

"It—" Fenway choked out as quietly as she could. "It surprised me, is all."

"I'm sorry, Fenway." Piper's embrace was stronger and more solid than Fenway expected.

Fenway exhaled in short bursts as her breath caught. "He told me he loves me, Piper. He told me he loves me, and I don't know what to do."

"McVie?"

"Yes."

"Oh wow. When did he tell you that?"

"He pulled me to the ground right after the shooting and whispered it in my ear right before he ran out to go help." Fenway pulled out of Piper's hug and wiped her eyes with the back of her hand. A little mascara came off with the tears.

"Oh." Piper turned and dug a travel pack of tissues out of her backpack, then handed it to Fenway. "Why don't you know what to do?"

"Because I haven't told him."

"Told him what? That you love him back?"

"No—I mean, I haven't told him what happened. What Professor Delacroix did."

"I see."

"How can I love him if I haven't told him? He doesn't know about Professor Delacroix. He doesn't know why the prosecution thinks my father killed him. What if he thinks..."

"What if he thinks what?"

"You know. That I brought it on myself?"

Piper's jaw dropped. "You do *not* think that *any* woman brings that on herself."

"Well—no, but if I had just—"

"Stop right there." Piper folded her arms. "McVie doesn't think of you like that. He doesn't think of *anyone* like that."

Fenway's breaths came more regularly. "I—I appreciate you saying that, Piper. But you can't know how he'll react. Even if he's a good guy. You can't know."

"I can," Piper said simply. "Because he *does* know."

Fenway sank into the carpet even further. "What did you say?" she squeaked.

"He knows. What—you think your dad gets arrested for murder and McVie doesn't do his research? That he doesn't come to me to dig into case files he doesn't know how to access on his own? You don't think he's smart enough to figure it out even *without* a pile of evidence staring him in the face?"

"Oh no." Fenway's voice was small.

"What do you mean, 'oh no'?"

Fenway's hands clapped her forehead, then dug into her curls, pulling her hair back. "He figured it out on his own. He knows I didn't tell him myself. He'll think I don't trust him."

"Oh, Fenway," Piper said. "That's not what he thinks. He thinks it's none of his business whether you tell him or not."

Fenway looked up at the ceiling, the lights glinting off the sharp angles of the fixtures. "He thinks I'm a horrible person for keeping this from him."

"He does not. Didn't you just say that he told you he loved you? This morning?"

Fenway's breathing evened out a little more, and she pulled her hands out of her hair, then dabbed her eyes and her cheeks with a tissue.

Piper cocked her head. "Feel better?"

Fenway nodded.

"Okay. Need another tissue?"

Fenway shook her head. "But I need your fingerprints."

"Wow, Fenway, you never stop with the investigation, do you?"

Fenway forced a smile.

"Yeah," Piper said, rolling her eyes, "my fingerprints. No problem."

Fenway wiped her eyes again. "Do I look okay? Like I've been crying?"

"Maybe a little. But it's okay."

Fenway wobbled on her knees, then grabbed the edge of the desk and pulled herself up. She retrieved the inkpad and placed two fingerprint cards in front of Piper.

"When ADA Kim brought me in last week—you know, after the whole break-in thing—she insisted on fingerprinting me." Piper completed her right hand first and pulled another tissue out of the pack. "Even though the county already took my fingerprints when I was hired. She was trying to make me feel like a criminal."

"Jennifer's okay." Fenway turned her gaze across the courtroom.

Leda Nedermeyer covered her mouth with her palm for a moment, then took her hand away, scrunched up her mouth, then swallowed.

Pills? Leda Nedermeyer had obviously dry-swallowed something.

"Fenway?" Piper asked.

"What? Oh—sorry. What did you say?"

Piper pushed her left thumb hard on the ink pad. "I said I'm not sure I trust her."

"Leda?"

Piper glared at Fenway. "Did you leave the solar system? No, not Leda. We were talking about ADA Kim."

"Oh." Fenway paused. "Listen, she sometimes rubs me the wrong way too, but it's just because she follows the law. It's irritating, like when she insisted you resign. I wouldn't have done it. But that doesn't mean you can't trust her. She's one of us."

"Didn't you say the sheriff's office had a mole?"

"Someone who worked in the jail or security is what I meant, Piper. Someone who could let someone into the jail and who knew the security footage."

"That could be ADA Kim."

"Look, I know you've got a chip on your shoulder about her, but she's only doing her job. She's between a rock and a hard place half the time."

"And she could make ten times more in private practice. Law school loans, maybe medical bills? She could be a prime candidate to take some money to look the other way."

Fenway scratched the back of her hand. "Well, I guess she makes as much sense as anyone else."

"Who else have you thought of?"

Fenway was quiet.

"What?" Piper said, finishing the card for her left hand and sliding the cards and ink pad back toward Fenway. "One of the guards? Or maybe it's one of the sheriff's deputies. Celeste Sandoval? Brian Callahan? Maybe Officer Todd Young? I mean, he kept you safe from the white supremacist group, but I'd guess he's on the take anyway."

Fenway paused. In spite of Piper's sarcastic tone, she actually *had* considered Officer Young. A couple of strange things had happened the nights when he was assigned to her protection detail.

But crazy bumps in the night and unusual glances didn't mean anything. There wasn't even any proof there *was* a mole in the department. No unusual payments. No one suddenly showing up with a new Ferrari.

"Okay, you made your point, Piper. I'll keep my eye out. I won't treat her differently than anyone else as a suspect." Fenway gathered up her cards and pad and walked down the side toward Rose Morgan. She passed Leda Nedermeyer, still sitting on the aisle, who was wiping her hands with a paper napkin.

Rose looked up, perched on the arm of a chair in the back row, and narrowed her eyes.

"Absolutely not, Jennifer!" a deep voice roared.

Fenway snapped her head around.

Evans Dahl pulled himself to his feet, his face pouring sweat, his nose beet red, his tie even more off-center than before. "Are you asking *all* these people for their fingerprints? That makes my blood boil."

Jennifer stammered. "We're trying to eliminate—"

"You're trying to skirt around the Fourth Amendment," Evans said. "I won't have it. Listen up, everyone!"

He didn't have to say it—everyone's eyes were on him.

"These county law enforcement officers have asked you to let them search your belongings and provide your fingerprints to them. That is, in my opinion, a recipe for disaster. If you haven't trod all over your own Fourth Amendment rights yet, do not do so. You have no compelling reason. Do not provide your fingerprints to these people!"

The room was quiet. Fenway turned her head back to Rose Morgan, who shrugged.

Evans Dahl winced as he hopped on one foot. "I should burn your license for this, Ms. Kim."

"Asking people to cooperate with an investigation—" Kim stammered.

"*Asking* people?" Evans spat. "You're holding them—you're holding all of us hostage in this courtroom until you identify the killer! And if someone doesn't provide their fingerprints, you're going to assume they're guilty!"

"We're not—" Fenway said weakly.

"Don't even start with your intent, Miss Stevenson," Evans Dahl said condescendingly. "You, personally, have killed suspects before. You, *personally,* have assaulted suspects. You even drove one suspect to suicide. And now you're trying to get around the law you supposedly love because there are eleven other people in the room with you."

Fenway's eyes bulged. What was he accusing her of?

The defense lawyer's eyes shone brightly. "Oh, you don't like those accusatory statements? Good. Next time, think about what you're doing when you try to get around the Constitution. Do I think you're a nefarious murderer? I do not. But with a different set of rules in place and a different set of people in charge, you better believe you'd be rotting in jail for murder and negligent homicide—you name it, those in power would boil you in oil if they could. Don't make a mockery of the system by ignoring the rules yourself."

Fenway bristled. *How dare he.*

"Who has yet to provide fingerprints?" Evans Dahl said, raising his hand. Rose Morgan stared right into Fenway's eyes as she raised her hand. No one else in the courtroom put their hand up.

"Well," Dahl said, "if you're checking fingerprints and don't get a match, either whoever it was is no longer in the room, or it's me or Rose. But you're getting no further."

Fenway's eyebrow cocked. He called Rose Morgan by her first name. Did they know each other already?

"Sorry, Miss Stevenson," Rose said. "Upon advice of counsel, I'm afraid I must decline to provide my fingerprints."

"You don't have to agree with him," Fenway said. "You know what would really piss me off? If you proved me wrong."

Rose smirked. "Yeah, that would piss you off, wouldn't it?"

Fenway nodded. "I'd be so angry. So do it. Put your prints on these cards and prove you didn't kill Professor Cygnus."

Rose crossed her arms and smiled lightly at Fenway. "Upon advice of counsel, I'm afraid I must decline—"

"Yeah, yeah," Fenway said. "You can't blame me for trying."

Fenway turned on her heel and went back to the front of the courtroom, up the steps to the side of the witness stand and behind the judge's desk.

"That's right, Miss Stevenson," Evans called. "If you can't take the heat, get out of the kitchen. Let me know if there's anything else in the Bill of Rights you need clarified."

Cheeks burning, Fenway glanced sideways at Piper. "I don't want to take advantage of someone's physical inabilities, but I'm glad he's got a sprained ankle so he can't come up here and stop me from comparing the fingerprints we already got."

"I'll let you know if he starts up here," Piper said quietly.

"I'm officially filing a complaint with the Ethics Board," Evans said. "Be glad you don't practice law, Miss Stevenson, or you'd find yourself unemployed and flipping burgers."

"Tell him to shut up or I'll break his other ankle," Fenway muttered.

Piper chuckled and went back to her laptop. "I've made some headway in the money laundering case too," she said. "Two of the code names—"

Fenway's eyes darted back up. Bryce Heissner had walked in front of Nathaniel Ferris, sitting with Charlotte, and was speaking in low tones. Fenway strained to hear him.

"I don't know why anyone is crowing about the Bill of Rights when we *all* know who's steering the ship," Heissner murmured. He pointed at Nathaniel Ferris. "You've gotten yourself in a lot of rough water the last six months."

Charlotte stood, visibly shaken. "Now listen here—"

"No, *you* listen, Miss Sure-Shot California." Bryce's tone was mocking.

Charlotte's face fell.

Miss Sure-Shot California? Charlotte had been a beauty queen with a gun?

"Yes," Heissner jeered, "I know about your shooting trophies and your beauty pageants. I know about your guns. I know about the bull's-eyes your targets consistently have, week after week, month after month. Your husband didn't pull the trigger, dear Charlotte, because he couldn't hit a stadium if he was standing in it." Heissner paced in the side aisle next to the nook where he'd been interviewed, where Ferris had punched him. "But *you're* a different story. Beauty queen—well, royal court, anyway—I guess you weren't pretty enough to win the national event. Even if you proved you were deadly from a thousand yards." He cackled. "Don't women like you only exist in James Bond movies and in the imaginations of thirteen-year-old boys? Yet here you are."

Charlotte's eyes narrowed.

"See, now that your husband is no longer my boss, I don't have to hold my tongue around you. And it's clear to me. You shot the gun that killed Cygnus because you didn't want him blabbing your husband's name to the cops. And whether you were doing his bidding or if you were acting on your own because you didn't want to lose your golden ticket, it doesn't really matter. You're both going down. Maybe you'll both be in jail, or maybe one of you will be in jail and the other one will live on the streets. Either way is fine by me. As long as you *never* set foot on Ferris Energy property again."

Charlotte's jaw was clenched tight, but she said nothing.

"Probably should warn you, Nate," Heissner said to Ferris, "we'll have to change the name of the company since your name is doing such irreparable harm to our image. And our lawyers are already drafting a lawsuit to make sure *you* pay for it, since it was your actions that did it."

"That's enough!"

Fenway jumped at the powerful voice—it had come out of Judith Cygnus.

"My husband of forty years is lying dead in the room with you," she shouted, getting to her feet, "and you're too much of an asshole for it to even *occur* to you to be a decent human being."

"I—" Heissner said.

"Shut the hell up," Judith Cygnus snapped, stepping into the center aisle. "The love of my life was murdered in front of us not three hours ago and you're gloating. You're *happy* he's dead because that means you get more money. If I had a baseball bat, I'd come over there and beat you within an inch of your life. You disgust me, sir."

"Don't give me that," Heissner bellowed, advancing toward her step by step. "Your beloved husband knew what he was doing when he agreed to launder that money. And you can't tell me you didn't understand what was going on. You may not have convinced him to do it, you may not have orchestrated it, but you knew what was happening." Less than an arm's length from Judith Cygnus now, he stopped and cocked his head, and a demented smile came over his face. "So yeah, I'll gloat, I'll be an asshole, and I'll lord it over my former boss for the rest of his pathetic life." He pointed at her face, his finger an inch from her nose. "And there's not a damn thing you can do about it."

Nathaniel Ferris scrambled between the rows of chairs into the aisle and slapped Heissner's hand away. "All right, that's enough, Bryce."

Bryce Heissner reared back and threw a punch at Ferris's jaw.

Ferris jumped backward into the center aisle, the blow glancing off his chin. Standing with his back to Fenway, he drew himself up to his full height.

Heissner took another step, then yelped and went down to the floor, clutching his knee in pain.

Ferris stepped out of Fenway's line of sight, revealing Judith Cygnus, a fire burning in her eyes and a chair in her hands.

"I'm a dead woman walking," Judith said, her voice steel-cold. "You think I won't kill you? You think I'm scared you'll beat up a poor old woman like me if I try to defend myself? Think again, Mr. Heissner. I have nothing to lose." She raised the chair to shoulder height. "You threaten me again and I *will* kill you. Not a jury in America will convict me, and when I get to the pearly gates, Saint Peter's going to tell me how kick-ass it was to see me take down a bully like you." She spat, and a glob of saliva landed on Heissner's shoulder. "Are we clear?"

"Bitch," Heissner whined.

"Bryce!" Cynthia Schimmelhorn barked from the back of the room.

Heissner scanned the faces of the people who had gathered around and finally settled on Jennifer Kim. "Aren't you going to arrest her for assault?"

"I didn't see anything," Kim said evenly.

"Bryce!" Schimmelhorn shouted again, her tone sharper this time. "Get back here and sit down. You're making an ass of yourself, and you're getting beat up by an old lady. It's *not* a good look for you."

Bryce rolled onto his side and gingerly straightened his knee, his face contorted in pain. Nathaniel Ferris took two steps to the side, giving Heissner more room, and Judith Cygnus set the chair down, right side up, and locked it into place with the chairs next to it.

Fenway looked at Judith with amazement. *No wonder she could tolerate life with Virgil Cygnus for forty years.*

Bryce Heissner may have been an oppressive bully, but he had pulled everyone's focus off Fenway and onto himself. Even Evans Dahl seemed more interested in casting dirty looks at Heissner than in lecturing Fenway on the constitutionality of her fingerprinting.

Right. The fingerprints.

Fenway got out the card with the fingerprint found on the gun and compared the cards. She started with Judith Cygnus's, but hers were all whorls and loops—not an arch in sight. The same with Charlotte's fingerprints.

ADA Kim appeared by Fenway's side and dropped off her cards: Schimmelhorn, Heissner, and Nedermeyer. Fenway went through those next. Schimmelhorn had arches on the second and third fingers of her left hand, but nothing tented nearly as much as the print on the gun. Heissner had arches on both his thumbs, but the angle was wrong. Nedermeyer had an unusual type called accidental whorls, and Fenway had never seen someone with more than three—Nedermeyer had seven.

Fenway didn't expect any positive results from Amanda and Xavier, and their ulnar and radial loops didn't match. Piper's prints didn't have a single tented arch either.

She steeled herself.

Nathaniel Ferris was the name on the last card.

She almost didn't want to know. Even though Rose Morgan was the best suspect out of everyone in the courtroom, Bryce Heissner had gotten under her skin. She worried that this was her father's fingerprint. Fenway's stomach did a flip as she compared the prints.

Plain whorl.

Central pocket loop whorl.

Another central pocket loop whorl.

Ulnar loop.

And the right thumb: *another plain whorl.*

Fenway had been holding her breath and exhaled. She'd finished the card for her father's dominant hand. The chance that he'd used his left hand to put the gun behind the speaker enclosure was small. Not zero, but small. She pulled the second card in front of herself.

Central pocket loop whorl.

Ulnar loop.

Another ulnar loop.

Yet another ulnar loop.

And the left thumb—

A tented arch.

Oh shit.

CHAPTER ELEVEN

Fenway stared at the left thumbprint for what seemed like a very long time. Jennifer finally cleared her throat, and Fenway blinked.

The ridge was fairly dynamic. She looked at the card with the partial print found on the gun. She took a deep breath and willed her hands not to shake as she placed the two prints next to each other.

The print on the gun was likely only the top two-thirds of the finger, but the lines looked very similar to the naked eye.

Wait.

Yes, the hill of the tented arch was just as high, but her father's fingerprint showed lines that merged above the right side of the arch. On the print on the gun, the lines didn't merge. And they grew toward a circular path a little earlier.

It wasn't a match after all.

The relief washed over Fenway like high tide, and she shook her head at Jennifer. "Nothing."

"No matches?"

"I *thought* there was a thumbprint match on that last one. But no, it's different."

"Okay." Jennifer Kim lowered her voice. "So you're still thinking Rose Morgan is the killer?"

"Of everyone in the room, she makes the most sense."

"Right. I'm not sure if we can get the sheriff's department to hold her, but I'll do my best to see if we can keep eyes on her until we get something to stick." She paused. "Surely she has her fingerprints on file somewhere."

"I don't know. I mean, I *think* when we took her in last week, we fingerprinted her, but I wasn't there. I don't really know. But if there —" Fenway clamped her mouth shut.

Jennifer Kim tilted her head. "What is it?"

I almost told ADA Kim about McVie and me suspecting that there's a mole in the department. She frantically searched her brain for something—anything—that she could say that wouldn't make it look like she was hiding something.

"I was about to say, if there was any doubt that we could take fingerprints, what with Rose's lawyer showing up, we might have erred on the side of caution."

ADA Kim shook her head. "I know these rules are in place for a reason, but wow, sometimes it makes it difficult to do our jobs."

"Right. But that's kind of the point, isn't it?"

Jennifer laughed. "Says the woman who was yelled at for violating everyone's Fourth Amendment rights."

Fenway tapped her chin and squinted for a moment. "Did I? I didn't think I was getting anyone's prints without their consent."

Kim screwed up her mouth. "Well, maybe it's a gray area. In this situation, with everyone stuck in the courtroom, it's not like everyone is free to go. People might think they have no choice but to give their fingerprints up. Or look guilty."

Fenway felt a pang of shame. "Like I'm doing with Rose."

"I guess so," Kim said. "I mean, only two-thirds of the people in here gave their prints, and you're still betting it was Rose. But I haven't given my prints. Neither has Evans. Or you."

"Oh, come on. The two of you were next to Cygnus when the shots were fired. And obviously I know I didn't do it."

"But *we* don't know that. The other people don't know it wasn't me. They don't know it wasn't Evans. They weren't watching. Or they weren't at the correct angle."

Fenway stuck her hand out in front of her, palm up. "Okay, fine then. Look for yourself. I won't match."

"I believe you didn't do it, Fenway," ADA Kim said. "But you don't need to convince me. You need to convince *them*."

"Seriously, people think I might have been the shooter?"

"No one's willing to say anything, not even Bryce Heissner, but I bet at least a couple of them are thinking it." Jennifer took Fenway's hand and examined her fingertips. "Not this hand. Not a single print with that kind of mountain shape on it."

"Tented arch."

"Right, tented arch. Jeez, how do you remember all that?"

Fenway shrugged. "I only took those forensics classes last year."

"And I never took forensics in law school." She let go of Fenway's right hand and took her left. "Swirl, swirl. Okay—this is an arch, but it doesn't have nearly the kind of hard tent-shape that the print on the gun has. And then you've got some, uh, loops on the last two." She dropped Fenway's hand. "Congratulations. You're not the murderer."

"Now you."

Jennifer hesitated, then put both her hands face up for Fenway to study.

"Everything okay?"

"It reminded me of something."

"Of what?"

ADA Kim shrugged. "It's stupid. When I was a teenager, I went to a palm reader, and she said I would die an early death. It freaked me out. I couldn't sleep for a week. The palmist was very convincing, and it didn't seem like she'd tricked me until much later. Like—when I found her file in our records. She'd been arrested for bank fraud, wire fraud, home invasion, embezzlement—she was a real piece of work."

"Sounds like she'd fit right in with our investigation." Fenway forced herself to smile as she studied the ADA's fingerprints. Not a single tented arch on either hand. She tapped Jennifer's fingers. "You're good."

"Anyway, enough about my traumatic childhood. Looks like we're back at square one."

"We've got a print. We've got the murder weapon. We've got a shell casing. And Piper's bound to find something in her search."

Jennifer motioned with her head to the side. Fenway followed her next to the flagpoles.

"What's up, Jennifer?"

"Look, I know you and Piper are friends, but what the hell is she doing with a laptop in here?"

"Oh." Fenway shuffled her feet. "Well, she's the best forensic financial analyst I know."

"How many others do you know?"

Fenway gritted her teeth. "My father hired her to work on his case."

"He *what?* With her insider knowledge?"

"Her job experience with the county didn't hurt."

"That's *such* a conflict of interest," ADA Kim said. "She's lucky we don't arrest her."

"For what?"

"She's caught breaking and entering. We fire her, and she knows she's skating on thin ice. Then the first person she starts working for is the defendant of one of the biggest murder-for-hire cases this county has ever seen."

"It was a serious job offer, and she happens to be *killing* it," Fenway said. "If anyone can track down who made those payments look like they came from my father, Piper can. What do you think she's been doing all morning? Playing the new *Halo?*"

"You're treating this like a joke."

"Okay," Fenway snapped, "that's enough. Get off your high horse. Unless she's in direct violation of her separation agreement or her employee agreement, you don't have any right to tell her who she can and can't work for."

Jennifer Kim folded her arms. "Okay, obviously you introduced her to the little career fair with your dad. Haha, fine, I get it. It's hilarious. But now, she has to stop."

Fenway put her hands on her hips. "You aren't the boss of her—and you can't threaten her with anything having to do with the Central Auto Body break-in without a direct violation of her separation agreement. Do you have a *direct* violation?"

Jennifer grumbled. "You're not great at keeping your law enforcement friends, Fenway."

"I'm great at keeping my *real* friends, though," Fenway shot back, then spun on her heel and stomped down the two steps at the side of the witness stand.

She got to the gate to the gallery and had no idea where she was going.

Rose Morgan in one back corner. Bryce Heissner in the other. Nowhere to sit and collect her thoughts.

This was already a very long day, and it was getting longer.

———

Fenway found her way over to the nook, pointedly avoiding eye contact with Bryce Heissner, and sat down on the chair she'd brought in earlier.

Her breaths came shallow and fast.

I need to think.

The images all bombarded her, jockeying for position in her head in front of each other, and Fenway closed her eyes.

I'm trapped in the courtroom with a killer, and I don't know how to get out of this.

My father is being set up to take the fall for everything—murder, money laundering, even buying oil from an embargoed country and selling it to terror-

ists. What's a little of treason when you're already going to jail for murder and money laundering?

What's Charlotte going to do? Will they seize all my father's assets? Will Charlotte have to move in with me?

Oh no. Oh no oh no oh no.

I'm trapped in a courtroom with a killer, and I'm more worried about the remote possibility of living with my stepmother. I'm a horrible person.

Fenway opened her eyes. There was a spot on the wall in shadow, an artifact of paint that hadn't been properly applied. She looked closer; it wasn't a shadow at all. It was the black paint, the cellphone-signal-destroying black paint, showing through.

If she got out of this—because someone *had* tried to kill her, that bullet had whizzed right by her ear—she'd have to deal with what McVie had said to her.

She closed her eyes again, and suddenly she was back on the floor, feeling the weight of McVie's taut, muscular body on her, his breath on the skin of her neck. She smelled like his bedsheets, and he smelled like cardamom and fennel and leather, and he pressed his body into hers. Like she was the most important thing in the world, like he treasured her more than anyone else.

And she knew that duty called. That McVie physically needed to run toward the fire, to pull as many people as possible from danger. But he hadn't thrown his body in the way of anybody else. It had been her, taken to the floor, and his words in her ear.

I love you, Fenway.

A chill started at the nape of Fenway's neck and slithered down her spine. He hadn't strained or forced his words. They were authentic. He didn't say he loved her to manipulate her or get her to say it back. He knew there was no time for Fenway to reciprocate.

He said it because he didn't know what fate awaited him once he got up from the floor and ran out of the courtroom.

He said it because it was true.

He said it because he wanted her to know in case it was the last thing he said to her.

And she didn't know if she could say it back.

She looked up at the ceiling. What was wrong with her? McVie was kind and decent and handsome and an excellent kisser. He was a little tone-deaf sometimes, but he was more teachable and more willing to make himself better than most of the guys she'd dated.

And he listened to her, which was also a little different.

Fenway hadn't had a lot of serious relationships. Not many long ones, anyway. And while she'd known McVie for six months, they'd only *just* started dating.

The pressure wasn't fair. It was *way* too soon. She didn't even know if she had the capability to love another person. Not in that way.

And dammit, she had a murder to solve. With only the items in her purse and her fingerprint kit, and with only Piper's text messages to communicate with the outside world.

"Fenway?"

Fenway tilted her head down. Piper stood at the edge of the nook, left arm wrapped around the edge of the wall, laptop balanced on her right hand. "What is it?"

"I found more information connected to the money laundering. You have a minute?"

Fenway smiled sadly. "Until McVie lets us out of here, I have all the time in the world."

Piper nodded. "No update on that front. I've been keeping McVie informed of everything that's going on, though. Texted him that we have a fingerprint for the gun, but no match with most of the people in the room."

"Has he responded?"

"Not yet."

"I'd like to—" Fenway started, then blinked and looked down.

"You'd like to what?"

"When he texts back, would you let me know? And maybe I could message him for a bit?"

Piper tilted her head and smirked. "You know I'll be able to read anything you guys text. I'm not sure I can unsee that kind of stuff. I'll have nightmares for weeks."

Fenway grinned. "Yeah, I know. We'll get extra goopy with the baby talk just for you."

"Ugh." Piper rolled her eyes.

"It'll be *worse* than you and Migs," Fenway said, lacing her fingers behind her head and stretching her spine up and her legs out. "I'll use all the kissing emojis, too."

"You would never. McVie is too old to understand emoji."

Ouch. As if she needed to be reminded about their age difference. Something to ask about when she found another therapist. But she pushed down her visceral reaction and smiled widely. "I can teach him all about emoji and he can teach me about eggplants and peaches."

Piper winced, looking like she wanted to clamp her hands over her ears were she not holding her laptop. "Okay, fine, you out-grossed me that time. And no problem. I know it's hard not being in contact with the outside world."

"You've been texting Migs."

"I have." Piper cleared her throat. "Anyway, do you want to see what I've found?"

Fenway nodded and sat up straight, turning the chair in front of her around. Piper sat in the chair and turned the laptop so they both could see it.

"Okay," she said, "now, look, there's a code name here, *Effect3125*. I've followed every place that it shows up in the ledgers and in the files I sent to you."

"Does that code name mean anything?"

"Not that I can find. Besides, I think they're too clever for that now. Probably just a name and number combination assigned randomly. That prevents geeks like me from digging around in personal data and getting the name of a pet dog or an old elementary school. It's most secure when these mean nothing—and I think they've followed that rule."

"Okay."

"So you see that this set of payments—" Piper pointed to a list of numbers "—and *this* set of deposits—" she clicked and another spreadsheet popped up "—has regular transactions twice a week. Wednesdays and Fridays."

"Gotcha."

"Well, almost two weeks ago, the regular payment went through, and the deposit was made. Then—nothing."

"Okay."

"Now look. There was a cash deposit made to the account from an ATM in Yuma, Arizona, yesterday morning, right around ten o'clock."

"This is *Effect3175*'s account?"

"Yes."

"Yesterday." Fenway looked up at Piper. "Is that supposed to be significant?"

Piper had an exasperated look on her face.

"Okay—do you see that the payments are all from Central Auto Body's ledgers?"

"Oh—and Domingo Velásquez's son was killed on Friday, then he disappeared."

"Yes. All before he could make the deposit."

"And everyone thinks Velásquez is on the run."

"You think the deposit was made by Domingo Velásquez?"

"I do. Right before he crossed the border into Mexico. You ever been to Los Algodones?"

Fenway shook her head.

"Cute little town. Mostly for retirees to go get cheap prescriptions that cost too much in the States."

"And that's where you think he went?"

"That's where I think he crossed. He has a sister in Hermosillo. That's about an eight-hour drive."

"Shit." Fenway exhaled hard. "I thought he might be able to help us."

"His family's still here. He might come back."

"The question is," Fenway said, "why is Rose Morgan still here? She was having an affair with him. But I think it went a lot deeper than sex. When he found out about his son, he went to Rose, not his wife. I think Domingo was in love with her." She paused. "So why didn't the two of them strike out for Mexico together? It's not like she had anything left to do for the money-laundering group. Her job was making sure Domingo stayed on the up-and-up."

"Maybe you got too close to her, Fenway. With the cops crawling around her house, maybe he had to cut his losses. Maybe she *wanted* him to cut his losses. Maybe she thought she'd catch up with him later or something." Piper squinted. "Or maybe she was only pretending with Domingo Velásquez. Pretending to have feelings for him so she'd be able to get as close to him as the money launderers wanted. And when he disappeared, when he was no longer useful to them, her job ended."

"It's time I had a talk with her."

Piper tilted her head. "Didn't she decline to say anything without a lawyer present?"

Fenway shrugged. "I can still *talk* to her. She doesn't have to respond." She stood up.

"Do you want the laptop?" Piper scrambled out of her chair, closing the laptop and following Fenway out of the nook.

"We'll keep it informal. I don't need exact dates and figures, right?"

"I don't know. I've never done this before."

"I'm getting used to playing things by ear. You know how you hear in cop shows that you never ask a question you don't know the answer to?"

"Sure."

"For me, that only applies in court. In the interrogation room, you have to ask questions you don't know the answer to." Fenway tapped her temple as they crossed the courtroom behind the last row of chairs, Piper just a step behind her. She stared right at Rose Morgan, who had her head turned, her eyes fixed on the back of the chair in front of her, in a trancelike state.

Rose jumped when Fenway stopped next to her.

"I've got nothing to say, I told you," Rose said through gritted teeth.

"You just have to listen," Fenway said. "So your boyfriend, the one who disappeared, who came to you instead of his wife when his son was killed? It looks like he made a deposit yesterday at an ATM in Yuma, Arizona. That's about a twenty-minute drive to a border crossing. And another eight hours to his sister's house in Hermosillo. You think it's reasonable to conclude that he went there?"

Rose pressed her lips together.

"Right, I forgot. You're not talking." Fenway cleared her throat. "So today is the start of Domingo's brand-new life. Do you think he woke up this morning wishing you had made the trip with him? Wishing you were next to him?"

Rose turned her head and looked down at the arm of the chair.

"I wondered why you hadn't gone with Domingo," Fenway said, leaning closer, "and then it hit me. You don't really love him. You were *pretending* to be in love with him to get close to him. So he'd tell you where the ledgers were, so he'd tell you where the backup drives were, so he'd tell you how to cover your tracks. You didn't love him. It was a way to get him to trust you. You basically sold your body for money."

Rose flinched, and Fenway tasted rust in her mouth. But she pressed on.

"That's not quite accurate," Fenway continued. "You didn't sell your body for money—you exchanged it for *information* about money. When he bought you flowers and little gifts, when he took you to Santa Barbara for dinner so no one around here would see the two of you together, all of that was for show, wasn't it?"

"You don't know what you're talking about," Rose Morgan mumbled.

"I don't?" Fenway asked, batting her eyelashes and placing the palm of her right hand theatrically on her upper chest. "Perhaps you can tell me how it is, then. Because from where I'm standing, it looks like he fell hard for you and you took advantage of that. You sold him out to your bosses."

Rose flinched. "I told you, I'm not saying anything."

"That's your right." Fenway stepped to the row of chairs in front of Rose and put one foot up on the last chair in the row, still facing Rose. "Maybe I'm wrong, Rose. I've been wrong before, and I'll be wrong again. I'm telling you what it looks like from my perspective." She paused and studied Rose's face.

Rose's long curly hair hung in front of her eyes, and she was looking down at the carpet.

"Or," Fenway said softly, "maybe *you* were the one in love." She watched Rose's eyes, still unreadable. "Maybe he's the one who betrayed you. Is that it? Did you say you'd slip away from the sheriff's office and meet him?"

Rose sank in her seat.

Fenway nodded. "And he wasn't there. Domingo was already on the run."

Rose lifted her hands to cover her face.

"Oh—Rose," Fenway said, reaching out a hand to touch her shoulder.

Rose shrugged her hand off.

Fenway took a deep breath and continued. "I'm sorry. You were supposed to get close to him. I bet your bosses loved it when you started having the affair with him. I don't know who came on to who first—"

"I did," Rose croaked miserably. "I seduced him in the office one night when everyone had gone home. Central Auto Body was one of the best businesses we had, and lots of people paid in lots of different ways, so we wanted to make sure there was no skimming." She sighed. "He seemed like such a good guy. Trapped in a loveless marriage. Oh, God, I *cannot* believe I fell for that. For every line in the book. Not an original thought in his head." She closed her eyes. "And the way he —" She shook her head. "I cannot *believe* I fell for that," she said again.

"We've all been there, girl," Fenway said.

"Don't *girl* me, Miss Stevenson," Rose said. "You don't know what

I've been through. You don't know how tough I had to be to survive the last five years. You don't know anything about me."

"I know enough to figure out that you and Domingo Velásquez were in love and that he's in Mexico and you're not."

Rose laughed sharply.

"But why are *you* here, Rose? To get information, maybe? To find where Domingo Velásquez went? Maybe you were meeting your boss here to ask where he was?"

Rose Morgan sank even further into her seat.

"You've got many interesting interpersonal relationships, Miss Morgan," Fenway said. "I bet if I keep digging, we'll find out how you're connected to Yesterday Audio. Once we get out of here, we'll find out who that Sig Sauer is registered to. Maybe we'll figure out how you're connected to the registered owner. Or maybe it's registered to *you*."

"I didn't kill anyone," Rose said, almost inaudibly.

"And what will you do now? Run after Domingo to Mexico? You think he'll be glad to see you? Will he introduce you to his sister, you think?"

Rose shrugged. "He's not with me now, is he?"

"No, he isn't. Now I'm thinking that he abandoned you and left with your share of the money. I mean, it's not the billions and billions the scheme is making in profit, but it's still a lot of money. It's enough so he can live in reasonable comfort in a place like, I don't know, Hermosillo. For example. But maybe not enough that he would want to share it. No matter *how* good you are in bed."

Rose swallowed hard. "You didn't strike me as this mean when we first met, Miss Stevenson."

"And you didn't strike me as such a softie, Miss Morgan."

"Well, there you go. I'm not a gold digger, and Domingo Velásquez isn't a wronged man. He left his wife, and he left me, and all I want to do is go see him and beg him to take me back. Some tough bitch I am."

Fenway took her foot down from the chair. "I'm sorry that he betrayed you," she said, "but it still doesn't tell me why you did it."

"I'm not admitting to knowing anything about any money laundering operation. I'm only admitting to being a fool in love."

Fenway scoffed. "I'm not talking about money laundering. I'm talking about murdering Professor Cygnus."

Rose stared at Fenway. "Really? You still think I'm the one who killed him?"

"You don't talk to me, you don't give me fingerprints—and you're the only one who won't. Tell me, what would *you* think if you were me?"

"That the killer had escaped with the rest of the crowd? Given the two hundred people who ran out of here, I'm pretty sure the odds are with someone from that big group, not the lucky thirteen people in here."

"Yet you won't let me take your fingerprints."

"Just because I know my way around the Constitution doesn't mean I'm guilty of anything, Miss Stevenson." Rose set her jaw. "And as much as I appreciate the shoulder to cry on, I think I'll go back to shutting my damn mouth."

CHAPTER TWELVE

Fenway walked back to the nook slowly and noticed a few pairs of eyes following her. None burned more harshly than those of Evans Dahl, who looked sickly and pained but whose flaming anger at Fenway talking to Rose was evident.

"I've got some other interesting stuff that I found too," Piper said.

"On more than just the money laundering? On my father's murder case, maybe?"

"Nothing else on that yet," Piper said, "though since ADA Kim was planning to introduce more charges and Bryce Heissner is prepared to take over as CEO when your dad gets fired, I have a few more roads to go down."

"You almost seem to relish this," Fenway said.

"I kind of do," Piper said. "I mean, I know that what you and your dad and your stepmom are going through is horrible, and I wouldn't wish it on anyone. But figuring out how all the pieces of this fit together is, uh, an adrenaline rush, I guess."

"It's okay, Piper. You can enjoy this. I do, too. It's probably why I stuck around as coroner."

Piper breathed a sigh of relief. "Yeah. I guess you understand what it means. It's like one of those massive video game puzzles masquerading as an adventure game. Only it's real."

"And you don't regenerate when you get killed," Fenway said drily.

"Right."

They were back in the nook, and each of them took a seat where they'd been before.

"So what is it?"

"So—first of all, I still think Judith Cygnus is a viable suspect," Piper said. "He was cheating on her, and she didn't want to be the laughingstock of the county anymore."

"She's known about the affair the whole time," Fenway said. "She said she was relieved that he had someone to, uh, *experience* his passion for Shakespeare with. Apparently, there was only so much *Merchant of Venice* she could take."

"It's a nice story," Piper said. "But I know a few poly people, and they're not like that at all. And everyone else I know gets pissed off when their partner cheats on them."

"It's not poly, Piper. It's—I don't really know what it is, but I think I believe her." She remembered how hurt she'd been when McVie had tried to repair his marriage to Amy, even though she'd cheated on him. "I don't know if I should tell you this, Piper, but you know Craig tried to get back together with Amy. Even after he found out that Amy had been cheating on him. And with Amy, it wasn't a one-time thing. It was something that went on for months. It wasn't all about the sex, either. But he still thought they had something worth saving." She looked down at her hands. "And the Cygnuses were together for twice as long as Craig and Amy were. They raised kids together. They built a life together. That's not something you throw away, I guess." Fenway laughed. "I mean, I wouldn't know, not really. I haven't even had a serious relationship yet. Not one that's lasted more than a few months. But Craig went through a lot of effort, and it just brought him pain."

Piper nodded. "I guess. I mean, I'd *kill* Migs if he cheated on me, but he and I haven't been going out that long. Maybe if we'd been together for years, it would feel different."

Fenway shrugged. "What do I know? Nothing. Only that it's not a foregone conclusion that Judith Cygnus wanted her husband dead just because he had a decade-long affair. It's not something you'd see on a TV sitcom, but it didn't mean they didn't have a happy marriage."

Piper was quiet for a moment.

"Did you have anything else?"

"Yeah. The real reason I wanted to talk to you. You know how I said that Leda Nedermeyer had been at UCLA as a student when your professor from Western Washington was a grad student?"

"Yeah?"

"Well, that's not all I found out about Leda." Piper leaned forward. "Professor Cygnus *sued* her for copyright infringement three years ago."

"Sued—three years—" Fenway couldn't get the words out, but then her thoughts arranged themselves. "So, Cygnus and Nedermeyer are having an affair. And it's been going on for about a decade. So what happened three years ago?"

"I guess Professor Nedermeyer wrote a textbook on reading classic literature. It's not that popular, but there are a few universities who use it as part of their curricula." Piper looked sideways at Fenway. "Including, obviously, Professor Nedermeyer's own English classes."

Fenway's mouth twitched. "This is my shocked face."

"So anyway, about a month after it comes out, Professor Cygnus sues Professor Nedermeyer, stating that she took the chapter on Shakespeare directly from his writings and notes."

"What happened?"

"They settled out of court."

"Of course they did."

Piper leaned forward. "I can dig more if you want."

"Maybe it was a lovers' quarrel that got out of hand." Fenway sat back. "I guess she makes a decent suspect, too. There's too much animosity between her and Cygnus."

"Isn't that from a cop show too? How you don't like coincidences? Professor Nedermeyer has an awful lot of coincidences with Cygnus."

"Yeah, but sometimes a cigar is just a cigar," Fenway said.

"Yeah, but sometimes it's the motive behind a killing."

Fenway grinned. "Oh, Piper, you haven't even been gone from the sheriff's office for a full workday and I already miss you."

Piper's face fell. "Oh—I can't believe I didn't tell you the most important thing about the ledgers!"

"What?"

"You remember when I found Peter Grayheath's name in the ledger? There was a code name in that line, too. *Carpe8765.*"

"*Carpe*—like 'carpe diem'?"

"Right. And *Carpe8765* is all over the spreadsheets. And most of the payments to that name—especially about four business days after the empty tankers leave port in East Timor—come from *another* code name. But it's not like the other code names. It's just a set of initials."

"Not a word-and-number combination like the others?"

"No. And because it's so different from the other code names, it makes me think that maybe *this* is the leader of this merry band of treasonous murderers."

"I suppose. Or it could be someone who was just very insistent on these initials. Or maybe it's a company name. What's the code name?"

"It's L.I.W."

"Really? L.I.W.?" Fenway tapped her foot. "That's—an odd combination of letters."

"I suppose it could be a person's initials, but that seems—well, wrong. Not a real person, anyway. Maybe a movie character, or a character out of a book?"

Fenway squeezed her eyes shut. She could feel a connection that she should make, but it wouldn't come.

"I tried searching for it online," Piper continued, "but it doesn't seem to stand for anything. There's a tiny village in Poland about fifty miles east of Warsaw spelled L-I-W. It's also the airport code for a regional airport in Myanmar that only has one commercial flight a day."

"Maybe someone is from Poland or Myanmar?"

Piper shrugged. "I did a cursory search of everyone who's connected to Ferris Energy and any of the companies who've been laundering money. I can't find any connections. No one was born in that tiny Polish village, for example."

Fenway blinked hard. "I—I don't know," she mumbled.

"What?"

"It's like I can *feel* like I have the information in my brain to make the right connection. It's in one of those file cabinets in my head, but in the back room, where it's all dusty. And I don't know what cabinet it's in or what file folder. But it's in there, I know it is."

"File cabinets in your brain?"

"You—you don't do the same thing when you're trying to think of something and it's not *quite* there?"

Piper shook her head.

"My brain is weird." Fenway squeezed her eyes shut and pinched the bridge of her nose. "Dammit, it's *in* there somewhere. If I can figure out where I've seen it before...."

"Could the L.I. stand for Long Island?"

"It's possible." Fenway sighed. "No. That doesn't sound like it's on the right track. I mean, it's possible that *I'm* not on the right track either, so maybe Long Island *does* mean something."

"I can see if anyone has any ties to Long Island."

"Thorough as always, Piper." Fenway opened her eyes and dropped her hand to her lap. "Anyone you've uncovered so far—and anyone in this courtroom, too."

"You don't think Judith Cygnus is the mastermind behind all this, do you? Or Charlotte?"

Fenway shrugged. "Leave them until last, but no, I don't think so."

"You want me to check the two lawyers?"

"Everyone in the courtroom."

"Should I leave you alone to puzzle out L.I.W.?"

"L.I.W.... L.I.W." Fenway chewed on the letters for a moment, then threw up her hands. "No. It'll come to me. I'll leave the door to the file room open in my mind and try to figure it out. Maybe I'll wake up at three in the morning with everything solved."

"That'll be a little late to catch the killer, if he's in *here*."

"Or she," said Fenway. "And if McVie keeps up this glacial pace, three in the morning isn't out of the realm of possibility."

"If you can figure out who it is," Piper said, "it might be the key to the entire thing. If I get a name, I can match the L.I.W. payments up to other financial transactions in their accounts."

"Maybe you could run it against the dozen people in here."

Piper shook her head. "That's a nice idea, but it's way too much work. I've already started comparing the ledgers to the financial information your dad has given me, but he's got so many accounts with so many transactions, it'll take at least a week to sort through all of it. Maybe only an hour for someone like Judith Cygnus, but even so."

"Is it possible that Professor Cygnus is L.I.W.?"

"With so many large transactions? It's unlikely, but possible, I suppose. I haven't done any research on his financials yet."

"Okay." Fenway leaned forward. "I'll have a chat with Professor Nedermeyer and tell her that we know about the copyright lawsuit. See how she reacts."

"And what about her time at UCLA?"

"Maybe," Fenway said. "I'm trying to solve one murder at a time, though."

Piper nodded and left the nook with her laptop.

Fenway leaned back in her chair again. What would she say to Leda Nedermeyer? How did she expect Leda to answer?

She stood slowly, turning the question over in her mind, trying to figure out how to say it so it didn't sound too accusatory. Leda had already flown off the handle at Judith Cygnus, and Fenway didn't want any drastic actions to wreck this investigation.

She scoffed aloud. *Investigation.* As if this were a by-the-book, formal investigation instead of a make-it-up-as-you-go-along set of enquiries. She just hoped anything she would uncover would be helpful in the long run.

Just getting a piece of evidence that could be submitted at trial, she knew, would be a win. Having her wits about her enough to get not only a shell casing but the gun itself was commendable, even if there was no one around to commend her. Her father might have been proud of her if he weren't so wrapped up in his own trial. Yes, Fenway was always angry with her father for his self-involvement, but this time she felt justified.

She took a deep breath in and exhaled slowly and fully, feeling the tension—some of it, anyway—leave her body, then she walked out of the nook toward Leda Nedermeyer.

Pride and Prejudice was open on the professor's lap, but her eyes were glazed over. "Professor?" Fenway asked gently, and Leda Nedermeyer jumped. "Oh—Miss Stevenson. I didn't notice you there. Lost in my own thoughts, I'm afraid."

"Yes. I'm sorry, Professor Nedermeyer. I'm sure this is a difficult time for you. I'm—I'm sorry for your loss."

Leda crinkled her nose. "I suppose everyone in the courtroom knows of my affair with Professor Cygnus."

"I hate to tell you this, Professor, but it's an open secret on campus. I don't think Professor Cygnus was as careful about his personal life as you might have been."

"I didn't know that Judith knew about us until today," Professor Nedermeyer said, folding a corner of the book and closing it. "You must think I'm quite a fool to be having an affair with a married man for eleven years and thinking no one would notice."

Fenway shrugged, remembering her tryst with McVie before his legal separation from Amy. "I hear that people in glass houses shouldn't throw stones. So you won't be hearing anything from me."

"Men are awful," Nedermeyer said quietly.

"Many of them, yes," Fenway replied. She took a seat and turned her body to look at the professor's face, remembering Piper's conversation earlier: *what crawls out.* "Professor Nedermeyer, I have to look under a lot of rocks when I do a murder investigation."

"I expect so, yes."

"And then I have to ask people about what crawls out from under those rocks. Sometimes they have everything to do with the murder. Sometimes nothing. Do you understand?"

Nedermeyer nodded. "You're going to ask me about the fight that Virgil and I had last week."

Fenway tried not to let the surprise register on her face. She nodded. The question about the copyright infringement could wait. "Can you tell me what the fight was about?"

"Well—he never goes home during his preparation for the Shakespeare production." Nedermeyer pursed her lips. "For the last several years, he and I spent many of those evenings together. He often gets to my house late, but he wakes me up. We talk about the progress in the play, and about the meaning of various objects referenced in the play, or words where the scholars disagree, and we both get, well—a bit impassioned." She closed her eyes and shuddered slightly. "It's—uh, one of my favorite times of the year." She placed the book on the chair next to her. "He never really spent that much time with me otherwise. Yes, maybe the odd afternoon here or there, but those six weeks, with the play preparation and the performances—it was magical."

"But last week, something changed."

"You're damn right something changed," Nedermeyer said. "He couldn't concentrate, didn't even want to talk about what kind of weapon Othello should have in his hand during the climactic scene. He was pacing up and down, then finally he said it was a mistake to come over."

"Ah." Fenway nodded. "And you didn't like that."

"Of *course* I didn't like it. Listen—ever since my divorce thirteen years ago, I haven't seriously dated. My ex-husband was a professional athlete."

"A professional athlete?"

"Opposites attract, Miss Stevenson." Leda smiled coyly, giving Fenway a glimpse of what Professor Cygnus found so attractive. "Doug spent three years in the NFL with Carolina, then blew his knee out. After surgery and rehab, no one wanted him. His contract was up—he hadn't really been used as more than a backup anyway—and no one else signed him. He was depressed and wanted to lie around the house, but I had finally finished my Ph.D. and I was ready to go into the academic world. I got a job on the tenure track at Tryon College, but Doug just turned himself off. Not excited about my job. Not excited when I got promoted after my first year—which, I don't know if you know academia—never happens."

"Not the most supportive husband."

"Precisely." Nedermeyer cleared her throat. "Then when I got the offer at Nidever and wanted to move across the country, he put his foot down and said I couldn't take it. Well, I fought with him, and he started throwing things, and I got scared. Then I told him I was sorry and that I wouldn't leave North Carolina, but the next day instead of going to work, I went to see a divorce lawyer. And I accepted the job at Nidever for the next academic year, and when the lawyer drew up the papers, I signed them and left them on the table and drove away with two suitcases that I'd sneaked out to the trunk of the car the night before, after he'd passed out drunk."

Fenway bit her lip. Sometimes people confused her with a confessor, but she sensed that Nedermeyer was going somewhere with the story and didn't want to interrupt.

"Anyway—I got to Nidever, and I threw myself into my work. I didn't date. Suddenly, here's this handsome, older professor who *wants* to talk with me about the things *I'm* interested in. And although he's stayed handsome, you should have seen him a dozen years ago. Some of the undergraduates were quite taken with him."

"He taught Cynthia Schimmelhorn."

"Oh—yes, she's quite the celebrity alumna at Nidever. But that would have been a good ten or fifteen years before my time," Nedermeyer said.

"Do you think Ms. Schimmelhorn and the professor ever..." Fenway let her voice trail off and looked at Nedermeyer.

But the professor only shrugged. "If he did, I never knew. He didn't talk about her. I was probably as moony-eyed over Professor Cygnus as those giggling undergraduate girls were, but I could go toe to toe with him when he got those wild hares. He'd go off on some crazy idea that spun him around until he couldn't see the logic in anything—but he'd still want to argue about it." She shook her head. "I don't see how Judith stayed with him for forty years. *I* was the only woman who could tame him—and his flights of fancy." She paused. "And the first time we argued —I was in my third year by then, and already assistant chair to the English Department—he said, 'Leda, the two of us have been arguing for an hour,' and I said, 'I'm here for as long as it takes for you to realize you're wrong.' And then he stepped forward and took me in his arms and —well, Miss Stevenson, I'm not ashamed to say I'd never been kissed like that in my life until that moment. Virgil made me feel everything I felt when I was falling in love with Doug plus everything I feel when I read a great book, all rolled up into a single kiss. You ever read a book like that?"

"Maybe once or twice," Fenway said.

"For me, I know it's so stereotypical, but *Emma*."

"Jane Austen," Fenway said, nodding to Nedermeyer's copy of *Pride and Prejudice.*

"Right."

"So what was different two weeks ago? How come he didn't engage with you?"

"At first I thought it was Judith's health," she said, "but then he said that Jessica Marquez had questioned him about the accounts. I assumed it was about The Guild's finances, but, you know, the more I hear, the more I think it was this scholarship fund that everyone's been whispering about."

"And you fought."

"Virgil never fought about money—but there we were, fighting about money." Leda paused. "Now, listen, I don't make a CEO's wage as a professor, but as the head of the department, I do all right. But I never moved out of that tiny house I bought a couple of years after I moved to Estancia. I thought I could wait it out until Virgil left his wife, but now—well, I have quite a bit of money socked away. I came out quite well in the divorce—half of that NFL money was mine—and I told him I would be glad to lend him whatever he needed to cover it. But that just seemed to make him more agitated. He had a pained look on his face and he said, 'But love is blind, and lovers cannot see the pretty follies that themselves commit.'"

"Is that from *The Merchant of Venice?*"

Nedermeyer nodded. "Jessica. It's when she realizes she's betrayed Shylock, but goes and leaves him anyway."

Fenway nodded. "I think Professor Cygnus treated his relationship with Jessica Marquez like a Shylock-and-Jessica relationship too. And I think he felt betrayed when she told her bosses about him skimming money."

"I suppose. He always did love inserting himself in those roles." Nedermeyer tapped her chin. "Anyway, we fought, and he said he was leaving—and I asked if he was coming back, and he, of course, gave me another quote."

"Which was?"

"'I would be, sweet madam, if my miseries were in the same abundance as my good fortunes are.'"

Fenway shook her head. "I can't place that one. Is that still *Merchant?*"

"In a way," Nedermeyer said. "It's the first thing Nerissa says to Portia, but she says *you* and *your*, not *I* and *my*."

"Putting himself in the play again," Fenway said.

"I suppose." She tapped her fingers on the book. "Still—it's odd. He always said the text was sacred. He'd never make any kind of change, even one that small. Not only that, but he inverted the meaning—Nerissa is trying to tell Portia that everything is going to be all right, but Virgil was all doom and gloom."

"Unless he was telling *you* something?"

"Even then," Nedermeyer said, and a pall of sadness came over her face. "Oh, Virgil," she whispered. "I would have given you that money. And you'd still be alive."

"One more thing," Fenway said quickly, trying to stave off Nedermeyer's tears. "Do you know a Solomon Delacroix?"

"Solomon who?"

"Delacroix. He would have been a grad student at UCLA when you were there."

"I got my undergraduate at UCLA. I didn't mix with many grad students."

"I know sometimes they work as teaching assistants and they lead small discussion groups for large lecture courses, though. Maybe he was one of your TAs?"

"Doesn't ring a bell, sorry."

Fenway nodded, rising from her chair. Then she stopped. "Oh—one more thing, Professor."

"Yes?"

"Did Professor Cygnus sue you for copyright infringement a few years ago?"

Leda shook her head, rolling her eyes. "That was both the stupidest thing ever—and the most Virgil thing ever."

"How do you mean?"

"I've been working on a theory about *A Midsummer Night's Dream* for a decade or so. Namely, that the play-within-a-play isn't meant to be played for laughs. That the faeries interfere and imbue dark magic upon the workmen, turning it into a brilliant dramatic tragedy."

"That's—kind of odd."

"Yes. But Virgil loved the idea. He ran with it. Even did a production that year of *Dream* where he inserted that interpretation." Leda chortled. "But in typical Virgil fashion, he fell so in love with my idea, he thought he'd come up with it."

"Really?"

"It's not the first time he stole one of my ideas, but it's the first time he took me to court over it."

"What did you do?"

"I showed him my notes from before we met. He couldn't believe the idea was mine, even then, but he withdrew the lawsuit."

Then Evans Dahl's voice boomed across the courtroom, and Fenway's head snapped up.

"Are you still trying to get around—"

"People are talking *willingly,* Mr. Dahl," Fenway shot back. "If you hadn't noticed, there's still a dead body up there, there's still a *gun* that was used to kill him, and there's a very real possibility that someone in this room is the killer."

As soon as the words were out of her mouth, she knew she'd made a mistake. She'd talked about the gunshot residue as if she assumed the killer had escaped with everyone else. No one liked being in the courtroom, but they'd assumed they were at least safe. The faces fell around her.

"What do you mean?" Xavier Go got to his feet. "Didn't the killer leave when everyone else did? I thought you were fingerprinting us to eliminate us as suspects! To show the sheriff that we could get out of here!"

"I was, but I—" Fenway began.

"It seems to me," Evans Dahl said, "that it's very convenient that *you're* the one doing the investigating when your father has an obvious motive for wanting the professor out of the way."

"Obvious motive?"

"The professor was about to name names," Dahl said.

"My father didn't kill anyone," Fenway said. "He was at the wrong angle. He wasn't even by the—"

"I don't mean that *he* could have killed the professor, Miss Stevenson," Evans Dahl said. He turned his face toward her, eyes burning with heat. "I mean *you* could have."

CHAPTER THIRTEEN

Fenway's jaw dropped open. "Me?" she said. "But I couldn't have shot from the back of the room. I was in the front row, right behind..." Fenway trailed off as Evans Dahl nodded.

"That's right," he said. "You *were* right there. It's a much easier shot to take from three feet away than from across the room."

"You would have seen me," Fenway insisted. "Jennifer, you too. The gun would have been right next to you—you would have known it was coming from the front row."

"Would we?" Evans Dahl said. "I know I was concentrating on everything Professor Cygnus was saying. I wasn't paying attention to anything but whether I could minimize the professor's jail time."

"And I was focused on it too," ADA Kim said. "Sorry, Fenway, I know you're a law enforcement representative, but Evans is right. You had the clearest, closest shot."

"You looked at my fingerprints less than a half hour ago, Jennifer! You said there was no match."

"I'm not great at fingerprint analysis," Kim said, her face impassive.

"I came in with Xavier and Amanda!" Fenway protested. "How was

I supposed to get the gun from its hiding place behind the speaker enclosure? They would have seen me!"

"Maybe you had it all along. Maybe you sweet-talked your way past the officer at the metal detector," Bryce Heissner said.

"You *are* the county coroner," Amanda Kohl said. "I mean, why did you even bring the fingerprint kit in here?"

"Maybe it was to hide the gun," Heissner said.

"I refilled the fingerprint powder this morning, and I didn't have time to go back to my desk before the arraignment started."

"Every excuse you have is just a little too convenient," Heissner said. "Is it a coincidence that you just *happen* to have your fingerprint kit on the day there's a shooting in the courtroom?"

"I was sitting next to the sheriff. Don't you think he would have been able to tell?"

"Rumor is the two of you are romantically involved," Dahl said. "That doesn't exactly make him an unbiased third party."

"Look—if I *had* shot from that close, there would be gunshot residue. And stippling. You can look for yourself. There's no stippling."

Evans Dahl scoffed. "Might as well tell a toddler to make Hollandaise sauce," he said. "I wouldn't know how to look for stippling if you paid me."

"If I had my GSR pads, you'd see I don't have gunpowder on my hands, either."

"Something else that's a little too convenient—losing the GSR pads when they're the one thing that could prove your guilt."

Fenway looked at ADA Kim, who shook her head.

The blood pounded in Fenway's veins, but she pursed her lips and counted slowly in her head, backward from twenty, to stay calm. "I don't have an issue with you taking my fingerprints, Mr. Dahl. Compare my prints to the partial print I found on the gun. You'll see it's not mine."

Evans Dahl was quiet, but Fenway could see the wheels spinning in his head.

"Oh," she said as the realization dawned. "Are you thinking

somehow I *planted* the fingerprint there? That you can't trust anything I say now that my father is being accused of murder?"

Evans Dahl held up his hands. "I'm not the one who said that."

"Need I remind you that my father and I barely talked for twenty years? That he hardly knows anything about me?"

"Hey," Charlotte said. "That's not fair."

"Really, Charlotte?" Fenway asked. She rounded on her father. "What part did I play in *You're a Good Man, Charlie Brown* in fifth grade, Dad?"

Nathaniel Ferris was silent.

"How about formal dances in high school? I went to three homecoming dances, the junior prom, and the senior ball. You remember the name of any of my dates?"

Ferris scrunched up his face.

"First names are fine, Dad."

He shook his head.

"One of them was my boyfriend for over a year. Nerdy black kid? On the debate team? No?"

Charlotte started again. "Fenway, your mother was never—"

"Stay out of this, Charlotte," Fenway snapped. "You remember my high school graduation? I do. It was one of the most important days of my life. Remind me—where did the two of you sit? Oh, right—back here in Estancia because the two of you were getting married that weekend."

Charlotte blanched.

Fenway turned back to her father. "I played a sport for all four years in high school, Dad. You remember what that was?"

"Basketball," Ferris said roughly.

"Aw, that one was too easy. I'm a tall black girl, after all. Of course I played basketball, right?" She nodded up and down, up and down, then narrowed her eyes and stared at her father as she shook her head side to side. "*Volleyball*. I can't shoot a basket to save my life."

"Look, Fenway," Ferris began, "I know I didn't participate very much when you were growing up, but that doesn't—"

"While I'm delighted to witness this family meltdown," said Evans Dahl, "what does this have to do with whether or not Mr. Ferris committed a crime?"

Fenway put her hands on her hips. "I'm trying to show you, Mr. Dahl, that my father and I aren't that close. That I would *never* in a million years commit murder for him because he has no idea who I am."

Nathaniel Ferris opened his mouth, then closed it, and his lower lip trembled slightly.

A pang of guilt rippled through Fenway's stomach. "Sorry," Fenway said. "I guess I should have gotten my point across differently." She glared at Evans Dahl. "Are you happy now?"

"This is supposed to convince me that you didn't do your father's bidding?" Evans Dahl asked coldly. "Assumes facts not in evidence. Not that I'm saying you're lying, but you haven't shown any proof that your father *hasn't* gotten you to kill the professor."

"You're a defense attorney, Mr. Dahl," Fenway replied coldly. "You should know better than to request that I prove a negative." She walked down the row to where her fingerprint kit was sitting, picked it up, and then brought it to Evans Dahl, setting it down in front of him. "I'll tell you what I'll do. I'll provide my fingerprints to your satisfaction, then you can compare them to the print I lifted off the gun. You okay with that?"

Evans hesitated.

"What is it? Are you not confident in your ability to compare fingerprints?"

"Even forensics labs make mistakes," Dahl said.

"Well, if you won't, Evans, I will," ADA Kim said, walking up to both of them. "There's too much at stake. Miss Stevenson needs to include her prints, and *I'll* make the comparison. Evans, you can watch me, if you want to, to make sure I'm not lying about anything." She looked from Evans's face to Fenway's. "Is that a deal?"

"Sure," Fenway said.

"I'll agree to that," Evans muttered.

"Then you'll provide your fingerprints too, Evans?" ADA Kim pressed.

"No," Evans said. "I'm trying to dissuade Miss Stevenson from gathering evidence to catch someone else without including herself in the suspect pool. That doesn't mean *I'm* willing to ignore my Fourth Amendment rights."

"I think that's hypocritical, Evans," Kim started. "Listen, if you—"

A wave of exhaustion hit Fenway, and the fight left her. "No." She put a hand lightly on Jennifer Kim's shoulder. "It's fine. Let me do this."

Jennifer Kim nodded and pulled the ink pad out of the kit, along with eight more fingerprint cards—four for the left hand and four for the right hand. She handed one of each to Fenway.

"I know I can be a klutz, Jennifer, but I think I can do it with just one card." She pressed her left index finger to the pad and then pressed her finger on the card.

"No, that's not what I mean," ADA Kim said. "I think we need to redo the prints from your dad and your stepmom."

Fenway paused with her ring finger on the pad. She looked up at Jennifer and narrowed her eyes. She opened her mouth—but then rotated her shoulders one at a time and nodded. "Good. I'm glad you're providing oversight. It'll help if this goes to trial."

Jennifer cocked her head and blinked twice, as if daring Fenway to say something else, but Fenway lowered her head and kept fingerprinting herself.

"Now the right hand," Evans Dahl said, pointing.

Fenway paused with her right hand above the ink pad. "I'm sorry?"

"I said, do your right hand now."

"What does it *look* like I'm doing? Am I not going fast enough for you?"

"Hey, watch your mouth, missy."

Fenway stared into Evans's eyes, and he leaned forward, his nose inches from hers.

"You have something to say to me?"

Fenway's mind raced. He was pushing all her buttons, all the vocabulary that was insulting but that didn't officially cross the line. He was up to something—some sort of weird power trip—but she couldn't figure out what. She didn't want to be the one to blink first, but she wanted to get the hell away from him. Breaking her stare with him, she finished inking her fingers and filling out the card.

She took a cloth from her kit and wiped off her fingers, then got up and went through the gate and behind the judge's bench.

"I can't get away from these people," she muttered to Piper.

Piper smirked. "And they can't get away from you. I'd say it's a fair fight." Her eyes focused on the screen and her lips moved. "Fenway?"

"Yeah?"

"Someone's been messing with these account files."

"What?"

Piper shook her head. "I have the ones I downloaded last week, and *those* are fine. But look—someone's entered new payment information. Not the amounts, but the code names. In fact, whoever did it replaced 'L.I.W.' with another username I haven't seen before."

"A new user?"

"Yes. And it's *bigwheel6809*."

"Six-eight-oh-nine?"

"Yes."

"That's a clumsy reference to my father. And the date of his wedding to Charlotte. June sixth, 2009."

"Ferris wheel—yeah, I get it," Piper said. "It's like they weren't even trying to make it subtle."

"Maybe it was the best they could do on short notice. They didn't have time to research anything deeper in his past."

Piper rubbed her forehead with her palm. "These entries weren't here last week—or if they were, they all were attributed to this L.I.W. person. Someone's gone through a lot of trouble to make it look like your dad was the brains of *all* of this—the money laundering, the embargoed oil, the hidden supertankers—everything."

"Can you get the old files over to—I don't know, the cops? At least to McVie? Maybe the D.A.'s office? If it's exculpatory evidence, don't they need to see it?"

Piper shifted uncomfortably. "Uh, Fenway, I was telling you all that because you're the daughter of the accused, not because you're a law enforcement representative. I'm turning everything I find into Imani Ingram. I'm not paid to send the stuff I find to anyone but her. And your dad, of course." She looked at Fenway. "Is it going to be a problem for you *not* sharing this with ADA Kim?"

Fenway set her jaw. "Absolutely no problem at all."

"Okay. I don't want to put you in a difficult position.'

Of course it's a difficult position. But I'd go crazy if I didn't know. "I understand, Piper. You don't have to worry about me."

"Plus," Piper said, "I haven't been able to prove who changed these ledgers. If somebody used a remote access tool, they hid their tracks very well."

"Do you think the prosecution has found these new ledgers? Is that why they're planning to add so many charges to the indictment?"

Piper rubbed her chin. "I don't know that I'd trust what Bryce Heissner said about adding those charges."

"Jennifer Kim didn't deny it."

"No, but she didn't confirm it either," said Piper. "All the other information I've seen is circumstantial—and pretty flimsy."

"Like what?"

"Mostly that your dad was in a position of power at Ferris Energy when the hidden tankers and embargoed oil were coming through their port. Any halfway-decent prosecutor could argue that as CEO, he should be expected to know the details of every single corner of his business." Piper narrowed her eyes. "But this looks like a real ledger, and it's certainly believable that it's your father's code name."

"But it's *too* obvious, isn't it?" Fenway asked.

"Yes, but the only argument against it is that someone might be trying to frame him."

"Which they are."

"That's true, but it might be too hard to believe. If we didn't have records of the other ledgers, I don't know that we could convince a jury that your dad *didn't* authorize all the criminal activity at Ferris Energy."

Fenway raised her head and looked across the courtroom at Rose Morgan, who was now pacing back and forth behind the last row of chairs. "Rose is a hacker, too," Fenway mused. "I wonder if she's got enough knowledge to cover her tracks well enough to fool you."

"She might," Piper said. "Or maybe she has the resources. If she's working for the money laundering operation and they're footing the bill, they have nearly unlimited resources for the latest obfuscation software."

"But why haven't *all* the payments been so well hidden?"

"Probably because only the higher-ups have access to those kinds of resources. The ones who are doing the grunt work have to use their own tools. Free VPNs or low-level proxy servers, probably."

"A chain is only as strong as its weakest link."

"There are bean counters everywhere, Fenway—fortunately for us. Well, not me anymore. Fortunately for you." Piper lowered her voice. "And I don't know what you said to your stepmom, but thank you."

"You're thanking me? For what?"

"For the hourly rate. I made more over the long weekend than I did in a month at the sheriff's office."

"Oh, right. No problem. I thought if she and my father are going to work you to the bone, you should at least be well compensated for it." Fenway looked around the courtroom as ADA Kim was again taking fingerprints of her father and Charlotte. "Piper—am I being paranoid, or do you think Jennifer Kim is trying to undermine me?"

Piper followed Fenway's gaze and set her mouth in a tight line. "I might not be the best person to ask," she murmured. "After what happened last week, you know I'm not a fan of Jennifer Kim." She turned to Fenway. "You've been too trusting of her. Just because she's a prosecutor doesn't mean she's trying to get at the truth about Professor Cygnus's murder or even about the money laundering and the embargoed oil."

"You think she's in on it?"

Piper turned back to the screen and began typing. "I'm not sure I'd go *that* far. I think she's in it for herself and herself only. Maybe she's only interested in keeping her conviction rate high so she can get promoted. But whatever it is, *stop* giving her so much information."

Fenway wasn't usually this trusting. Was it the bump on the head she'd gotten? Or maybe, with a killer in the courtroom, she was reaching for people who would be on her side, against the killer—and she knew Jennifer Kim hadn't pulled the trigger. She nodded.

But Piper was right—just because the ADA wasn't the killer didn't mean she was on Fenway's side.

"I'll update McVie about our situation," Piper continued. "I hope he opens the doors soon. Then we can get some real resources."

"Yeah." Fenway watched as ADA Kim took the four completed fingerprint cards back from Nathaniel and Charlotte Ferris.

"Anyone have a tissue?" Charlotte asked, holding her hand up palm out, her fingers covered in black ink.

"I've got plenty," said Leda Nedermeyer, pulling a wad out of her purse.

Charlotte stepped past Nathaniel and walked across the aisle toward Leda.

ADA Kim went through the galley gate and set the four fingerprint cards down on the prosecutor's table. Placing the fingerprint lifted from the gun above the cards, she bent down, placing her hands flat on the table, and studied the prints.

Oh, no. My father's thumbprint with the tented arch.

Fenway hurried down the side of the judge's bench. Kim wasn't trained in fingerprint recognition, and at first glance—

"What the *hell* is this?" Kim roared, holding up Nathaniel Ferris's left-hand card.

"They *don't* match!" Fenway shouted back.

"They certainly do!" Kim yelled. "Evans—*someone*—get Nathaniel Ferris separated! *Now!*"

Bryce Heissner sprinted down the center aisle and leaped over the row of chairs around Evans Dahl.

Nathaniel Ferris slowly got to his feet, a confused look on his face.

Heissner ran at full speed at Ferris—then jumped.

Ferris turned to the side at the last second, but Heissner hit him full force, throwing him to the ground and landing on top of him.

"How do you like it now, *sir*," Heissner growled. "You're going away for a *long, long* time."

Ferris wheezed and moaned in pain.

"You *idiot!*" Fenway yelled, snatching the card from ADA Kim's hand.

"I should have you arrested too!" Kim yelled. "Stay away from me!"

"The fingerprint lines *above* the arch don't match, Jennifer!"

"The prints *do* match—you've been covering up for him!"

"No, they don't!" Fenway yelled. "Yes, they both have the same kind of tented arch, but there's a break above the arch in my father's print and *not* in the killer's print." She pointed an accusatory finger at ADA Kim. "You're accusing my father on evidence that *doesn't match*."

"It abso—"

"Mr. Dahl!" Fenway barked, grabbing the fingerprint card from the gun and striding toward the defense attorney. "Take a look at these two prints."

Evans Dahl gingerly lowered his injured leg onto the floor and leaned forward. Fenway tried to stop her hands from shaking.

"May I?" Dahl asked gently. He took the cards from Fenway's outstretched hands and studied them for about ten seconds. Then he shook his head. "These prints don't match, Ms. Kim. As much as I'd like to see Professor Cygnus's killer identified and held, the fingerprint from the gun doesn't match Mr. Ferris."

ADA Kim glared at Fenway.

"And I think that means," Evans said, turning to Heissner, who was still holding Nathaniel Ferris on the floor, "you need to get off Mr. Ferris."

Heissner turned his body to look at Evans Dahl, then pushed

himself up to a sitting position and turned his head toward Cynthia Schimmelhorn, who nodded.

"You still deserved that, and more," Heissner jeered, pushing himself to a standing position.

Fenway climbed over the seats and knelt down next to her father, who was still lying on his side. "Are you hurt, Dad?"

He gasped for breath, then coughed. "Uh—knocked the wind out of me."

"Move slowly. Let me know if anything hurts."

"I'm sorry, Fenway. I'm sorry for everything. I thought I knew how I could make it up to you, but I guess I don't."

"Let's not talk about that," Fenway said, her gut bubbling. *I told Jennifer these prints looked similar but not the same. She knows they didn't match. What the hell is going on?* "First, I want to make sure nothing's broken."

"Right, okay." He grabbed the seat of the chair next to him and pulled himself into a sitting position, grunting in pain.

"What? What is it?"

"My shoulder. Twisted it or something."

Fenway reached out and unbuttoned the top button of Ferris's white dress shirt and loosened his tie. She placed a hand delicately on his shoulder. He winced but didn't gasp or pull away.

"Strained muscle," she said. "I don't think you have any worse damage than that, but still, you should see a doctor when this is over."

Charlotte slid into the seat next to Ferris. "Are you hurt, Nate?"

"They've got a decent medical staff in prison, right?"

Fenway grinned. "At least you haven't lost your sense of humor."

Ferris gave her a smile in return, but it didn't reach his eyes. "But no joke, Fenway, I'm in a terrible spot. I can't believe everything happened under my nose, and I didn't see it."

She took his hand and looked into his eyes. "Listen, Dad, I know we don't get along right now, but I believe you. You're being framed. Framed for all of it."

"Framed?" whispered Charlotte, her eyes wide.

Shaking his head, Ferris squeezed Fenway's hand affectionately. "Even so, it all happened on my watch. Miss Patten showed me what's been happening. How did I not know about it? Do you know how hard it is to hide a supertanker?"

"It's easy if no one's looking for it."

Ferris exhaled long and low. "That's the problem, Fenway. I surrounded myself with yes-men, and I didn't want to hear about any of the problems we had. I made it easy for them—whoever *they* are—to buy embargoed oil, to refine it using *my* equipment, and to sell it to terrorists. It all happened right in front of me, and even though I had no idea it was happening, I'm still the one responsible."

Fenway nodded. "Okay, Dad, the confessional will be open a little later. Let's get you back to your seat and maybe we can get out of here before dinner." She stood and held a hand out to her father. With one hand on the seat of the chair and Fenway holding his other hand, Ferris pulled himself up.

"You okay?"

"Shoulder still hurts. My ribs, too. But I'm fine."

"Okay, good." Fenway turned to walk away, and Ferris put a hand on her shoulder.

"I'm scared, Fenway. I'm about to lose my company."

"Good. Then you'll have more time to spend with your daughter."

Ferris scoffed. "I'm serious, Fenway."

"So am I, Dad."

Charlotte reached over and took Ferris's hand.

Piper opened the gallery gate.

"You looking for me?" Fenway asked.

Piper nodded.

"Did you find something?"

Piper motioned her head toward the back of the courtroom, and Fenway followed her.

Next to the double doors, Piper turned to face Fenway and took a deep breath. "So," she said, "this is big."

"Big?"

"I found the master ledger, Fenway. All the payments—at least all the ones I've found in the smaller ledgers so far—are in there. And then some. I've connected more code names to actual people. Did you know the bagel shop on Tenth Street is a cover for the money laundering scheme too?"

"I *knew* it. No one's ever in there, and their bagels suck." Fenway cleared her throat. "So that's good, right? And what about our friend L.I.W.?"

"Yep. All over the ledgers. Several notes in the margins specify that a transaction or a decision requires L.I.W.'s approval. Changing the schedule of the supertanker. Ordering the hit on Dr. Tassajera."

"What? That's in there?"

"Not so explicitly—it's all referenced by the code names, but yes. I've uncovered what I *think* is an order to Peter Grayheath to purchase plastic explosives, too."

"That would be the hit on Domingo Velásquez."

"Right."

"If that faked ledger gets entered into evidence, though—the one where L.I.W. was replaced by—what was it? *Bigwheel6809?* Will that be enough to convince a jury that my father is behind the oil conspiracy?"

"No, we have the real ledger, the one before the names were changed. That proves the ledger with *bigwheel6809* is fake."

Fenway smirked. "I don't think you should tell my father about this until you're sure. He can get a little crazy."

"I've already texted Imani Ingram. She's got other investigators she can use, too."

Fenway nodded. "I know it sucks that you had to resign from the county, Piper, but I'm really glad you're on my father's team. You've done more in a few days than his team of lawyers could do in a few weeks."

"Don't thank me until they drop the charges."

Fenway nodded and glanced over Piper's shoulder. About twenty feet away, Bryce Heissner was pacing between the rows of chairs, limping slightly. Everyone in the courtroom was getting restless. Fenway glanced over to the other side at her father and Charlotte, then at Judith Cygnus, then at Leda Nedermeyer. "Should we let McVie know that it's turning into *Lord of the Flies* in here? He might decide we should be released sooner than later, before my father's head ends up on a stick."

"Yeah. Even if they have to open up the whole building to do it." Piper turned and began going up the aisle toward the judge's bench. Fenway followed. Just as they reached the gallery gate, Piper said in a low voice, "Oh—Fenway—one more thing. You and McVie were right."

"We were right? About what?"

"I found proof. There *is* a mole in the sheriff's department."

CHAPTER FOURTEEN

Fenway blinked and leaned on the gate. "You got proof there's a mole? Are you *sure?*"

"Almost positive," said Piper. "I have the mole's code name—it's kind of silly. *37cuckoo37.*"

"Yeah, that *is* silly. How do you know that's the mole?" They continued to walk past the witness stand and up to the dais.

"Because," Piper said, "there's a payment of ten thousand dollars to the *cuckoo* the morning after Dylan Richards was killed in his cell. And a note written in the margin of one of the handwritten ledgers we got from Marisol Velásquez last week."

"Which was?"

"Leo is cuckoo."

"Did you just say 'Leo is cuckoo'?"

"Right. I puzzled over that for a while. I hadn't seen any payments to anyone with a code name of *cuckoo* or the name of *Leo*, but as soon as I noticed the timing of that payment, everything clicked into place."

Fenway nodded. "Law enforcement officer."

"Right. I should have known that—and it *did* pop into my head—but I rejected it because this was a criminal enterprise, not an internal police thing. Then as soon as I saw that payment and the *cuckoo* code name on the day after Dylan was killed, I remembered how much work Domingo Velásquez did for Ferris Energy and for their security teams, and how many of *them* were former law enforcement."

"Do you think *cuckoo* means anything?"

Piper shrugged. "I only found out about *cuckoo*'s existence a few minutes ago. Give me at least a half hour to figure out their social security number and their favorite fruit."

Fenway chuckled. "Excellent work, Piper. You're not holding back any other information, are you?"

Piper shook her head. "Nothing that seems very relevant, anyway. I started looking at some financials. Cynthia Schimmelhorn seems interesting, but she's so rich she's got most of her payments listed in secure systems. I did get an interesting cross-reference when I started looking at Evans Dahl, though."

"Evans Dahl? Why would you look at him?"

Piper folded her arms. "Because he pissed me off. Talking about you like that."

"Aw, thanks, Piper. You're like the feisty little sister I never had."

Piper grunted. "Well, I found a payment from Cynthia Schimmelhorn to Evans Dahl. It just went through this morning. He must have accepted it over the long weekend."

"What's it for?"

"I think," Piper mused, "it's for defending Professor Cygnus from the murder charge."

"What?"

"There's no record of payment from either of the Cygnus accounts, and Evans Dahl doesn't come cheap," Piper said. "Maybe Evans is taking it purely for the publicity, or maybe he's working out a payment arrangement with the Cygnuses."

"Maybe." Fenway leaned on the desk. "But why Evans Dahl? He's a decent attorney, I suppose, but there are many criminal attorneys better than him. His reputation isn't that great, and he's expensive."

"Cynthia Schimmelhorn is right there. You could go ask her why she hired him."

Fenway nodded.

"And," Piper whispered, "have you noticed that she's got the chief operations officer of Ferris Energy wrapped around her little finger?"

"Yeah, I have noticed that."

"He looks at her all the time before he makes a move. Approval or something."

"I mean," Fenway said, "she *is* the most powerful person on the board of directors. Besides, Mr. Heissner seems to have an issue with impulse control."

"But even so," Piper said, "it's odd, isn't it?"

Fenway giggled. "What, you think maybe they have some sort of weird power-sex relationship?"

Piper's eyes went wide. "No, that wasn't what I was thinking at *all*." She made a face. "Thanks for the visual."

"What were you thinking?"

"Um—that Cynthia was the one trying to get your father kicked out. That Bryce is basically her lackey. Doing her dirty work for him."

"Her heavy?"

"Uh—yes, I guess so."

"And you think *Cynthia* is behind everything?"

Piper bobbed her head sideways and forward. "I don't know. I suppose the notion occurred to me."

The wheels turned in Fenway's mind. "I suppose that does make a certain kind of sense."

Piper shook her head. "But she's doing the power grab so blatantly. She must have enough leverage to squeeze your dad out without a billion-dollar oil-to-terrorists scheme."

"Plus, she's rich," Fenway said. "So I don't know why she'd do it."

Piper looked thoughtful. "She made a *lot* of money when Ferris Energy took over the division of Petrogrande that she led. I researched it—I don't have the number in front of me, but it was almost ten million dollars. Honestly, I'm surprised she's so angry at your father."

"Maybe she wanted to get a lot more out of the deal."

"She came out pretty well."

Fenway paused. "Could you do some research into Bryce Heissner? He told me he was in the Navy—made it up to Lieutenant Commander."

Piper nodded. "So his prints are on file anyway."

Fenway paused a moment. "Have Schimmelhorn and Heissner been on the board since Ferris Energy took over?"

Piper shook her head slowly. "I don't know about Heissner, but Schimmelhorn disappeared for a while. A year, maybe two. Then she ran operations at another energy group in Mexico, then she was at a natural gas company in the Pacific Northwest. It was about five years after the leveraged buyout before she joined the board of directors. She lobbied the other directors pretty hard."

"How do you know that?"

"Your dad gave me access to corporate email."

"What? Is that—is that *legal?*"

Piper nodded. "Sure it is. Just like the county can access all of our email."

Fenway pulled a chair out and sat, motioning Piper to take a seat next to her. "Okay, walk me through the timeline here," she said.

"Right. About eight years ago, she was the general manager of Petrogrande Western. Operations in Colorado, Nevada, California. Ferris came in and scooped it up. Ferris Energy had been investing in the lands where Petrogrande Western leased and in the real estate properties where their offices were. Ferris Energy then bought a bunch of stock in Petrogrande—the international firm—and convinced them to carve off Petrogrande Western and give it to Ferris Energy."

"*Give* it?"

"Ferris owned the oil fields and the buildings—pretty much everything except the equipment and the workers. And they obviously wanted the profit. I'm sure there was a threat made—*give us Petrogrande Western or we'll make it impossible to do business on our land.*"

"That's nasty."

"That's business. That's how your dad got his reputation for being ruthless."

"What did Petrogrande get in return?"

"Besides the money from the stock purchase? I don't think they got anything. The press release says they got about fifty million dollars out of it, but that's a fraction of what it was worth. Cynthia Schimmelhorn had to spend a few days in intense negotiations trying to save Petrogrande Western, but she couldn't do it. And she was the first one let go, although they gave her a severance package and let all her stock options vest. That's the ten million dollars I mentioned before."

"And she just disappeared for a couple of years?"

"Maybe she just wanted to take some time off. I know she's been divorced, but I don't know the timing yet. Maybe she was trying to save her marriage."

"Ah, that makes sense. And she had a daughter, too. Did I tell you that Cynthia's daughter was named Nerissa after the character she played in *The Merchant of Venice*, directed by Professor Cygnus?"

Piper nodded. "I don't think you mentioned it to me, but now that makes sense why she'd pay for his murder defense. If he made such a big impact on her, she might have needed to give back."

"Right."

"Nerissa went to Western Washington, too, just like I did."

"Oh, wow. A fellow Husky."

Fenway scoffed. "No, no, Piper, that's the *University* of Washington. Western Washington is the Vikings."

Piper chuckled. "Pardon me for not being up on my college mascots." She paused. "Did you know Nerissa?"

Fenway shook her head. "She was younger than I was by a year or two, I think. She died by suicide. Not sure what the story is there."

"I could look into it. Maybe that has something to do with Schimmelhorn disappearing."

Fenway turned and looked at Cynthia Schimmelhorn, sitting in the back row of the courtroom. "I don't know if it's relevant, but sure. I'll talk to Schimmelhorn in the meantime."

"Do you think that'll get us closer to finding out who the killer is?"

"At this point," Fenway said, "if it doesn't get me Rose Morgan's fingerprints, I'm not sure *what* will get me closer to catching the murderer. But the payment is a little odd. Maybe something will shake loose—who knows." She lowered her voice. "Truth be told, I think there's something fascinating about her. She's gotten a long way in the energy industry, especially for it being so male-dominated. I kind of want to be her when I grow up."

"Really?" Piper followed Fenway's gaze to Cynthia Schimmelhorn. "She seems so sad to me. She might be rich, but she's unhappy."

Fenway sighed. "You're right. How can she not be, with her daughter gone?" She stood up and stretched her long arms up above her head. "Okay, wish me luck."

"You're not being shipped off to war, Fenway. I'll see you back at the judge's desk in five minutes."

"You're no fun." Fenway stuck her tongue out at Piper. "Let me know if McVie responds."

Piper went through the gallery gate, and Fenway turned the other way, back down the center aisle. Cynthia Schimmelhorn sat primly in her seat, her legs elegantly crossed.

"Hi, Ms. Schimmelhorn."

"Hello, Miss Stevenson. What can I do for you?"

"I just had a couple more questions."

Cynthia sighed and leaned back. "Of course. I'm not sure when the sheriff plans to let us out, but I hope it's soon. I don't want to miss my lunch meeting."

At the mention of lunch, Fenway's stomach growled, and she put a hand on her stomach and grinned. "Aw, man, you woke it up."

Cynthia laughed and shook her head. "It's unusual, Miss Stevenson. So many people don't feel like they can joke around me."

Fenway shrugged. "You *do* come off as a little serious."

Schimmelhorn nodded. "I suppose so. I am a rather somber person."

"So—my questions."

"Yes."

"They have to do with Professor Cygnus."

"I should hope so. This is an investigation of his death, is it not? Even though your hands are a bit tied?"

"I don't have access to the things I usually do, that's for sure." Fenway sat down in the row in front of Schimmelhorn. "I found a payment you made to Evans Dahl recently. Can I ask what that was for?"

"It was for legal representation."

"For yourself, Ms. Schimmelhorn?"

Cynthia tightened her smile and stared at Fenway. "No." She paused and blinked.

Fenway waited for a moment, but Schimmelhorn would offer nothing further without prompting. "For who, then?"

A calmness passed over Cynthia Schimmelhorn's face as she continued to pause, but finally leaned forward and said, "Professor Cygnus."

"Why did you pay for his representation?"

Schimmelhorn examined her fingernails. They were short, with a clear coat. Nothing over the top, but it looked like a professional manicure. "Because, Miss Stevenson, Professor Cygnus was a great inspiration to me when I went to university. I was a rather spoiled child, and I was used to trying very little but scoring high marks on tests. Professor Cygnus and I fought terribly when I was at school here, but I learned an enormous amount from him. Not just about Shakespeare. Not just how to perform in a play. I learned about myself. What I could do with effort. What I could do if I applied my intelligence to solving problems and not just trying to skate by doing as little as possible." Schimmelhorn raised her eyes to the ceiling and clicked her tongue. "It was the most valuable lesson I've ever been taught." Her voice took on a dreamy quality. "I even named my daughter after the character I played. I found a depth in Nerissa that at first I refused to believe was there. But I just wasn't looking hard enough." She blinked and focused on Fenway again. "Anyway, perhaps it was poor judgment to get a decent attorney for the professor, but it was the right thing to do."

"Why did you choose Evans Dahl, Ms. Schimmelhorn?"

"What do you mean?"

"I mean—look, nothing against him, he's a decent attorney. But that's just it. He's a *decent* attorney. There are much better attorneys in the area. You'll forgive me for saying so, but I don't think money is as much of an issue for you as it was for Professor Cygnus."

Schimmelhorn smiled. "Well, Miss Stevenson, as you are no doubt aware, this was a three-day weekend, and the professor was arrested Friday night and arraigned first thing on the docket the next business day. I may be able to afford expensive lawyers, but they can all afford to say no to me when they have weekend plans with their families. Or their mistresses." Schimmelhorn smiled innocently.

Fenway nodded. "Fair enough."

"Is that all?"

"With the questions?" There was something scratching at the back of Fenway's brain, but she had no idea what it meant. Only one line of questioning was left. "Just about. I just wanted to know how long you've been on the board of directors of Ferris Energy."

"Almost three years." Cynthia Schimmelhorn sighed. "I knew I was a diversity hire, but I didn't care. I'd been away from the oil industry for a few years, and I wanted to come back."

"Weren't you forced out originally when Ferris Energy made Petrogrande sell their Western division?"

Schimmelhorn nodded. "Yes. It was, shall we say, rather backhanded." She set her mouth in a thin line.

"Is it fair to say you're not over it yet?"

"All's fair in love and business, Miss Stevenson."

"You must admit it's a little strange that Ferris Energy still let you on their board of directors."

"By then, your father barely gave me a second thought. Even though it was the most painful experience of my life, and even with my unusual Dutch surname, it simply didn't register with him."

"Okay—yes, that sounds like my father. But why would you even want to be on the board of a company you obviously detested?"

Cynthia nodded. "There's such a thing as changing a company from the inside, Miss Stevenson. In fact, it's the only way positive disruption is possible."

"What changes did you want to see?"

"I wanted to see the removal of stagnant ideas. From a personal perspective, I wanted diverse voices to be giving those fresh ideas. It's one thing to have groupthink at a company. It's quite another one when the room doing the groupthink is full of people from the same demographic." She sighed. "I did get Arlene Petersbury approved. And Jamal Kincaid, which was a struggle because he'd spent so much time in the public sector. Seven external members on the board, and now we have two women and two African-Americans. That, believe it or not, is in the top five percent of Fortune 1000 companies."

"I believe it," Fenway said. "And you fought to save Petrogrande Western."

"A little too hard, I'm afraid," Schimmelhorn said. The muscles in her neck tightened visibly.

"You think you could have stayed on at Ferris Energy if you hadn't pushed so hard?"

Schimmelhorn laughed derisively. "Not a chance."

Fenway blinked. "You still sound angry."

"I am." Schimmelhorn smiled again, her eyes dancing with animation. "Angry enough to kill? I don't know—killing people is just giving into your base urges, isn't it? And don't we as a species like to think we're better than that?" She clapped her hands together. "Now, when Nathaniel Ferris drops dead and foul play is suspected," she whispered, "I shall be honored to be considered a suspect. But are you seriously asking whether I'm angry enough at Mr. Ferris to kill my beloved Shakespeare professor?"

Fenway absently nodded, not as an affirmative answer to her question, but as an acknowledgment of the absurdity of the question. "One last thing, then I'll leave you alone. Did you know or did you suspect that anything was going on with the embargoed oil, the hidden super-tankers, the money laundering—any of it?"

Cynthia Schimmelhorn shook her head. "I get compensated in stock for my work on the board of directors, Miss Stevenson. Do you think I'd have risked millions of dollars of my investment if I *had* known about it?"

"You didn't see *anything* that made you suspicious? No ledgers, no secret communications about supertankers, no areas of the docks that were off limits but where you could still see activity happening?"

"I never went to the docks. I'm sure none of the board did. And as for suspicious activity—if I *had* seen something, don't you think I'd want to protect that investment?"

"You might not have blown the whistle," Fenway pointed out. "You might have just wanted to sweep it all under the rug."

"Not without putting a stop to it first," Schimmelhorn said, glaring at Fenway. "Really—hiding a *supertanker*. That takes balls, if you'll pardon the expression. Or a monumental amount of stupidity." She smirked. "Or, in your father's case, perhaps an overgenerous amount of *both*."

Fenway grinned back at Cynthia Schimmelhorn. "Yes, that sounds like my father."

Schimmelhorn leaned forward. "I do think your father is an evil son of a bitch, Fenway. You must know that."

"It doesn't surprise me. Sometimes I'm close to that impression myself."

Her eyes softened. "But you have to know that he loves you very much. He knows he has to make up for two decades of lost time, and it will *kill* him if he doesn't figure out how to move past this with you."

Fenway was startled. "How—how in the *world* do you know all this?"

Shrugging, Schimmelhorn said, "I'd like to tell you I'm a magical creature who can take all the pain and suffering away. Or perhaps I can chalk it up to the sorcery of women's intuition." She smiled. "Or perhaps it's the woefully pedestrian explanation that your father speaks more loudly on personal calls during board meetings than he likes to think he does."

Fenway chuckled. "That also sounds like my father." She started to get up and then hesitated. "Um—look, I don't know if this is appropriate for me to say, but I just lost my mother earlier this year, so…" She cleared her throat. "I went to Western Washington too. I'm not sure if it was at the same time as your daughter—I only went for two years—but I know it can be a tough place to go to school. A lot of commuters. People can be cruel."

"So could the professor your father had killed."

Fenway's stomach dropped. "I—uh…"

"I may not think much of your father," Cynthia Schimmelhorn said, "but I do admire him for that. If that Delacroix bastard had *touched* Nerissa—much less recorded it and put it on the web for sale— I'd have wanted to torture him and watch him die, slowly, painfully, as gruesomely as possible." She straightened up. "Perhaps I don't have the right mindset to kill the man who wronged my daughter, but perhaps I do." She moved her hands outward slightly, as if she couldn't be bothered to shrug. "At any rate, I admire him for it. And you can tell him so, should you wish."

"We can prove he's innocent of Delacroix's murder," Fenway said, then immediately regretted saying it.

"*What?*"

"I mean—well, I've probably said too much."

"If you've found evidence your father didn't commit the crime, surely it will be public knowledge soon enough."

"That's true," Fenway admitted. "Okay—there are payments that my father supposedly made to the hit man, but we can prove it's not really his account—someone opened it in his name."

"Who?"

"We haven't figured that out yet, but we've already sent the documentation to his lawyer. What she does with it is anybody's guess."

Schimmelhorn nodded. "I don't think his lawyer will just sit on it and let him rot in jail." She folded her arms. "Is there another suspect?"

Fenway shrugged. "We're working on it."

"Oh—well. I rescind my admiration of your father, then."

"Yeah."

Fenway stood up with a sudden desire to end the increasingly strange conversation, and her stomach rumbled again.

"Let's hope this is over soon," Cynthia Schimmelhorn said. "We wouldn't want you to miss a meal."

IV

11:00 AM

CHAPTER FIFTEEN

Fenway turned away from Cynthia Schimmelhorn, and Bryce Heissner's eyes bored into her from across the aisle. Heissner sat sideways on one of the wooden chairs, his legs splayed, his right elbow up on the back of the chair.

"What is it, Mr. Heissner?" Fenway asked wearily.

"I'm just wondering how much longer you'll keep up the charade that your daddy dearest is innocent," Heissner said, tapping the back of the chair in an oddly timed rhythm with his fingers. "Surely there's so much smoke around him, you must think there's *some* fire in all of that by now."

"Doesn't mean he's the source of the flame," Fenway retorted. "In fact, I could say the same about you."

"About me?"

"Yes, Mr. Heissner. You're just as involved in Ferris Energy as my father is. More, in fact, since you hold all the purse strings. If there's something that affects the bottom line, you have the final say, don't you?"

"If you think I have more control over Ferris Energy than your dad—"

Fenway shook her head and took five steps toward Heissner until she was only two or three feet from him. "I don't think you have more control over the public relations, or over what companies Ferris Energy buys or sells, but I *know* you have more control over where things come out of the budget, or how much money one division gets in discretionary spending."

"So?" Heissner crossed his arms and glared at Fenway.

"So, Mr. Heissner, it means that if anyone is hiding anything having to do with Ferris Energy finances—like moving huge amounts of ill-gotten money around—*you'd* have visibility into it."

Heissner set his jaw, seething. "That's quite an accusation."

"Accusation?" Fenway feigned surprise. "I'm accusing you of knowing what's going on with your own company's finances? And you're *angry* with me?" She laughed, a fake, too-loud noise, and Heissner winced slightly. "I can't call you a competent COO? You get mad at your wife when she calls you a good lover, too?"

Heissner's cheeks went red. "That's not what you meant, and you know it."

Fenway smiled as wide as she could. "Yes, I do know it, Mr. Heissner. I am, in fact, accusing you of knowing a lot more that you're letting on about the whole thing."

"What *whole thing?*"

"The hidden supertanker. The refining of the embargoed oil. The money laundering. And especially the murders."

Heissner shook his head. "The people who are doing all of this—whoever they are—had us all tricked. They were using decommissioned maintenance yards and holding tanks. It goes deep within the organization, but they didn't touch the official bank accounts of Ferris Energy, and they *certainly* didn't inform me about it." He set his jaw. "How many people at the company do you think had the ability to coordinate that kind of monstrous project while keeping me in the dark?"

"I'm not sure how Ferris Energy works, Mr. Heissner," Fenway said, "but I bet that you'll identify my father as the only person who could pull that kind of thing off."

Heissner chewed his tongue for a moment before giving Fenway a chilling smile. "Well, I can't say that Nathaniel Ferris had a stupid daughter, can I? He expected you to be a lot less dogged about all the murders he'd like to have covered up, didn't he?"

Fenway glanced over at her father and Charlotte. Charlotte was tending to him, a look of concern on her face. Neither was listening to anything that was being said in the courtroom. "I can't really speak to what his expectations were, Mr. Heissner," Fenway said, "but I believe my close ratio on homicides speaks for itself."

"You've got a couple open cases," Heissner said.

"A couple of open cases that aren't even a week old," Fenway said. "And one that's not even a day old."

Heissner shrugged. "I suppose."

"So how much do you know, Mr. Heissner?" Fenway asked. "Are you aware of the ledgers?"

Heissner flinched. Very slightly, but enough that Fenway knew she should keep digging.

"Do you know how many of the businesses in Estancia have gotten wrapped up in the money laundering?"

"Only what I've been told by the police," Heissner said. "I can assure you that I've been completely unaware of all of it—because your dear ol' dad knew exactly where to hide everything."

"I'm just astonished at how little people know," Fenway said, batting her eyelashes at Heissner. "The money laundering scheme involves half the businesses in this town, yet no one seems to know anything at all. With that huge university down the road, you'd think we'd be teaching our residents some critical thinking skills."

Bryce Heissner stared at Fenway for a moment, then started to laugh, softly and slowly at first, and then louder and heartier, until his entire body shook with laughter and tears leaked from his eyes.

"I'm glad that in a serious situation like this, you can still find moments of levity," Fenway said.

Heissner laughed harder.

"Look, I know that we don't have the leverage to compel you to provide financial documents to prove or disprove your innocence." Fenway scratched the top of her head. "But Mr. Heissner, this house of cards is about to fall. Schemes like this are only as strong as their weakest links. And Professor Cygnus was about to flip. Whoever was behind the scheme was able to snuff out that leak." Fenway put her hands on her hips. "There are surely other leaks out there. You've got *so* many people involved—"

"I don't have any people involved in anything," Heissner said with disdain.

"—and now there are an *enormous* number of people in law enforcement looking at this money laundering scheme. Someone involved is bound to talk before you can kill them."

"I am not responsible for any of this, Miss Stevenson."

Fenway rolled her eyes. "It's the *general* you. The *royal* you."

"Well, whichever *you* you are, you can stop it. Stop your insinuations, stop your accusations. Just stop."

"Will *you* stop assaulting my father?"

Heissner sniffed loudly. "Look, I don't like being held in here any more than you do." He coughed into his elbow. "Actually, somehow I get the feeling that you're actually getting off on this. It's like a crazy puzzle to you, isn't it? Other people do crosswords or sudoku or jigsaw puzzles. You solve murders."

Fenway shrugged. "I'm pretty good at it so far."

"Well, you've been remiss in your interviewing," Heissner said.

"What do you mean?"

"You've interviewed me. You've interviewed Ms. Schimmelhorn—twice now. You talked to your father, but I doubt that was an interview. You spoke to the professor's widow and that other lady over there." Heissner pointed to Leda Nedermeyer. "You tried to talk to Rose a couple of times."

Fenway cocked her head. "How do you know Rose?"

Heissner shook his head. "Doesn't matter. The point is, you're all over the place. You haven't interviewed your dad or your stepmom.

You haven't interviewed the two students either. You ever think maybe they have a motive for wanting their professor offed? And maybe they know how to shoot?"

"Are you trying to tell me how to do my job?"

"You seem to have a pretty good idea how I should be doing mine." Heissner stretched his arms over his head as if he couldn't be bothered.

"I'll bear that in mind, Mr. Heissner. Is there anything else I can do for you?"

"Some food would be nice."

"It sure would. I'll see if I can get in touch with the outside world. Hopefully it won't be too much longer now."

Fenway turned and walked up the aisle, through the gallery gate to the safe confines behind the judge's bench.

"He's a real piece of work," Piper whispered as Fenway sat down.

"My father tends to hire assholes," Fenway said. "I think it's a job requirement."

Her gaze landed on the gun, still in the evidence baggie on top of her fingerprint kit. "So much for being assured of the chain of custody," she mumbled.

"What did you say?"

"Nothing. I need to put the gun in the evidence locker."

"Oh, right. Do you need the code again?"

Fenway closed her eyes. *Corners, then up and down the middle column.* "I think I have it."

"Okay. It'll lock up after five tries, so if you screw up the first couple, let me know."

Fenway grabbed the gun in the evidence baggie and walked around the side to the front of the judge's bench, where she pushed the corner of the door and popped it open again.

9-3-3-1, 0-2-8-5.

A red light and a soft but firm buzz.

Oh—that's right. Two nines at first, and only one three.

9-9-3-1, 0-2-8-5.

A green light, and the safe door unlatched. Fenway placed the gun inside next to the shell casing, closed the safe, then pushed the mahogany door shut over it.

As she walked around the judge's bench to go sit next to Piper, she hoped the safe would pass muster with any judge to allow the gun and the shell casing into evidence.

"Did you get anything from Ms. Schimmelhorn?" Piper asked as Fenway sat down next to her.

"She denied knowing anything about the embargoed oil or the hidden supertanker. But she's still mad about being forced out of her company." Fenway put her elbow on the desk and rested her chin in her hand. "It feels like there's something I'm missing here."

Piper nodded. "You know, when you think you're close to putting it together, you're usually right. What is it? Is it about Schimmelhorn or Heissner?"

Fenway shut her eyes. Lights popped on and off in her head. She tried to follow her threads of thought like streamers, but with no defined beginning or ending. She pictured the file cabinet in her mind so she could open it and figure out what was buried in her brain that she couldn't access. "I'm not sure," she muttered.

There was silence for a moment.

"Can I tell you something else I found?"

Fenway sighed. "Yes. I don't think I'll be able to think of it now."

"So I found a birth certificate."

"A birth certificate?"

"Yes. From nine years ago."

"Okay. What does this have to do with anything?"

Piper hesitated. "Look, this is probably a HIPAA violation. It's probably against the law for *me* even to know about it."

"If it's not pertinent to the investigation, I don't want to know about it."

"No. It's definitely pertinent."

Fenway was quiet for a moment.

Piper hesitated. "Leda Nedermeyer is listed as the mother."

"Really? But she—" Fenway replayed her conversation with Nedermeyer, complaining about not being able to have children. Adoption? Stillbirth? Crib death?

"And there's no one listed as the father."

"That—that was *after* she started at Nidever."

"She'd been here for three years and spent the spring semester that year on sabbatical."

"Sabbatical? After only three years?"

Piper shrugged. "I haven't dug up the communications from the university, but my guess is that giving her a semester of paid sabbatical made the most sense from a public relations standpoint. You know, rather than having students ask questions about her pregnancy and possibly causing issues with their rock-star Shakespeare professor."

"Cygnus's name isn't listed, though," mused Fenway. "It might have been someone else."

"No way. Not with Nedermeyer taking a sabbatical after less than three years on the job and then getting promoted when she came back. I don't think even the university president would get that much consideration."

"Are you sure it's Cygnus?"

Piper nodded. "The evidence wouldn't stand up in court. But there's no other logical conclusion."

"Just because the father's name isn't listed doesn't mean it's Cygnus. It could easily have been another professor. Or a student, even."

"If the father had been a student, Nidever would have fired her, not promoted her. This isn't a situation in which one *ever* gets promoted— unless the father's the most powerful person on campus."

Fenway glanced up at Judith Cygnus. "I wonder if his wife knew about the baby. About the pregnancy." She paused. "Any word about what happened to the child?"

"I haven't found out. Not sure I'll be able to—some of the records are sealed."

Fenway nodded. "That probably means adoption."

"A *closed* adoption, probably. Especially if the father's name isn't listed on the birth certificate." Piper paused. "I don't think that gives anyone motive to kill Professor Cygnus, though."

"Judith might, if she just found out. It's one thing to know your husband is having an affair. It's another thing to find out his mistress had his baby."

Piper scoffed. "That's so old-school soap opera."

"Well, it's true. For certain people." Fenway turned her head to the left to glance at Leda Nedermeyer. "I can't wait to get out of here, Piper. Has McVie responded yet?"

"They're just getting the last of the people searched. He says it'll be another hour, maybe an hour and a half, tops."

Fenway tilted her head at Piper. "Weren't you going to come get me so I could text McVie?"

"You were in the middle of your conversation with Cynthia Schimmelhorn. I didn't want to interrupt." Piper pushed her laptop over to Fenway. "You can text him now."

Fenway shook her head. "If it'll just be another hour, I can wait." She exhaled. Besides, she didn't know what she would say to him.

Did she think she loved him? Had she ever *been* in love before? Did she even know what that would look like?

"I'll talk to Leda Nedermeyer again," Fenway mumbled. "And I guess I should interview Xavier and Amanda too. As much as I think Bryce Heissner is an asshole, he's right that I haven't covered all my bases."

"Is that what he was saying to you?"

"Among other things. He's like a creepy uncle." Fenway turned to study Heissner, who was leaning back in his chair with his eyes closed. "He also called Rose Morgan by her first name with no prompting from me. So he knows her."

"Did you ask how?"

"He didn't answer, but it's got to be through the money laundering. He's a COO, and she's the one who's done the oversight on Domingo Velásquez and the Central Auto Body books."

Piper looked thoughtful for a moment. "Didn't you say that Rose had done some petroleum engineering work for Petrogrande before?"

"Something more complicated, but yeah."

"Maybe it's innocent. Cynthia Schimmelhorn worked at Petrogrande, right? Perhaps she and Heissner had a professional relationship with Rose Morgan before."

"That would be a hell of a coincidence."

"And you don't like coincidences in murder investigations."

Fenway stared at the double doors, with eyes glazing over.

CHAPTER SIXTEEN

Fenway turned everything over in her mind. Rose was in the back of the room—that made sense. Cynthia Schimmelhorn saw someone with a hoodie and with brown skin. That could have been Rose, too—Cynthia's preconceived idea of what a shooter looked like could have easily transformed Rose's black, curly hair into a sweatshirt hood in her mind, as well as swapping genders out.

Did Rose show up just to kill Professor Cygnus? Try as she might, Fenway couldn't come up with a motive. Rose should be long gone by now—not in the courtroom at all.

"You okay, Fenway?" Piper asked.

"Piper," Fenway murmured.

"Yeah?"

"I've been thinking," Fenway said slowly, "that Rose Morgan is the murderer all this time. But look at everyone who's in the courtroom now. Why in the world would Rose show up to the arraignment?"

"Like you said, to murder Professor Cygnus."

"She's got opportunity, and she's involved with the money laundering scheme—but does she really have the motive?"

"Cygnus was about to tell the prosecution more names. So Rose Morgan killed him so he couldn't."

"But why would it be *her* name she wanted to silence? It's not to prevent us from looking at her as a suspect. We're already doing that."

Piper smirked. "Not *her* name. Her boss's name. Whoever that is."

"Right. Yes. That makes sense." Fenway stared into space for a moment. "But that doesn't adequately explain why she showed up this morning. If you're planning to kill somebody, you don't want to call attention to yourself. And she knew that the sheriff's department was looking for her."

"For what?"

"Resisting arrest, for one thing. For assaulting a peace officer, for another."

"Are you talking about when you surprised her in The Guild office and she threw that book at you?"

Fenway turned and stared at Piper. "It was a big Shakespeare hardbound collection. Must have weighed ten pounds. It hit me in the face, remember?"

"She threw a book at you, so now you'll throw the book at her?"

Fenway rolled her eyes and groaned.

Piper leaned back in her seat. "So why haven't you arrested her yet?"

Fenway folded her arms. "I don't exactly have handcuffs. There's no way to take her into custody."

Piper cocked her head. "And for another thing, what you have on her is weak, and it's your word against hers."

Fenway nodded. "I'm a law enforcement representative, and that should count for something, but I'm not sure it does."

Piper stared at the ceiling. "Do you think if you took her into custody, she'd flip on whoever hired her?"

Fenway chortled. "Absolutely not. She knows how to keep her mouth shut, and she's already lawyered up once. I'm afraid we'd be wasting our time if we arrested her."

"Maybe she knows that. That could be why she showed up here—she knew you wouldn't do anything. Or it could have been a decoy. Her boss sent her here so that everyone would watch her, giving the real killer a chance to make their move."

Fenway threw up her hands. "That's a chess match, Piper. Thinking ten moves ahead. It's a possibility, but I think the answer is a lot simpler than that."

Piper shrugged. "That's why you get elected County Coroner and I sit at my computer." She glanced again at Bryce Heissner. "If you *are* going to talk to Xavier and Amanda, I suggest you do it before you talk to Leda about the pregnancy. Then Heissner will think you're listening to him. If he sees you interviewing Leda again first, he might confront you again."

"Good thinking." Fenway's stomach rumbled again, but she ignored it. She glanced up at the clock above the double doors—it wasn't even noon yet—then dropped her gaze to Xavier and Amanda, sitting three-quarters of the way back, spread out on four chairs in the center of the row. Amanda had turned toward Xavier, reciting another monologue, and Xavier was recording her.

Fenway walked around the witness stand, then down the center aisle again, stopping at the row where Xavier and Amanda sat. Amanda stopped mid-sentence and looked up at Fenway.

She nodded at Amanda. "Can I speak to you, please?"

Amanda glanced at Xavier, tilting her head, and the look on the young man's face was just as worried as hers. She cleared her throat. "Sure, I guess so."

Hmm. What was that about? Is there something to dig up after all? Maybe this won't just be window dressing for Heissner's sake.

"And Xavier, just so you know, recording on that smartphone might set people on edge. You might want to put it away." Fenway motioned with her head toward the nook, and Amanda stood and followed Fenway behind the last row of seats.

When they entered the nook, Fenway held her hand out toward

the chairs, and Amanda sat in the chair with her back to the wall—the one Fenway had been sitting in for all the other interviews. Fenway tapped her foot, annoyed that Amanda took her chair and annoyed at herself for not saying anything.

This was Fenway's third interview with Amanda in a week. She'd questioned Amanda in the North American Shakespeare Guild office, then again with McVie in her dorm room at Nidever—which didn't end well. Amanda likely didn't trust Fenway—and had really opened up to Dez instead. In different circumstances, Fenway would definitely have gotten Dez to do the interview.

Taking the chair in the middle of the cramped space, Fenway tried to organize her thoughts. Amanda shifted in her seat and blinked several times quickly.

"How have things been going since Professor Cygnus's arrest, Amanda?"

Amanda looked down at her hands and played with the locket on her necklace. "Hard."

Fenway tilted her head and continued watching Amanda's face, waiting for her to keep speaking.

A deep crease formed between her eyebrows, then Amanda took a deep breath and looked up at the ceiling. "I—I just can't believe what's happened the last few days. The only reason I even chose Nidever was because of Professor Cygnus's program." She swallowed hard, and tears began to form in the corner of her eyes. "I just figured it had been some horrible mistake. That the cops had to pin the murder on someone, and Professor Cygnus was famous, and some cop figured they'd get their name in the news arresting him." Amanda dropped her gaze to Fenway, and a look of terror came over her face. "Oh—oh shit, that's not—I mean—"

Fenway held up her hand. "I get it. That's why all those students were protesting today. It's hard to believe that Professor Cygnus could have been capable of murder."

"I didn't mean that you were trying to get on the news—"

Fenway laughed. "Oh, that's the *last* thing I want right now."

"Anyway," Amanda continued quickly, "we barely got the show off on Friday night. We started about thirty minutes late—we didn't even know if we wanted to continue."

"Why did you?"

"It was all Xavier—he was amazing. He basically took over the show. He told us we had to prove to Professor Cygnus that he had taught us well—so well that we could have a fantastic performance without him." Amanda chuckled, even though her voice sounded like it would break at any moment. "It was the best performance of *Othello* we ever put on. Denise wasn't even her usual annoying self. When Xavier cried out after killing me—I mean, you know, killing Desdemona— there were real tears. Then afterward, when we usually have notes after the performance, we all gathered onto the stage and sat there for about fifteen minutes before we realized that no one was coming out to give us feedback. That everything we'd worked so hard for was in jeopardy."

Fenway nodded.

Amanda continued, "My summer in London with the theater tour —gone. The auditions that Professor Cygnus could set us up for— other acting jobs, theater companies, directors that he knew—gone." Tears started coming down Amanda's cheeks. "But Jessica Marquez was *actually* murdered and Professor Cygnus had *actually* killed her, and I was just thinking about my stupid auditions in L.A. I felt like the worst person ever."

Fenway cocked her head to the side and wished she had a box of tissues for Amanda, but she didn't. She'd even left her purse up on the judge's desk next to Piper.

Fenway believed the tears—but Amanda's shoulders were still tense. There was no relief in this confession. Yes, she felt terrible that she'd been selfish—but was she hiding something else?

"Anyway," Amanda continued, "the reality of it—that Jessica was dead, that Cygnus wasn't coming back—hit all of us then. Suddenly, this play that had been our *lives* all semester—it didn't matter at all anymore. We had a nearly sold-out show on Saturday night, but not even Xavier could get us prepared for it. We were *awful*. Our performance was as bad on Saturday as it was awesome on Friday. People fucked up their lines, missed their blocking—Denise started going off on a couple of the actors during intermission. And no one stuck around after."

Fenway nodded.

Amanda sank down into her chair. "We'll probably cancel the second week of shows. And I think this will be the end of the North American Shakespeare Guild."

Was that anger or just resignation in Amanda's voice? "But you came here to support Professor Cygnus anyway," Fenway said gently.

Amanda smiled sadly and shook her head. "I don't know what I expected. It might be dramatic, or everything would be a big misunderstanding. But it was over so fast. I guess I didn't really know what an arraignment was. I was surprised he didn't say anything. I had a glimmer of hope that maybe he wasn't guilty, and life could go on as before. The Guild could go on. But he didn't even acknowledge us."

There was definitely a touch of anger there. Fenway decided to push the emotional button and see what happened. "Did that make you angry? Cygnus only caring about saving his own skin?"

Amanda looked at Fenway like she was crazy. "Angry—angry enough to kill him, you mean? What good would that have done?" An edge crept into Amanda's voice. "Even though he didn't even look at us, he was still the only thing that could save The Guild. He's the reason so many Nidever grads jump-start their careers in Hollywood or on Broadway. His connections." She shook her head. "At first, like I said, I was freaked out about Cygnus being in prison. But Xavier had a good point. Even if Cygnus was in jail, maybe he couldn't set up auditions for us, but he could still write us letters of recommendation. It's not like Hollywood producers would suddenly ignore his eye for talent just because he's a murderer."

Fenway sat back. That wasn't the right path—Amanda had no

motive. There were still questions she had to ask, but Fenway didn't think she'd find out anything she didn't already know.

"Where were you when he was shot?"

"Xavier and I were stunned. Neither one of us thought it would be so quick. The prosecutor went to the defense table to speak with Professor Cygnus and his lawyer. We talked about maybe catching a quick word with him before they took him away again. You know, get a pep talk or something that would help us figure out how to go on, or at least get a sense of whether he was guilty or innocent. Xavier and I were about to walk up to the front when the shooting started."

"How many shots did you hear?" Fenway knew she heard two, but with all the commotion afterward she wanted to be sure she had corroboration.

"Two." Amanda looked up at the ceiling and stuck her tongue partway out between her lips. "At least—at least I think it was two."

Fenway nodded. But something kept grinding at the back of Fenway's mind. The crease between Amanda's eyebrows, if anything, had deepened.

"Can I go?" Amanda asked, fiddling with the locket on her necklace.

There was something there, all right, and Amanda was dying to tell someone. Fenway just had to press her a little more.

Fenway leaned forward and put her hands on her knees. "You know, when they take your oath in a courtroom like this, they ask if you swear to tell the truth, the whole truth, and nothing but the truth."

Amanda shifted her weight and blinked rapidly.

"You're not under oath here, Amanda, but I don't think I need to tell you how serious it is to mislead the police."

Amanda swallowed, keeping her back straight.

"You might be telling me the truth, but it's not the *whole* truth, is it?" Fenway glared at Amanda.

The younger woman broke off eye contact and looked at the ground. "I don't know anything more about the professor's murder. I told you where I was. I told you what I heard. Why can't I leave?"

Oh—Amanda wasn't afraid of the police. Whatever she was hiding, it wasn't something illegal. The bad-cop tactic was making Amanda more nervous and more hostile. Fenway had to switch up her strategy.

"Look, you respected the professor, right?" Her tone was softer.

Amanda nodded, still looking at the floor.

"He was a good teacher. A good director. A good *man*. He was just in over his head. You don't have to think he was evil." Fenway leaned back. "I was right there. He wanted to tell ADA Kim who some of the higher-ups were—to do the right thing." She paused, and Amanda's shoulders started to shake. "He was trying to make up for what he'd done. And someone shot him."

"I don't see what that has to do with me."

"Amanda, come on. I know you're smarter than that. Professor Cygnus was working with some bad people."

Amanda flinched.

Oh—that's why she's scared. Bad people.

Fenway leaned forward, but now her body language was relaxed, her shoulders loose. "I believe that you don't know anything else about who killed him. But you know something that can help us."

Amanda scrunched up her nose. She might have been a great actor, but she'd be a horrible poker player.

"I know that you're scared of telling me what you know," Fenway continued. "But all I want is the truth. The sheriff, the sergeant you talked to last week, even me—we protect our sources."

Amanda looked up and took a shaky breath.

"What is it?"

"So many people have died, Miss Stevenson."

"Because we didn't know they had information. We couldn't protect them."

"But—Professor Cygnus was killed right in front of you. You couldn't protect *him*. What makes you think you can protect *me*?"

Fenway nodded. "If we had known about his information earlier, we could have done something. But he'd also gotten into bed with some very bad people. They knew where his weaknesses were. They don't know about you."

Amanda turned the locket over in her hand again, back and forth, back and forth.

"If you don't tell me, Amanda, I can't protect you."

Amanda leaned back in her chair and lightly bumped the back of her head against the wall, then focused her eyes on the ceiling. Her voice dropped to a whisper. "So—by now you know there was another PC in The Guild office. One that's missing."

"The one that you used most often. Since you worked more hours than any other student."

"Right." Amanda sighed.

"You found a spreadsheet, right? One where the numbers didn't match up with the public report for the scholarship fund."

Amanda nodded. "I found it on Jessica's laptop one day when it was connected to the main network. I'd been working on the scholarship fund, and I thought at first it was a file I'd overlooked. And then when I opened it, I couldn't believe it. I copied it to my desktop and then I had to figure out what to do." Panic lit in Amanda's eyes. "You have to understand, Coroner, I have to submit scholarship fund paperwork with my *signature* attesting that the numbers are all correct. I could have been expelled—or even arrested—if I'd signed off on those numbers if I'd been aware they were false. This was my *future* we're talking about. And Jessica wanted me to sweep it under the rug."

"Sweep *what* under the rug, exactly?"

"The millions and millions of dollars in scholarship money that was missing! I only saw a spreadsheet from last quarter, but come on— sixty-five million dollars that comes in unaccounted for, that suppos- edly gets awarded to students who don't exist? No way. That's more than the university's whole annual budget. And I checked—those students aren't enrolled at Nidever. There's not even a listing of them in Nidever's student records."

"Really? How do you know?"

Amanda blushed. "There's—there's this guy who works in the

records office. He kind of has a crush on me. I was, uh, flirting with him at lunch last week, and I kind of saw the passwords on his phone."

Fenway shook her head. "You *kind of* saw the passwords in his phone?"

Amanda hesitated and looked down at the floor, still fiddling with her locket. "He left his phone unlocked on the table when he went to get our sandwiches."

Fenway paused for a moment, taking it all in. Sixty-five million dollars in one quarter. Piper had calculated that the whole embargoed-oil-to-terrorist-rebels scheme was netting the group over one billion dollars a year. She'd assumed that dozens, if not hundreds, of local businesses were taking part in the laundering, none being able to launder more than a few million a year. But one poorly overseen scholarship fund was responsible for laundering about thirty percent of it all by itself.

And Cygnus got in trouble—may have even gotten himself killed—for skimming half a million to pay for Judith's cancer treatment.

"You found the PC, didn't you?" Amanda said quietly.

Fenway cocked one eyebrow. She'd figured the computer was long gone, maybe destroyed. "We're still looking."

"It's in the costume closet in DiFazio Hall. Xav—I mean, *I* hid it really well. It's a mess in there. No one cleans that closet up until the end of our show run, and now that there might not even be a Guild next year, who knows—it might be ten years before that computer is found."

Fenway ignored the slip of the tongue. "Amanda, that spreadsheet is very important. There's an investigation into some *huge* crimes. Global-scale, billion-dollar stuff. And the murders are happening because the criminals in charge of it all are trying to save their own hides. They're killing people who know too much, or who might talk."

"Is that why Professor Cygnus was killed?"

"I don't know for sure, but yes, I think it was."

Amanda squinted at the floor. "Well, then, I guess you better take this."

She popped open the locket on her necklace. A small black piece of plastic, less than half an inch on each side, fell into her hand. She held it out to Fenway.

"What's this?" Fenway asked.

"A microSD card—the smallest flash storage I could get my hands on," Amanda said. "And my insurance policy against anything happening to the PC. That's the spreadsheet. That's where you'll find the sixty-five million dollars."

CHAPTER SEVENTEEN

THE MICROSD CARD WAS TINY, BUT IF ANYONE COULD GET THE information from it, it was Piper. Fenway thanked Amanda for being so forthcoming. She walked to the front of courtroom, around the witness stand, and to the judge's bench, where she set the card next to the laptop.

Piper stopped typing and looked up. "What's this?"

"It's the Holy Grail," Fenway replied. "This is the spreadsheet from Jessica Marquez. The one with all the payments in and out of the scholarship fund."

"Where did you get it?"

"Amanda copied it. See if any of the usernames or code names match with any of the dates and times of the payment information you have in the master spreadsheet. All we need is getting lucky on the right name, and maybe everything will fall into place."

Piper's eyes lit up. "I think I have an adapter in my bag."

"Really? I don't know that I've ever seen one of these so small before."

"They're usually for mini cameras, or smartphones. A couple of e-readers support them too. Honestly, I wasn't planning to get the adapter, but your father didn't even blink at the price tag on this laptop, so I figured what the hell."

Fenway looked at the clock on Piper's screen. "It's been about fifteen minutes. Any update from McVie on when we're getting out of here?"

"Nothing yet. I texted Dez, Rachel—some of my texts aren't getting through, but no one's responded. I tried another IP phone, but I configured the firewall myself to block all that kind of traffic."

"I want to make sure I talk to Leda while we're still in here," Fenway whispered. "I really should talk to Xavier first to appease Bryce, but I want to make sure that Judith didn't know about the baby. Or if she did, that she's known about it for a while."

"Long enough so that she'd have killed him long before now?"

"Exactly." She walked down the steps around the witness stand again. How many times had she gone back and forth in the two hours they'd been stuck in here?

Leda Nedermeyer sat in the last seat next to the side aisle in the fifth row on the prosecution's side. Fenway stepped sideways through the fourth row and sat down heavily in the chair in front of Leda. "Hi again, Professor," she said.

Nedermeyer glanced up from *Pride and Prejudice*. "Hello again, Coroner. I take it you didn't come over to chat about the role of garden pathways as motifs in Jane Austen."

Fenway sighed. "I'd rather discuss that than what I'm about to say, Professor, believe me."

Nedermeyer put her book down, then crossed her arms. "I don't believe you, but I appreciate you trying to protect my feelings."

It wasn't worth going through the past of Fenway's failed attempt at being a literature major, so she simply smiled. "We're doing background research on everyone in the room, Ms. Nedermeyer." Then she paused, looking in the professor's face.

Nedermeyer blinked and tilted her head. "And?"

"And we found a—a piece of information in your past. Something that connects you to Professor Cygnus. Beyond the simple affair the two of you had."

Nedermeyer was silent.

"About nine years ago, Professor. It would have been on August fifth."

The professor sighed and nodded. "Yes, Coroner, it's true. Virgil showed me exactly where he drew the line with our relationship. His daughter had just graduated college, so there was no need to stay together with Judith for appearances. We could have been happy, I think. If he had wanted to. But—but I didn't want to stop seeing him, and I wanted to keep my job, and—"

She looked down at her knees.

"It was a closed adoption. Those papers should have been confidential. I didn't even think Virgil's name was supposed to be on the birth certificate."

"I'm sorry, Professor. I really am. But I have to ask. Does Judith know about the baby?"

"How should I know? I didn't have any idea she knew about the affair until now. I don't know how much Virgil told her about us."

"Would she be angry with him? I mean, it's one thing to have an affair. It's another thing when your husband's mistress is pregnant."

"I don't know. They had an unusual relationship." A wistful smile touched the corners of Leda's mouth. "I suppose he and I did too."

Fenway hesitated. "Were—were *you* angry with him, Ms. Nedermeyer?"

"What?"

"Well—if he made it clear that if you wanted to keep seeing him, you had to give up the baby, and if staying with him, as you said earlier, ruined your chances for a family..." She let her phrase trail off, hoping it didn't sound too forced.

Leda crinkled her nose. "Yes. You know what? Yes. I was mad as hell. I got him for six weeks out of the year, and Judith got him the rest of the time, and I gave up *everything* for that man. I waited for *years* for him to be free of her, to be free of everything she represented so he and I could be together." She leaned forward and put her finger inches from Fenway's nose. "But I didn't kill him," she said, her voice rising, "because then I wouldn't have gotten what I wanted. I didn't want *him* dead; I wanted *her* dead. And I just had to wait another six months at most." Leda put her arm down as she stood, drawing herself up to her full height until she was looking down at Fenway, who was still sitting down. "I'd already waited ten years! I already gave away my baby with him! How much of an *idiot* would I have to be to kill the man I loved when I was so close to getting him?"

"I had to ask," Fenway murmured.

A bloodcurdling scream—and the figure of Judith Cygnus, racing at Leda, sprinting like a woman half her age.

Leda's eyes went wide, and she backed up—right into the side wall.

Judith Cygnus—all hundred pounds of her—slammed Leda into the wall with her body, then grabbed a fistful of her hair and pulled, gasping. "You—don't get—to lie—about Virg—"

Leda squealed. Fenway bolted out of her seat and tried to wedge herself between the two women, but Judith hung on to Leda's hair firmly.

"*Let go!*" Fenway shouted in Judith's ear. The older woman flinched, and Fenway shot her fist out, hard and fast, about two inches above the inside of Judith's elbow.

Judith yelped in pain and let go of Leda, who spun out of her grasp.

Fenway put her body between the two women, who eyed each other warily.

"You take back what you said," Judith screeched, her eyes dilated and her voice raspy.

"I don't even know what you're talking about," Leda murmured, arms straight out in front of her body, palms out. "What are you pissed off about? That I said you'd die of cancer in six months? Sorry to be the one to break it to you."

"The lie about the baby," Judith said through gritted teeth.

"*Stop it,*" Fenway growled. "I'm trying to find your husband's killer,

Mrs. Cygnus, and it doesn't get me any closer to the truth if you insist Professor Nedermeyer hide things from me."

Judith put down her arms and wilted into the closest chair, her head in her hands. "What am I going to do?" she moaned. "What am I going to do?"

"*You* have your daughter," Professor Nedermeyer hissed at Judith. "I have no one. You can feel better knowing that when I die, I will be alone, without anyone around. They probably won't even find my body until it starts to smell. My cats will probably have eaten my face."

Judith raised her head and glared at Leda.

Then Judith began to giggle.

"What's so funny?" Leda demanded.

"I just—I just got this image of you lying on some horrible linoleum floor, and a big orange cat just snacking on your nose." She bobbed her head up and down. "*Om nom nom nom. Tastes like tuna.*"

Fenway had to turn her head so Leda wouldn't see the smile on her face.

Leda shook her head. Fenway thought she would start screaming or crying.

Instead, she snickered. "One does read some awful stories."

"And cats *are* assholes," Judith said. "Do you actually have cats?"

"No," Leda said. "I think I'm considered quite loony enough by the Nidever community without being a crazy cat lady too."

"Your face is probably too small to properly feed more than one or two cats anyway," chuckled Judith, and then Leda was laughing, too.

"I'm sorry, Judith," Leda said. "I—I'm sorry I fell in love with Virgil, and I'm sorry I was such a shit to you all these years."

"I was a shit to you, too," Judith said.

"Oh, don't," Leda said. "You're the scorned woman in this situation."

"Are you two hugging it out now?" Fenway said, half annoyed and half amused.

Both women glared at Fenway.

"I'm going back to my seat," Judith declared.

"I'll come with you." Fenway stood up. She nodded at Leda, who looked amused, if a bit dazed. Judith walked slowly through the empty row, Fenway a few feet behind her. Everyone else in the room, even Rose Morgan, was staring at Judith.

She took several steps toward her seat and began coughing. She stopped as she caught her breath.

"Are you all right?" Fenway asked.

Judith nodded, inhaling slowly. "I'm in no shape for that."

Fenway walked slowly over to Judith's seat.

"Funny," Judith said as she sat down, "you'd think no one in the courtroom has ever seen an old woman completely lose her mind before."

Fenway took a seat next to Judith.

"Oh, now," Judith said, "I've just had to relive the worst news I'd ever gotten in my life. I'd successfully forgotten it. And you and Leda just made it come rushing back. I suppose you'll ask me questions about it now."

"You were angry enough about the baby to attack Leda. You might have hurt her."

"I certainly would have. Leda Nedermeyer doesn't know how to stand up for herself, never mind fight anyone. She's weak."

"So that makes me wonder, Mrs. Cygnus—were you angry enough at your husband for all of this—for the murder of Jessica Marquez, for essentially taking himself away from you for the last six months of your life—maybe even giving you flashbacks to when you first found out about Leda's baby—to hide a gun in here over the weekend and then shoot your husband?"

Judith looked pensive. "That would have taken a huge amount of planning that I simply no longer have the energy to do." She sighed. "Speaking of which, that fight with Leda took quite a bit out of me. I'll be feeling *that* this evening. Probably too exhausted to think tonight."

Fenway nodded. "Okay. Thanks for the chat." She got up. "Can I get anything for you?"

"My medication," she said. "I'm late for it."

"You don't have it with you?"

Judith shook her head. "It's in my case in the car."

"I'll see how soon we can get out of here. Last time I checked, it wouldn't be very much longer." Fenway got up and placed a comforting hand on Judith Cygnus's shoulder.

"Fenway?"

She looked across the aisle at her father, who was beckoning her over. Fenway stepped in front of Judith and walked over to her father.

"What is it, Dad?"

"This board vote that Heissner talked about—I need to see where I stand with that. Is there any way you can get in touch with Mel?"

"Mel?"

"Mel Cherrington. From the board. I know him; he's in my corner. If I can present my side of things, I'm sure the board will be fine with me staying on."

"Even if you're charged with murder?"

Ferris waved his hand. "It's all in the way you phrase it. Besides— I've got the best lawyer in the state, and a researcher who'll be able to prove I was framed."

"But—come on, Dad, Schimmelhorn and Heissner have leverage to force you out. And you won't be able to present to *anyone* if Heissner was right and they're adding charges."

"Let me worry about that." Ferris cleared his throat. "Aren't you doing something with the computer where you can contact the sheriff?"

"Dad, Craig is in the middle of a murder investigation. He doesn't have time for this. And I should hope that I don't have to remind you that Piper is working her ass off to find evidence that keeps you out of any more trouble."

"Yes, yes, yes, I understand all that, but look, I could get kicked out of the company even though I'm innocent. If I'm cleared, it won't matter—it's not like they'll give me back the CEO position, or give me all my shares back. I've got thousands that I'm still waiting to vest—"

"*Dad.*" Fenway's tone was sharp.

Nathaniel Ferris closed his mouth.

"Do you have any idea how pissed off this makes everyone around you?" Fenway continued. "There's a dead man lying twenty feet away from you, and you're talking about vesting stock options. Options that will be the difference between you making one hundred million dollars or two hundred million dollars next year."

"There's a lot more than—"

"*You will be fine.*" Images of grocery shopping with her mother at nine years old flickered across her mind: the bargains in the cart, the coupon clipping, the normal food she couldn't get. The Sunday evenings when neither she nor her mother ate dinner, and probably the times she didn't see her mother go hungry while she ate. "Seriously, the worst thing that will happen to you is that you'll have to sell the mansion and just live in a normal house. You'd probably be able to sell your Red Sox memorabilia for hundreds of thousands of dollars."

Shock registered first on Nathaniel Ferris's forehead, then cascaded down his face. "I—I don't—"

"It's because you have your whole identity wrapped up in that oil company," Fenway said, trying to will herself into a calm passivity. "Listen, Dad, the last couple of weeks, first with Charlotte being falsely accused, and now you—haven't you been happier connecting with Charlotte rather than your stakeholders?"

Ferris grunted.

"I didn't get your money when I was growing up, and that's okay." Fenway forced a smile onto her face even as more confusion registered on her father's. "You were mad at Mom for leaving and taking me with her and not telling you. I get that. I get that you left me to my own devices to pay for college. It made me resilient, even if I'm up to my eyeballs in debt. And you gave me a way out when I needed it. An apartment I can afford, a job I'm good at, and a chance to put things right with a father I never really knew." She sighed. "But the time and the effort you put in with Charlotte—all the stuff you do that isn't stuff you pay for? That's what I need, too. I don't need the money. I don't need the fancy Porsche or the mansion on the beach. I need to, I don't know, walk through a museum with you. Get burgers at In-N-Out. Talk to you about how my day went. That kind of stuff." She cocked her head.

Her father's eyes and mouth had turned up in disbelief. "You—you didn't get my money when you were growing up?"

"What money? I told you months ago that we had to go on food stamps!"

"I just figured what I was sending wasn't enough."

"Wasn't—" A buzz started in Fenway's brain. "What you were sending? You weren't sending *anything*. Your lawyers made sure of that. Look, I get it—Mom essentially kidnapped me. So she didn't get anything, no alimony, no child support, nothing."

Ferris's eyes went wide. "What do you mean, no child support? I gave your mother ten thousand a month until you turned eighteen!"

"You—you what?" Fenway's voice barely registered.

Her mother, who'd always scrimped and saved and worked two jobs just so they could have a roof over their head. Who, that first year, slept on a bench in the closet that wasn't even big enough for her to stretch out fully. Her mother, who said they'd have to make do with food stamps for a while.

Had Fenway actually *seen* the food stamps?

Her mother, who said being poor was the price to pay for Ferris not pursuing a kidnapping charge.

Who was so proud when they didn't have to miss a meal for a whole month. And then it became a whole year.

Her mother, who always calmed Fenway when she was angry with Nathaniel Ferris.

Her mother, who was so proud of the small house they bought.

"What—what are you saying, Dad?"

"And I don't understand you saying that you went into debt for college. I paid for every class you took—unless there were some your mother didn't tell me about. I paid for that master's program at Seattle U. What did you do with the—" He paused, the realization dawning on his face. "She—she didn't give you any of the money?"

"We didn't *have* any money, Dad! We were poor! I went to school and went into debt so I could get *out* of poverty. So I wouldn't have to live like my mother. Why do you think I—" Her words caught in her throat. If he'd given her mother the money, then what happened to it? All that money, and Fenway had to eat rice and ramen? Hardly ever in new clothes, unless her mother had sold a painting.

"Why didn't you tell me before?" Fenway asked. "All this time, I never thought you sent us anything at all." Ten thousand dollars a month for ten years of child support. That was over a million dollars. And all that money for her education—where the hell did it go?

"I—" Ferris fumbled. He took a deep breath. "You never told me you never got my money. You said you were on food stamps, you said you owed money on your college loans, but you never told me you never got any money at all."

Fenway shook her head. "And you never asked me where it all went?"

Ferris grabbed the back of the chair for support. "Oh, Fenway. Oh, no. No wonder you hate me. No wonder you think I never did anything for you. I'd ask to come see you, but your mother said you didn't want me there."

"What did you think after I told you I was mad at you for missing my graduation?"

"That I misread the situation. That you were being a typical teenager, I guess. Saying you wanted one thing but really wanting something else. You know, saying you were embarrassed of me but secretly wanting me to be there. I figured I just botched it."

"And you thought ten thousand a month wasn't enough to keep us off food stamps?"

Ferris looked uncomfortable. "Well, it's been quite a while since I, uh, did a lot of shopping for myself. I'm used to a certain lifestyle. Maybe I'm a little out of touch."

"A *little* out of touch? Like, you're one of those rich guys who doesn't know how much a gallon of milk costs?"

Ferris looked at the floor. "I don't know what to tell you, Fenway.

I'm sorry. I'm sorry I didn't make sure that everything was happening properly. I'm sorry I gave your mother the checks for your education and didn't pay the tuition directly to the school."

"If you gave my mother the money, then what the hell happened to it? You don't buy a hundred grand worth of art supplies in a year."

Her mother's voice rang in her head. *You haven't seen the price of oil paints lately.*

"Did she have a problem? Drugs, maybe?" That didn't seem right—her mother never seemed high around her. She tried to think back, this time with a clear head. *It's always those that are closest to an addict who never see it.* But Joanne Stevenson Ferris didn't have the cloying cleaning-product smell of meth or the floral metallic scent of cocaine. She didn't have the lethargy of pills or the mania of uppers. Yes, the cigarette stench on her clothes and in her hair that she'd come home with was due to the creative meetings often happening on the smoke breaks that the art director took so frequently, but that was a common job hazard. There was no alcohol on her breath—or rarely, anyway, and only in the evenings.

Ferris spun on his heel and spoke to Charlotte for a moment before returning with a checkbook.

"How much do you owe on your college loans?" he said.

"I don't—I don't want your money, Dad."

"I don't care. I promised I would pay for your college. And I broke the promise. So I'm making up for it."

"I don't know what happened to it—maybe Mom invested it or something, or maybe she—"

"Dammit, Fenway, that money was supposed to be yours for college. The fact that I gave it to the wrong person—it's like going to a restaurant for lunch but accidentally dropping a hundred-dollar bill on the street and watching the wind take it away. I've still got to pay for lunch. I'm not dining and dashing." He opened up the checkbook. "Who do I make it out to?"

Fenway gave her father a frown. "What?"

"The college loan company. Is it all with one organization?"

"Uh—yeah. Education Lending Fund of Washington. ELFW. That's what I write on the checks when I pay."

"How much?"

"I—uh, I don't know the exact amount. It's about ninety-four thousand, I think."

"Ninety-four thousand?"

Fenway grimaced. "Seattle University is pricey."

Ferris dashed off the check and ripped it out, handing it to her. "There you go. ELFW. An even one hundred thousand dollars, because I know you and you tend to lowball bad news."

"You don't have to—"

"I certainly *do* have to." Nathaniel Ferris closed his eyes and pinched the bridge of his nose. McVie sometimes made fun of Fenway for doing the same thing when she was thinking hard—she must have gotten that from him. "Now it makes sense why you were so mad at me for flying the private jet to Sea-Tac to get your car. And for me getting you a new car in the first place."

Fenway's throat was dry.

"Here you are, barely making your college loan payments, and I'm burning thirty grand every time my plane takes off."

"I'm sorry, Dad—"

"There's nothing to be sorry about," he said, but his voice broke. "I'm glad I found out before I went to jail so I could at least put *that* right."

Fenway had no idea if her father was lying about her child support or the college tuition, but she wasn't going to argue about finally getting enough money to pay off the college loans. If she had to do it all over again, maybe she wouldn't have gotten the expensive master's in forensic nursing, but it was certainly relevant to her current job.

"I—uh, thank you, Dad," she said.

He nodded and turned away.

Fenway looked down at the hundred-thousand-dollar check in her hand and suppressed an urge to vomit.

CHAPTER EIGHTEEN

FENWAY WALKED THROUGH THE GALLERY GATE AND BACK TO THE judge's desk. Piper scrolled through a spreadsheet on the screen but stopped when she glanced at Fenway's face.

"What's wrong with you? You look like you've seen a ghost."

"I don't—" Fenway coughed and cleared her throat. "Can you—can you look up some stuff for me? You're all about tracking payments and stuff, right?"

"I wouldn't put it that eloquently, but yeah." Piper smirked, but her smile faltered when she saw Fenway wasn't laughing.

"My father says he paid my mom ten grand a month for child support. Starting about twenty years ago. But, uh, I don't think I got a dime. Can you see if my mom received any payments like that from any of my father's accounts? And—uh, if she did, can you tell me, uh—you know..."

There was silence between them, looming like a cold shadow.

"You'd like to know what happened to it?" Piper finished.

"Yeah."

Piper shifted in her seat.

"Oh. You're uncomfortable with that."

Piper held up her hand. "I *would* help you. I really would. But I work for your father now. I can't use his bank account information like that."

Fenway frowned and sighed.

"I mean," Piper continued, "if the shoe was on the other foot, wouldn't you be pissed off if your employee did something like that?"

"No, I get it, Piper. You're right." Fenway massaged her own neck with her right hand. "I could get you my mom's information, though, right? Bank account numbers, that kind of thing?"

"Sure, that's fine. I won't even charge you my special Ferris 'Friends and Family' hourly rates." She smiled.

Fenway tilted her head up and stared at the elegant brushed-nickel lighting fixtures over the courtroom. Whoever designed the courtroom had studied Frank Lloyd Wright's designs closely. The room had a stateliness to it, but also a certain art déco panache.

"Seriously, Fenway? Not even a tiny little smile?"

Fenway put her palms on the desk and leaned forward. "Sorry, Piper. I—I just don't know what to believe right now. I thought my mom..."

Silence for a moment. Then Fenway hung her head.

She felt a hand on her shoulder.

"I'm sorry, Fenway," Piper murmured, and Fenway leaned into Piper's hand. "You, uh, you need anything?"

Fenway scoffed. "I need another clue, Piper. I need to solve this— not just Cygnus's murder, but the entire thing. I need to know who's behind the money laundering. I need to know who paid Peter Grayheath to kill my professor at Western Washington. And I need to know who's making it look like my father is responsible for everything." She sighed. "And I'm stuck in this courtroom without most of my tools. Without being able to talk to witnesses."

"Sorry."

"It probably wouldn't matter anyway. Everywhere I turn is a dead end. I thought maybe with the right leverage on Professor Cygnus, we'd get a name."

Piper lowered her voice. "We got Jessica Marquez's spreadsheet with all the transactions into the scholarship account. And I found a way into the master ledger. I'm checking and correlating and doing all the things I'm good at. Something will shake out, Fenway. You've got to believe that."

Fenway shut her eyes. For years, her mother had done her best, had always put Fenway's welfare and well-being first.

Except now there was a million dollars missing from her childhood.

Her mother had let her go to bed hungry. Not just once. Not just twice. Over and over and over again, for months.

"Yeah," Fenway said, opening her eyes. "Something will shake out. I've got to believe that."

"I did get some information on Heissner's Navy career."

"Anything interesting?"

"A couple of items, actually. He spent the first part of his naval career in Indonesia but requested a transfer in the mid-nineties."

"Do you know why?"

Piper shrugged. "Those records are sealed."

"Sealed?"

Piper raised her hands. "Doesn't necessarily mean anything. I just don't have access."

"Can you get it?"

"Not today."

"Anything else?"

"When he was honorably discharged from the Navy, he started working at Petrogrande too. Not their Western Division, but it looks like he spent most of his time in South America.

Fenway perked up. "Does it say if he worked in La Mitad?"

"I haven't gotten that far—and I've got a lot of research on everyone else. He landed at Ferris Energy about five years ago, after the Western takeover. That's barely scratching the surface."

Fenway put her chin in her palm. "I wonder how many other employees of Ferris Energy have a background with the Navy."

"I'm looking to see who at Ferris Energy has connections to La

Mitad. I started with their personnel files, but I'll go through their personal histories too—what I can find online, at any rate." Piper turned back to her laptop. "And I'll see if McVie has an update for us."

"I suppose I could interview Xavier. He's the only one I haven't talked to yet. Well—Rose, but she's not talking to anyone."

A ding from Piper's laptop.

"What's that?" Fenway asked. "Did McVie respond? Can I text him?"

Piper shook her head slowly. "No—that's weird. It says my last message wasn't delivered."

"Maybe McVie is somewhere he can't get a signal."

"Maybe." Piper typed and stared at the screen. "I still have internet access, so that's not it." Then her face fell. "Oh. No, I don't. It just—it just went offline. So it's not him, it's me." She craned her neck around to the back of the laptop and checked all the connections and adapters. "Everything *looks* okay," she murmured. "I better make sure." She pushed her chair out and was under the desk a moment later.

"Hey," Fenway said, "do you need me to pull on any cords up here or anything?"

"No," Piper said from under the desk. "You go ahead. I bet the problem isn't even in this room."

"Holler if you need me." Fenway made the trek around the witness stand again, and an image came into her mind of a cartoon character wearing a track into the carpet. "I put the over-under at twenty more times," Fenway mumbled to herself. She made eye contact with Xavier, who was leaning back in his chair. He sat up and flexed his fingers in both hands.

Suddenly, Cynthia Schimmelhorn was in front of her. "Okay, Coroner, you're the closest to being in charge here. It's almost noon. I can't speak for everyone else, but we need to get out of here. I've already missed several meetings. Obviously the sheriff's department won't find the murderer today, and we haven't even had water. I'm now very glad I went to the ladies' room before the arraignment began this morning." She motioned toward Judith Cygnus. "You have a sick woman in here who's being kept from her medication. You have university students who are missing class. A professor who can't teach today." She pointed a finger that came close to Fenway's chin, and her voice was firm and loud. "You need to let us out."

"Do I look like *I* want us to be stuck here?" Fenway said. "I'm going crazy in here too. I want to get back to my desk where I have internet access and a phone where I can actually do research. I want to get the evidence I've collected over to the lab in San Miguelito. I want to get back to work. I'm not catching a killer in here, that's for sure. And I want to go to Dos Milagros and get a couple of lengua tacos. Maybe even three or four." Fenway shook her head. "You think I have some magic wand I can wave and unlock the door? Maybe have some sort of space-time-continuum portal appear in the wall so everyone can get out?" She turned toward the wall and held her hands up in clawlike shapes. "Abracadabra! Shazam! Electric boogaloo! Presto-change-o!"

She stared at the wall for a moment, then turned back to Cynthia. "Sorry, Ms. Schimmelhorn. Must be the electromagnetic paint interfering with my magic. I can direct you to a complaint form when we get out of here."

"There's no need to take that tone with me."

"Oh, but it's fine for you to take it with me?"

Schimmelhorn glared at Fenway.

"You think if Sheriff McVie thought it was safe for us," Fenway said, "he'd keep us in here just for his own amusement?"

Schimmelhorn shook her head. "You seem to be able to contact the sheriff. So contact him and tell him we all need to be let out."

"The internet's down," Fenway said. "We have no cell service in here, we have no way to get out, and now the internet's down. I don't know how long it'll be out."

"I have no use for you anymore," Schimmelhorn said coldly.

"Oh, that hurts my feelings," Fenway snapped. "Another nice rich white lady who has *no use for me.*"

Her father's voice sounded next to her. "That's enough, Fenway."

Fenway turned to her father, standing next to her. "Oh—now you decide to participate, Dad? What do you care? She's already told you Ferris Energy is firing you. She doesn't care if you're guilty or not. The other shoe has already dropped. The fat lady has sung."

"Please," came a voice from behind them. "I need my medicine."

Fenway turned around. Judith Cygnus was holding onto the back of a chair for balance. "I'm supposed to take it within a very specific time frame. It's important."

"Are you sure you don't have it with you?"

Judith shook her head. "It's in a case on the passenger seat."

That's right—Judith had said she'd left it in her car earlier. "I'm sorry," Fenway said. "I don't have any way—"

Leda Nedermeyer jumped out of her seat and ran down the center aisle to the double doors. She pushed the handle and threw her body against it with a loud thump. The doors didn't budge. "*Let me out!*" she screamed. "Let me out!" She threw her body against the doors again. "Get me out of here!"

Xavier jumped out of his seat and ran to the double doors, grabbing Professor Nedermeyer by the shoulders before she could heave herself into the doors again. He spoke into her ear in low tones as the professor was still shaking, and slowly, Professor Nedermeyer calmed down. Xavier continued to speak quietly and calmly to her as he led her to a seat in the back row.

As if choreographed, everyone's head swiveled from staring at Professor Nedermeyer to staring at Fenway.

Fenway cleared her throat. "Well," she said, "*that* ought to get their attention."

Judith Cygnus sat down heavily in the chair behind her.

"I hope you think of *something*," Schimmelhorn hissed, then turned to walk to the last row.

Fenway stood for a moment, her potential interviewee still talking with Leda Nedermeyer. She took a step forward, then hesitated. Was there really any need to talk to Xavier? What could he possibly tell her that she didn't already know?

She mentally kicked herself. *Anyone* could provide more insight.

Hadn't she thought the same thing about Amanda? And hadn't Amanda been the one to provide the scholarship fund's master spreadsheet, the one where all the bodies were buried?

Xavier stood up and hurried over to Fenway. "Miss Stevenson—something's wrong with Professor Nedermeyer."

Fenway rushed over to Leda Nedermeyer, Xavier following close behind. The professor looked punch drunk, her head not quite staying upright as she tried to track who was in front of her.

"Professor," Fenway said, kneeling in front of her, "are you all right?"

"I—I will be fine." Nedermeyer slurred her words and tried to push Fenway away, but missed her shoulder completely. She regained her balance and stared Fenway in the eyes. "It's nothing. I just need to eat, is all."

Fenway's stomach growled in empathy, and she ignored it. She remembered that Nedermeyer had dry-swallowed something a couple of hours ago. "Have you taken any medication today?"

"I'm perfectly fine. I don't need any more medication." Nedermeyer's pupils were dilated, her eyelids heavy.

"No, no, Professor. I meant, did you take medication *already?*"

"Well," Nedermeyer said haughtily, if unsteadily, "you have to understand that this situation is stressful. It makes me anxious." She leaned forward, her elbows on her knees, and this seemed to stabilize her a little more. "I'm sure my doctor would understand if I needed to take an additional dose or two."

"Or *two?*" Fenway leaned over to Xavier. "Go get Professor Nedermeyer's purse and bring it here."

"You're looking for medication?"

"Yes. Anti-anxiety meds or something—she had a couple of prescription bottles in her purse when I went through it earlier. Then I'll know what I'm dealing with. Not many of these meds are supposed to make you loopy like this."

"Loopy?" Xavier asked, grinning. "Is that the technical term?"

Fenway narrowed her eyes. "Just get the purse, Xavier. And hurry."

Xavier dropped the smile from his face and rushed off to get Leda's purse.

"Professor, what are you taking?"

"I'll tell you what I'm taking," Nedermeyer said, snapping to lucidity. "I'm taking too much bullshit from everyone, is what I'm taking." Then her eyes unfocused, and she giggled.

"That's a good one, Professor," Fenway said. "But I'd like to know. Is it Zoloft? Prozac?"

"Oh, I *bet* you'd like to know. They'd fetch a pretty penny on the black market. No sir, I'm not going to tell you."

Black market? "Dammit," Fenway murmured, "it's divenamine." She pushed herself up from her kneeling position and stood up. "Okay, Professor, it's time to go for a walk."

Xavier appeared at her side, holding a beige plastic bottle with a white cap, a telltale prescription label taped around it. "I found two pill bottles. Ator—atorvastatin?"

"For high cholesterol."

"And this one is, uh, divenda—no, divena—"

"Divenamine," Fenway said, taking the professor's hand in hers and lightly clapping her palm across the knuckles. "And it's got a ton of side effects. And if she took more than three of these in the last eight hours, and I think she did, we're looking at a potential comatose patient if she goes to sleep."

"What?" Xavier's jaw dropped.

"I don't have time to explain the whole list of symptoms right now," Fenway said. "We just have to keep her moving until she starts to come around."

"That's weird."

"I've walked enough overdosing patients through hospital corridors to know." Fenway tried to look in Nedermeyer's eyes, but her lids kept drooping. "With her size, and if she only took a triple dose, a half hour should do it. Moving around will get it out of her bloodstream."

Xavier nodded. "Sounds a lot like what you're supposed to do if someone takes too much Dive Bomb."

"Oh—if you know Dive Bomb, this is essentially the same stuff, only in official pharmaceutical form. And you know what happened to some of those kids."

"Yeah, but not the coma thing. I had a kid at my high school stab someone while he was on it."

"Right." Fenway nodded. "It can trigger violent reactions as well as imitating the symptoms of drunkenness. Doesn't destroy the liver quite as badly as years of heavy drinking, but the unconsciousness after an overdose can be worse than alcohol poisoning."

"What do we need to do?"

"Get her up and walking."

"Okay, Professor," Xavier said loudly. "Let's get up and move around."

"I don't feel like it," Nedermeyer said, sticking out her bottom lip. "I want to take a nap."

"Nope," Fenway said, sitting in the chair to Leda's right and placing the professor's arm around her shoulder.

"Let me help," Xavier said, moving to Leda's left, wrapping his arm around her back. "You've got stuff to do, don't you?" He looked up at Fenway. "Is there any more water?"

"I'll check," Fenway said. "Do you have her?"

"I got her. She's light."

Fenway rushed through the gate and up the steps next to the witness stand, where there were three sets of cabinet doors next to the walkie-talkies. The first was empty, as was the second.

In the third, she found two flats of bottled water with heavy plastic wrap.

She pulled the first flat out and lifted it on top of the back counter. Pushing a finger through the plastic on the top, she started to tear a hole—then she stopped.

She ran to the judge's bench and pulled a black pen and an old receipt from her purse.

"You need anything?" asked Piper, looking down from her computer.

"I'll tell you later." This was crazy—but it might work.

She made the hole larger and pulled a dozen bottles out. She looked over her shoulder, but no one was watching her. Uncapping the pen, she debated for a moment, then marked eleven of the twelve bottles, putting them back and arranging them to look like they hadn't been removed. She made the same marks on the receipt—and then a letter next to each mark. L, R, B, K, W, E, S, M, N, X, A.

"It's like Murder Wheel of Fortune," she said under her breath.

She hefted the flat of water and held it steady with one arm. She steeled herself, took a breath, and then descended the steps.

"We found some water!" she announced as she pushed the gallery gate open.

"Great," Xavier said. "Professor—why don't you take some water?"

Fenway hooked her fingertips under the screw top of the first bottle. "Here you go."

Leda grabbed it out of Fenway's hand. "Oh, thank you, dear—I'm so thirsty." She struggled with the cap.

Fenway held her hand out. "I can help—"

"No, no, don't take my water. I'm perfectly capable of doing it myself."

Xavier shook his head. "Come on, Professor. We've got to walk some of this off."

"Would anyone else like some water?" Fenway said, and Bryce Heissner practically snatched a bottle out of Fenway's hand as she pulled it off the flat.

Fenway passed out water to each of them. Amanda politely declined, and Xavier was too busy with Professor Nedermeyer, but Fenway returned to the open cabinet with nine fewer bottles. She set the flat down on top of the cabinet and watched everyone open the water bottles and drink.

"What are you up to?" Piper whispered, appearing at her side.

Fenway chuckled. "I'll tell you in a minute." She watched as Nedermeyer tripped over her feet, and she hurried down to the center aisle.

"I didn't mean to be the other woman," Nedermeyer was saying as

Fenway steadied her on the opposite side. "I just—he was just too good. I never met anyone I could talk to like that."

"I get it," Xavier said, taking a few tentative steps with the professor. "Don't worry, no one thinks you're a ho."

"Ha!" Nedermeyer said loudly, taking a couple of unsure steps forward. "Me! A ho! I'd be lucky to be considered a *cougar*."

Xavier winced at the term. He cautiously walked forward, trying not to step on Nedermeyer's toes.

"Yeah," Fenway said, "we all have lapses in judgment."

"Right," Xavier said, "I know that. I'm not naïve enough to think I'm the only one who's ever screwed up."

Fenway laughed as she tried to move Nedermeyer's arm to a more comfortable position. "Yeah, well, I remember being twenty—it wasn't that long ago—and thinking everyone was judging me for every single mistake I made. The truth is, people just don't care that much, and the people who *do* watch you will criticize everything you do anyway, whether it's a mistake or not."

"My mom says being a grownup sucks," Xavier said

"Yeah, it does," Fenway admitted. "And being able to eat cake for breakfast doesn't make it a fair trade."

"I *like* cake," Professor Nedermeyer said. "But not carrot cake. That's not *real* cake."

"What's your favorite cake, Professor?" Xavier asked, again in the loud voice.

"She can hear you, Xavier," Fenway murmured. "You can use your inside voice."

"Sorry."

"My *very* favorite cake," Nedermeyer declared, "is a snickerdoodle cake."

"Snickerdoodle?" Xavier asked.

"That's what I said."

"Isn't a snickerdoodle a cookie, not a cake?"

"Well," Nedermeyer slurred, watching her feet as they shuffled forward, "it's true that a snickerdoodle *is* a cookie, but it's—it's quite a delicious, tasty cake as well." Her head rolled slightly. "You know, I had it when Virgil and I took a trip several years ago. Wonderful. To the Oregon Shakespeare Festival."

"I hear that's a great festival," Fenway said.

"The cake," Leda proclaimed, soldiering on, "is made by a bakery just south of the Oregon border. It is a delightful vanilla almond sponge in three layers, filled and frosted with cinnamon buttercream and dusted with brown sugar. Virg and I purchased one on the way up, and we demolished it before the second act of *Henry V.* Just before leaving Ashland, we stopped at a small restaurant that specialized in wild game, and I almost choked on the buckshot that was still in my pheasant."

"Oh, that sounds awful," Fenway said, commiserating.

"So Virg promised me another snickerdoodle cake on our return trip. True to his word, we ordered another on the drive home, this time with a white chocolate ganache, but I think the cinnamon buttercream is the superior choice." Her eyes turned dreamy, and she stopped moving her feet. "The bakery closed last year. It pains me to think I'll never eat another snickerdoodle cake like that again."

"No one else makes it, huh?" Xavier said, gently prodding her forward.

"Really, Mr. Gonsalves, it's not that uncommon." Leda giggled again. "I hope you don't keep that *ridiculous* new surname of yours."

"You mean changing my name to Xavier Go?"

Leda sputtered with laughter and nearly tripped. "I don't care what your agent told you. It makes me think of, well, you know."

Xavier arched an eyebrow.

"*The toilet,*" Leda said in a stage whisper. "'Oh, look, Xavier has to *go.*'"

"You said there were lots of side effects with this medication?" Xavier murmured to Fenway. "Is 'turning into a six-year-old' listed?"

"Keep moving, Professor," Fenway said.

"I'm not a *child,*" the professor said.

Fenway turned her face so Nedermeyer wouldn't see the grin touch her lips. She glanced up at the judge's bench and Piper beckoned her. "Oh—something must have come up in our research."

"I've got her," Xavier said. "If you want to go be a detective again."

"Remember, keep her walking until she comes around. Then she won't be a coma risk."

"What if she wants to go to sleep after she comes around?"

"That should be fine. Just not while she's acting drunk." Fenway dropped Leda's arm and took two strides—then ADA Kim blocked her path.

"Hi, Jennifer—" Fenway started.

"You are being far too chummy with your father," Kim snapped. "Do you know how many people watched you take a check from him about ten minutes ago?"

"That wasn't—"

"What? That wasn't *what*, Fenway? That wasn't for looking the other way when you found out he hired someone to kill Professor Cygnus, just like he hired someone to kill your professor in Bellingham?"

Fenway set her jaw. "You're not even making sense. Talk about going after someone without evidence!"

Jennifer Kim pursed her lips.

"Yes, that's what I said, Jennifer. The fingerprint doesn't match my father's, so now you're throwing wild accu—"

"They're not wild accusations. He did it once, he can—"

"This will be easily resolved once we try to match that fingerprint. Look, the gun and the bullet are both in the safe right now. I don't have them—"

"You're the one who knows the combination, Fenway! Of course you have access to them." She tapped her foot and screwed up her mouth. "And taking a payment from him in front of everyone? Do you have any idea how guilty this makes you look? How guilty it makes *him* look?"

"Fathers give their adult children gifts every day," Fenway said, backing away from Kim.

"Don't you walk away from me, Fenway! This looks like a breach of ethics! You just got elected, but don't think this will get swept under the rug."

"I've got an investigation to conduct," Fenway growled. "If you don't think a father can pay for his daughter's education—"

Kim gasped. "So you admit it? You admit you took a payment for going easy on him?"

"I did no such thing," Fenway snapped. "He's owed me that money for years."

"So—rich guy finally pays off his debt to his daughter if she doesn't interview him too harshly?"

Fenway clenched and unclenched her fists. She closed her eyes and stepped outside herself, and for a moment saw herself take the check from her father.

How incredibly *stupid*. And how horrible that must have looked to anyone else in the courtroom.

"Okay—okay, Jennifer. I get how it must have looked, but I swear, we weren't talking about anything but family stuff. You know I didn't see him for twenty years. He'd made a promise to pay for my school to my mother, and he didn't. That's all."

"I don't give a damn, Fenway!" Jennifer's voice raised, and a few of the others in the courtroom were starting to pay attention. "You took a payment from a murder suspect."

Fenway looked across the courtroom. Everyone but Leda had their eyes on her.

Jennifer Kim folded her arms. "You need to recuse yourself now—or I'm opening an investigation into you accepting bribes."

CHAPTER NINETEEN

EVERY NERVE IN FENWAY'S BODY WAS ON EDGE, AND HER BREATHS came shallow and short. ADA Kim was not a tall woman, but *though she be but little, she is fierce*, as Shakespeare would say.

Fenway drew herself up to her full height. "There's no official investigation here, Jennifer," she said as calmly as she could. "And once those doors are open, I'm more than happy to dump this murder case on someone else." She pointed at Professor Virgil Cygnus's dead body, still in front of the defense table, draped with her father's suit jacket. "I made a determination—hours ago, that you were party to—that the shooter was on the defense side of the courtroom. You've accused me of being the shooter, when I was so close to you that you would have seen me with a weapon. You accused me of taking money from my father so he wouldn't be the shooter—when he was clearly nowhere near where he had to be."

"But we're all supposed to just take your word for it?"

"I'm a sworn law enforcement officer," Fenway said. "You know me, Jennifer. You know my word means more to me than a bribe, or ensuring a good relationship with my father. He been pissed off at me for just about every arrest I've made since I've been appointed, so there's no reason for you to think I'd just blindly support him."

ADA Kim was silent.

"Yes, Jennifer, you are absolutely correct that taking a check from my father in the courtroom right now was an idiotic thing to do. I don't know what I can do about that except tell everyone here that he'd made a promise to pay for my college, and he didn't. And he didn't realize it until I blew up at him about ten minutes ago, so he cut me a check."

Evans Dahl raised his hand. "I'm not a fan of yours, Miss Stevenson, but I was close enough to hear the two of you, and I can vouch for the content of the argument. And I'd be willing to swear that the check wasn't offered as a bribe." He paused. "Not unless you've got a very complicated con going on." He looked out of the corner of his eye at Fenway's father. "Which, I suppose, I wouldn't put past our dear Mr. Ferris."

Kim was silent.

Fenway turned around slowly, still feeling the daggers from Kim's glare digging into her back. The path between the gallery gate and the witness stand seemed to take a month to navigate, and it felt like cement in her shoes with each of the three steps to the dais.

"Hey," Piper said. "Sorry about that."

"Don't worry about it," Fenway said, even though she had a horrible feeling in the pit of her stomach. "Listen, before I forget—did you hear me say Leda Nedermeyer is taking divenamine for anxiety?"

Piper nodded. "I didn't hear exactly, but yes, it was something like that."

"It's got some serious side effects for a certain percentage of the population. Violent outbursts, for one."

"You think Professor Nedermeyer could have shot and killed Professor Cygnus?"

"She has motive if you don't take her grandiose love for him at face value," Fenway said. "With the medication's side effects, it's possible."

"But—what about the premeditation? Contacting the audio

contractor to have them hide the gun? What about the fact that her prints didn't match?"

"I know, I know," Fenway said. "Just—see if you can find any information on violent acts when people are on divenamine, would you?"

"As soon as the internet comes back up."

"It's still down? I thought for sure you had something for me that you just found on the internet."

Piper stared out over the courtroom as if surveying land. "I didn't find it on the internet; I found it in the ledgers. I have two numbers that don't match that should. And I want to know why."

"What?"

"Okay." Piper looked down at the monitor and pointed. "Money laundering makes monetary gains look like legal transactions, which means people pay taxes on that money, right?"

"Right."

"So—tell me why, in this master spreadsheet, Central Auto Body has a number under 'taxes paid' that's a full seventy thousand less than the check the Franchise Tax Board received?"

"Isn't one of the spreadsheets the public one and one the *real* ledger?"

"No. This *is* the master ledger. It says there was a tax payment made. But this number and the amount the tax board got? Seventy thousand dollars difference."

"Seventy thousand exactly?"

"No. Seventy-one thousand, four hundred and six."

Fenway's mind was blank. "I have no idea."

"That's how they caught Al Capone, you know. Tax fraud."

"Right." Fenway stared at the spreadsheet over Piper's shoulder, as if the numerals would rearrange themselves to magically provide the answer.

Piper rubbed her chin. "It just seems strange because this whole money laundering scheme was put into place to *avoid* things like tax fraud."

"Could it be a genuine mistake? Someone using the wrong calculation?"

Piper sat up. "Or maybe someone was trying to steal money." She clicked on the screen, and the spreadsheets zoomed back into a grid with about twenty spreadsheets in small windows on the screen. "Okay, what do we know so far? We know that the spreadsheet from Central Auto is supposed to be accurate. But it's not. Who was supposed to ensure that they were accurate?"

Fenway nodded. "Rose Morgan. But she fell in love with Domingo Velásquez. And now he's fled the country."

"Right. And he hasn't taken any Central Auto Body money to do it."

Fenway snapped her fingers. "Piper—you said he got money out of an ATM. Can you find out how much that account has in it?"

"Well—no, not at this very moment because the internet's down. But when he got money, it had one hundred sixty thousand and change."

Fenway paused. "That's a lot more than seventy thousand."

Piper smiled. "I've got it." She clicked on two of the spreadsheet graphics. They looked identical. Piper clicked on the tab labeled RECIPIENTS on the first spreadsheet, and did clicked the same tab on the second. She scrolled to the bottom on each.

"Hmm," she said. "I guess I was wrong."

"What is it?"

"Well, I thought the scholarship spreadsheet—the one with all the fake student names on it—would have a different number of entries." She pointed to the screen. "But look. Exactly 1,428 in both."

"Why did you think they'd be different?"

"Because I *think* Rose Morgan and Domingo Velásquez stole about two hundred twenty-five thousand dollars, give or take. If they planned to escape to Mexico, that would keep them comfortable for a while."

"But the missing amount is seventy thousand."

"Aha—but that's the difference in taxes paid. I thought Rose might have made an extra contribution to the scholarship fund—it's a nonprofit—which would have reduced Central Auto Body's tax burden. If you donate two hundred twenty-five thousand dollars, you don't pay taxes on it."

"Then where did that money go?"

"Well, that's just it. I expected three, maybe four, additional students in the scholarship fund in the spreadsheet from the file that Amanda gave us, as opposed to the spreadsheet we had before." Piper shook her head. "But there aren't. Look—1,428 rows of names in both."

Fenway nodded. "There's got to be another way. Maybe each of the student names were issued an extra amount of money?"

Piper scrolled up. "Nope. The same in all of them—$74,580."

"Holy shit. That's how much it costs to go to Nidever?"

"Yeah. That's not just tuition, though. That's room and board, a stipend for books, class materials, and all the fees, too—health center, campus rideshare, everything like that."

"That's still really expensive."

"Almost no one goes to Nidever without some sort of scholarship, Fenway. That's probably why no one blinked at a scholarship fund that's worth so much."

"It just seems insane. My *master's* program wasn't even that much."

Piper shrugged. "It's gone up since I applied, but it was pretty expensive even six years ago. I got a scholarship that paid for half the tuition, but it was still too expensive for me to accept."

Fenway squinted at the screen. "Hang on a second," she said. "Start at the bottom and scroll up. Slowly. So we can read the row numbers."

"Why?"

"Because I want to see if there are any hidden rows in the second spreadsheet."

Confusion showed on Piper's face. "If you hide row 25 in a spreadsheet, Fenway, it skips from 24 to 26. That'll be obvious."

"That's right, but if you hide row 2576 and it skips from 2575 to 2577, it's not so noticeable." She pointed to the spreadsheet. "I bet there are four hidden rows in different spots in the spreadsheet, and I bet you wouldn't have noticed if I hadn't said anything."

Piper went up to the *View* menu and selected *Unhide all rows*. Then she began to scroll, squinting at the sheet.

One row was blank with zeroes in the total. A thousand rows below that, another blank row. Then another after more scrolling. And another. Four in all.

"See? They added the rows in the middle instead of at the end—and then in the version sent back to—oh, I don't know, let's just call it 'headquarters'—they just zeroed those lines out then hid the rows."

"It's an interesting tactic," Piper murmured. "They took money from the Central Auto Body account and *donated it* to the scholarship fund, then dispersed that money to—I guess it was fake students."

"And those students had accounts that Domingo Velásquez had access to." Fenway rubbed her hands together. "So let's see if there are hidden rows."

"Match those blank rows to the ones in the other spreadsheet," Fenway said.

"Then we'll have the names on the accounts—and maybe we'll be able to see who found out about the fake students."

Fenway shook her head. "Skimming money from a laundering operation," she said. "There really is no honor among thieves."

Piper clicked on the names, copying each one into a note.

"I've got the four names," Piper said. "As soon as the internet is back up, we can cross-reference these bank account numbers—and maybe if Domingo Velásquez hasn't drained all of them yet, we can freeze these assets. Make him come back home. Or at least, make it so Rose Morgan can't join him."

Fenway nodded, looking across the courtroom. Judith Cygnus was sitting down, slumped to the side, the half-drunk bottle of water in her hand. She looked pale. "Mrs. Cygnus isn't looking too good," Fenway said. "When you get internet access back, make sure you tell McVie that she needs her medicine—maybe there's a way he can get it from her car."

"I've told him she needs her medicine—McVie said he's trying to get the doors open. I don't know why they're still locked."

"Anyone finished with their water bottle yet?"

"Oh—a couple." Piper looked to the back of the room. "Heissner looks like he's done with his. So does Rose."

"This might work after all," Fenway said. "Come with me." She walked over to the cabinet in back of the bench, emptying the remaining bottles from the flat, just leaving the cardboard and the hard plastic wrap with a gaping hole in the top. "Grab as many bottles as you can."

"What, you take the empty flat and I try to juggle eight bottles of water?"

Fenway shot Piper a look of warning. "Trust me, Piper. Take as many bottles as you can."

"Do you have something up your sleeve?" Piper asked, piling seven bottles into her arms.

"Absolutely." Fenway turned and walked down the steps. "Anyone need more water?"

"Me," said Leda Nedermeyer, tripping up the center aisle with Xavier supporting her. She dropped her empty plastic bottle into the hole in the cardboard flat Fenway carried and took a second bottle out of Piper's arms.

"I'm fine for now, thank you," said Cynthia Schimmelhorn, slipping her empty bottle inside the plastic. A few people took another bottle —Judith Cygnus, Nathaniel Ferris, and Amanda Kohl. Rose Morgan nodded in thanks and returned her empty bottle to the cardboard flat, then turned and sat in the back row in the corner. Fenway watched her slouch in her seat as everyone else put their bottles in the flat as well.

"You didn't touch any of those," Piper whispered to Fenway as they turned back up the aisle.

Fenway nodded. "Excellent observation, Piper." They walked through the gallery gate and then up the steps around the witness stand to the dais.

"My heart was beating really fast," Piper said. "I was afraid someone would figure out what we were doing."

"Yeah, I could have gotten in trouble with ADA Kim. Again."

Fenway put the cardboard tray full of bottles on the floor and opened the fingerprint kit.

"No," Piper hissed. "Not yet."

"Not yet?"

"Not unless you want the smell of the fingerprint dust to give us away." Piper paused. "Wait a few minutes, and then go find something else you can fingerprint in front of everyone, so it doesn't look like we just grabbed everyone's water bottle and then started fingerprinting *something.* People will put two and two together very quickly."

"Right. Good call."

"If Rose's fingerprints are on the gun—"

Fenway smirked. "We didn't get Rose's prints, or Jennifer's. And Evans Dahl was the one who made a stink about it."

Piper's eyes widened. "That's how you can get the bottle fingerprinting done without calling attention to it. Use me."

Fenway furrowed her brow. "Didn't I get your prints earlier?"

"Yes, you did, but *Jennifer* doesn't know that, does she? I'm surprised ADA Kim complained about your father and Charlotte and insisted on doing those herself, but didn't mention me." Piper drummed her fingers on the desk. "Actually—I'm *really* surprised by that. Why didn't she?"

A chill ran down Fenway's spine. "Oh no."

"What?"

"Maybe—maybe Jennifer Kim doesn't want to call attention to the fact that *she* hasn't had her fingerprints taken either."

Piper cocked her head and sat down in front of her laptop. "But that doesn't make any sense. She couldn't have shot him. She was standing right next to him."

Fenway nodded. "I know. But maybe—maybe the killer had gloves on, and Jennifer's the one who hid the gun in the first place?"

"No one had gloves on when the shooting happened."

"Maybe someone did, and I just didn't see it."

Piper shook her head. "You went through all the purses, briefcases, and pockets of everyone in this room except for Rose."

"You're right." Fenway took the seat next to Piper. "Can you think of any other reason that ADA Kim wouldn't suggest that you need to be fingerprinted?"

Piper shrugged. "Maybe she thought I had."

"Well, *she* didn't take your fingerprints, so she would have assumed that I did. And she made a huge fuss over me taking my father's prints—she even took his prints herself."

"True—but I don't have the money your father has. Maybe she figured you could only get corrupted by familial bonds and a pile of cash."

Fenway blinked. The information refused to organize itself in her head. Piper was just as likely to take cash from Nathaniel Ferris as Fenway was. The only thing that made sense was that Jennifer Kim didn't want her fingerprints taken. That might have even been the reason she volunteered to print half the people in the room—so that she wouldn't have to give hers.

She was lost in thought and missed what Piper said. "Oh—sorry, Piper. I was in my own little world. What did you say?"

"I said you should go tell ADA Kim that you haven't taken my fingerprints. Maybe say that you know she has trust issues with you and offer for her to take the fingerprints so it doesn't look shady. Something like that. Then you can come up here to run fingerprint tests on the water bottles, and it won't look so suspicious."

Fenway nodded. "I suppose that might work."

"And if she hears that you're fingerprinting me, that'll give her another opportunity to volunteer to fingerprint herself."

"That's smart," Fenway said, grinning. "You'll be a detective yet."

Piper rolled her eyes.

"Should I have Jennifer come up here? She can watch me finger-print you."

Piper considered for a moment. "I think that's the only way to do it. Otherwise, you'll have to get the kit back here again, right? And that might raise some people's suspicions."

"I don't have to take the whole kit. We could just go down there with the ink pad and the fingerprint cards."

"I'd actually rather have her come up here. This is starting to feel like my home court."

Fenway nodded and stood up. ADA Kim sat about halfway down the gallery seats with her elbows on her knees, leaning forward, covering her face with her hands.

"Jennifer?" Fenway called. ADA Kim didn't move.

We're all going a little stir crazy. When the even-keeled Jennifer Kim starts losing it, I know we're in trouble.

"Jennifer?" Fenway called, a little louder.

This time, ADA Kim raised her head, then looked left and right, and finally up to the judge's bench. Fenway beckoned her.

Kim pointed to herself, and Fenway nodded.

"Think we can pull this off?" Piper whispered.

"I believe in you," Fenway whispered back. Piper elbowed her in the side.

Jennifer Kim walked through the gallery gate and started to turn to her right, toward the defense table, and then flinched at the sight of Professor Cygnus's body. *It's bordering on cruel to leave him in here like that.* Kim turned left and walked around the witness stand and up the steps.

"You okay?" Fenway asked as the ADA approached.

"When are we getting out of here?" Jennifer asked. "I don't know how much more of this I can take."

"We've lost internet," Piper said. "So I can't get in touch with McVie."

"There's a spot in the nook where I got signal for a couple of minutes," Fenway said, "but then I lost it."

Jennifer took a deep breath. "Maybe I'll try going in there. See if I can get a signal."

"I asked you up here," Fenway said, "because we didn't get Piper's prints. She's agreed to get fingerprinted, but since you're aware of the close working relationship Piper and I have, I thought you'd want to be here when I take her prints and when I compare it against the print on the gun."

Jennifer nodded. "Yeah, okay. Then you'll check for internet access again?"

Fenway cocked her head and looked at Jennifer. "Are you okay? You need more water?"

Kim shook her head. "No. I'm just—I'm just getting a little cabin fever. I'm hungry, too, so maybe it's low blood sugar."

Fenway's stomach rumbled in empathy. "Yeah, I hear that." She opened the kit, then set out the fingerprint cards and the ink pad. "Let's see if this takes your mind off everything." She paused. "Hey— you know, breathing exercises always calm me down when I'm stressed out. Deep breaths, focus on counting to ten in, and then ten out."

Jennifer nodded. "Right. Yeah." She closed her eyes and inhaled, then breathed out. Fenway didn't imagine she got much past the count of five.

"Okay," Fenway said, and Jennifer opened her eyes again. "Piper, let's start with your right hand."

Jennifer watched while Piper filled out first the right-hand card, then the left.

"Remember, the fingerprint we're looking for is a tented arch," Fenway said. "I don't even have to take the print we found on the gun to see that none of Piper's prints are a match. They're all loops and whorls."

"Pull out the print you found on the gun just to make sure," Kim said.

Fenway took a deep breath herself. "Sure." She pulled out the baggie with the gun fingerprint and held it above the cards. "You want to compare the prints yourself?"

"Uh—yes, I guess so." Jennifer stepped around Fenway and stood next to her at the desk, then leaned over the fingerprint array.

She stared at the cards for almost a full minute, though it seemed much longer. Fenway had to stop herself from tapping her foot or sighing loudly to get Jennifer Kim to hurry.

Finally, Kim pushed the cards away from her. "No, you're right. It doesn't look like a match."

"Great, thanks," said Fenway.

"Hey," Kim said, looking at the laptop screen. "What's this? Is this —is this the missing scholarship fund spreadsheet we've all been looking for?"

Piper closed her laptop. "It's client work for Mr. Ferris. I can't show it to anyone but family members."

Jennifer smirked. "Fine. But if it *is* the missing spreadsheet, I expect to be informed as soon as possible."

"I still have some work to do to confirm... some things," Piper said.

Kim widened her eyes. "If that spreadsheet has information identifying the head of the money laundering scheme, Miss Patten, you are legally obligated to release that information to us."

"I don't work for the county anymore—"

"So that's almost everyone's prints," Fenway interrupted. "Everyone except Rose Morgan and Evans Dahl, who have both declined to comply." She snapped her fingers. "Oh—we didn't get your fingerprints either, Jennifer. I looked at your fingertips, but we didn't print them."

Jennifer Kim shook her head. "Sorry, Fenway. I've changed my mind. I'm in solidarity with my fellow counselor on this one."

"What?" Fenway narrowed her eyes. "You're the one who insisted that *I* give my fingerprints. Isn't that a little hypocritical?"

Kim shrugged. "Not when I'm pointing out *your* hypocrisy. You're the one insisting on taking everyone's prints—"

"You did it too!"

"Ah, but as an officer of the court, I'm required to serve the cause of justice. But I'm under no obligation to give up my Fourth Amendment rights because of it."

Fenway set her jaw.

"Sorry if you don't like my answer, Fenway. Feel free to talk to a judge who'll compel me to comply." Jennifer Kim took three steps back. "Or once we're out of here, you can simply check my prints in the system. I had to be fingerprinted when I accepted this position." She began to turn away, then stopped. "Was there anything else?"

Fenway folded her arms. "I guess not."

"Thanks for volunteering to provide your fingerprints, Piper," ADA Kim said. "Maybe we should cross-check those fingerprints with the ones we found after the Central Auto Body break-in. I hear nobody's been arrested in that case yet."

Jennifer Kim turned her back and walked off the dais.

Piper shot her middle finger up at Jennifer Kim's back.

V

NOON

CHAPTER TWENTY

PIPER DROPPED HER HAND AND SUPPRESSED A LAUGH AS SHE watched ADA Kim go back and sit down. "She's a kick in the pants, as my grandmother would say."

"You almost sound like you admire her," Fenway said.

"Well, I mean, I don't agree with her, but you've got to appreciate someone who can be that brazen."

"I suppose." *Like my father.*

"It doesn't matter anyway," Piper said. "We've got everyone's fingerprints now. If the print from that gun is from someone in the courtroom, we'll find it."

"Well—not necessarily, Piper. What if the print on the gun is from someone's left hand, but they only held their water bottle with their right hand?"

"Yeah—okay, but it does significantly increase our probability, right?"

Fenway nodded. "Sure. Most people would both grab a gun and drink from a water bottle with their dominant hand."

"Great. So let's get to work."

Fenway dug in the kit and handed Piper a pair of blue nitrile gloves, then took out a pair for herself. "Move your laptop," she said. "The fingerprint dust gets everywhere."

"Okay. How do you want to do this?"

"The bottles are round, so they'd roll if I put them on the table. You hold them for me and rotate them." Fenway paused.

"One thing," Piper said. "How will we know whose is whose?"

Fenway grinned, getting the old receipt with the letters and numbers. "I numbered the bottles."

"Really?"

"Yes. One through twelve—well, eleven. I used Roman numerals, though. I could make the marks less noticeable if they were straight lines. No real way to hide VIII, but I, II, and III were easy."

Piper bent down and retrieved an empty water bottle from under the desk. She stared at the label for a moment. "Where?"

"Under the bottling information on the back of the label. I tried to make it look like a stamp."

"There it is. I'll be damned."

"That's three," Fenway said. "And who does III correlate with?"

Piper checked the receipt. "That's B. Bryce Heissner?"

Fenway nodded. "All right. I'll get the tape, and hopefully we'll get this done in no time."

"Who's W?"

"Oh, those are all first names except for Judith, Jennifer, Cynthia, and Charlotte—W is for *widow*, K is for *Kim*, S is for *Schimmelhorn*, and M is for—"

"Mom? Like stepmom?" Piper guessed.

Fenway snorted. "Monster. Like stepmonster."

There were only nine bottles to test. Xavier, Amanda, Piper, and Fenway hadn't taken water. Fenway was most concerned about the fingerprints on Rose Morgan's water bottle.

Piper stopped. "Do you hear that?"

Fenway listened. "Rain," she said. The patter on the roof grew louder as the rain intensified.

Piper nodded and held the plastic bottle as Fenway brushed the fingerprint dust on the surfaces and tried to collect as much as possible that had fallen onto the table. Piper rotated the bottle a few times, and by the time they were finished, Fenway had lifted nine distinct prints off Rose's bottle. Jackpot—three of Rose's fingerprints had tented arches, and the one partial didn't have a tented arch.

As soon as she transferred all of Rose's prints to a card, Fenway's heart raced as she pushed the cards next to each other.

She stared at them, willing one of the prints to match.

But no luck.

None of the tented arch prints matched the one on the gun. One was close, but a notch just below the tent and a more tightly packed swirl pattern above the tent meant that Rose hadn't had the gun in her hand.

Fenway didn't believe it. She looked again.

No.

She wanted to scream in frustration, but that might have alerted the others in the courtroom to what she was doing.

"Is Rose a match?" Piper asked.

Fenway shook her head. "I would have put *money* on it. A lot of money."

"We've got two more to compare. Let's not give up hope yet."

Fenway's throat was dry, but she swallowed and nodded. "Right."

She tried to work just as quickly when Piper enthusiastically held the plastic bottle in front of her, but she didn't have her heart in it. Evans Dahl didn't have any arches at all—though Fenway only got five useable prints from him. The ADA's fingerprints made up for it, though—all ten of hers were on the bottle. But she only had two arches out of the ten fingers.

Something itched at the back of Fenway's brain.

Had she seen these fingerprints before?

No—that was silly. Even if she had, how could she remember them?

"Piper," Fenway murmured, "we *didn't* take Jennifer Kim's fingerprints earlier, did we?"

"I don't think so. You're the one who compared all the cards."

"Right." She looked through the cards again. Schimmelhorn, Heissner, Ferris, Ferris, Kohl, Gonsalves, Nedermeyer—the one with all the accidental whorls, she remembered—and Judith Cygnus. And then the duplicate cards for the two Ferrises, then Fenway's own card, then Piper.

I'm missing something.

She compared the prints that she pulled off Kim's water bottle and held them up to the others.

They perfectly matched the cards labeled Cynthia Schimmelhorn.

Fenway cursed under her breath.

"What is it?" Piper asked.

"I think I messed up. Look—ADA Kim and Cynthia Schimmelhorn's prints."

Piper looked. "Oh no."

"Yeah. I *thought* those prints looked familiar. So I compared them to everyone else's—and those prints are Cynthia Schimmelhorn's, not Jennifer Kim's." Fenway's lip curled. "I—I can't believe I did messed up the bottles. I was *extremely* careful."

"Maybe they switched."

"But then *both* of their prints would be on the bottle, right?"

"Hey," Piper said, "we all make mistakes."

"Yeah, well, this isn't like making a typo. Because of my screwup, we might not catch a killer." Fenway pulled the cards toward Piper. "Take a look, Piper." She tapped the card on the left. "These are the ones we just pulled off the bottle." Then she tapped the two cards on the right, labeled CYNTHIA SCHIMMELHORN. "These are an exact match. Can you explain it any other way than a massive error on my part?"

Piper shifted her weight in her chair uncomfortably. "I—uh....You're right, I guess." She set her jaw. "What about with the Roman numerals? Maybe you wrote a VI when you meant to put in IV or something like that? Or maybe something upside down? An IX that should be an XI?"

Fenway closed her eyes. "I don't—I don't see any way I could have done something like that. But now you've got me doubting my memory."

"Don't beat yourself up, Fenway."

"No—it's—it's not that. See, in my head I know I'm right. I either made a huge mistake, or someone outsmarted me." Fenway gave Piper a pained smile. "And frankly, neither of those choices are acceptable." Fenway threw up her hands. "What I want to know is, if Cynthia Schimmelhorn's fingerprints are on Kim's bottle, then whose fingerprints are on *her* bottle?"

"You're not suggesting that you screwed up more than one bottle, are you?"

"I—I don't know what I'm suggesting. Maybe we should check all the other bottles just to make sure that the fingerprints all match the cards we think they match with."

"Yeah, okay. Let's check."

"I'm sorry, Piper." Fenway smacked her hand on the counter. "I'm so angry with myself for messing this up."

Piper put a hand on Fenway's shoulder. "It's possible that the killer was *way* ahead of us. When we handed out those water bottles— maybe they changed some of the Roman numerals. It's easy to change a VII into a VIII."

Fenway grunted. "Yes. You're right. Maybe that's what happened."

"That makes you feel better? That the killer knows we're onto them?"

Fenway leaned forward in her chair. "Not when you put it like that."

"All right, let's just work through these. It's like a logic puzzle, right?"

Fenway nodded. "Right. We've gotten sets of prints we know for sure are accurately matched with their owners. We've got eight water bottles we *don't* know for sure are matched with their owners, but we can match the bottles with the prints we *can* identify, right?"

"Right. But we have three bottles with prints we hadn't taken before—Rose Morgan, Evans Dahl, and Jennifer Kim."

"And we know Jennifer's is wrong."

"So maybe someone switched the bottles around, or changed the labels. Or something."

Fenway nodded. "Great. Let's get cracking."

The two of them worked steadily for the next forty-five minutes. As Fenway expected, Cynthia Schimmelhorn's bottle didn't match any of the existing prints. Neither did Evans Dahl's bottle.

Piper checked the internet again. Still no connectivity.

The other water bottles all matched their respective fingerprint cards, however.

Fenway had fingerprint powder all over her gloves, and she was relieved to take them off. A bit of powder got on her slacks, but they were black anyway. Piper had a hard time taking her gloves off, so Fenway helped her.

"And now, the moment of truth," Fenway said.

She pulled the card with the print from the gun toward her and compared them to Evans Dahl. A single arch, and the rest loops and whorls. Then she took a deep breath and slid the prints from the bottle labeled for Cynthia Schimmelhorn next to the gun card.

One tented arch.

And it was a perfect match.

CHAPTER TWENTY-ONE

"I don't believe it," Piper said, staring at the two prints with the exact same tented arch pattern. "I just—I don't believe it. I always knew she had it in for me—but I didn't think she was capable of murder."

"Who?"

"Jennifer Kim."

Fenway bowed her head and put her hand on her forehead. "That—that might be the conclusion the killer wants us to come to."

Piper's face was awash in confusion. "What are you talking about?"

"I mean," Fenway said, "that if the killer wanted us to *think* it was ADA Kim, they might swap more than two bottles."

Piper frowned.

"Look—if Rose is the killer—"

"—which she's not—"

"If Rose *were* the killer, though," Fenway continued, "and she realized we were doing the old 'get-the-fingerprints-off-a-bottle' trick that I've seen dozens of times in cop shows, she might not *just* switch her bottle with Kim's."

"No? But I'm sure she's seen how much animosity there is between you and her. It wouldn't take much to push you over the edge to think *she's* the murderer."

"That's true, but I'd be even *more* suspicious if it looked like ADA Kim were trying to trick us, right?"

Piper tilted her head up. "Uh... I suppose it might."

"So instead of just switching her bottle with Jennifer Kim's bottle, Rose switches her bottle with Cynthia Schimmelhorn's, *then* switches Cynthia's bottle with Jennifer's, knowing that we've already got definitive proof that Cynthia's fingerprints are real. Now we suspect Kim more than anyone else."

"That—that seems too complicated."

"But it might be what happened. And it's a lot simpler than it sounds."

Piper scrunched up her nose. "How are we supposed to explain that Jennifer Kim was standing next to Professor Cygnus when he was killed? How do you explain that?"

"Rose doesn't need to be proved innocent, Piper. She just has to get away from the courthouse. Then she'll hightail it as fast as she can to go meet the love of her life down in Mexico."

Piper furrowed her brow.

"You don't think so?" asked Fenway.

"Uh... well, you've investigated more murders than I have, but that still seems a little overly complicated. A lot of things would have to align just right for that plan to go smoothly."

Fenway sat down in her chair. "I don't know. It wouldn't be the first time I've been accused of overthinking."

Piper nodded. "You know the old saying—when you hear hooves, think horses, not zebras."

"Unless you're in Africa," Fenway said.

Piper leaned forward. Her laptop dinged, and a text message popped onto the screen.

"What is it?" Fenway asked.

Piper groaned. "There's good news and bad news. The good news is, the internet's back up. The bad news is, McVie just sent a message that the locking mechanism on the courtroom doors has failed."

"Failed? So the doors won't unlock?"

"That's correct."

"Can't he just break the doors down?"

"I don't know, Fenway, I just saw the message. Hold on."

Piper read the text and Fenway leaned to her right so she could read it over Piper's shoulder.

Mechanism in doors failed – mechanic working on it

Fenway folded her arms and sat up straight again. "Isn't there some emergency exit out of here? Aren't public offices *legally* required to have them?"

Piper typed and pressed *Enter.* The laptop dinged again. Piper read. "Uh… yes on the legal requirement, but the side door had the same locking mechanism fail."

"He knows we can get sued, right?"

Piper squinted at the screen. "I'm not going to ask him that."

"What the hell? We're locked in here?"

"No. He says he'll break the door down."

Fenway blinked. "Break the door down?"

"They need to get a special piece of equipment here. Half an hour, he says."

"We were *supposed* to get out of here an hour ago."

Piper scooted the laptop in front of Fenway. "You wanted to text him. Here you go."

Fenway nodded.

PATTEN: *Hey Craig it's Fenway*
MCVIE: *hi Fenway how you holding up*
PATTEN: *Wish I'd never gotten out of bed this morning*
MCVIE: *me too last night was fun ;)*
PATTEN: *Hey careful this is Piper's machine*

> MCVIE: *sorry — we're tryin to get u out as fast as we can*
>
> PATTEN: *Everyone else out of the courthouse?*
>
> MCVIE: *yes*
>
> PATTEN: *How much do u know about the situation in here*
>
> MCVIE: *i know u found the gun with a print on it*
>
> MCVIE: *and a few of the people aren't doing well medically*
>
> PATTEN: *Judith Cygnus needs her medication — it's in her car*
>
> PATTEN: *I'm afraid she won't make it if she doesn't get it soon*
>
> MCVIE: *we're doing everything we can*
>
> MCVIE: *i have an electrician tryin to override locking mechanism*
>
> PATTEN: *Were u the one who turned off the internet*
>
> MCVIE: *it was an accident sorry*

Fenway's fingers hovered over the keyboard for a moment. Should she open up that Pandora's Box and discuss his confession of love?

She didn't know how she felt. And she didn't want to mislead McVie. She liked him—a lot, even—but she didn't know if she loved him. She didn't know if she could love anyone. But she didn't want McVie to wonder whether Fenway had gotten the message.

And the killer was in the room with them. Fenway had neglected to mention that.

> PATTEN: *So you should know that the fingerprint on the gun matched someone in this room but we don't know who*

There was silence. Then three dots, then they disappeared. Then reappeared and disappeared again.

MCVIE: *prof Cygnus killer is in there but u dont know who?*

PATTEN: *It's a long story, too long for texting*

PATTEN: *But yes*

PATTEN: *Maybe Rose Morgan*

PATTEN: *Maybe Evans Dahl*

PATTEN: *Maybe Jennifer Kim*

MCVIE: *u sayin the ADA killed Cygnus?*

PATTEN: *I'm saying that the fingerprint on the gun belongs to one of the people in here*

PATTEN: *We have everyone else's fingerprints but theirs*

MCVIE: *so the killer might not be in there at all*

PATTEN: *No a fingerprint we lifted from a water bottle matched*

PATTEN: *I DID tell you the story was too long to text*

PATTEN: *Just trust me the killer's in here*

MCVIE: *i do trust you*

Fenway groaned. This was it. This was McVie's way of giving Fenway an opening. He might as well have asked her outright if she'd heard his declaration of love.

Well, no sense in beating around the bush. If this is it, it's been a fun, if painfully short, ride.

PATTEN: *I heard you tell me you love me*

And... nothing. No return message, no three dots, no acknowledgment. She was holding her breath, and she exhaled.

Maybe McVie was waiting for something else. She grimaced. Yeah —she hadn't given him much to go on. She didn't have much to go on herself.

PATTEN: *I wish I knew how I felt*

> PATTEN: *We're just getting started with the whole dating thing*
> PATTEN: *Things are going well so far*
> PATTEN: *And I like you*

She took a deep breath and remembered to breathe out again. That first text was hard, but now that she had started she wanted to explain herself. Or maybe she just wanted to talk with him.

> PATTEN: *I'm glad you told me though*

Finally, the telltale three dots appeared. It seemed like a month before the text finally came through.

> MCVIE: *i know it's way too early to tell you i love you*
> MCVIE: *but i've known how i felt for awhile now*
> MCVIE: *and when i heard those shots and i thought something might happen*
> MCVIE: *i wanted u to know u were loved*
> MCVIE: *you ARE loved*

Fenway stared at the screen for a moment. Would Craig think it was okay that she didn't feel the same way? She started typing a response.

> PATTEN: *I might be in love with you too*

Her finger hovered over the *Enter* key. She couldn't think straight. She didn't even know who the killer was. The people of the town had elected her not a week before to the County Coroner position. She wasn't Acting Coroner anymore—she was the real thing. She didn't have to feel the shame of having McVie appoint her, with everyone whispering that she only got it because of her father's connections.

She'd won the election, and won handily, and solved a murder during the election cycle. She was the real thing.

But she still didn't *feel* like she was the real thing. Especially not when it came to relationships, or when it came to Craig McVie. Her friends from high school were getting married and having kids. Almost all her friends who weren't married were engaged.

The prospect of having her own family filled her with—she wasn't sure what. The idea was far off in the future, as if the day she could settle down and start a family could be years away—decades even.

But she didn't have decades. If she were lucky—if she were *really* lucky—she'd have a single decade from right now to decide if marriage and kids and settling down were what she wanted. In ten years, she'd be thirty-nine, and it's possible that her biological clock would be ticking.

But Craig McVie was already in his early forties, and he *had* a daughter who was now a teenager—Megan was halfway through her junior year. Maybe she could have the marriage and settling down part with him—but could she have the kid with him? Did she even *want* to have kids?

She pinched her eyes shut. *Yes, this is overthinking it.* The question was pretty simple. Did she love him or not? And she didn't have to be scared about him not returning her feelings because he'd already laid it out on the table.

And since the killer *was* in the room with them, if something happened and she was killed, would Craig McVie always wonder if Fenway loved him back?

Maybe she should say it anyway. Just in case something happened. Even though she didn't mean it—

Oh.

She didn't mean it.

Maybe she *could* love him in the future. This might be a grown-up relationship for once in her life, rather than an interconnected series of one-night stands that just happened to be with the same person.

She wished she could talk to someone about it. She wasn't close with any of her friends from Seattle anymore—not where she could just call them up and dump on them for an hour. There was Rachel, but as the public information officer, she worked too closely with McVie. There were Dez and Piper and... well, that was it.

Fenway really wanted to talk to her mom.

And then the nauseating punch of betrayal hit Fenway in the gut.

Ten thousand a month. A hundred twenty thousand a year.

And all of it gone... and Fenway had no idea where.

Maybe she could talk to Charlotte about it. Charlotte might even like it—the two of them talking like real girlfriends to each other. They'd never had a stepmother/stepdaughter relationship—there were only six years between them, after all—but maybe they could have a friendship. That might even serve the double duty of pissing off her father.

Fenway looked back at the screen to delete what she'd written, but McVie had already written.

MCVIE: *ok gotta talk to the electrician see u soon*

And that was it. Fenway didn't have the chance to tell him she loved him. Whether it was the truth or not.

She unfocused her eyes and stared down at the table, trying to shape her thoughts around McVie, around what to do about the finger-prints and the bottles, about how to save her father, about how to solve the murder of Professor Cygnus.

She blinked and her eyes focused for a moment on Rose Morgan's fingerprint work. She reached her hand out for it and picked it up.

This wasn't an area covered by police procedure. Besides, Fenway told herself, the police lied to interviewees all the time. She wouldn't be doing anyone any harm.

She picked up the fingerprint card and got up, walking around the side of the witness stand.

"Fenway?" Piper asked, but Fenway ignored her and kept walking.

Rose Morgan, sitting in the back row, looked up at Fenway as she stomped down the aisle. Rose slowly got to her feet and drew herself up to her full height—several inches shorter than Fenway, but still an imposing figure in the way she carried herself.

"So," Fenway said as she strode in between the chairs to get to Rose, "do you want to tell me what you're doing here?"

"What *I'm* doing here?" Rose said. "Um—did you not know that Jessica Marquez was not only my coworker but my *friend?* I came to see her murderer get arraigned."

"But you knew I was looking for you. You knew *all* the sheriff's deputies were looking for you. You're not getting out of here without getting questioned—about everything. About Domingo Velásquez, about your plans to go to Mexico, about where you have the USB stick—and we've got enough compelling charges that your lawyer won't be able to get you out on your own recognizance this time."

"What can I say?" Rose said. "Some things are just so important that you take that risk." She laughed. "I thought I'd get in and out without anyone recognizing me. Then when the shooting started— well, it's not often I'm caught off guard, but I sure as hell was caught off guard."

"You didn't come here to meet with your employer?'

"My employer? Central Auto Body? They don't employ me anymore. Marisol Velásquez made it clear I'm not welcome there again. She gave me my last paycheck too, so I know she's done her homework on how to get rid of me." Rose examined her nails. "Person-ally, if I found out that *my* husband had planned to run off with a woman half his age, I'd make her a cyanide cocktail instead of breaking out the final paycheck. But hey, I guess that's why I don't get the big bucks."

"What would you say, Rose, if I told you I found your fingerprint on the gun that killed Professor Cygnus?"

Rose Morgan guffawed. "That's funny. Usually *I'm* the one lying to the cops."

"So you'd say it was a lie?"

"It's definitely a lie. I've never seen that gun, I've never seen that air conditioning vent thing—"

"It's a speaker enclosure."

"Whatever. I've never seen anything like it, is my point. No—if you found *my* prints on that gun, I'd say you were high." She folded her arms. "How'd you get my prints, anyway?" She slapped her forehead. "Of course. The internet must be back up. You found my prints in the police database."

"It doesn't matter how we got them," Fenway said. "It matters that you're—" And suddenly the folly of what she was doing hit her. She'd wanted to get McVie out of her head, and going whole hog into solving the case seemed like the way to do it. But it had been thoughtless, and she'd overplayed her hand. *Dammit, Fenway, you're better than this.* She shook her head from side to side to clear the cobwebs and staggered to sit in a chair that was several seats from Rose.

"Hey," Rose said, genuine concern on her face, "are you okay?"

"I know someone in this room killed him," Fenway said softly, "and you fit the profile. You work for the money launderers."

"I don't—"

Fenway held her hand up. "You absolutely do. This isn't on the record, and I may not be able to prove it, but don't try to deny it."

Rose sat down one seat away from Fenway. "Hypothetically speaking, let's say I don't try to deny it."

"If we're discussing hypotheticals, Rose, let's say you were to hypothetically figure out a way to skim a quarter million dollars from the scheme without your bosses being any the wiser."

"Okay."

"Let's say you were to make a large donation to a nonprofit organization from one of the accounts you oversaw, and you were able to fake tax payment paperwork."

"Well, first, I'd have to be an excellent forger, or a really good hacker. That computer and scanner they have in The Guild office probably wouldn't cut it."

Fenway smiled, even though she was emotionally and physically drained. The exhaustion hit her like a freight train. "Somehow I don't think either of those things are a problem for you."

"Maybe not, but I'm interested in this hypothetical scenario anyway." Rose crossed her arms. "I'm interested to see how this plays out."

"There are four scholarship students—they're fake students, just like most of the ones that Jessica used to give to your bosses—but these student names don't show up in either the real student list *or* the list of fake students that your bosses are using to launder money. These four students have real bank accounts set up... but you and Domingo Velásquez are co-signers on their accounts. So the year of tuition, room and board, books, whatever—that gets cleared into those accounts, and no one is the wiser." Fenway tapped her temple. "And the payment for spring semester just went in, didn't it? On Friday?" Fenway paused. "Was this the first year? Or had it been going on since the beginning of the money laundering scheme? Two whole years? Half a million dollars? Or was one year and a quarter million enough for you?"

Rose tapped her chin with her index finger. "Don't you think it would be much easier to get away with skimming money if everything was in place from the moment it started?"

Fenway nodded. "Yes, I do. But they found out, didn't they?"

Rose shrugged. "It wasn't just Domingo and me. There were a few others, too."

"Who were they?"

Rose smiled. "You're the cops. You haven't found any other suspicious withdrawals?"

"We might if you told us who to look for."

Rose shook her head. "All communications were anonymous. That way, if they caught one of us, that person couldn't rat us out to the cops."

"And do you know who found out?"

Rose nodded. "Yes. It was Jeremy Kapp. He had this meticulous bookkeeper overseeing his account and a lot of the smaller accounts too. Officially, he was on Kapp's payroll. This bookkeeper knew IRS rules like the back of his hand and knew exactly what we could do to stay out of trouble." Rose chuckled and lowered her voice. "Well, one day, the bookkeeper comes in and finds all these discrepancies. With some of the smaller businesses we used, you kind of expect petty cash to be taken from the till—I think drug dealers use the term 'breakage.'"

Fenway nodded.

"Anyway, this exceeded the breakage they were willing to accept, and it happened both with Dr. Jacob Tassajera and with Central Auto Body."

"This magic bookkeeper didn't find anything in The Guild's scholarship fund? Like the half-million that Cygnus stole?"

Rose shook her head. "He wasn't looking there—Kapp wasn't coordinating that account. That one was too big. Jessica Marquez was running lead on that one."

"But Kapp was coordinating yours?"

"I oversaw Central Auto Body. Kapp's guy had all the little businesses. Central Auto Body was one of Kapp's fake landscaping clients. I don't know how the bookkeeper found the issues with *our* books too, but he did."

Fenway exhaled. "So everything started hitting the fan."

"Right. First, Jeremy Kapp gets killed." Rose leaned forward, her palms on her knees. "Look, the group was up in arms about it. Everyone said that someone who was skimming money was responsible for killing him." She sighed. "The order comes down—it's pretty harsh. The two people who couldn't establish their whereabouts the night Kapp was killed—"

"You ran your *own* investigation?"

"We had to. We had to keep it within ranks. And so the order came down—kill Dr. Tassajera and Domingo." Rose shook her head. "I couldn't let that happen. I was planning to hide Domingo in the hopes that we could lay low until the Friday after Election Day—then we'd have all the money in the account." She set her jaw. "But then Peter

Grayheath—that asshole—can't make things look like an accident. He wants to *send a message*."

"So he bashes Dr. Tassajera over the head with a golf club, and Domingo Velásquez's kid gets blown ,up in Domingo's minivan." Fenway leaned forward. "And now, the million-dollar question, Rose. Who are *they?* Who are your bosses?"

Rose smiled. "Why, Miss Stevenson, I told you this was all hypothetical. There'd be all kinds of problems if I named names." She leaned back in her chair. "I thought we were pretty much home free after you captured Kapp's killer. There was no need to search for anyone else. Of course, they'd tighten the ranks." A dark cloud passed over her face. "But then Jessica was killed."

"And you had to do something."

"Things were going so well for two years, Miss Stevenson. We were all making money hand over fist. Yes, Domingo and I got a little greedy, and unfortunately, we took the wrong people into our confidences—and in another stroke of bad luck, we weren't the only ones stealing from the organization." She looked at Fenway; Rose's eyes were both stubborn and pleading. "We had to get out, Miss Stevenson. Yeah, we'd made some bad decisions, but after it came out that Professor Cygnus had stolen half a million, we couldn't stay in." Rose narrowed her eyes. "And then *you* had to screw everything up."

"Me?"

"Yes, you. You had to cart me off for questioning at the sheriff's office."

"And Domingo Velásquez was still at your house."

"Not for long, of course. He took my car and took off to Mexico by himself."

Fenway cocked her head. "You're not planning on joining him when this is over?"

Rose squinted. "Is that a joke?"

"Should it be?"

"You tracked his movements and his bank withdrawals, right?"

"Sure. Yuma, Arizona. Like I said, I assume he's going to his sister's in Hermosillo."

"Didn't you see that he withdrew *all* the money? And don't you think it odd that he left without me?"

"You don't plan to meet him later?"

"Ha. If I could figure out how to get away with his murder, maybe. But I know I'd be the number one suspect. Well—maybe his wife. Hell, maybe I should call her up so we can plan offing him together." Rose smiled. "Hypothetically, of course."

Fenway looked at the ground. "So you're saying he took all the money that the two of you stole from the money launderers. Why are you back here? Surely the people who run the laundering business are looking for you, too. Aren't you worried you'll be killed just like Dr. Tassajera?"

Rose nodded. "Yes, I sure am. But I don't have a lot of choices." She put her arm over the back of the chair next to her. "People do some funny things when they're backed into a corner, Miss Stevenson." She looked up at the ceiling. "I didn't think they'd do anything in a public place like the courthouse. I see now I was wrong—and I'm probably lucky that it was Professor Cygnus on the business end of that bullet and not me."

"He was about to name names."

Rose giggled. "Well, I'm not *that* stupid. All the names I'm giving you are ones you already know."

"You're helping me piece some things together. That's helpful. I can't imagine your bosses are very cool with that."

"What have I done? I've given you some information about Peter Grayheath. You've already got him in custody for one murder."

"You and I already know that you won't testify, and unless you have some hard evidence you can give me, it doesn't really help."

"It tells you where to focus your efforts." Rose looked down her nose at Fenway. "And if I'm perfectly honest, it'll keep you from looking at my bosses."

"Someone hired Grayheath to kill Dr. Tassajera."

Rose smiled. "Yes, but that same person hired him to kill your professor up at Western Washington, too, and Grayheath hasn't talked yet." She leaned forward again. "His sister's got MS, and I think you'll find that her medical bills were just anonymously paid. If Grayheath doesn't want her or her three kids out on the street, he'll keep his mouth shut. And he's a good enforcer on the inside, too."

Fenway nodded. "That makes sense."

Rose cocked her head. "Did you hear what I said, Fenway? I said I knew your dad was set up to take the fall for the murder of your professor."

Fenway kept nodding. "I heard you, Rose. We've already found enough evidence to free my father, though. We can prove that bank account was opened by someone else, and that's pretty much the thread that connects everything else together for the prosecution. Without that bank account, they don't have a case. We'll probably even get it dismissed with prejudice."

Rose chuckled. "Wow—I thought I was keeping a few steps ahead of you, Coroner, but I obviously have to watch my back. You're catching up."

"So," Fenway said, tapping her fingers on the seat of the chair next to her, "I take it Cygnus didn't come to you when he wanted to take some extra money for himself."

"It wouldn't have been a hard thing to do," said Rose. "Dr. Pruitt wasn't a monster."

"Dr. Pruitt—the president of the university? He's the one behind everything?"

"No! Of course not! You searched Dr. Pruitt's computer—surely you knew he was one of the intermediaries."

"Right." Fenway searched the file drawers in her brain for the code names that Piper had told her. *Carpe diem*—that wasn't right, but it was *Carpe* with a four-digit number. And then it came to her: *Effect3175*.

"So are you *Effect3175*, or is that your boyfriend?"

Rose jumped in her seat. "You know about the code names?"

"Of course we do. We've been trying to figure out who the code names belong to for a couple of days now." Fenway pointed at Rose. "We narrowed *Effect3175* down to either you or Domingo Velásquez. Domingo accessed an account that we connected to *Effect3175* yesterday. But now that I know that he stole all your money, I'm now betting that you're *Effect3175*. Plus, lots of payments were made and received by that name—and the big bosses, whoever they are, obviously trusted that person. Until a few days ago." Fenway slouched back in the chair and put her feet up on the row in front of her. "That sounds a lot like you."

A sly smile crept across Rose's face. "You know," she said, "hypothetically speaking, of course, if we'd let you in on this, and if you weren't so damn honest, you'd have been a great resource. It's a shame you're working *against* us instead."

"The real shame is that Jeremy Kapp couldn't keep it in his pants," Fenway said. "If he hadn't gotten himself killed, I'd never have uncovered all of this."

"Oh, we probably would have imploded eventually," Rose said. "Human nature, greed, all that. If I'd gotten away with half a million, someone else would have tried to get away with ten times that."

"So, tell me," Fenway said, remembering the code name for the mole, "is *cuckoo37* crazy, or do they have a thing for clocks?"

Rose grinned. "Well, first of all, it's *37cuckoo37*, and, well, aren't we all just a little bit crazy?"

"Just a hint. Another clue."

Rose shook her head. "I've said too much already. I like riddles way more than I should."

Oh—that code name means something.

"What about L.I.W.?"

Rose raised her eyebrows. "You're definitely not getting anything from me there."

"Just give me a third of it. Does the L stand for Leda?"

Rose snorted. "Yeah. The whole criminal scheme is masterminded by a woman who's high half the time and so thirsty for Professor Cygnus she can't think straight."

"Lincoln? Lawrence?"

Rose looked around the room, then lowered her head and beckoned Fenway closer. "Okay, okay, I'll give you the L."

Fenway leaned forward. "Really?"

"It stands for *lickety-split*. Like, you better get us out of this courtroom *lickety-split* before we start behaving as if we don't like each other."

Fenway leaned back. "Great. So helpful."

"Licking Infected Walruses," Rose said. "Low Incandescent Wattage. There's an actual sentient soft-white bulb that set up this whole thing."

"Okay," Fenway said, getting up.

"It may not have seemed like a bright idea at first—"

"Gotcha, Rose, thanks."

"No problem. If you ever need me to shed light on anything else, just let me know."

Fenway made the march back through the gallery gate and up to the judge's dais again.

"That didn't sound fruitful," said Piper.

"On the contrary," Fenway said. "It was very helpful. Get your spelunking hat on—we're going to catch a mole."

CHAPTER TWENTY-TWO

Piper's eyes widened. "What did you find out, Fenway?"

Fenway pulled her seat to the rear of the dais, its back to the rest of the courtroom, and motioned to Piper to pull her chair over too. "I tried to get her to tell me who a couple of the code names belonged to," she said, sitting down.

"And she told you?"

"No, but remember you said that the word and number combinations didn't mean anything?"

"Yes," Piper said. "Was I wrong?"

"I think so. At least for our mole."

"*37cuckoo37?*"

"That's the one. I asked Rose about *cuckoo37,* and she corrected me with *both* the 37s. So I think the name means something."

"Hmm. It could be lots of things. It could be a reference to a year, like 1937, or a month and a day, like March 7th, or it could—jeez, even be a reference to a Las Vegas jackpot—three 7s, you know."

"Like if one of the sheriff's deputies hit a jackpot on March 7th?"

"Sure. Who's in the pool of suspects?"

"I don't think there's anyone who we *shouldn't* look at, except probably McVie, since he's the one who said there was a mole to begin with, and you and me."

"What about other county employees?"

"The key is, they would have to have access to the jail. If they couldn't open Dylan Richards' cell, they aren't the mole."

"Gotcha." Piper paused. "That's a lot of people who we know, Fenway. Some of whom we really trust."

Fenway nodded sadly. "It sucks, I know. We've got to know, though. Whoever it is, they're responsible for at least one death that we know of—and probably some others indirectly, especially if they've warned the money launderers about what we're doing or somehow misdirected our investigation."

Piper hesitated.

"What is it?"

"Well—I told you, I still have access to the county's network. They haven't turned off my account yet."

Fenway shrugged. "You were directed to access the files by a law enforcement representative. You have plausible deniability. If anything, I'll be in one to get in trouble."

"But I don't—" Piper began.

"Seriously, Piper," Fenway interrupted, "we're talking about four murders in the last two weeks. If we don't catch this person, more people will die. And this is the first whiff of a clue we've had in months about the mole."

"The *what*?"

Fenway and Piper both startled and spun around. The voice belonged to Jennifer Kim, who was peeking over the top of the bench.

Fenway exhaled. "Don't sneak up on us like that, Jennifer."

"Sorry, but you were talking to Rose Morgan for a really long time. Did she say anything to you?"

"She didn't reveal any information about any of the leaders of the money laundering ring, if that's what you mean. I pressed her hard on two of the code names—"

"I'm sorry, the *code names*?"

Fenway rolled her eyes. "Listen, Jennifer, we have about twenty different avenues of inquiry we're going down. Yes, there are code names in the files. I was trying to get the code names out of Rose, but she wouldn't budge. But as I was talking to her, I thought of other ways we could try to match the identities up to the code names."

"Did she give you those ideas?"

"You mean, is she suddenly on our side now?" Fenway chuckled. "Not a chance. I started looking at the code names a little differently, that's all. Don't you dare go easy on her when we finally arrest her."

Kim nodded. "Okay. And—did you say there was a—"

Fenway shot her a warning look. *"Don't say it,"* Fenway hissed. "Whoever killed Professor Cygnus is still in here, and I don't want them warning anyone or thinking they have to shoot their way out."

"We're on the same side, Fenway."

"It sure seems like we've got different ideas about how to solve problems," Fenway said. "I respect you most of the time, Jennifer, but you can't go around accusing me of things I haven't done."

"I'm just saying that taking the check from your dad looks bad. You know I'm right."

"But calling me out in front of the whole courtroom wasn't cool, Jennifer. You know me better than that."

ADA Kim took a step back, then nodded solemnly. "You're right. It wasn't cool. I'm sorry. I should have spoken to you privately."

"Okay," Fenway said. "And now, if you don't mind, we still have a murderer to catch."

Jennifer turned slowly and walked back through the gallery gate.

"I've got another idea," whispered Piper. "I'll look at the key card usage at the jail, too. Entrances and exits. I'll cross-reference any time somebody goes to an area they don't normally access with the days that payments are made to their bank accounts. See if anything else sticks out."

"Yeah, but the guards all have access to the jail—and they're always in and out of there."

Piper shrugged. "Maybe it's a long shot, but at this point, what do we have to lose?"

"All right." Fenway looked across the courtroom again. Jennifer Kim had taken her seat, and Leda Nedermeyer was stretched out across a few chairs.

Xavier and Amanda were trying to make eye contact.

"Oh," Fenway said. "You keep working on the personnel files, Piper. Amanda and Xavier want to tell me something."

She started walking back around the witness stand, and to her relief, Amanda and Xavier walked toward her as well. She sat on the steps next to the witness stand and waited.

"Professor Nedermeyer sobered up before you let her lie down, right?" Fenway asked sharply.

Xavier nodded. "I would have asked you if it was okay, but—well, you looked really busy."

She nodded. "If she was coherent, the worst of it was out of her system. Is that what you wanted to tell me?"

"No," said Amanda.

"Oh. Well, then, what?"

"We thought of something," Amanda said. Her voice had a note of sadness in it. "I don't know if it'll be helpful."

Fenway leaned against the wall. She was getting a little lightheaded from the lack of food. She hoped the electrician could get the doors open soon. "Anything at this point might be useful," she said.

Amanda darted her eyes at Xavier, who nodded. "Well," Amanda began, "Professor Nedermeyer has been a little bit out of it this semester. I'm a freshman, so I didn't notice anything was wrong, not really, but she missed a couple of classes in September and then a couple more in October.

"I sat in on a couple of her classes, too," Xavier said. "And it was odd. Long, awkward pauses, and sometimes she'd just ramble."

"I forgot about a paper I had until the night before," Amanda cut in, "and I turned in a pile of hot garbage."

"It wasn't that bad—"

"It was a *pile of hot garbage*," Amanda said forcefully. "And I got it back with a 92 written on the front and not a single comment on the whole paper. Honestly, I was embarrassed. I was praying to get a C on it, but there I was, with a 92."

Fenway nodded. "Well, sometimes people have a problem with certain prescription medications."

"That's it," Xavier nodded. "Such erratic behavior. I know most of the students didn't care—she was passing all of us and letting our mistakes slip past her—"

"You two were in the same class?"

Xavier shook his head. "Amanda's got her for English 1B, and I have her for Comparative Literature 206. But it's the same in both our classes—she's distracted, she's sometimes insulting to her students or to other professors." Xavier paused. "Look, my aunt was on pills for a long time and it took a while for her to kick it. She had a pill dealer for a few months before my mom found out about it. I know how nasty some of this stuff is."

"Was your aunt on divenamine?" Fenway asked.

"Not quite—it was an anxiety medication, but it's the one they took off the market last year because it was so addictive." Xavier stared up at the ceiling, blinking hard. "Anyway, my aunt wound up being okay, but she had a lot of people worried. And I don't think Professor Nedermeyer has the interfering, bossy family members that my aunt did. I just don't want her to—well, die. I know divenamine is hard on the body, and if she's double or triple dosing, it's just a matter of time before she hurts herself."

Fenway nodded.

"You said she was okay when you left her?"

"Yes. I walked her around for forty minutes. She wasn't acting drunk or slurring her words. But she was tired."

"That's plenty of time to get it out of her system. And she went to sleep?"

"I just woke her up five minutes ago. She was still lucid."

"Good," Fenway said. "Well, it seems like we dodged a—uh, we, um, aren't in hot water with her."

If either Xavier or Amanda noticed Fenway's faux pas, neither of them said anything.

"How are the two of you doing?"

"All right, all things considered," Xavier said. "But we've missed a whole day of classes."

Amanda nodded. "I had a midterm in stats today, too."

"I'm sure your professors will excuse you today for being on lockdown." She considered for a moment. "You just wanted to tell me that Professor Nedermeyer's been acting strange all semester?"

Amanda shifted from foot to foot. "I just—well, when Xavier told me that one of his friends stabbed someone when they were high on the same stuff, I was worried."

Fenway attempted a smile but didn't quite make it. "I appreciate you telling me. I think this required a lot of forethought and planning. Someone who was just experiencing a drug side effect wouldn't have been able to put everything in place."

Amanda looked worriedly at Professor Nedermeyer. "I guess."

"You don't like Ms. Nedermeyer?"

"I don't know," Amanda said. "I guess she's okay. I just wish she'd leave Professor Cygnus alone." She sunk down. "Oh—shit. I guess I—I wasn't thinking." Her breath caught. "He's really gone." She turned and buried her face in Xavier's chest, and he wrapped his arms around her.

"She's been strange all semester," he mumbled, and the two of them turned back to their seats.

Fenway sighed and watched them go. *They don't seem to have any problem telling each other how they feel. And they haven't been seeing each other as long as Craig and I have.*

She walked to her chair and sat down heavily, then noticed Piper's face, scrunched up in concentration.

"You're onto something?"

"I think so, but I can't believe it's this obvious," said Piper. "Officer Todd Young."

"Officer Young? The one who was assigned to protect me after the car bomb incident?"

Piper nodded.

Fenway remembered waking up from a nightmare the night after the car bomb exploded, feeling like she was choking. And Officer Young had been in the room already. He'd said she was screaming and he'd rushed into protect her—but maybe he'd really been choking her.

After the car bomb, Fenway had stayed with her former assistant Rachel, who had been promoted to public information officer. Rachel hadn't trusted Officer Young from the start. Fenway had dismissed Rachel's mistrust a couple of weeks ago—but now, with Piper suspecting Young of being the mole, perhaps Rachel had been onto something.

"What makes you think that it's him?"

"Okay, do you know when his birthday is?"

Fenway shook her head. "It never came up in conversation. I take it he was born on March 7?"

"No—good guess, but no. He was born in Boston on July 26, 1988." She paused. "Your dad's a big Red Sox fan, right? Do you remember what happened on that day?"

"Umm," Fenway said, searching her memory banks. That had been two years after the heartbreak of losing the World Series to the Mets. That had been the year the Oakland A's had lost to the Los Angeles Dodgers—as if the baseball fans around Estancia would have allowed her to forget it. Kirk Gibson pumping his arm after hitting the game winner off the best closer in baseball, limping around the bases as if he were in his late seventies instead of his late thirties, but giving the Dodgers a World Series win. Her father's beloved Red Sox had dominated the AL East that year. Had they made it to 90 wins? Maybe not. Fenway knew they got swept by the A's in the division series. It had been after Nathaniel Ferris had married Joanne Stevenson, but before Fenway had come into the picture.

But July 26? Obviously a famous day in Red Sox lore. A long home run? No—certainly not longer than the one Ted Williams hit, where they still had one of the outfield seats painted red. What in the world could it be? That would make Officer Todd Young—

Oh.

"That was Jasper Todd's no-hitter," Fenway said. A 31-year-old left-handed call-up from Triple-A Pawtucket, Jasper Todd had made five spot starts for the Sox when Oil Can Boyd went on the DL. He'd dominated in every one of his five starts, making the Boston press go crazy—her father still had the news articles in a scrapbook. Jasper Todd wasn't a fireballer, but his curve was filthy, and the bottom fell out of his split-fingered fastball. He had a dozen strikeouts in his debut right after the All-Star Game, then a heartbreaking 1-0 loss to the hated Yankees—his only run unearned, by the way—and then... the glorious no-hitter.

It was against the Kansas City Royals, a team not far removed from their own World Series appearance, but at the front end of a decade of bottom-dwelling. Jasper Todd walked only two batters in the game, both in the first inning, and Mike Greenwell made a diving catch of a pop fly that caught the wind just right to end the seventh inning.

Fenway had watched the tape of that game with her father a few times, and when Todd Benzinger caught the ball at first base to end the game, it was pandemonium at Fenway Park. Players streaming out of the dugout, Jasper Todd looking like a five-year-old who'd just met his favorite Ninja Turtle, Van Halen's "Jump" blasting through the stadium speakers. Fenway had to give it to Todd Young's parents for naming him Todd instead of Jasper.

"And what was Jasper Todd's uniform number?"

Fenway blinked. She didn't know, but she could guess. "Thirty-seven."

"Right you are," Piper said.

"And where does the *cuckoo* come from?"

"So Todd Young also has a bunch of pictures of the hip-hop artist Forty Fresh on his Facebook page."

Fenway shrugged. "Lots of people like Forty Fresh."

"Right—but Officer Todd is an admin for their fan page."

"Really? How many admins are there?"

"Well," Piper said, "about a dozen, but that's still relatively few in the grand scheme of things."

"I don't know what's so odd about that. I listen to Forty Fresh too. I've got their big album from a few years ago on vinyl, even. Or—I did, up in Seattle."

Piper cocked her head. "And what's the name of their debut album from 2007?"

Fenway blinked. "Well, since we're talking about where *cuckoo* came from, I'll guess that it had something to do with that."

"It's called *If the Cuckoo Doesn't Sing.*"

Fenway nodded. "I can honestly say I've never heard of that album."

"It wasn't very popular, but hardcore fans would know it. The name of the album is a famous quote by one of the three daimyo who unified Japan in the late sixteenth century."

"Remind me never to compete against you at trivia night."

"But," continued Piper as if Fenway hadn't spoken, "that's not the whole quote. The end of the quote is, *kill it.*"

"'If the cuckoo doesn't sing, kill it'?"

"Right."

"Kind of morbid, don't you think, Piper?"

"Exactly. So we've got a connection to the number thirty-seven and a connection to cuckoos."

"It's a connection all right, but both of those are a stretch."

"If you're going for a username that no one else will understand, though," Piper mused, "wouldn't you want the references to be obscure?"

Fenway furrowed her brow but nodded. "And now can you cross-reference payments with Officer Young's bank accounts, or maybe his purchase history?"

"And I'm aligning them with card key usage, like I said. Officer Todd was on duty the night that Dylan Richards was killed. I'm looking for a door opened by Officer Todd's keycard that leads into the area where Dylan Richards was being held. And if a payment or a big deposit went into his account the next day, chances are pretty good he's the mole."

Fenway paused. "Is there any way you can bring up a map of that section of the jail?"

"Sure. Give me a minute."

Less than thirty seconds later, Piper had the blueprints of the jail on the screen.

"What doors have card key entry?"

"These four here," Piper said, pointing to the screen. "From the common room to the main jail hallway, and then there's a door to the gated yard, and then the side hallway here, and finally the guard station here."

Fenway cocked her head. "Isn't there one more?"

Piper frowned. "Not on the blueprints."

"No, it wouldn't be on the original blueprints. The administrative annex they built a couple of years ago—that abuts this hallway here, right?"

Piper's mouth dropped open. "Right, of course it does. I didn't go over there very often, but yes, there's a door in the annex with a card key reader on it."

"Can you get the records from that one too?"

Piper nodded. "It'll take a little work for me to get the identification number for that reader, but yes, I can do it."

Fenway nodded. "Besides Todd Young, are there any other suspects?"

Piper shook her head. "I thought of a few things. Cuckoo clocks, obviously. I can't check out whether any of the deputies or county employees own cuckoo clocks—that's the kind of purchase people often make on vacation anyway. Although it turns out that Jennifer Kim was born in Triberg, Germany."

"Germany?"

Piper nodded. "Her father's company sent him there for a couple of years."

"And what's so special about Triberg?"

"Home of the world's largest cuckoo clock."

Fenway laughed. "And just how large is the world's largest—"

"Forty-nine meters high."

Fenway nodded. "That's a big cuckoo clock. So she grew up there too?"

"Nope. How's your California geography knowledge?"

Fenway shrugged. "Pretty good, I guess."

"Jennifer Kim's family moved to a town north of San Francisco—Novato, when she was about eighteen months old."

Fenway nodded. "I've heard of it."

"Then her parents got divorced, and she moved inland to a city called, uh, *Vallejo*." She used the full Spanish pronunciation, with the double-L sounding like a Y. Fenway didn't have the heart to correct her to the local way of saying it.

"So Jennifer Kim never spent any time with that cuckoo clock growing up."

"Nope."

"And when was she born?"

"July."

Fenway sighed. "I thought maybe we'd get lucky and she'd be born on March seventh. Anyone else with the number thirty-seven?"

Piper shook her head. "Not that I've found."

"One thing, though." Fenway rested her chin on her hand. "Thirty-seven appears twice. We certainly know the meaning of one of them in Officer Young's life. Shouldn't there be another?"

Piper scrunched her face up. "Yeah. That bothered me, too. I mean, maybe it's a personal thing that you wouldn't find anywhere else. Maybe one of his heroes died at age thirty-seven, or maybe his high school had thirty-seven people in his favorite art class or something. Not all of this information is online."

Fenway nodded. "You're right. And of course, we don't know for sure that 'thirty-seven' and 'cuckoo' aren't relevant for any of the other employees either."

"Right. But so far, Officer Young seems like the one that makes the most sense."

Fenway sighed. "Just like Rose Morgan makes the most sense to shoot and kill Professor Cygnus."

"Oh," Piper said, leaning forward. "You don't think so. Not anymore."

"I can't put my finger on it," Fenway said. "But no, I don't think so. Not after I talked with her. She was willing to talk with me a little too much—sort of like she knew that if I really dug into it, I wouldn't find anything."

"But you haven't eliminated her, even though her fingerprints didn't match."

Fenway scratched her nose. "It's just a feeling I get."

"Your feelings aren't usually wrong, Fenway."

"That's not true," Fenway said. "I'm wrong about half the time. I really thought it *was* Rose Morgan. Now, whether it was or not, my hunches have finally betrayed me. I don't know which one it is."

There was a moan from the gallery, and Fenway got partway out of her seat to see who it was.

Judith Cygnus was standing hunched over in the aisle, holding onto the back of a chair for support.

"She's white as a sheet," Piper whispered.

Judith looked up and locked eyes with Fenway for a moment.

A sinking feeling in Fenway's stomach.

"Judith?" Fenway called. "Are you all right?"

Not even a flicker of recognition.

Her right arm began to twitch.

Fenway leaped over the judge's bench, knocking over the ceremonial gavel with her right knee. She landed on her feet and bolted through the gallery gate.

She was ten feet from Judith when it happened.

Judith's eyes rolled into the back of her head.

She sank like a stone to the floor of the aisle.

And started to shake violently.

CHAPTER TWENTY-THREE

Judith's head hit the floor with a sickening thud. Fenway dove for Judith's head with her hands, cradling it so the violent shaking of her body wouldn't injure her head any further.

Three pairs of shoes appeared in her peripheral vision. "Get away!" Fenway yelled. "She's having a seizure! Give her room!"

With surprising ease, she moved Judith onto her side.

"Open her mouth!" Leda screamed. "Open her mouth! She could swallow her tongue!"

Fenway shook her head at the old wives' tale. "No! That's not how it works!"

Leda wailed. "Oh—Judith—I'm so sorry. I'm so sorry. I'm so sorry."

"Shut up, Leda," Fenway snapped. She hadn't looked at her phone for what time it was when the seizure started, and time seemed to stop as soon as Judith hit the floor.

"Time?" Fenway asked.

"But I—" Leda began. Judith was still shaking.

"Time?" Fenway yelled.

No one answered.

"What's the fucking time?" Fenway screamed.

"12:21," Xavier called.

"Is she—" said a female voice. Cynthia? Amanda? Rose?

"Shut up!" Fenway yelled. Judith's head tried to bounce out of Fenway's hands. She tried to feel where Judith's head had hit the floor. No blood. "Dad! Go to the door and yell 'medical emergency' as loud as you can."

Her father's footsteps clapped the floor as he ran, shouting.

"Piper! Help clear the aisle."

Piper hurried over as Fenway looked down into Judith's face. "Don't die on me, Judith," Fenway whispered. "Show these people you're made of stronger stuff."

But maybe Judith didn't want to go back to her empty house and fight this terrible cancer without her husband. Without the infuriating man she'd spent the last forty years with. Maybe Judith wanted it this way.

Fenway could only hear the blood pounding in her ears and the roar of rain hitting the roof.

Judith's legs kicked out violently, and the backs of her heels smashed against the chair legs. "Move those," Fenway said, and her voice was hoarse.

Fenway had dealt with epileptic patients in the ER in Seattle, as well as a few in the clinic who'd had seizures brought on by cancer. Her textbook pages flashed through her mind. *In a study of 5,000 cancer patients, seizures occurred in 12.4% of those patients, and additionally was the main cause of 5% of all neurological manifestations.*

The helplessness overwhelmed her, even as Piper moved chairs and Xavier and Amanda looked on with worried faces. Fenway couldn't do anything—there wasn't anything *to* do, except make sure Judith injured herself as little as possible, and then check for injuries when she came to.

A cacophony of sound enveloped Fenway. Her father yelling about the medical emergency, the squeak and grind of chairs on the floor, the labored, uneven breathing of Judith Cygnus, and above it all, Fenway's heart and the rain.

Judith likely wouldn't remember anything—none of her seizure patients ever did. This might well be Judith's first seizure. She was late with her medicine, she hadn't eaten anything since before nine o'clock, and the cancer had put her in a weakened state. She was probably especially frail after her outburst at Leda.

When would McVie get them out of this courtroom? It had been far too long. She was hungry, she was tired, but she was far from the worst one off. Leda had almost overdosed on her medication, Evans Dahl had a badly sprained ankle—he almost certainly needed to go to the emergency room. And Judith needed an ambulance. As if her medical funds weren't strained enough. Maybe Fenway could drive her to the hospital.

Fenway closed her eyes.

The shaking started to subside, and Fenway relaxed her hands. Her whole body had tensed up, and she was shaking too. Nerves, or the whack on her forehead, or the lack of food. Or maybe it was simply the strain she'd been under.

The shaking subsided even more, then stopped. "Time?" Fenway called, but her voice had no power behind it, and she was drowned out by her father yelling for emergency services.

"Time?" she called again, looking up at Xavier.

"12:23," Xavier said.

That was only two minutes? Fenway felt like a lifetime had passed with Judith's head in her hands.

Judith's eyes fluttered.

Then they opened. She blinked, trying to focus.

"What am I doing on the floor?" she asked, a note of panic in her voice.

"You had a seizure," Fenway said.

"I'm lying on my side."

"That's to keep your airway clear."

Amanda walked up to them with a black *Nidever Forever* sweatshirt wadded in her hands and shook it out. Fenway blinked a few times. Judith's skirt was wet—her bladder had let go during the seizure.

Amanda draped the sweatshirt quickly over Judith's hips, hiding the front of her skirt.

"Who's yelling?" Judith said.

"My father," Fenway replied. "We're trying to get you an ambulance. You hit your head pretty hard on the way down. But you're not bleeding, which is good." The bump on Fenway's forehead throbbed again, as if it were jealous of all the attention Judith's head was getting. "Have you had any seizures before, Judith?"

"One, back in March," Judith said.

"You have epilepsy?"

Judith tried to shake her head. "No. The doctor said it was brought on by the cancer."

"You take anything for it?"

"Yes. I take, uh, what's it called? Gabapentin."

"That's an epilepsy drug, isn't it?"

"I don't know. It's what my doctor prescribed." She winced. "I have a terrible headache."

"Dad!" Fenway called. Nathaniel Ferris stopped. "She's awake now. Hopefully they're coming with an ambulance."

"I don't think anyone is out there," Ferris said. "And if there is, I don't know if they can hear us through the door."

"Okay, it's fine," Fenway said. "We'll figure this out." She looked down at the woman lying halfway in her lap. "All right—Judith, how do you feel?"

"Like shit," Judith said.

Fenway nodded. "Any pain? You said your head hurt?"

"Like someone's trying to squeeze my brain from the inside."

"Your head hurt anywhere else?"

"Like how?"

"You hit your head when you went down. I wasn't able to get to you in time."

"Well, I tell you, this day keeps getting better and better," Judith said, shifting her weight. "What the hell?" She pushed herself up. "Oh, that's just great. I pissed myself."

"It happens during seizures. It's nothing to be embarrassed about."

Judith laughed. "The next time you piss all over yourself, I'll tell you it's 'nothing to be embarrassed about.'"

Fenway nodded. "Yeah."

"And can you just put my head down? My ear is right next to your stomach, and it's grumbling so loud I figured a medevac helicopter was landing on top of me."

Fenway chuckled and moved, with Judith pushing herself up to her elbows. "Nice to know you haven't lost your sense of humor."

"The day I do is the day I die," Judith said.

"We don't need any more of that today," Fenway said, then caught herself. "Oh—I mean—sorry."

But Judith hadn't been listening. "I was kind of hoping I'd wake up and this whole day would just be a bad dream." She sighed. "No such luck." She cackled, and then her voice broke. She put her hand over her face. "What the hell am I going to do now?" she said, her voice low. "What the hell am I going to do?"

"Piper," Fenway said, "see where McVie is, would you?"

"Sure."

"You sent him a text?"

"About five minutes ago. I have another few ideas about what we can do to communicate with him."

"Really?"

"I tried a trick to get around the firewall ports that are blocked on the IP phone. No luck—but I started to download Skype and Signal and Discord. Do you know if he has any of those apps on his phone?"

"Maybe Skype. I don't think he has the others. Just do what you have to do, okay? We're all ready to be out of here, so let's go before there are any more medical emergencies."

Piper nodded and went through the gallery gate to go back to the judge's bench.

"I—I don't think I want to get up," Judith said. "I know I'm in the middle of the aisle, but my head is splitting."

"That's fine," Fenway said. "You're okay right there."

"Can you imagine being the designer for this courtroom?" Judith said, staring at the ceiling. "All this beautiful dark wood, the architectural design of the chairs and the lighting, and the first day it's in use, it gets shot up and an old lady pees right in the middle of the floor."

"You could have just said you preferred neoclassic style," Fenway said with a crooked smile. "There's no need to get urine involved in your critique."

Judith laughed, and it turned into the dry, hacking cough that Fenway had heard in the Cygnus's house the week before.

"Sorry," she said, when the coughs died down.

"Any word from McVie yet, Piper?" Fenway called.

No answer.

Fenway turned to the judge's bench, but since she was sitting on the floor of the aisle, she couldn't see anything behind it. "Piper?"

"Uh—yeah, Fenway, I'm here." Piper's voice was shaky.

Fenway pulled herself to her feet. "Everything okay?"

"You better—you should just come up here." Piper's voice didn't have the edge of confidence it usually had.

Fenway looked down at Judith. "I'll be right back."

"Thank you, Miss Stevenson."

"For what?"

"For taking care of me. You didn't have to."

Fenway smiled at Judith, then she hurried through the gate and up the side steps. Piper sat at the desk, pushed back about five feet, her head in her hands.

"What happened?" Fenway said, and her eyes widened.

The decorative gavel sat askew on Piper's keyboard.

Piper's laptop screen was smashed right in the center. The screen was dark.

CHAPTER TWENTY-FOUR

Fenway spent a minute processing the broken screen, like her eyes couldn't correctly translate the information to her brain.

"I almost finished processing all the card key data," Piper moaned. "The program was about to spit out all the employees who were most likely to be the mole based on financial statements, who opened what doors when—and the people in the jail building at certain times."

"Sounds like a complex algorithm."

"It wasn't that complicated. And the information is all publicly available."

Would someone have broken the computer to prevent them from finding out who the mole was?

Fenway popped her head up and surveyed the courtroom, scrutinizing everyone. It obviously wasn't Judith Cygnus—although it was possible she'd been in cahoots with the person who had done it.

But if Judith had faked the seizure, she should win every acting award in existence. Fenway had never seen anyone who could shake the specific way that a seizure shook one's body. Maybe actors in cop shows.

Fenway wondered if anyone in the room had close ties to Officer

Todd Young. Maybe Leda? Maybe Officer Young was another lover of hers?

Fenway couldn't ignore the itch in her brain anymore, though. Officer Young fit the profile of *37cuckoo37* in a lot of ways, but if he was the mole, he wasn't the one to break the laptop. Fenway doubted that anyone in the room was close enough to Officer Young to care about hiding his identity.

If the killer assumed the laptop was about to reveal the mole's identity, that would be enough of a reason to bash the machine.

But maybe the laptop was smashed for another reason.

She looked at Leda Nedermeyer. That business with her anxiety medication could have easily been a ruse. All she would have needed was knowledge of the symptoms, and acting talent would get her the rest of the way there. She looked at Leda—she was fussily arranging herself on her chair and looked like she was ready to lie down again. Plus, Leda keened about being sorry. She wouldn't have had the opportunity.

Xavier had helped move the chairs with Piper.

Amanda had covered Judith's body with her sweatshirt so Judith wouldn't be embarrassed about her bladder letting go.

Her father had been at the door, screaming for medical help.

That left six people. One of whom had smashed Piper's screen.

Cynthia Schimmelhorn, Bryce Heissner—and she wouldn't have put it past either of them.

Rose Morgan, of course. Still in the aisle behind the last row on the prosecution's side, she was like a bad penny—Fenway couldn't get rid of her. Just when Fenway was ready to eliminate Rose as the main suspect, she leapt to the forefront again. In fact, smashing that laptop was exactly the M.O. that Rose might have.

And Evans Dahl—that ankle injury was a sprain, and it appeared to make him feel worse, not better, but maybe he was faking it too. Maybe no one would notice him sneaking behind the judges' bench.

Also, Fenway didn't see Charlotte during the seizure. A few weeks ago, Fenway might have said that Charlotte had neither the brains nor the savvy to pull something off like smashing a laptop while everyone was paying attention to something else. Over the last two weeks, Fenway had seen that Charlotte likely had both the book smarts *and* the street smarts to do it.

Oh—and ADA Kim.

Hmm. Jennifer Kim was certainly popping up all over. First her fingerprints were on the wrong bottle, then she had The World's Biggest Cuckoo Clock near her birthplace. Plus, she was complaining constantly at Fenway and Piper. But no relation to the number thirty-seven.

There was that scratching in Fenway's brain again. *Something* was there, she just couldn't see what it was yet.

It wasn't doing her any good sitting at the judge's desk with a broken laptop, feeling sorry for herself. She grabbed the phone out of her purse. "Let me know if I can do anything, Piper. Otherwise, I'll be standing on my head in the nook over there, trying to get a useable cell signal."

"Your dad'll kill me," Piper said.

"Not likely. You've already found enough evidence to clear him of one murder." Fenway shook her head. "He'll probably be so thankful he'll give you his Porsche."

"That doesn't help fix the laptop."

"Well, sometimes we have to celebrate every single victory we get."

Piper nodded, and Fenway, clutching her phone, went around the witness stand for what seemed like the hundredth time that day, then through the gate.

She knelt at Judith Cygnus's side. The widow's eyes were closed, but she opened them, blinking a few times.

"How are you feeling, Mrs. Cygnus?"

"Still horrible, thanks for asking."

"Can I get you anything? Water, maybe?"

"Ha. So I can piss myself again? No, thank you."

"You need to stay hydrated."

Judith patted Fenway's hand. "I doubt I'll leave with much of my dignity intact, Miss Stevenson, but surely you can let me have this."

Fenway smiled. "Certainly."

"I can go to sleep, right? I won't get an aneurysm or anything?"

Fenway shook her head. "No. You hit your head pretty hard."

"Then put me through a concussion test or something. My head is killing me. I want to go to sleep."

Fenway looked up at Xavier and Amanda, sitting across the aisle and several rows back. "Hey—Xavier, grab Amanda and come down here." Then turning her face down to Judith, she said, "I'm sorry, Mrs. Cygnus, I know you just want to sleep, but I hope that medical personnel will arrive any minute. They'll be able to take you through concussion tests."

"I thought you used to be a nurse," Judith said. "You don't even know how to give someone a concussion test?"

"Nurse practitioner. And I've already asked you enough questions to determine that you need a balance and coordination assessment, which, no, I can't give you here." Fenway smiled tightly as Xavier and Amanda arrived. "Keep Mrs. Cygnus from falling asleep. She might have a concussion, and I want the medical personnel to get here before we do anything to jeopardize her health."

"But after the medical personnel get here, you can jeopardize my health all you want," said Judith, cackling, and then she coughed, a dry, coppery hacking that soon wracked her whole body.

When the coughing fit subsided, Fenway said, "Are you okay?"

Judith, catching her breath, nodded. "That'll keep me awake real good."

Amanda stepped forward. "You've got a daughter, right? Where does she live?"

Fenway stood, not waiting for Judith's answer to Amanda, hurried down the aisle, turning left after the last row to get to the nook.

"What happened?" Cynthia Schimmelhorn asked as Fenway turned the corner around the last row of chairs.

"Did you see anyone go up to the judge's bench when Judith was having her seizure?"

"Did I see—no, of course I didn't. I was concentrating on the commotion around you saving the professor's wife."

I didn't save her—but now wasn't the time to correct her. "You didn't see anyone going up the aisle or the side, or coming back? You didn't hear a smashing sound?"

Cynthia shook her head.

"All right."

"What's happened?"

Fenway hesitated. Cynthia Schimmelhorn might be the person who had broken the laptop. She certainly wasn't anyone that Fenway could trust. But this wasn't exactly confidential information, and Cynthia had been the person who'd first complained about being stuck in the courthouse. "Someone smashed Piper's computer. So—no way to contact McVie to let him know Judith had a seizure. No way to research anything so maybe we could find the murderer."

Cynthia Schimmelhorn laughed.

Fenway stopped, trying not to let a look of horror slide over her face.

"I'm sorry for laughing," Schimmelhorn said. "I know it's not funny. That's not what I'm laughing at."

"What's so funny, then?"

"Here you are, stuck here in this locked courtroom for hours, that bruise on your forehead looking nastier by the minute. And you can't think about anything but solving this case." She chuckled again. "To think I was concerned that your father was recommending someone incompetent for the coroner job."

"What?"

"Oh—I was in the board meeting when your dad found out that your mother died. Immediately—and I mean *immediately*—he started thinking about how he could convince you to come down from Seattle and join him."

Fenway was taken aback. "Really?"

"Yes. He asked if anyone knew of any jobs at the county. Someone reminded him that you were a nurse, and he opened his laptop and started researching you. Facebook profile, graduating class, everything. At the time I was annoyed. Now I see he might have known what he was doing."

"Is that when you found out that your daughter and I both went to Western Washington?"

"I'd known before, actually, but he did bring up that you graduated at the top of your class." Schimmelhorn leaned forward. "I know you don't like many of the things he did—"

"Or didn't do," Fenway said under her breath.

"—but your dad should know that you love him. It's probably the most important thing you can say to a parent."

Fenway nodded somberly, remembering that Schimmelhorn had lost her daughter seven or eight years earlier. If she thought about it too much—and the one-hundred-thousand-dollar check in her purse—she might just go crazy. "Thanks for the advice," Fenway said, stepping around her. "I've gotta see if I can get any service in here so I can make sure they know we're having a medical emergency."

"Of course," Cynthia said.

Fenway walked into the nook. She held her phone above her head again, but there was no signal. She turned and spun, then took her shoes off and climbed carefully onto a chair. She raised her phone above her head again.

There.

Two bars.

She immediately pushed the phone app and called McVie.

The screen turned into the black background of the phone app. CRAIG MCVIE—MOBILE appeared on the screen, and below that, it read CALLING.

Fenway pushed the speakerphone button and waited.

Please pick up. Please, please, please pick up.

Three beeps.

CALL FAILED.

She went back to the main screen. Still two bars. Not great, but better than one, and it should be enough to call.

One of the bars disappeared.

She twisted the phone in her hand, but there was no change. She raised it further, and the last bar disappeared.

NO SERVICE.

Fenway wanted to scream in frustration. There was a medical emergency, and they were locked in. The side exit was locked—a lawsuit waiting to happen for sure. If Judith died, Laura Cygnus would have one hell of a wrongful death suit against the county.

Then she heard it—and felt it.

There was a thunderous bang against the double doors. Then another one.

They were breaking down the doors.

Then a siren began to wail—so loud she almost fell off the chair she was standing on. She clapped her hands over her ears, dropping her phone to the floor, then felt another bang, now two, now three, and then there were no more bangs against the door, just the wailing siren, buzzing like a chainsaw in her brain.

Almost by instinct, Fenway jumped off the chair and ran to the speaker enclosure—but the siren wasn't coming from there. It was coming from up high, inside the walls, above the ceiling. The siren echoed through the courtroom, off the mahogany, making it difficult to think.

The evidence safe—maybe the system was connected there.

Fenway raced down the center aisle, pushing through the gallery gate, and slid open the mahogany panel. Sure enough, the lights were lit and flashing red, and the readout said ZONE 3 ATTACK. Fenway tried to remember the code to the safe Piper had given her earlier.

She closed her eyes and tried to shut out the siren. *Three of the four corners—and then up and down the center column.* There was a repeated number. And Fenway remembered that the first half of the eight-digit code was all divisible by three, and the second set were all even numbers.

Kind of. The first half ended with a one, and the second half began with a zero. Which her high school math teacher would argue was neither odd nor even.

She reached out with her right index finger and pushed the buttons.

9-9-3-1.

0-2-8-5.

The green light next to the blinking red lights came on, but the siren didn't go silent. Instead, the display read: TURN OFF ALARM.

Well, duh. It was a good security measure, not allowing the safe to be opened while the alarm was going off, but she didn't have time to praise the design of the system.

Piper had changed the safe code from the default. Had anyone changed the alarm code?

In desperation—and in the middle of doing it, wondering how many chances she had—she entered 1-2-3-4-5-6-7-8.

The siren stopped.

A ringing stayed in Fenway's ears, but she swallowed hard. Her ears popped a little, the ringing diminishing with it.

She turned her head. Xavier and Amanda were still with Judith, who was sitting up now, looking scared out of her mind but otherwise okay. A bit of color had come back into her face.

She craned her neck. Evans Dahl, up on both feet, was ready to flee.

She stood, still in her bare feet—she'd abandoned her shoes in the nook—and slowly went around the witness stand and up the steps to the dais.

"You okay, Piper?"

"That was loud," Piper said, giving Fenway a nervous laugh.

"Why aren't they breaking down the side door?"

"Because it's a security door. Since the defendants go in and out of there, the committee ordered a steel door—almost impossible to smash through." Then Piper's head suddenly snapped up. "Hold on," she said. "Hold on." She pulled her backpack that was sitting on the desk toward her and took out a small tablet.

"You can't get anything from that," Fenway pointed out. "That doesn't have an Ethernet port. It can't read USB sticks, either."

"I actually have a converter," Piper said in a low voice, "but that's not what I mean." She pointed to a soft blue light on the broken laptop. "Whoever smashed my screen didn't turn the computer off." She carefully reached to the keyboard and pulled her sleeve over her hand, brushing some of the broken glass off the function key and the top row. She held down the FUNCTION and ALT keys, and with her right index finger pressed F15. Another blue light appeared on the top of the machine.

"Now," she said, "I can get it."

"What are you doing?" Fenway whispered.

"I turned Bluetooth on. I had it off because I didn't want anyone getting into the machine, but I've got an RDP app on my tablet, and I can continue working."

Fenway nodded. "You know, I felt like I *almost* understood that."

"Bluetooth—the same thing that allows you to connect your head-phones and your wireless mouse—pushes data back and forth too. I'm running a remote desktop on my tablet and using Bluetooth to control the laptop, even though the monitor got smashed." Piper sighed. "It's slow, and I won't be able to access some of the applications, but it's better than nothing."

Piper woke the tablet up and launched an app, then immediately started typing on the screen.

"Are you in?" Fenway murmured.

"Impatient much?" Piper said. "Just calm down. I've got a few security hoops to jump through."

Fenway fought the urge to stare at the tablet over Piper's shoulder as she typed. Finally, Piper leaned back. "Oh wow. I wasn't sure that would work, but it did. I'm in."

Fenway nodded. "We've got to make it look like we're despondent, though," Fenway whispered. "The person who broke your laptop is in this room. They've got to think we don't have any way to figure out who the mole is."

"Since it's on my tablet, maybe I won't even sit near the laptop. You can say that I'm devastated that the laptop's broken." She paused. "Which I am—but I'm glad I found a workaround." Piper glanced up at the double doors. "Do you think McVie will try bashing his way in again?"

Fenway shrugged. "I hope so. Or that they can figure out how to trick the doors into opening." Fenway sat down next to the broken laptop. "Did you do any searches on Yesterday Audio? Maybe try to find out who was assigned to install those speaker enclosures over the weekend?"

Piper grimaced. "I started to, but then I got sidetracked. But it should be easy enough to figure out." She began tapping on the tablet. "Are you interested in the business, too, or just the workers?"

"Just the work—" Fenway stopped. "You know, there's a very good chance that Yesterday Audio is one of the money laundering businesses too."

Piper nodded. "I'll look up the business license. See who owns it."

"Okay. While you're doing that, I guess I better do what I can to help Judith. I swear, if one more person gets injured today, I'm going to scream."

"Stay away from the double doors, then. McVie might bring in a tank next."

Fenway turned and stepped down from the dais, through the gate and knelt next to Judith Cygnus. Amanda and Xavier crouched next to her, deep in conversation.

"Oh, I see you're talking with me *now*," said Judith. "I was so boring that you left me with these two." She pulled herself up slightly. "But the joke's on you. Amanda might know more about the poetry of Adrienne Rich than anyone in the county. Besides me, of course."

"My mom has a signed copy of *The Fact of a Doorframe*," Amanda said. "It's not worth a lot because my mom read it so much and it's all ratty, but books are meant to be read. Right, Mrs. Cygnus?"

"Exactly right," Judith said, patting Amanda's hand.

"I take it you're feeling better."

"My headache's going away," Judith admitted.

"Good."

"I probably don't even need an ambulance. Just a change of clothes."

"I wish I could help you there," Fenway said.

"Well, Amanda and Xavier were telling me that you protected my head when I had the seizure. So thank you. I might have gotten badly hurt if you hadn't done that."

"It was my pleasure," Fenway said automatically, putting on her nurse voice. She stood up. "Let me know if you need anything." She walked across the aisle to Evans Dahl. "How's your ankle doing?"

"Swelling up like crazy," Dahl said. "I'll be glad to get out of here and put some ice on it."

"Can I take a look at it?"

"Don't bother," Dahl said. "I can put weight on it. It's just sore."

"You need to see a doctor, though," Fenway said. "And do it soon because there might be some injury to the soft tissue that won't get better by itself. And—I might have missed a hairline fracture or a pinched nerve."

"If you're going to nag me, I'll nag you too. *You* need to make sure you keep the Fourth Amendment in mind."

"Touché." Fenway turned and walked back three rows. Leda Nedermeyer had stretched out over four chairs, lying on her side, facing out. "Professor Nedermeyer?" she said gently.

"Ummm."

"Are you feeling all right?"

"Not really. I don't know why I took more pills. I guess I was feeling particularly anxious."

"I'm sorry. Did Xavier take good care of you?"

"He did." She paused. "I believe I told him I didn't like his stage name."

"You might have."

"Did I mention something scatological?"

"It's possible." Fenway couldn't stop a grin from sliding over her face.

"Oh dear. I do like him. He's a good person. I hope he wasn't offended. Xavier really is an angel in disguise, you know. Such a thoughtful student, and such a calming presence in class, too."

"An angel in disguise, huh?"

Then something clicked in Fenway's head.

An angel in disguise.

Fenway turned as Leda said, "I'll be all right, then? Nothing else?"

"Drink four or five more glasses of water today. Make sure you stay hydrated." Fenway hurried up the aisle and was back on the dais.

Piper looked up from her tablet, an excited grin on her face. "I think I found the mole."

Fenway nodded. "And I think I figured out who murdered Professor Cygnus."

CHAPTER TWENTY-FIVE

"Okay, you first," said Fenway.

"So there were two payments made to this *37cuckoo37* person in the ledger—one the day before Dylan Richards was killed, and one two days after."

"And who used the keycards?"

"There was quite a bit of action on the keycards that night, but we weren't looking for any pattern because there were so many people going in and out." Piper paused. "Besides, once his murderer was caught, it didn't seem that important to catch the person who let him in."

"I sense a breakthrough moment coming," said Fenway.

"Yep. The key is that door to the annex, which was used only twice that night—once on the outside to get in, and once on the inside to get out—about thirty minutes apart, and definitely within the time frame of Dylan Richards' death."

"That doesn't necessarily prove anything."

"Yes, but it's the only time that person used their keycard in that door. Ever."

Fenway cocked an eyebrow. "Still not conclusive, but definitely interesting. Who?"

Piper leaned forward. "Jennifer Kim."

Closing her eyes, Fenway grimaced. She'd defended the ADA as someone who followed the rules a little too closely. How could she not have seen this? "Were those two payments made in her account?"

"It's harder to access bank records of an ADA than I thought. I'm still working on it."

"So the cuckoo is from the town where she was born?"

Piper shrugged. "I guess so. Or maybe she really likes Cocoa Puffs. But the two thirty-sevens—I'm still working on the second one. But the first is Highway 37. She grew up in Novato before her parents divorced and in Vallejo after. Highway 37 connects the two cities."

"And—hang on, you said she was born in July?"

"Right."

"What day?"

"The third."

Fenway rolled her eyes. "I can't believe I didn't put that together. She was born in Germany. Europeans put the day before the month. So July third is *three seven* in Germany." More puzzle pieces fell into place in her mind. The fingerprints. The broken laptop. The speaker enclosure.

"Okay—now what's your big epiphany?" Piper asked.

"All right—bear with me for a moment. I want to make sure we've got the evidence to back this up."

"Okay, fine." Piper picked up her tablet. "That sounds like you need me to do some digging."

"Should be fairly straightforward," Fenway said. "First of all, did Cynthia Schimmelhorn's daughter take any classes from Professor Solomon Delacroix?"

Piper's eyes widened. "Wait—you think your Russian lit professor might have done the same thing to Schimmelhorn's daughter as he did to you?"

"It's only a working theory," Fenway said, thinking of the threats

Schimmelhorn had made that Fenway had assumed were hypothetical. "But I know my father didn't hire Peter Grayheath to kill him."

Piper tapped on the tablet, her fingers flying.

"Did you get any texts from McVie? Or Dez, or anyone at all?"

"One thing at a time," Piper mumbled.

"Sorry." Fenway looked out across the courtroom and spied Jennifer Kim. The lines of worry in her face, the stress in her shoulders, it all made sense now.

Cynthia Schimmelhorn stood at the back of the room. "Did she really blame my father that much?" Fenway murmured to herself.

Piper took her hands off the tablet and took a deep breath. "Okay, I got it. Nerissa Schimmelhorn was, in fact, enrolled in Professor Solomon Delacroix's Russian lit class. Eight years ago, spring semester."

"Did she complete the class?"

"No. Oh—that's interesting."

"What?"

"She withdrew on March eighteenth." Piper tapped several items on the tablet, scrolled, then tapped again. "That was—" Piper swallowed hard.

"That was what?"

"A little over a month," Piper murmured. "A month before she killed herself. According to this news article, her body was found on April twentieth."

Fenway closed her eyes. "And when did my father do his little power struggle move with Petrogrande Western?"

"April nineteenth," Piper said. "The memo to Petrogrande shareholders hit their inboxes about seven o'clock on the morning of the nineteenth."

Fenway opened her eyes and was quiet for a moment.

Piper sniffled and hunched over the tablet, pulling her hair down over her shoulder to hang down. It hid her face. She tapped rapidly, hardly pausing. One minute went by, then another, Piper still typing and tapping and scrolling furiously. Then she paused, and pushed the tablet over to Fenway, keeping her head down and her face hidden.

Fenway scooted her chair closer to the table and read the screen. It was an old travel database, but there was no mistaking what it said.

> ### *Schimmelhorn, Cynthia*
> **TRANSACTION** · *17 April*
> *$568.45 Purchase*
> **ITINERARY** · *19 April*
> *Depart LAX 13:51 · Arrive PDX 15:45*
> *Depart PDX 17:05 · Arrive BLI 18:15*
> **TRANSACTION** · *19 April*
> *$368.45 Refund/Cancel*

"She was planning to see her daughter on April nineteenth," Fenway said. "And she canceled that morning because my father had Ferris Energy take over her division."

"Tap the other window," Piper whispered.

Fenway did.

Phone logs.

From a 310 area code to a 360 area code. Los Angeles to Bellingham. Mother to daughter. Starting on March twenty-first, back and forth, first twenty minutes, then two hours, then another two hours, barely skipping a day. A final call on April nineteenth, placed at 9:28 AM.

Then two calls that evening from the 310 number. One minute—it must have gone to voice mail.

The next day, another four calls, one minute each.

The next day, fifteen calls, one minute each.

The next day, eleven calls, the last one at 2:44 PM.

Fenway pushed the tablet back over to Piper and sat back in her seat.

"How did—" Piper's voice broke, and she cleared her throat. "How did you know?"

"Leda called Xavier an angel in disguise," Fenway said, "and that's when it hit me. Angel in disguise. Lady-in-waiting. L.I.W. Nerissa, in *The Merchant of Venice*, is Portia's lady-in-waiting."

"L.I.W.," Piper repeated.

"And Cynthia Schimmelhorn has been waiting for eight years to destroy the company—and the man—who took her daughter away."

"I feel sick," Piper said.

Fenway crossed her arms. "And I feel worse that we *still* have to prove it."

Piper nodded. "Now that we know exactly who L.I.W. is, though, I can dig into more financial records and see how to connect Cynthia Schimmelhorn to the L.I.W. accounts. I know I can't do it through the normal financial channels because of the privacy rules in the Caymans, but I bet there's an electronic trail. Just like the one that proves your dad didn't hire Peter Grayheath."

Fenway gave Piper a tight smile and leaned forward, her hands on her knees. "That sounds like it'll take time."

"Yeah. We'll probably get out of here before I make any headway at all."

Fenway paused and looked up at the ceiling—the mahogany of the crown molding, the angles on the lighting fixtures with their nickel-plated arms jutting to spread the light across the large courtroom. "They must know we're getting close."

"Yeah." Piper sighed. "My poor laptop. I barely had it three days."

"This entire operation has netted over a billion dollars just this year, right, Piper?"

"If my calculations are correct."

"That's enough to go around, certainly. Everyone in charge here—Cynthia Schimmelhorn, Jennifer Kim, and who knows who else—they've got more than enough money to walk out of here and disappear. Move to a country with no extradition treaty and live like royalty the rest of their days."

"You don't think Rose Morgan falls into that category?"

Fenway furrowed her brow, thinking. "No. From what she told me,

I bet she isn't getting the big bucks from this operation. I think they paid her well, but it wasn't the millions that the ringleaders are getting. Rose is too desperate for cash, and she knows she's fallen out of favor with them."

"From what she told you?"

Fenway nodded slowly. "I know I shouldn't trust anything she says, but it was more the stuff she implied. She didn't come right out and say she needed money or that she was being cut out of anything."

Piper cocked her head at Fenway. "I think Rose Morgan is extremely good at manipulating people, and I think you might overestimate your ability to see through her."

Fenway bristled. "Look, Piper, I know—" Then she paused. "Hm. Maybe you're right." She'd vacillated between thinking Rose was guilty for everything and then thinking she was far less responsible. Maybe Rose *did* know how to talk to Fenway to elicit maximum sympathy.

"You want to stall for time?"

Fenway shook her head. "We can't. Judith Cygnus needs a doctor. We've got to get out of here. We've got to get Kim and Schimmelhorn taken into custody—if we don't, they'll be in Mexico in a matter of hours."

"They were working together," Piper said. "So which one of them do you think pulled the trigger?"

Fenway opened her fingerprint kit and pulled out the fingerprints from the bottled water. "I didn't make any mistakes with the bottles, Piper."

Piper tilted her head. "Then—how—"

"Jennifer Kim offered to take Cynthia Schimmelhorn's fingerprints this morning," Fenway said. "Only she put her *own* fingerprints on that card and labeled them with Schimmelhorn's name."

"Oh—so when the bottle labeled as Jennifer Kim's came back with the prints on Schimmelhorn's card—"

"Exactly." Fenway nodded. "It sent us in the wrong direction. I assumed the cards were right and the bottles were wrong—not the other way around."

"That's proof enough, isn't it?" Piper said. "Maybe not that Schimmelhorn hired Peter Grayheath to kill all those people, but certainly for the murder of Professor Cygnus."

"It's enough to have the lab take Schimmelhorn's prints. If she gets taken into custody."

"So if you think Schimmelhorn is planning to escape as soon as the doors open," Piper asked, "how do you want to handle this?"

Fenway had grandiose plans of confronting Schimmelhorn in front of everyone and exposing the truth. Even though the fingerprint match on the water bottle was the only concrete evidence they had—and who knows if that would stand up in court—maybe Schimmelhorn's sense of revenge would get the best of her and she'd confess.

Shaking her head, Fenway looked across the courtroom. Schimmelhorn was too savvy for that. She'd never admit anything, and if she knew Fenway was onto her, she'd resist all efforts to cooperate with the sheriff. Cynthia Schimmelhorn would be out of the country five hours after getting out of the courtroom, that much she was sure of—unless Fenway could figure out how to convince the sheriff's office to hold her.

"Piper," Fenway said, "tell McVie that we have a fingerprint match for Cynthia Schimmelhorn on the gun that killed Professor Cygnus. Ask him to bring GSR swabs too. I don't know if that will be enough to for them to put Schimmelhorn in custody when they get out of the courtroom, but it's better than nothing."

"Oh—well, that's actually one thing I haven't figured out," said Piper. "The tablet is searching for a cell signal when the messaging app comes up, and when I launch the messaging app through the remote desktop interface, it brings up the tablet's messaging app, not the laptop's. It's a glitch—it definitely shouldn't be doing that—but I'm not sure I can fix it. Definitely not in the next fifteen or twenty minutes."

Something itched in Fenway's brain again, and she closed her eyes.

Oh yes.

The bullet whizzing by her right ear—dumb luck that she'd bent to the side just as the bullet had been fired.

And Cynthia Schimmelhorn's voice from an hour ago.

"But you have to know, Fenway, he loves you very much. He knows he has to make up for two decades of lost time, and it will kill *him if he doesn't figure out how to move past this with you."*

It will *kill* him if he doesn't figure out how to move past this with you.

Schimmelhorn's revenge plot wasn't just about destroying Nathaniel Ferris's company, or damaging his reputation, or framing him for the murder of her daughter's rapist. She also wanted him to feel the pain of losing a daughter. And knowing that he could have stopped it.

Cynthia Schimmelhorn had tried to kill Fenway. And if given the opportunity, she'd do it again.

BANG.

Fenway's head snapped up. The double doors reverberated. The sheriff's department was trying to break down the doors again.

Fenway, a mixture of relief and panic flooding her mind, raced around the side of the witness stand and through the gate. She had to stop Cynthia Schimmelhorn from fleeing as soon as the doors were open.

BANG.

This time, the bangs were louder and heavier, the instrument used to deliver the blows much bigger. The double doors shook, and a crack appeared in the wall above the left-hand corner of the frame.

The doors weren't budging. The wall might split before the doors would open. Piper and the others who had picked the security system had done an excellent job of keeping people out. Unfortunately, they'd done just as good of a job keeping people in.

BANG.

The siren went off, and Fenway immediately clapped her hands to her ears. Cynthia Schimmelhorn was in sight, and she didn't know if the doors would break open.

But the walls *were* cracking. One crack zigzagged from the middle of the top of the doorframe and disappeared behind the art déco clock. If McVie and his team noticed the cracking on the other side, they might stop. Or, given that they knew it was a medical emergency, the doorframe might get ripped from the wall, and the clock would be stopped at two minutes to one forever.

Fenway hoped the wall wasn't load-bearing.

The siren was so loud she couldn't think straight. There was no way she'd be able to capture Cynthia—or convince McVie to—with the shrill wailing of the alarm. She took a last look at Cynthia, behind the last row of chairs on the defense side, near the speaker enclosure, and at Rose Morgan, mirroring Cynthia behind the last row of chairs on the prosecution side, standing warily in front of the other speaker enclosure.

Swearing at herself, she turned and ran to the safe in the wall of the judge's bench and yanked the cover open.

The siren was louder here, and Fenway said her thanks to the universe that no one had changed the alarm code from the default.

She punched in 1-2-3-4-5-6-7-8, and the siren fell silent.

But so had the banging.

Fenway looked behind her. The crack in the drywall above the door went all the way to the ceiling in a near-45-degree angle. It *must* have been visible from the other side.

"Keep going!" she screamed. "Medical emergency! Break the door down!"

Nothing.

Cynthia Schimmelhorn turned from the double doors. She met Fenway's eyes.

Schimmelhorn's brow furrowed, and she tilted her head ever so slightly to the left.

She knows. She heard it in my voice.

Fenway was livid with herself. Any advantage she might have gotten from the element of surprise was gone.

And without the sheriff's team bursting through the door, and without any way to prevent Schimmelhorn from escaping on her private jet to wherever, Fenway had to make a split-second decision. She didn't know what Piper had found to back up her theory, but she couldn't wait any longer.

Besides, eleven to two were pretty good odds.

"Ladies and gentlemen," she bellowed, feeling more like a carnival barker than a coroner, "we know who killed Professor Virgil Cygnus."

VI

1:00 PM

CHAPTER TWENTY-SIX

Then Piper's voice sounded behind Fenway. "And we know who's behind the money laundering scheme too—and we know everyone involved."

Fenway's head spun to look at Piper. Fenway tried to give Piper a *what are you doing* look, but Piper seemed to ignore her and barreled on.

"For two years, one of you in this room has masterminded a complicated scheme from the maintenance docks at Ferris Energy," Piper continued. She pulled her straight red hair behind her shoulders with her left hand and pushed a ponytail holder onto it with the right. "You hid a supertanker in plain sight at the Ferris Energy docks for four days every month."

Fenway was giving off her best *shut up, Piper* vibes, shooting daggers with her eyes, but Piper kept talking.

"The tanker brought crude oil from La Mitad—an embargoed country, for those of you who follow current events. The ship was disguised en route. Once docked, the crude went out to be refined, and it was replaced with refined gasoline or diesel fuel." Piper paced slowly across the wide center aisle. "Then the tanker set sail for East Timor, where the fuel went to the rebels and their tanks and jeeps, and other vehicles that they need to fight the American-backed government.

"If you think this sounds too complex for a single person to run, you're right." Piper stepped toward the flags and then walked down the steps to the area in front of the defense table where the body of Professor Cygnus still lay. "This kind of complicated operation requires funds and manpower. It needs a supertanker—and those aren't cheap. It requires labor—in La Mitad to load the oil, in East Timor to unload the fuel, and right here in Estancia, to swap one out for the other."

Piper walked across the front of the judge's bench, stopping dramatically in front of the Dominguez County seal. "The tankers were piloted by former Navy sailors, some of who were discharged less honorably than others."

Bryce Heissner, across the room, stiffened.

"Some of you had access to the right people in La Mitad who didn't mind selling their oil to an off-book customer during the embargo."

Cynthia Schimmelhorn furrowed her brow.

"Some of you might have even sympathized with the rebels in East Timor and wondered if the United States military was even on the side of the good guys." She paused, and Heissner turned, muttering.

"It might have been a complex scheme," Piper continued, "but it was very lucrative. When the money started coming in, you had to pay laborers, you had to buy more infrastructure to support it. But after the initial investment costs, over a billion dollars came in that first year. It was over a billion five the second year." Piper scanned the room, and her eyes came to rest on Rose Morgan's face. "It seems like treason is a relatively small price to pay for making a billion dollars a year."

Rose glanced around the courtroom, locking eyes for a moment with Cynthia Schimmelhorn, but didn't say anything.

"But then," Piper continued, "two workers at Ferris Energy figured out what you were doing. And they had to be silenced. That wasn't hard—you had the security team leader from Ferris Energy in your back pocket. He poisoned them and made it appear to be a gas leak accident caused by their own negligence. But there wasn't that much risk—if it all came crashing down, you had a great fall guy." Piper extended her arm in Fenway's father's direction. He looked at Piper and set his jaw.

"For another year or so, things went smoothly. But then Jeremy Kapp was killed, and everything started going up in smoke."

"I didn't *want* to do it!" blurted Evans Dahl.

Fenway's eyes widened.

"But Kapp insisted," Dahl continued. "He knew I was barely making ends meet, and he threatened to report me to the bar association for misreporting time. Look—I *did* take money for clients who didn't exist, and yes, I *did* participate in the laundering, but I was being blackmailed."

"Shut up, Evans," snapped Bryce Heissner.

Piper pointed at Heissner. "Ah, Mr. Heissner," she said. "At first, I thought you might be innocent in all of this. Imagine my surprise when I found several names on the tanker's manifest matching people you served with on an aircraft carrier in the South China Sea. I wasn't nearly as surprised when I researched the holding company that controls Yesterday Audio and found your name listed as the owner." She clicked her tongue. "It had been removed from most of the electronic paperwork, but not all of it. I don't suppose you'd recognize an email sent on Saturday to the ADA asking her to authorize Yesterday Audio to come in and perform those repairs."

Fenway stared openmouthed at Piper. She'd been able to dig so far in the short time she'd had.

"That's confi—" Heissner started, then snapped his mouth shut.

"Bryce?" Nathaniel Ferris asked, incredulous.

"It is better to keep one's mouth shut and be thought a fool, than to open one's mouth and remove all doubt," Cynthia Schimmelhorn said pointedly.

"And then there's the matter of the code names," said Piper.

Schimmelhorn, Heissner, Dahl, Morgan, and Kim all swiveled their heads toward Piper, their eyes wide.

Oh no. It's not eleven against two. It's eight against five. And one of those eight is Judith Cygnus, who's leaving here in an ambulance.

If she's lucky.

Piper paused. Fenway wasn't sure what she was doing, but then she saw it in Piper's face: she was listening.

Piper was listening for the banging on the door again, or any sign that McVie and the cavalry would save the day. She was stalling for time—not time so that she could catch the killer, but time so that Schimmelhorn would be concentrating on anything but escape.

But with five people involved in the conspiracy, was that even a good idea?

And Fenway had another thought that sent her close to panic: *what if those five weren't the only ones in the courtroom involved in the conspiracy?*

"The code names?" said Charlotte. "What code names?"

Fenway stepped forward. "We have the ledgers kept by a few of the companies involved in the money laundering," she said. "Those involved had enough sense to use code names instead of their real names. We concluded"—Fenway shot a look at Jennifer Kim—"that the code names were chosen arbitrarily. Almost all of them followed the same nomenclature: a random word and a four-digit number. But two important code names didn't follow that template. And those had meaning."

"And one of them in particular," Piper said, "refers to someone who works in law enforcement. In fact, this person worked very hard to have me fired from the county."

Fenway took another step forward to stand at the gallery gate. "Probably because she knew you were getting too close to figuring out code names—and what some of the payments were for." She turned to her right and addressed her father and Charlotte. "Piper found the entry Domingo Velásquez wrote in the ledger, noting that Peter Grayheath was paid to murder Professor Solomon Delacroix," she said. "That's why I insisted that you pay her to keep looking."

"It's funny, Ms. Kim," Piper said, "if you hadn't insisted on my resignation, I wouldn't have started working for Nathaniel Ferris—and

I wouldn't have gotten access to the Ferris Energy files and the Ferris Energy databases and networks. Unloading the crude oil from the supertanker and filling it up with refined fuel—all of that took place on Ferris Energy property. So I was able to uncover equipment logs and financial transactions I wouldn't have otherwise. You tried to protect yourself, but I wouldn't have figured out *you* were the mole if I were still working for the county."

Kim, sitting in a chair on the aisle, set her jaw, her right arm casually draped over the back of the chair next to her. "I don't know what you're talking about. Mole? What mole?"

Fenway leveled her gaze at the assistant district attorney. "You know very well that someone has been keeping the people in charge of the money laundering apprised of the sheriff's office's progress on the case. And we know that someone let the killer into Dylan Richards' jail cell the night he was killed."

"If you had any proof that I was this supposed mole," Kim said, "you wouldn't be grandstanding like this. I only give this kind of complicated speech to juries when I haven't proved my case."

Piper shook her head. "I'm no lawyer, and there's no jury," she said. "But see if you can connect the dots. I know two huge payments were made to someone with the code name *37cuckoo37*, one day before and one day after the murder of Dylan Richards. And on the day in between, I discovered activity on your card key from the annex into the back hallway—the one leading into the county jail."

"Now who do you suppose," Fenway said, "was born in Triberg, Germany, home to the world's largest cuckoo clock? And whose birthday is the third of July, who spent her childhood growing up in both the cities that bookend California Highway 37?"

The color drained from Jennifer Kim's face.

Behind her, Cynthia Schimmelhorn narrowed her eyes, a look of anger over her face.

"And another thing," Fenway said. "Why are your fingerprints on the card you labeled for Ms. Schimmelhorn?"

Kim opened her mouth but didn't say anything.

"It's because the gun was hers," Fenway continued. "You jumped into helping me fingerprint right away. It was strange that you were so chummy, given how much we'd clashed over Piper's resignation. Now I know you were trying to protect your boss."

Jennifer Kim's mouth fell open.

"Here's the thing I can't figure out, Jennifer," Fenway said quietly. "You're one of the most law-abiding people I know. The only confusing things you've done were *all* to protect your boss. You fired Piper when she was getting too close. When I was about to search everyone's belongings, you pretended to faint—and I bet that's when your boss moved the gun from her purse to the speaker enclosure. So why are you protecting the bad guys?"

Jennifer Kim's face was hard and tight with anger, but slowly her features fell, her shoulders slumped, and her eyelids drooped. Finally, she shifted in her seat and sighed. "The night Dylan Richards was killed, Stotsky told me he'd be wearing a wire," Kim said. "I thought if I could get him to talk to Dylan, get him to confess on a recording, we'd have an open-and-shut case. Everything was too circumstantial otherwise."

"But Stotsky didn't record him—he killed him."

"I swear I didn't know what he had planned," Kim said, "but that didn't matter. I was an accessory to murder." She raised her head and glared at Schimmelhorn. "And then she told me about the deposits into my account. She owned me. She had an insider who could make evidence disappear, disconnect cameras, swap security tapes. Tell her that Cygnus was blabbing about names from the moment the jail door shut. So she asked me to get Professor Cygnus to a certain spot in the courtroom." She set her jaw. "I could have suppressed all those names, Cynthia. You didn't have to kill him."

"That's ludicrous," Cynthia Schimmelhorn hissed, still standing behind the last row of seats.

"Is it?" Fenway said, turning to face her.

"I loved Professor Cygnus," Schimmelhorn said. "He gave my life purpose and meaning. I didn't want him dead."

"But you were cornered," Fenway said softly. "He was about to give you up, wasn't he?" She took three more steps forward through the center aisle, until only ten feet separated them. "He was offering to tell the police everything—with McVie sitting right there, so not even your woman on the inside could prevent it getting out. He cared far more about spending the next six months with his wife than he did about protecting you." She folded her arms. "So you did what you had to."

"I have no idea what you're talking about. You're saying *I'm* the shooter? That's ridiculous."

"You planned it ahead of time," Fenway said. "A call to Bryce Heissner, your crony on the Board of Directors, ensured that Yesterday Audio would be in here over the weekend to hide the gun in the speaker enclosure for you. You got here before anyone else did this morning so you could remove the gun and stake out a seat on the *other* side of the column that would allow you to hide from view. I don't know if you were planning to kill him all along or if you just wanted to be prepared if he started talking." She looked at Jennifer. "But it appears your woman on the inside told you he was quite the blabbermouth."

Cynthia Schimmelhorn narrowed her eyes.

"You had your millions in the offshore account," Fenway continued. "I'm sure you had an escape all ready, too. Probably a chartered plane from Estancia to—where? Would Mexico have been far enough?"

A flicker of hate flashed across Cynthia Schimmelhorn's face.

"Oh!" A bolt of revelation hit Fenway. "I know. Hermosillo. You don't take kindly to people who steal from you, do you? Domingo Velásquez might have escaped the country with half a million dollars, but there's no way he'd escape from *you*, was there?"

"You tried to fire me, Cynthia," Nathaniel Ferris said in disbelief, getting to his feet. "We treated you well in the buyout. You got millions. Far more than other people in your position would have gotten. That must have been the reason the board said we could trust you."

"I was wondering if you'd make this all about yourself, Dad," Fenway said, turning to face him. "In this case, though, you're right. It *is* all about you. Cynthia Schimmelhorn wasn't just looking to escape the country with a billion dollars. She wanted you destroyed."

Confusion washed over Nathaniel Ferris's face. "She wanted me destroyed?"

"She sure did, Dad. You know she had a daughter."

Ferris blinked. "I mean—I guess so."

"Yes, you knew that. Her name was Nerissa. After the character Cynthia played in *The Merchant of Venice* when Cygnus was her professor." Fenway paused. "Did you know that Nerissa went to Western Washington, same as I did, and had Professor Delacroix for Russian lit?"

Ferris cringed.

"It was eight years ago, just about a year after *my* first semester." She tilted her head to the side. "Eight years ago—that's when you did your big power move for Petrogrande Western, right, Dad?"

Ferris looked at the ground. "I don't want to—"

"You *will* find out, Dad. Because that professor did the same thing to her that he did to me. And Cynthia, being a good mom, found out that her daughter was in trouble and bought a ticket to fly up there to help her."

Ferris looked up. "But what does that have to do with—"

"The memo saying Ferris Energy was performing a hostile takeover of Petrogrande Western crossed her desk the morning she was supposed to leave. So she had to cancel her trip."

"What—what happened?"

"I remember what happened," Charlotte said quietly. "You and I talked about this, Nate." She looked up at Fenway. "But I didn't know the buyout was related to the, uh—"

"Stop trying to sugarcoat it," Schimmelhorn growled. "You think you can't say the word *suicide* in front of me?" She shook her head and started to pace. "Fine. You figured out that I was the one to pay Peter Grayheath to kill that son-of-a-bitch professor at Western Washington. I only have two regrets about that. First, that I didn't kill him myself, and second, that the asshole didn't suffer *nearly* enough before he died."

"That makes two of us," Ferris said. "I should give you half of whatever you paid to take him out, Cynthia." He took a few steps down the row toward Fenway, but Fenway folded her arms. This wasn't an opening for him to try to heal their father-daughter relationship.

And where was McVie? Surely it had been five minutes, maybe even ten. Where were the police?

Ferris stopped, almost in the aisle, about an arm's length from Fenway, and studied her face. Then he sighed and turned to Schimmelhorn. "I—I'm sorry," he said. "I didn't know your daughter was in trouble. If I had known that would happen, I'd have never—" He put his head down and grasped the back of the chair in front of him.

Schimmelhorn kept pacing. "You said I planned everything ahead of time. I had an escape route, a car waiting to go to the airport. I just didn't know there'd be a lockdown procedure in place. My intelligence gathering must have failed on that particular item." She shot a withering gaze at Bryce Heissner but then smiled. "But you can't prove any of this. Yes, maybe there's a fingerprint on that gun, but who knows how it got there? Or when? It might be registered to me, and I might have reported it stolen. Or any number of other explanations. I'm sure my lawyer will jog my memory." She set her jaw. "I have no record. I'm a pillar of this community. Anything that I'm accused of will be publicly denounced as your beloved father exerting his considerable power in the sheriff's office to frame one of his corporate rivals." She thrust her chin at Jennifer Kim. "Particularly when the sitting assistant district attorney will decline to press charges."

She paced to the prosecution's side of the gallery, passing within a foot of Rose Morgan. "I may have some people in my employ who are more loyal to the almighty dollar than to me." She glared at Rose as she passed her, but Rose stepped back, standing right next to the second speaker enclosure.

"No can do, Ms. Schimmelhorn," Rose said, folding her arms and widening her stance. "No more."

Fenway paused. No more what? Was Rose turning on her boss?

Schimmelhorn spun around to face Fenway and smiled. "You haven't mentioned the other part of my plan, Miss Stevenson," she said, her voice dripping with honey. "Do you want to tell your father the rest of it, or shall I *show* him?"

Fenway didn't know where Schimmelhorn was going with this, but with Rose seemingly no longer on Schimmelhorn's side, she decided she could risk it. Xavier was only two rows away from Schimmelhorn. Who was unarmed. Between Fenway, Rose, Xavier, and maybe Nathaniel Ferris, they had more than enough muscle to subdue a fifty-year-old woman who was more at home in a high-end restaurant than a boxing ring.

"Cynthia Schimmelhorn, you are under arrest for the murders of Virgil Cygnus and Solomon Delacroix," she said.

Schimmelhorn chuckled, and then she began to laugh heartily. "And who'll take me in?" she asked between guffaws. "Your brand-new court-room is the jewel of Estancia, and you can't even unlock the doors!"

Schimmelhorn doubled over in laughter and put her hands on her knees to steady herself.

There was a note of fake mirth in that laugh. Maybe Schimmelhorn was taking this seriously.

Rose Morgan, still standing in front of the speaker enclosure, put her arms down and seemed to relax.

Fenway's eyes widened.

No, Cynthia Schimmelhorn was far from done.

Schimmelhorn's elbow came up hard and caught Rose in the jaw. In one fluid move, Schimmelhorn pulled the second speaker enclosure open with her left hand, reached inside with her right, and pulled out *another* Sig Sauer.

Fenway blinked.

Of course there was a gun in both speaker enclosures. I'm an idiot.

Silence washed over the room. The rain hammering the roof and

Cynthia's deep but measured breaths were the only noises. She pointed the gun at Jennifer Kim.

Kim squeezed her eyes shut and bowed her head.

"Dear, dear Jenny," Schimmelhorn said. "I won't waste a bullet on you. It's all over for both of us. And you know what?" She shrugged. "It doesn't matter. Yes, living out my life on a beach in the tropics would have been nice. But I don't really care." She took a step forward up the center aisle, closer to Fenway and her father. "Here's what I do care about, though." She casually moved the gun from Jennifer Kim to Nathaniel Ferris. "Now here's a man who kept me from my daughter when she needed me the most. Making me choose between my livelihood and the light of my life." She sighed. "Eight years and two hundred six days, Nathaniel." She smiled wistfully. "The only thing I want is for him to feel the same pain I've lived with for eight years and two hundred six days."

She pointed the gun at Fenway.

Fenway drew in her breath sharply, staring down the handgun barrel.

She heard the rain beating on the roof of the courthouse, unbearably loudly, the storm of the conspiracy pounding in her brain.

Schimmelhorn pulled the trigger.

The bang of the gun.

A loud *crunch* from outside the double doors.

The lights went out.

CHAPTER TWENTY-SEVEN

Fenway didn't expect the darkness to come so quickly. She didn't feel the bullet hit. Unbearable noise swam all around her—voices screaming, bodies hitting the floor, a couple from across the room, one right in front of her. A loud click. A rush of warm, stale air on her face.

Is this what it's like to die? When you don't even feel what hit you?

And then she blinked. Her eyes started to adjust.

The low light of a cell phone a few rows in front of her.

A dozen dim green LEDs swarming in from the double doors.

From several yards beyond the open doors, a dim, murky light from distant windows.

Are the doors open?

Did McVie finally break through?

Am I still alive?

Then a low hum, and orange bulbs, unseen in each corner of the room, flickered on.

The emergency lighting system.

Fenway blinked and took in the scene—two paramedics kneeling over Judith Cygnus. Schimmelhorn face down on the floor, Dez hand-cuffing her behind her back.

Xavier, two rows in front, holding his smartphone in front of him, recording the whole thing on video. Amanda next to him, wide-eyed, her hand over her mouth.

Fenway briefly wondered how much of it he had recorded. And how much of it they could use in court.

Then she looked down.

Nathaniel Ferris lay on the floor, face up.

A wound in his upper chest, on the left side, just below his shoulder. The bloom of blood on his white dress shirt grew from a carnation, to a rose, to a lily before Fenway's eyes.

He had leaped in front of her and taken the bullet.

"*Help!*" she cried, tearing her blazer off and putting it over the wound, both hands down, all her weight on it. "*Help! My dad's been shot!*"

Despite the motion all around her, she concentrated on the blood, warm and wet, soaking through the jacket. Charlotte appeared and said something. Fenway must have responded.

She looked in her father's face.

His cheeks were rapidly losing their color, but he managed a smile. He blinked twice and moved his lips.

"What, Dad? What?"

She couldn't hear him, but he moved his lips again, slowly, clearly.

I'm so proud of you.

Then a middle-aged white man in a paramedic uniform pulled her away, and another paramedic, this one a young black woman with her hair in a bun, began working on Nathaniel Ferris but blocked Fenway from seeing. All Fenway could see was the woman's overly neat bun, her hair pulled so tight it must be painful. She watched the bun dip down, then come back up, move from side to side, bob up when the stretcher arrived.

It's funny what you notice when you don't know what to do.

Fenway staggered back, out of the way of the medics and the arrests and the mêlée.

"She's got my briefcase!" Heissner yelled as an officer handcuffed him. "She's stealing my briefcase! Get her!"

In a daze, Fenway looked toward the floor in front of the second speaker enclosure where Schimmelhorn had dropped Rose Morgan with a well-placed elbow to the jaw. Rose wasn't there.

Piper passed Fenway down the center aisle, making a beeline for Dez, who was pulling Cynthia Schimmelhorn to her feet.

The double doors had been thrown open but not blown apart. She expected the emergency locks to engage when the power was cut, but the electrician must have had a way to outsmart it.

Fenway scanned the courtroom. Everything moved in slow motion. Heissner looked comical, like his jaw would come unhinged at any moment.

Evans Dahl was still in his seat, his foot up on the chair next to him, his head in his hands. No medical personnel were talking with him yet—they'd burst in, but they hadn't expected a live gunshot victim.

Jennifer Kim tried to look official as she walked down the aisle, but Dez stepped in front of her at the double doors. Then a burst of motion as Dez pulled Kim out of the way of the paramedics rushing out with Ferris on a stretcher, Charlotte running after them.

Leda Nedermeyer was sitting near the side wall, taking it all in, looking almost as dazed as Fenway felt.

Fenway's knees wobbled, and she sank to the floor, sitting, staring at the scene in front of her. The overhead bulbs came on again, and Fenway squinted at the sudden brightness, like when the house lights come up after a concert.

The whole thing was surreal.

Her dad had saved her life.

And maybe sacrificed his.

Fenway pulled her knees up and put her forehead down. Her breaths came short and hot, and as the room spun, she closed her eyes and counted as she slowed down her inhalation—one, two, three, four—ugh, she had to exhale—one, two, three, four, five, six.

The tears burned hot on her cheeks as they slid down her face. She wanted this day to be over, to be a dream. But she wanted parts of it to be real, too. Cynthia Schimmelhorn was the ringleader, and she'd been caught.

She concentrated on her breathing, counting to six, then to eight, then to ten. Her heart rate slowed to something resembling normal. She was still lightheaded.

Her stomach rumbled.

Oh—that was probably it. She hadn't eaten since shoving a granola bar in her face that morning. Although the idea of food nauseated her.

She had to get to the hospital. She had to see her dad through this.

It took a monumental effort to raise her head, but she did it. The courtroom had mostly cleared out. Two officers were ushering Xavier and Amanda through the double doors—probably to take their statements, Fenway assumed, but maybe also to look at the footage on Xavier's phone. She was glad that Xavier hadn't listened to her about putting his phone away.

Two other officers were putting crime scene tape around Cygnus's body. Fenway briefly wondered how she would get her father's suit jacket back to him. The weight of the day was so heavy on her shoulders she couldn't stand up. She couldn't even move.

A shadow appeared in the doorway, and then McVie entered. He looked tired, his boyish good looks marred by his unkempt hair and the dark circles underneath his eyes. He caught Fenway's eye and gave her a slight smile.

Fenway wasn't sure if she was glad to see him or not.

McVie walked up the center aisle and eased himself onto the floor beside Fenway, his knees up. He was quiet for a minute, then stretched his legs out in front of him.

"I need—" Fenway croaked, and her voice broke. She cleared her throat and tried again. "I need to go to the hospital."

"Okay. I'll drive you." McVie clambered to his feet and held out his hands in front of him. "Come on."

Fenway reached out, almost without thinking, and grasped McVie's outstretched hands. He pulled her up and into a hug.

"I—I, uh, I'm glad you're okay, Fenway."

"And I'm glad you're okay," she whispered.

"Let's get you to your father," he said, but drew her closer.

Fenway buried her face into McVie's shoulder and shut her eyes tight.

———

McVie sped in his beige Highlander down the darkened streets to St. Vincent's Hospital, wipers at top speed. Fenway stared straight ahead and replayed almost every conversation that she'd had with her dad since returning to Estancia six months ago. McVie glanced over a few times but didn't say anything. Charlotte wasn't answering her texts, but that wasn't surprising.

As soon as McVie killed the engine, Fenway was out of the car, hurrying into the hospital building through the pouring rain and the gray light.

The admin at the front reception desk told Fenway that Nathaniel Ferris was in surgery and he directed her to a waiting room down the hall from the intensive care unit.

Fenway took a deep breath as she walked into the waiting room. Charlotte sat in a straight-backed chair in the corner, her head in her hands. Making as much noise as she could so she wouldn't startle her, Fenway stepped closer to Charlotte, who slowly looked up into Fenway's face.

Then Charlotte crumpled into tears. Fenway knelt and held her, feeling the tears come back to her eyes too.

"Did the doctors say anything?" Fenway asked quietly.

"They took him in and said they were prepping him for surgery," Charlotte choked out. "I haven't heard anything since."

"How does it look?"

"They—they said they didn't know." Another tear ran down Charlotte's cheek.

"He's got to make it through," Fenway said. "The doctors know what they're doing."

Charlotte held Fenway tighter.

Fenway closed her eyes and saw everything clearly. The murders of the Ferris Energy workers who had gotten too close to finding out what the supertankers did, all because of Cynthia Schimmelhorn.

The killing of Solomon Delacroix in Bellingham, Schimmelhorn framing Nathaniel Ferris for the murder-for-hire.

The dead bodies of the business owners who had skimmed off the top, betraying Schimmelhorn's trust.

The look in Schimmelhorn's eyes just before she fired the gun in the courtroom.

The bloodstain blossoming on her father's chest.

"He saved my life," Fenway said.

And her father *hadn't* been the deadbeat dad she thought he was. She didn't know what her mother had done with the money, but she was determined to find out.

Charlotte and Fenway embraced for a few minutes, and slowly Charlotte's sobs got further and further apart, then stopped.

Fenway turned her head. McVie was silhouetted in the doorway, hand on the door frame. He took a cautious step forward, and the hard fluorescent lighting illuminated his face.

Past the unkempt hair and the dark circles beneath his lower lids, kindness and concern shone in his eyes.

And she closed her eyes and remembered the courtroom that morning, the bullets flying, the whisper of McVie's confession of love in her ear.

"He saved my life," Fenway said softly.

ACKNOWLEDGMENTS

Many thanks to my editors, Max Christian Hansen and Jess Reynolds, and Ziad Ezzat of Feral Creative, who has designed all the Fenway Stevenson covers.

Thank you to all the early readers: Siobhan Ordorica, who initially steered the book in the right direction, and Blair Semple, Dana Luco, Michelle Damiani, Beverly Ange, Devin McCrate, Timarie Trexler, and Dr. Christina Bellinger (my trusted medical expert!) who spent their valuable time catching errors and getting my book to be the best it could be. I'd also like to thank Cheryl Shoults and A.L. Book Promotions for helping my novels rise as high on the booksellers' charts as they have.

Special thanks to "The Two Marks"—Stay and Desvaux—for creating the 200-words-a-day BXP 2020 challenge that accelerated the first draft of this manuscript, and to Charlie Lemoine for being my "accountability partner" throughout this process, even when COVID-19 had him down for the count.

To all my fellow student actors from the 1993 American Shakespeare Company production of *A Midsummer Night's Dream*: I hope you enjoyed your names showing up as characters and places in the last two books.

To my wife, my children, and my mother: I'm deeply grateful for your encouragement and support, without which these books would never have seen the light of day.

WANT MORE FENWAY?

The Fenway Stevenson Mysteries

Book One: The Reluctant Coroner

Book Two: The Incumbent Coroner

Book Three: The Candidate Coroner

Book Four: The Upstaged Coroner

Book Five: The Courtroom Coroner

Book Six: The Watchful Coroner (coming soon)

Collection

Books 1–3 of The Fenway Stevenson Mysteries

Dez Roubideaux

Bad Weather

To order more books in the Fenway Stevenson series, go to

www.books2read.com/rl/fenway

Sign up for *The Coroner's Report,*

Paul Austin Ardoin's biweekly newsletter:

www.paulaustinardoin.com

I hope you enjoyed reading this book as much as I enjoyed writing it. If you did, I'd sincerely appreciate a review on your favorite book retailer's website, Goodreads, and BookBub. Reviews are crucial for any author, and even just a line or two can make a huge difference.

www.ingramcontent.com/pod-product-compliance
Lightning Source LLC
Chambersburg PA
CBHW051627180726
48284CB00006B/1622